The Betrothed

The Betrothed

by Alessandro Manzoni

©2011 SMK Books

Wilder Publications, LLC.
PO Box 3005
Radford VA 24143-3005

ISBN 10: 1-61720-149-9
ISBN 13: 978-1-61720-149-3

Chapter I.

That branch of the Lake of Como, which turns toward the south between two unbroken chains of mountains, presenting to the eye a succession of bays and gulfs, formed by their jutting and retiring ridges, suddenly contracts itself between a headland to the right and an extended sloping bank on the left, and assumes the flow and appearance of a river. The bridge by which the two shores are here united, appears to render the transformation more apparent, and marks the point at which the lake ceases, and the Adda recommences, to resume, however, the name of *Lake* where the again receding banks allow the water to expand itself anew into bays and gulfs. The bank, formed by the deposit of three large mountain streams, descends from the bases of two contiguous mountains, the one called St. Martin, the other by a Lombard name, *Resegone*, from its long line of summits, which in truth give it the appearance of a saw; so that there is no one who would not at first sight, especially viewing it in front, from the ramparts of Milan that face the north, at once distinguish it in all that extensive range from other mountains of less name and more ordinary form. The bank, for a considerable distance, rises with a gentle and continual ascent, then breaks into hills and hollows, rugged or level land, according to the formation of the mountain rocks, and the action of the floods. Its extreme border, intersected by the mountain torrents, is composed almost entirely of sand and pebbles; the other parts of fields and vineyards, scattered farms, country seats, and villages, with here and there a wood which extends up the mountain side. Lecco, the largest of these villages, and which gives its name to the district, is situated at no great distance from the bridge, upon the margin of the lake; nay, often, at the rising of the waters, is partly embosomed within the lake itself; a large town at the present day, and likely soon to become a city. At the period of our story, this village was also fortified, and consequently had the honour to furnish quarters to a governor, and the advantage of possessing a permanent garrison of Spanish soldiers, who gave lessons in modesty to the wives and daughters of the neighbourhood, and toward the close of summer never failed to scatter themselves through the vineyards, in order to thin the grapes, and lighten for the rustics the labours of the vintage. From village to village, from the heights down to the margin of the lake, there are innumerable roads and paths: these vary in their character; at times precipitous, at others level; now sunk and buried between two ivy-clad walls, from whose depth you can behold nothing but the sky, or some lofty mountain peak; then crossing high and level tracts, around the edges of which they sometimes wind, occasionally projecting beyond the face of the mountain, supported by prominent masses resembling bastions, whence the eye wanders over the most varied and delicious landscape. On the one side you behold the blue lake, with its boundaries broken by various promontories and necks of land, and reflecting the inverted images of the objects on its banks; on the other, the Adda, which, flowing beneath the arches of the bridge, expands into a small lake, then contracts again, and holds on its clear serpentining course to the distant horizon: above, are the ponderous masses of the shapeless rocks; beneath, the richly cultivated acclivity, the fair landscape, the bridge; in front, the opposite shore of the lake, and beyond this, the mountain, which bounds the view.

Towards evening, on the 7th day of November, 1628, Don Abbondio, curate of one of the villages before alluded to (but of the name of which, nor of the house and lineage of its curate, we are not informed), was returning slowly towards his home, by one of these pathways. He was repeating quietly his office; in the pauses of which he held his closed breviary in his hand behind his back; and as he went, with his foot he cast listlessly against the wall the stones that happened to impede his path; at the same time giving admittance to the idle thoughts that tempted the spirit, while the lips of the worthy man were mechanically performing their function; then raising his head and gazing idly around him, he fixed his eyes upon a mountain summit, where the rays of the setting sun, breaking through the openings of an opposite ridge, illumined its projecting masses, which appeared like large and variously shaped spots of purple light. He then opened anew his breviary, and recited another portion at an angle of the lane, after which angle the road continued straight for perhaps seventy paces, and then branched like the letter Y into two narrow paths; the right-hand one ascended towards the mountain, and led to the parsonage (*Cura*); that on the left descended the valley towards a torrent, and on this side the wall rose out to the height of about two feet. The inner walls of the two narrow paths, instead of meeting at the angle, ended in a little chapel, upon which were depicted certain long, sinuous, pointed shapes, which, in the intention of the artist, and to the eyes of the neighbouring inhabitants, represented flames, and amidst these flames certain other forms, not to be described, that were meant for souls in purgatory; souls and flames of a brick colour, upon a ground of blackish grey, with here and there a bare spot of plaster. The curate, having turned the corner, directed, as was his wont, a look toward the little chapel, and there beheld what he little expected, and would not have desired to see. At the confluence, if we may so call it, of the two narrow lanes, there were two men: one of them sitting astride the low wall; his companion leaning against it, with his arms folded on his breast. The dress, the bearing, and what the curate could distinguish of the countenance of these men, left no doubt as to their profession. They wore upon their heads a green network, which, falling on the left shoulder, ended in a large tassel, from under which appeared upon the forehead an enormous lock of hair. Their mustachios were long, and curled at the extremities; the margin of their doublets confined by a belt of polished leather, from which were suspended, by hooks, two pistols; a little pow-der-horn hung like a locket on the breast; on the right-hand side of the wide and ample breeches was a pocket, out of which projected the handle of a knife, and on the other side they bore a long sword, of which the great hollow hilt was formed of bright plates of brass, combined into a cypher: by these characteristics they were, at a glance, recognised as individuals of the class of bravoes.

This species, now entirely extinct, flourished greatly at that time in Lombardy. For those who have no knowledge of it, the following are a few authentic records, that may suffice to impart an idea of its principal characteristics, of the vigorous efforts made to extirpate it, and of its obstinate and rank vitality.

As early as the 8th of April, 1583, the most illustrious and most excellent lord Don Charles of Arragon, Prince of Castelvetrano, Duke of Terranova, Marquis of Avola, Count of Burgeto, High Admiral and High Constable of Sicily, Governor of Milan, and Captain General of His Catholic Majesty in Italy, "fully informed of the intolerable misery which the city of Milan has endured, and still endures, by reason of bravoes and vagabonds," publishes his decree against them, "declares and designates all those comprehended in this proclamation to be regarded as bravoes and vagabonds,—who, whether foreigners or natives, have no calling, or, having one, do not follow it,—but, either with or without wages, attach themselves to any knight, gentleman, officer, or merchant,—to uphold or favour him, or in any manner to molest others." All such he commands, within the space of six days, to leave the country; threatens the refractory with the galleys, and grants to all officers of justice the most ample and unlimited powers for the execution of his commands. But, in the following year, on the 12th of April, the said lord, having perceived "that this city still continues to be filled with bravoes, who have again resumed their former mode of life; their manners unchanged, and their number undiminished," puts forth another edict still more energetic and remarkable, in which, among other regulations, he directs "that any person whatsoever, whether of this city or from abroad, who shall, by the testimony of two witnesses, be shown to be regarded and commonly reputed as a bravo, even though no criminal act shall have been proved against him, may, nevertheless, upon the sole ground of his reputation, be condemned by the said judges to the rack for examination; and although he make no confession of guilt, he shall, notwithstanding, be sentenced to the galleys for the said term of three years, solely for that he is regarded as, and called a bravo, as above-mentioned;" and this "because His Excellency is resolved to enforce obedience to his commands."

One would suppose that at the sound of such denunciations from so powerful a source, all the bravoes must have disappeared for ever. But testimony, of no less authority, obliges us to believe directly the reverse. This testimony is the most illustrious and most excellent lord Juan Fernandez de Velasco, Constable of Castile, High Chamberlain of His Majesty, Duke of the city of Freas, Count of Haro and Castelnuovo, Lord of the house of Velasco, and of that of the Seven Infanti of Lara, Governor of the State of Milan, &c. On the 5th of June, 1593, he also, fully informed "how great an injury to the common weal, and how insulting to justice, is the existence of such a class of men," requires them anew to quit the country within six days, repeating very nearly the same threats and injunctions as his predecessor. On the 23d of May, then, 1598, "having learnt, with no little displeasure, that the number of bravoes and vagabonds is increasing daily in this state and city, and that nothing is heard of them but wounds, murders, robberies, and every other crime, to the commission of which these bravoes are encouraged by the confidence that they will be sustained by their chiefs and abettors," he prescribes again the same remedies, increasing the dose, as is usual in obstinate disorders. "Let every one, then," he concludes, "carefully beware that he do not, in any wise, contravene this edict; since, in place of experiencing the mercy of His Excellency, he shall prove his rigour and his wrath—he being resolved and determined that this shall be a final and peremptory warning."

But this again did not suffice; and the illustrious and most excellent lord, the Signor Don Pietro Enriquez de Acevedo, Count of Fuentes, Captain and Governor of the State of Milan, "fully informed of the wretched condition of this city and state, in consequence of the great number of bravoes that abound therein, and resolved wholly to extirpate them," publishes, on the 5th of December, 1600, a new decree, full of the most rigorous provisions, and "with firm purpose that in all rigour, and without hope of remission, they shall be wholly carried into execution."

We are obliged, however, to conclude that he did not, in this matter, exhibit the same zeal which he knew how to employ in contriving plots and exciting enemies against his powerful foe, Henry IV., against whom history attests that he succeeded in arming the Duke of Savoy, whom he caused to lose more towns than one; and in engaging in a conspiracy the Duke of Biron, whom he caused to lose his head. But as regards the pestilent race of bravoes, it is very certain they continued to increase until the 22d day of September, 1612; on which day the most illustrious and most excellent lord Don Giovanni de Mendoza, Marchese de la Hynojosa, gentleman, & c., Governor, & c., thought seriously of their extirpation. He addressed to Pandolfo and Marco Tullio Malatesti, printers of the Royal Chamber, the customary edict, corrected and enlarged, that they might print it, to accomplish that end. But the bravoes still survived, to experience, on the 24th December, 1618, still more terrific denunciations from the most illustrious and most excellent lord, Don Gomez Suarez de Figueroa, Duke of Feria, Governor, & c.; yet, as they did not fall even under these blows, the most illustrious and most excellent lord Gonzalo Fernandez de Cordova, under whose government we are made acquainted with Don Abbondio, found himself obliged to republish the usual proclamation against the bravoes, on the 5th day of October, 1627, that is, a year, a month, and two days previous to the commencement of our story.

Nor was this the last publication; but of those that follow, as of matters not falling within the period of our history, we do not think it proper to make mention. The only one of them to which we shall refer, is that of the 13th day of February, 1632, in which the most illustrious and most excellent lord, the

Duke of Feria, for the second time governor, informs us, "that the greatest and most heinous crimes are perpetrated by those styled bravoes." This will suffice to prove that, at the time of which we treat, the bravoes still existed.

It appeared evident to Don Abbondio that the two men above mentioned were waiting for some one, and he was alarmed at the conviction that it was for himself; for on his appearance, they exchanged a look, as if to say, "'tis he." Rising from the wall, they both advanced to meet him. He held his breviary open before him, as though he were employed in reading it; but, nevertheless, cast a glance upward in order to espy their movements. Seeing that they came directly toward him, he was beset by a thousand different thoughts. He considered, in haste, whether between the bravoes and himself there were any outlet from the road, and he remembered there was none. He took a rapid survey of his conduct, to discover if he had given offence to any powerful or revengeful man; but in this matter, he was somewhat reassured by the consoling testimony of his conscience. The bravoes draw near, and kept their eyes upon him. He raised his hand to his collar, as if adjusting it, and at the same time turned his head round, to see if any one were coming; he could discover no one. He cast a glance across the low stone wall upon the fields; no one! another on the road that lay before him; no one, except the bravoes! What is to be done? Flight was impossible. Unable to avoid the danger, he hastened to encounter it, and to put an end to the torments of uncertainty. He quickened his pace, recited a stanza in a louder tone, did his utmost to assume a composed and cheerful countenance, and finding himself in front of the two gallants, stopped short. "Signor Curate," said one of them, fixing his eyes upon him,—

"Your pleasure, sir," suddenly raising his eyes from his book, which he continued to hold open before him.

"You intend," pursued the other, with the threatening and angry mien of one who has detected an inferior in an attempt to commit some villany, "you intend to-morrow to unite in marriage Renzo Tramaglino and Lucy Mondella."

"That is," said Don Abbondio with a faltering voice, "that is to say—you gentlemen, being men of the world, are very well aware how these things are managed: the poor curate neither meddles nor makes—they settle their affairs amongst themselves, and then—then, they come to us, as if to redeem a pledge; and we—we are the servants of the public."

"Mark now," said the bravo in a low voice, but in a tone of command, "this marriage is not to take place, neither to-morrow, nor at any other time."

"But, my good sirs," replied Don Abbondio, with the mild and gentle tone of one who would persuade an impatient listener, "but, my good sirs, deign to put yourselves in my situation. If the thing depended on myself—you see plainly, that it does not in the least concern—"

"Hold there," said the bravo, interrupting him, "this matter is not to be settled by prating. We neither know nor care to know any more about it. A man once warned—you understand us."

"But, fair sirs, you are too just, too reasonable—"

"But," interrupted the other comrade, who had not before spoken, "but this marriage is not to be performed, or (with an oath) he who performs it will not repent of it, because he'll not have time" (with another oath).

"Hush, hush," resumed the first orator, "the Signor Curate knows the world, and we are gentlemen who have no wish to harm him if he conducts himself with judgment. Signor Curate, the most illustrious Signor Don Roderick, our patron, offers you his kind regards." As in the height of a midnight storm a vivid flash casts a momentary dazzling glare around and renders every object more fearful, so did this *name* increase the terror of Don Abbondio: as if by instinct, he bowed his head submissively, and said—

"If it could but be suggested to me."

"Oh! suggested to *you*, who understand Latin!" exclaimed the bravo, laughing; "it is for you to manage the matter. But, above all, be careful not to say a word concerning the hint that has been given you for your good; for if you do, ehem!—you understand—the consequences would be the same as if you performed the marriage ceremony. But say, what answer are we to carry in your name to the most illustrious Signor Don Roderick?"

"My respects—"

"Speak more clearly, Signor Curate."

"That I am disposed, ever disposed, to obedience." And as he spoke the words he was not very certain himself whether he gave a promise, or only uttered an ordinary compliment. The bravoes took, or *appeared* to take them, in the more serious sense.

"'Tis very well; good night, Signor Curate," said one of them as he retired, together with his companion. Don Abbondio, who a few minutes before would have given one of his eyes to avoid the ruffians, was now desirous to prolong the conversation.

"Gentlemen—" he began, as he shut his book. Without again noticing him, however, they passed on, singing a loose song, of which we will not transcribe the words. Poor Don Abbondio remained for a moment, as if spell-bound, and then with heavy and lagging steps took the path which led towards his home. The reader will better understand the state of his mind, when he shall have learned something more of his disposition, and of the condition of the times in which it was his lot to live.

Don Abbondio was not (as the reader may have perceived) endowed with the courage of a lion. But from his earliest years he had been sensible that the most embarrassing situation in those times was that of an animal, furnished with neither tusks nor talons, at the same time having no wish to be devoured. The arm of the law afforded no protection to a man of quiet, inoffensive habits, who had no means of making himself feared. Not that laws and penalties were wanting for the prevention of private violence: the laws were most express; the offences enumerated, and minutely particularised; the penalties sufficiently extravagant; and if that were not enough, the legislator himself, and, a hundred others to whom was committed the execution of the laws, had power to increase them. The proceedings were studiously contrived to free the judge from every thing that might prevent his passing sentence of condemnation; the passages we have cited from proclamations against the bravoes, may be taken as a faithful specimen of these decrees. Notwithstanding this, or, it may be, in *consequence* of this, these proclamations, reiterated and reinforced from time to time, served only to proclaim in pompous language the impotence of those who issued them; or, if they produced any immediate effect, it was *that* of adding to the vexations which the peaceful and feeble suffered from the disturbers of society. Impunity was organised and effected in so many ways as to render the proclamations powerless. Such was the consequence of the sanctuaries and asylums; and of the privileges of certain classes, partly acknowledged by the legal power, partly tolerated in silence, or feebly opposed; but which, in *fact*, were sustained and guarded by almost every individual with interested activity and punctilious jealousy. Now this impunity, threatened and assailed, but not destroyed, by these proclamations, would naturally, at every new attack, employ fresh efforts and devices to maintain itself. The proclamations were efficient, it is true, in fettering and embarrassing the honest man, who had neither power in himself nor protection from others; inasmuch as, in order to reach every person, they subjected the movements of each private individual to the arbitrary will of a thousand magistrates and executive officers. But he, who before the commission of his crime had prepared himself a refuge in some convent or palace where bailiffs never dared to enter; or who simply wore a livery, which engaged in his defence the vanity or the interest of a powerful family; such a one was free in his actions, and could laugh to scorn every proclamation. Of those very persons whose part it was to ensure the execution of these decrees, some belonged by birth to the privileged class, others were its clients and dependants; and as the latter as well as the former had, from education, from habit, from imitation, embraced its maxims, they would be very careful not to violate them. Had they however, been bold as heroes, obedient as monks, and devoted as martyrs, they could never have accomplished the execution of the laws, inferior as they were in number to *those* with whom they must engage, and with the frequent probability of being abandoned, or even sacrificed, by him who, in a moment of theoretical abstraction, might require them to act. But, in addition to this, their office would be regarded as a base one in public opinion, and their name stamped with reproach. It was therefore very natural that, instead of risking, nay, throwing away, their lives in a fruitless attempt, they should sell their inaction, or, rather, their connivance, to the powerful; or, at least, exercise their authority only on those occasions when it might be done with safety to themselves; that is, in oppressing the peaceable and the defenceless.

The man who acts with violence, or who is constantly in fear of violence from others, seeks companions and allies. Hence it happened that, during these times, individuals displayed so strong a tendency to combine themselves into classes, and to advance, as far as each one was able, the power of that to which he belonged. The clergy was vigilant in the defence and extension of its immunities; the nobility, of its privileges; the military, of its exemptions; the merchants and artisans were enrolled in companies and fraternities; the lawyers were united in leagues, and even the physicians formed a corporation. Each of these little oligarchies had its own appropriate power,—in each of them the individual found the advantage of employing for himself, in proportion to his influence and dexterity, the united force of numbers. The more honest availed themselves of this advantage merely for their defence;

the crafty and the wicked profited by it to assure themselves of success in their rogueries, and impunity from their results. The strength, however, of these various combinations was far from being equal; and, especially in the country, the wealthy and overbearing nobleman, with a band of bravoes, and surrounded by peasants accustomed to regard themselves as subjects and soldiers of their lord, exercised an irresistible power, and set all laws at defiance.

Don Abbondio, neither noble, rich, nor valiant, had from early youth found himself alone and unaided in such a state of society, like an earthen vessel thrown amidst iron jars; he therefore readily obeyed his parents, who wished him to become a priest. He did, to say the truth, not regard the obligations and the noble ends of the ministry to which he dedicated himself, but was only desirous to secure the means of living, and to connect himself with a powerful and respected class. But no class provided for the individual, or secured his safety, *further* than to a certain point; none rendered it unnecessary for him to adopt for himself a system of his own. The system of Don Abbondio consisted chiefly in shunning all disputes; he maintained an unarmed neutrality in all the contests that broke out around him;—between the clergy and the civil power, between persons in office and nobles and magistrates, bravoes and soldiers, down to the squabbles of the peasantry themselves, terminated by the fist or the knife. By keeping aloof from the overbearing, by affecting not to notice their acts of violence, by bowing low and with the most profound respect to all whom he met, the poor man had succeeded in passing over sixty years without encountering any violent storms; not but that he also had some small portion of gall in his composition; and this continual exercise of patience exacerbated it to such a degree, that, if he had not had it in his power occasionally to give it vent, his health must have suffered. But as there were a few persons in the world connected with himself whom he knew to be powerless, he could, from time to time, discharge on them his long pent-up ill-humour. He was, moreover, a severe censor of those who did not regulate their conduct by his example, provided he could censure without danger. According to his creed, the poor fellow who had been cudgelled had been a little imprudent; the murdered man had always been turbulent; the man who maintained his right against the powerful, and met with a broken head, must have been somewhat wrong; which is, perhaps, true enough, for in all disputes the line can never be drawn so finely as not to leave a little wrong on both sides. He especially declaimed against those of his confraternity, who, at their own risk, took part with the oppressed against a powerful oppressor. "This," he said, "was to purchase trouble with ready money, to kick at snarling dogs, and an intermeddling in profane things that lowered the dignity of the sacred ministry." He had, in short, a favourite maxim, that an honest man, who looked to himself and minded his own affairs, never met with any rough encounters.

From all that has been said, we may imagine the effect the meeting just described must have had upon the mind of poor Don Abbondio. Those fierce countenances, the threats of a lord who was well known not to speak idly, his plan of quiet life and patient endurance disconcerted in an instant, a difficulty before him from which he saw no possibility of extrication; all these thoughts rushed confusedly through his mind. "If Renzo could be quietly dismissed with a refusal, all would be well; but he will require reasons—and what can I say to him? he too has a head of his own; a lamb, if not meddled with—but once attempt to cross him— Oh!—and raving after that Lucy, as much enamoured as— Young idiots! who, for want of something else to do, fall in love, and must be married, forsooth, thinking of nothing else, never concerning themselves about the trouble they bring upon an honest man like me. Wretch that I am! Why should those two scowling faces plant themselves exactly in my path, and pick a quarrel with me? What have I to do in the matter? Is it I that mean to wive? Why did they not rather go and speak— Ah! truly, that which is to the purpose always occurs to me after the right time: if I had but thought of suggesting to them to go and bear their message—" But here he was disturbed by the reflection, that to repent of not having been the counsellor and abettor of evil, was too iniquitous a thing; and he therefore turned the rancour of his thoughts against the individual who had thus robbed him of his tranquillity. He did not know Don Roderick, except by sight and by report; his sole intercourse with him had been to touch chin to breast, and the ground with the corner of his hat, the few times he had met him on the road. He had, on more than one occasion, defended the reputation of that Signor against those who, in an under-tone, with sighs and looks raised to heaven, had execrated some one of his exploits. He had declared a hundred times that he was a respectable cavalier. But at this moment he, in his own heart, readily bestowed upon him all those titles to which he would never lend an ear from another. Having, amidst the tumult of these thoughts, reached the entrance of his house, which stood at the end of the little glebe, he unlocked the door, entered, and carefully secured it within. Anxious to find himself in society that he could trust, he called aloud, "Perpetua, Perpetua," advancing towards the little parlour where she was, doubtless, employed in preparing the table for his supper. Perpetua was, as the reader must be aware, the housekeeper of Don Abbondio; an affectionate and faithful domestic, who knew how to obey or command as occasion served; to bear the grumbling and whims of her master at times, and at others to make him bear with hers. These were becoming every day more frequent; she had passed the age of forty in a single state; the consequences, *she* said, of having refused all the offers that had been made her; her *female friends* asserted that she had never found any one willing to take her.

"Coming," said Perpetua, as she set in its usual place on the little table the flask of Don Abbondio's favourite wine, and moved slowly toward the parlour door: before she reached it he entered, with steps so disordered, looks so clouded, and a countenance so changed, that an eye less practised than that of Perpetua could have discovered at a glance that something unusual had befallen him.

"Mercy on me! What is it ails my master?"

"Nothing, nothing," said Don Abbondio, as he sank upon his easy chair.

"How, nothing! Would you have me believe that, looking as you do? Some dreadful accident has happened."

"Oh! for the love of Heaven! When I say nothing, it is either nothing, or something I cannot tell."

"That you cannot tell, not even to me? Who will take care of your health? Who will give you advice?"

"Oh! peace, peace! Do not make matters worse. Give me a glass of my wine."

"And you will still pretend to me that nothing is the matter?" said Perpetua, filling the glass, but retaining it in her hand, as if unwilling to present it except as the reward of confidence.

"Give here, give here," said Don Abbondio, taking the glass with an unsteady hand, and hastily swallowing its contents.

"Would you oblige me then to go about, asking here and there what it is has happened to my master?" said Perpetua, standing upright before him, with her hands on her sides, and looking him steadfastly in the face, as if to extract the secret from his eyes.

"For the love of Heaven, do not worry me, do not kill me with your pother; this is a matter that concerns—concerns my life."

"Your life!"

"My life."

"You know well, that, when you have frankly confided in me, I have never—"

"Yes, forsooth, as when—"

Perpetua was sensible she had touched a false string; wherefore, changing suddenly her note, "My dear master," said she, in a moving tone of voice, "I have always had a dutiful regard for you, and if I now wish to know this affair, it is from zeal, and a desire to assist you, to give you advice, to relieve your mind."

The truth is, that Don Abbondio's desire to disburden himself of his painful secret was as great as that of Perpetua to obtain a knowledge of it; so that, after having repulsed, more and more feebly, her renewed assaults; after having made her swear many times that she would not breathe a syllable of it, he, with frequent pauses and exclamations, related his miserable adventure. When it was necessary to pronounce the dread name of him from whom the prohibition came, he required from Perpetua another and more solemn oath: having uttered it, he threw himself back on his seat with a heavy sigh, and, in a tone of command, as well as supplication, exclaimed,—

"For the love of Heaven!"—

"Mercy upon me!" cried Perpetua, "what a wretch! what a tyrant! Does he not fear God?"

"Will you be silent? or do you want to ruin me completely?"

"Oh! we are here alone, no one can hear us. But what will my poor master do?"

"See there now," said Don Abbondio, in a peevish tone, "see the fine advice you give me. To ask of me, what I'll do? what I'll do? as if you were the one in difficulty, and it was for me to help you out!"

"Nay, I could give you my own poor opinion; but then—"

"But—but then, let us know it."

"My opinion would be, that, as every one says our archbishop is a saint, a man of courage, and not to be frightened by an ugly phiz, and who will take pleasure in upholding a curate against one of these tyrants; I should say, and do say, that you had better write him a handsome letter, to inform him as how—"

"Will you be silent! will you be silent! Is this advice to offer a poor man? When I get a pistol bullet in my side—God preserve me!—will the archbishop take it out?"

"Ah! pistol bullets are not given away like sugarplums; and it were woful if those dogs should bite every time they bark. If a man knows how to show his teeth, and make himself feared, they hold him in respect: we should not have been brought to such a pass, if you had stood upon your rights. Now, all come to us (by your good leave) to—"

"Will you be silent?"

"Certainly; but it is true though, that when the world sees one is always ready, in every encounter, to lower—"

"Will you be silent? Is this a time for such idle talk?"

"Well, well, you'll think of it to-night; but in the meantime do not be the first to harm yourself; to destroy your own health: eat a mouthful."

"I'll think of it," murmured Don Abbondio; "certainly I'll think of it. I *must* think of it;" and he arose, continuing—"No! I'll take nothing, nothing; I've something else to do. But, that this should have fallen upon me—"

"Swallow at least this other little drop," said Perpetua, as she poured the wine. "You know it always restores your stomach."

"Oh! there wants other medicine than that, other medicine than that, other medicine than that—"

So saying, he took the light, and muttering, "A pretty business this! To an honest man like me! And to-morrow, what is to be done?" with other like exclamations, he went towards his bedchamber. Having reached the door, he stopped a moment, and before he quitted the room, exclaimed, turning towards Perpetua, with his finger on his lips—"For the love of Heaven, be silent!"

Chapter II.

It is related that the Prince of Condé slept soundly the night preceding the battle of Rocroi; but then, he was greatly fatigued, and moreover had made every arrangement for the morrow. It was not thus with Don Abbondio; he only knew the morrow would be a day of trouble, and consequently passed the night in anxious anticipation. He could not for a moment think of disregarding the menaces of the bravoes, and solemnising the marriage. To confide to Renzo the occurrence, and consult with him as to the means—God forbid!—He remembered the warning of the bravo, "not to say one word"—otherwise, *ahem!* and this dreadful *ahem* of the bravo resounded in the ears of Don Abbondio; so that he already repented of his communication to Perpetua. To fly was impossible—and where *could* he fly? At the thought, a thousand obstacles presented themselves.—After long and painful deliberation, he resolved to endeavour to gain time, by giving Renzo some fanciful reasons for the postponement of the marriage. He recollected that in a few days more the time would arrive, during which marriages were prohibited. "And if I can keep this youngster at bay for a few days, I shall then have two months before me; and in two months who can tell what may happen?" He thought of various pretexts for his purpose; and though they were rather flimsy, he persuaded himself that his authority would give them weight, and that his experience would prevail over the mind of an ignorant youth. "We will see," said he to himself: "he thinks of his love, but I think of myself; I am, therefore, the party most interested; I must call in all my cunning to assist me. I cannot help it, young man, if you suffer; I must not be the victim." Having somewhat composed his mind with this determination, he at length fell asleep. But his dreams, alas! how horrible—bravoes, Don Roderick, Renzo, roads, rocks, cries, bullets.

The arousing from sleep, after a recent misfortune, is a bitter moment; the mind at first habitually recurs to its previous tranquillity, but is soon depressed by the thought of the contrast that awaits it. When alive to a sense of his situation, Don Abbondio recapitulated the plans of the night, made a better disposal of them, and after having risen, awaited with dread and impatience the moment of Renzo's arrival.

Lorenzo, or as he was called, Renzo, did not make him wait long; at an early hour he presented himself before the curate with the joyful readiness of one who was on this day to espouse her whom he loved. He had been deprived of his parents in his youth, and now practised the trade of a weaver of silk, which was, it might be said, hereditary in his family. This trade had once been very lucrative; and although now on the decline, a skilful workman might obtain from it a respectable livelihood. The continual emigration of the tradesmen, attracted to the neighbouring states by promises and privileges, left sufficient employment for those who remained behind. Besides, Renzo possessed a small farm, which he had cultivated himself when otherwise unoccupied; so that, for one of his condition, he might be called wealthy: and although the last harvest had been more deficient than the preceding ones, and the evils of famine were beginning to be felt; yet, from the moment he had given his heart to Lucy, he had been so economical as to preserve a sufficiency of all necessaries, and to be in no danger of wanting bread. He appeared before Don Abbondio gaily dressed, and with a joyful countenance. The mysterious and perplexed manner of the curate formed a singular contrast to that of the handsome young man.

"What is the matter now?" thought Renzo; but without waiting to answer his own question, "Signor Curate," said he, "I am come to know at what hour of the day it will be convenient for you that we should be at the church?"

"Of what day do you speak?"

"How! of what day? do you not remember that this is the day appointed?"

"To-day?" replied Don Abbondio, as if he heard it for the first time, "to-day? to-day? be patient, I cannot to-day—"

"You cannot to-day? why not?"

"In the first place I am not well—"

"I am sorry for it; but we shall not detain you long, and you will not be much fatigued."

"But then—but then—"

"But then, what, sir?"

"There are difficulties."

"Difficulties! How can that be?"

"People should be in our situation, to know how many obstacles there are to these matters; I am too yielding, I think only of removing impediments, of rendering all things easy, and promoting the happiness of others. To do this I neglect my duty, and am covered with reproaches for it."

"In the name of Heaven, keep me not thus in suspense, but tell me at once what is the matter?"

"Do you know how many formalities are required before the marriage can be celebrated?"

"I must, indeed, know something of them," said Renzo, beginning to grow angry, "since you have racked my brains with them abundantly these few days back. But are not all things now ready? have you not done all there was to do?"

"All, all, you expect; but be patient, I tell you. I have been a blockhead to neglect my duty, that I might not cause pain to others;—we poor curates—we are, as may be said, ever between a hawk and a buzzard. I pity you, poor young man! I perceive your impatience, but my superiors—Enough, I have reasons for what I say, but I cannot tell all—we, however, are sure to suffer."

"But tell me what this other formality is, and I will perform it immediately."

"Do you know how many obstacles stand in the way?"

"How can I know any thing of obstacles?"

"Error, conditio, votum, cognatis, crimen, cultus disparitas, vis, ordo.... Si sit affinis...."

"Oh! for Heaven's sake—how should I understand all this Latin?"

"Be patient, dear Renzo; I am ready to do—all that depends on me. I—I wish to see you satisfied—I wish you well— And when I think that you were so happy, that you wanted nothing when the whim entered your head to be married—"

"What words are these, Signor?" interrupted Renzo, with a look of astonishment and anger.

"I say, do be patient—I say, I wish to see you happy. In short—in short, my dear child, I have not been in fault; I did not make the laws. Before concluding a marriage, we are required to search closely that there be no obstacles."

"Now, I beseech you, tell me at once what difficulty has occurred?"

"Be patient—these are not points to be cleared up in an instant. There *will* be nothing, I hope; but whether or not, we must search into the matter. The passage is clear and explicit,—'antiquam matrimonium denunciet—'"

"I'll not hear your Latin."

"But it is necessary to explain to you—"

"But why not do this before? Why tell me all was prepared? Why wait—"

"See there now! to reproach me with my kindness! I have hastened every thing to serve you; but—but there has occurred—well, well, I know—"

"And what do you wish that I should do?"

"Be patient for a few days. My dear child, a few days are not eternity; be patient."

"For how long a time then?"

"We are coming to a good conclusion," thought Don Abbondio. "Come," said he, gently, "in fifteen days I will endeavour—"

"Fifteen days! Oh! this is something new. To tell me now, on the very day you yourself appointed for my marriage, that I must wait fifteen days! Fifteen," resumed he, with a low and angry voice.

Don Abbondio interrupted him, earnestly seizing his hand, and with an imploring tone beseeching him to be quiet. "Come, come, don't be angry; for the love of Heaven! I'll see, I'll see if in a week—"

"And what shall I say to Lucy?" said Renzo, softening.

"That it has been a mistake of mine."

"And to the world?"

"Say also it is my fault; that through too great haste I have made some great blunder: throw all the blame on me. Can I do more than this? Come in a week."

"And then there will be no further difficulties?"

"When I say a thing—"

"Well, well, I will be quiet for a week; but be assured, I will be put off with no further excuses:—for the present, I take my leave." So saying, he departed, making a bow to Don Abbondio less profound than usual, and giving him a look more expressive than respectful.

With a heavy heart he approached the house of his betrothed, his mind dwelling on the strange conversation which had just taken place. The cold and embarrassed reception of Don Abbondio, his constrained and impatient air, his mysterious hints, all combined to convince him there was still something he had not been willing to communicate. He stopped for a moment, debating with himself whether he should not return and compel him to be more frank; raising his eyes, however, he beheld Perpetua entering a little garden a few steps distant from the house. He called to her, quickened his pace, and detaining her at the gate, endeavoured to enter into discourse with her.

"Good day, Perpetua; I expected to have received your congratulations to-day."

"But it must be as God pleases, my poor Renzo."

"I want to ask a favour of you: the Signor Curate has offered reasons I cannot comprehend; will you explain to me the true cause why he is unable or unwilling to marry us to-day?"

"Oh! you think then that I know the secrets of my master."

"I was right in supposing there was a mystery," thought Renzo. "Come, come, Perpetua," continued he, "we are friends; tell me what you know,—help a poor young man."

"It is a bad thing to be born poor, my dear Renzo."

"That is true," replied he, still more confirmed in his suspicions—"that is true; but it is not becoming in the clergy to behave unjustly to the poor."

"Hear me, Renzo; I can tell you nothing, because—I know nothing. But I can assure you my master would not wrong you or any one; and he is not to blame."

"Who then is to blame?" asked Renzo, carelessly, but listening intently for a reply.

"I have told you already I know nothing. But I may be allowed to speak in defence of my master; poor man! if he has erred, it has been through too great kindness. There are in this world men who are overpowerful, knavish, and who fear not God."

"Overpowerful! knavish!" thought Renzo; "these cannot be his superiors."—"Come," said he, with difficulty concealing his increasing agitation, "come, tell me who it is."

"Ah! you would persuade me to speak, and I must not, because—I know nothing. I will keep silence as faithfully as if I had promised to do so. You might put me to the torture, and you could not draw any thing from me. Adieu! it is lost time for both of us."

Thus saying, she re-entered the garden hastily, and shut the gate. Renzo turned very softly, lest at the noise of his footsteps she might discern the road he took: when fairly beyond her hearing, he quickened his steps, and in a moment was at the door of Don Abbondio's house; he entered, rushed towards the little parlour where he had left him, and finding him still there, approached him with a bold and furious manner.

"Eh! eh! what has happened now?" said Don Abbondio.

"Who is this powerful personage?" said Renzo, with the air of one resolved to obtain an explicit answer; "who is he that forbids me to marry Lucy?"

"What! what! what!" stammered Don Abbondio, turning pale with surprise. He arose from his chair, and made an effort to reach the door. But Renzo, who expected this movement, was upon his guard; and locking the door, he put the key in his pocket.

"Ah! will you speak now, Signor Curate? Every one knows the affair but myself; and, by heavens! I'll know it too. Who is it, I say?"

"Renzo, Renzo, for the love of charity, take care what you do; think of your soul."

"I must know it at once—this moment." So saying, he placed his hand on his dagger, but perhaps without intending it.

"Mercy!" exclaimed Don Abbondio, in a stifled voice.

"I *must* know it."

"Who has told you?"

"Come, no more excuses. Speak plainly and quickly."

"Do you mean to kill me?"

"I mean to know that which I have a right to know."

"But if I speak, I die. Must I not preserve my life?"

"Speak, then."

The manner of Renzo was so threatening and decided, that Don Abbondio felt there was no possibility of disobeying him. "Promise me—swear," said he, "never to tell—"

"Tell me, tell me quickly his name, or—"

At this new adjuration, the poor curate, with the trembling look of a man who feels the instrument of the dentist in his mouth, feebly articulated, "Don—"

"Don?" replied Renzo, inclining his ear towards him, eager to hear the rest. "Don?"

"Don Roderick!" muttered he hastily, trembling at the sound that escaped his lips.

"Ah! dog!" shouted Renzo; "and how has he done it? what has he said to you to—"

"What? what?" said Don Abbondio, in an almost contemptuous tone, already gaining confidence by the sacrifice he had made. "I wish you were like myself, you would then meddle with nothing, and certainly you would not have had so many whims in your head." He, however, related in terrible colours the ugly encounter; his anger, which had hitherto been subdued by fear, displayed itself as he proceeded; and perceiving that Renzo, between rage and astonishment, remained motionless, with his head bent down, he continued in a lively manner, "You have made a pretty business of it, indeed! You have rendered me a notable service. Thus to attack an honest man, your curate, in his own house! in a sacred place! You have done a fine thing, truly. To wrest from my mouth, that which I concealed, from prudence, for your own good. And now that you know it, what will you do? When I gave you good advice this morning, I had judgment for you and me; but believe me, this is no jesting matter, no question of right or wrong, but superior power. At all events, open the door; give me the key."

"I may have been to blame," replied Renzo with a softened voice, but in which might be perceived smothered anger towards his concealed enemy, "I may have been to blame, but if you had been in my situation—" He drew the key from his pocket, and advanced towards the door.

"Swear to me," said Don Abbondio with a serious and anxious face.

"I may have been to blame—forgive me," replied Renzo, moving to depart.

"Swear first," said Don Abbondio, holding him tremblingly by the arm.

"I may have been to blame," said Renzo, freeing himself from his grasp, and immediately springing out of the room.

"Perpetua! Perpetua!" cried Don Abbondio, after having in vain called back the fugitive. Perpetua did not answer. The poor man was so overwhelmed by his innumerable difficulties, his increasing perplexities, and so apprehensive of some fresh attack, that he conceived the idea of securing to himself a safe retreat from them all, by going to bed and giving out that he had a fever. His malady, indeed, was not altogether imaginary; the terror of the past day, the anxious watching of the night, the dread of the future, had combined to produce really the effect. Weary and stupified, he slumbered in his large chair, muttering occasionally in a feeble but passionate voice, "Perpetua."—Perpetua arrived at last with a great cabbage under her arm, and with as unconcerned a countenance as if nothing had happened. We will spare the reader the reproaches, the accusations, and denials that passed between them; it is sufficient that Don Abbondio ordered Perpetua to bolt the door, not to put her foot outside, and if any one knocked, to reply from the window that the curate was gone to bed with a fever. He then slowly ascended the stairs and put himself really in bed, where we will leave him.

Renzo, meanwhile, with hurried steps, and with a mind unsettled and distracted as to the course he should pursue, approached his home. Those who injure others are guilty, not only of the evils they commit, but also of the effects produced by these evils on the characters of the injured persons. Renzo was a quiet and peaceful youth, but now his nature appeared changed, and his thoughts dwelt only on deeds of violence. He would have run to the house of Don Roderick to assault him there; but he remembered that it was a fortress, furnished with bravoes within, and well guarded without; that only those known to be friends and servants could enter without the minutest scrutiny; and that not even a tradesman could be seen there without being examined from head to foot; and he, above all, would be, alas! but too well known. He then imagined himself placed behind a hedge, with his arquebuss in his hand, waiting till Roderick should pass by alone; rejoicing internally at the thought, he pictured to himself an approaching footstep; the villain appears, he takes aim, fires, and he falls; he exults a moment over his dying struggles, and then escapes for his life beyond the confines! And Lucy? This name recalled his wiser and better thoughts: he remembered the last instructions of his parents; he thought of God, the Holy Virgin, and the Saints; and he tremblingly rejoiced that he had been guilty of the deed only in imagination. But how many hopes, promises, and anticipations did the idea of Lucy suggest? And this day so ardently desired! How announce to her the dreadful news? And then, what plan to pursue? How make her his own in spite of the power of this wicked lord? And now a tormenting suspicion passed through his mind. Don Roderick must have been instigated to this injury by a brutal passion for Lucy! And she! He could not for a moment endure the maddening thought that she had given him the slightest encouragement. But was she not informed of his designs? Could he have conceived his infamous purpose, and have advanced so far towards its completion, without her knowledge? And Lucy, his own beloved, had never uttered a syllable to him concerning it!

These reflections prevailing in his mind, he passed by his own house, which was situated in the centre of the village, and arrived at that of Lucy, which was at the opposite extremity. It had a small court-yard in front, which separated it from the road, and which was encircled by a low wall. Entering the yard, Renzo heard a confused murmur of voices in the upper chamber; he rightly supposed it to be the wedding company, and he could not resolve to appear before them with such a countenance. A little girl, who was standing at the door, ran towards him, crying out, "The bridegroom! the bridegroom!" "Hush, Betsy, hush," said Renzo, "come hither; go to Lucy, and whisper in her ear—but let no one hear you—whisper in her ear, that I wish to speak with her in the lower chamber, and that she must come at once." The little girl hastily ascended the stairs, proud of having a secret commission to execute. Lucy had just come forth, adorned from the hands of her mother, and surrounded by her admiring friends. These were playfully endeavouring to steal a look at the blooming bride; while she, with the timidity of rustic modesty, attempted to conceal her blushing countenance with her bending arm, from beneath which a smiling mouth nevertheless appeared. Her black tresses, parted on her white forehead, were folded up in multiplied circles on the back of her head, and fastened with pins of silver, projecting on every side like the rays of the sun: this is still the custom of the Milanese peasantry. Around her throat she had a necklace of garnets, alternated with beads of gold filagree; she wore a boddice embroidered in flowers, the sleeves tied with ribands; a short petticoat of silk, with numerous minute plaits; crimson stockings, and embroidered silk slippers. But beyond all these ornaments was the modest and beautiful joy depicted on her countenance; a joy, however, troubled by a slight shade of anxiety. The little Betsy intruded herself into the circle, managed to approach Lucy, and communicated her message. "I shall return in a moment," said Lucy to her friends, as she hastily quitted the room. On perceiving the altered and unquiet appearance of Renzo, "What is the matter?" said she, not without a presentiment of evil.

"Lucy," replied Renzo, "all is at a stand, and God knows whether we shall ever be man and wife!"

"How!" said Lucy, alarmed. Renzo related briefly the history of the morning; she listened with anguish: when he uttered the name of Don Roderick, "Ah!" exclaimed she, blushing and trembling, "has it then come to this?"

"Then you knew!" said Renzo.

"Too well," replied Lucy.

"What did you know?"

"Do not make me speak now, do not make me weep! I'll call my mother and dismiss the company. We must be alone."

As she departed, Renzo whispered, "And you have never spoken of it to me!"

"Ah, Renzo!" replied Lucy, turning for a moment to gaze at him.

He understood well what this action meant; it was as if she had said, "Can you doubt me?"

Meanwhile the good Agnes (so the mother of Lucy was called) had descended the stairs, to ascertain the cause of her daughter's disappearance. She remained with Renzo; while Lucy returned to the company, and, assuming all the composure she could, said to them, "The Signor Curate is indisposed, and the wedding cannot take place to-day." The ladies departed, and lost no time in relating amongst the gossips of the neighbourhood all that had occurred, while they made particular enquiries respecting the reality of Don Abbondio's sickness. The truth of this cut short the conjectures which they had already begun to intimate by brief and mysterious hints.

Chapter III.

Lucy entered the lower room as Renzo was sorrowfully informing Agnes of that, to which she as sorrowfully listened. Both turned towards her from whom they expected an explanation which could not but be painful; the suspicions of both were, however, excited in the midst of their grief, and the displeasure they felt towards Lucy differed only according to their relative situation. Agnes, although anxious to hear her daughter speak, could not avoid reproaching her—"To say nothing to thy mother!"

"Now, I will tell you all," said Lucy, wiping her eyes with her apron.

"Speak, speak!" cried at once her mother and her lover.

"Holy Virgin!" exclaimed Lucy, "that it should come to this!"—and with a voice interrupted by tears, she related that a few days previously, as she returned from weaving, and was loitering behind her companions, Don Roderick came up with her, in company with another gentleman; that the former sought to engage her in idle conversation; that she quickened her pace, without lending him an ear, and rejoined her companions; in the mean while she heard the other gentleman laugh, and Don Roderick say, "I'll lay a wager with you." The day following, on their return, they met them again, but Lucy kept in the midst of her companions, with her head down; the other gentleman burst into laughter, and Don Roderick said, "We will see, we will see." "Happily for me," continued Lucy, "this day was the last of the weaving. I related the adventure immediately—"

"To whom didst thou relate it?" asked Agnes quickly, indignant at the idea of any one being preferred before her as a confidant.

"To Father Christopher, in confession, mamma," replied Lucy, in a tone of apology. "I told him all, the last time you and I went to the church of the convent; you may perhaps recollect my contrivances for delay on that morning, until there should pass some villagers in whose company we might go into the street; because I was so afraid—"

The indignation of Agnes subsided at once, at the mention of a name so revered as Father Christopher's. "Thou didst well, my child," said she; "but why not tell it also to thy mother?"

For this, Lucy had had two very good reasons; the one, a desire not to disturb and frighten her mother with a circumstance she could not have prevented; the other, the dread of placing a secret, which she wished to be buried in her own bosom in danger of becoming known to all the village: of these two reasons she only alleged the first.

"And could I," said she, turning to Renzo, in a gentle and reproachful voice, "could I speak to you of this?—Alas! that you should know it now!"

"And what did the Father say to you?" asked Agnes.

"He told me to endeavour to hasten my nuptials, and in the mean while to keep myself within doors; to pray much to God; and he hoped that if Don Roderick should not see me, he would cease to think of me. And it was then," continued she, turning again towards Renzo, without, however, raising her eyes, and blushing deeply, "it was then that I compelled myself, at the risk of appearing very forward, to request you to conclude the marriage before the appointed time. Who can tell what you must have thought of me? But I did it for the best, and from advice—and this morning I little thought—" She could articulate no longer, and burst into a flood of tears.

"Ah! the scoundrel! the villain!" exclaimed Renzo, pacing the room in a violent paroxysm of rage. He stopped suddenly before Lucy, regarded her with a countenance agitated by various passions, and said, "This is the last wicked deed this wretch will perform."

"Ah! no, Renzo, for the love of Heaven!" cried Lucy; "no, no, for the love of Heaven! There is a God who watches over the oppressed; but do you think he will protect us if we do evil?"

"No, no, for the love of Heaven!" repeated Agnes.

"Renzo," said Lucy, with a more resolved and tranquil air, "you have a trade, and I know how to work: let us go away into some distant place, that he may hear of us no more."

"Ah, Lucy! but we are not yet man and wife! If we were married, then, indeed—" Lucy relapsed into tears, and all three remained silent; the deep despondency of their countenances formed a mournful contrast to the festive character of their dress.

"Hear me, my children; listen to me," said Agnes, after a few moments; "I came into the world before you, and I know it a little better than you do. The devil is not so frightful as they paint him. To us poor people the skeins appear more entangled, because we do not know where to look for the end; but sometimes advice from a learned man—I know what I mean to say.—Do as I tell you, Renzo; go to Lecco; find the Doctor *Azzecca Garbugli*; relate to him—But you must not call him by this name—it is a nick-name. Say to the doctor—what do they call him? Oh dear! I can't think of his real name, every one calls him *Azzecca Garbugli*. Well, well, find this tall, stiff, bald doctor, with a red nose, and a face as red—"

"I know the man by sight," said Renzo.

"Well, very well," continued Agnes, "there's a man for you! I have seen more than one troubled wretch who did not know which way to turn himself; I have known him remain an hour with the Doctor *Azzecca Garbugli* (be careful you don't call him so), and go away laughing at himself for his uneasiness. Take with you these fowls; I expected to have wrung their necks, poor little things! for the banquet of to-night; however, carry them to him, because one must never go empty-handed to these gentlemen. Relate to him all that has happened, and he will tell you at once that which would never enter our heads in a year."

Renzo and Lucy approved of this advice; Agnes, proud of having given it, with great complacency took the poor fowls one by one from the coop, tied their legs together as if she were making a nosegay, and consigned them to his hands. After having exchanged words of hope, he departed, avoiding the high road and crossing the fields, so as not to attract notice. As he went along, he had leisure to dwell on his misfortunes, and revolve in his mind his anticipated interview with the Doctor *Azzecca Garbugli*. I leave the reader to imagine the condition of the unfortunate fowls swinging by the legs with their heads downwards in the hands of a man agitated by all the tumults of passion; and whose arm moved more in accordance with the violence of his feelings, than with sympathy for the unhappy animals whose heads became conscious of sundry terrific shocks, which they resented by pecking at one another,—a practice too frequent with companions in misfortune.

He arrived at the village, asked for the house of the doctor, which being pointed out to him, he proceeded thither. On entering, he experienced the timidity so common to the poor and illiterate at the near approach to the learned and noble; he forgot all the speeches he had prepared, but giving a glance at the fowls, he took courage. He entered the kitchen, and demanded of the maid servant, "If he could speak with the Signor Doctor?" As if accustomed to similar gifts, she immediately took the fowls out of his hand, although Renzo drew them back, wishing the doctor to know that it was he who brought them. The doctor entered as the maid was saying, "Give here, and pass into the study." Renzo bowed low to him; he replied with a kind "Come in, my son," and led the way into an adjoining chamber. This was a large room, on the three walls of which were distributed portraits of the twelve Cæsars, while the fourth was covered with a large bookcase of old and dusty books; in the middle stood a table laden with memorials, libels, and proclamations, with three or four seats around; on one side of it was a large arm-chair with a high and square back, terminated at each corner by ornaments of wood in the fashion of horns; the nails which had fallen out here and there from its leathern covering, left the corners of it at liberty to roll themselves up in all directions. The doctor was in his morning gown, that is, enveloped in a faded toga, which had served him long since to appear in at Milan, on some great occasion. He closed the door, and encouraged the young man with these words: "My son, tell me your case."

"I wish to speak a word to you in confidence."

"Well, say on," replied the doctor, as he seated himself in the arm-chair. Renzo stood before the table twirling his hat in his hand, and began, "I wish to know from one as learned as yourself—"

"Tell me the affair just as it is," interrupted the doctor, "in as few words as possible."

"You must pardon me, Signor Doctor; we poor people know not how to speak to such as you are. I wish then to know—"

"Bless the people! they are all alike; instead of relating facts, they ask questions; and that because their own opinions are already settled!"

"Excuse me, Signor Doctor. I wish, then, to know if there is a punishment for threatening a curate, to prevent him from performing a marriage ceremony?"

"I understand," said the doctor, who in truth had *not* understood—"I understand." And suddenly assuming an air of seriousness and importance, "A serious case, my son—a case contemplated. You have done well to come to me; it is a clear case, noticed in a hundred proclamations, and in one, of the year just elapsed, by the actual governor. You shall see, you shall see! Where can it be?" said he, plunging his hand amidst the chaos of papers; "it must surely be here, as it is a decree of great importance. Ah! here it is, here it is!" He unfolded it, looked at the date, and with a serious face exclaimed,

"Fifteenth of October, 1627. Yes, yes, this is it; a new edict; these are those which cause terror—Do you know how to read, my son?"

"A little, Signor Doctor."

"Well now, come behind me, and you will see for yourself."

Holding the proclamation extended before him, he began to read, stammering rapidly over some passages, and pausing distinctly with great expression on others, according to the necessity of the case.

"*Although by the proclamation published by order of the Signor Duke di Feria, on the 14th of December, 1620, and ratified by the most illustrious, and most excellent lord, Signor Gonsalez Fernandez de Cordova, &c. &c.—had by extraordinary and rigorous remedies provided against the oppressions, exactions, and other tyrannical acts committed against the devoted vassals of His Majesty; the frequency of the excesses, however, &c. &c., has arrived at such a point that His Excellency is under the necessity, &c. &c.—wherefore, with the concurrence of the Senate and Convention, &c. &c.—has resolved to publish the present decree.*" "*And from the tyrannical acts which the skill of many in the villages, as well as in the cities.*"—"Do you hear"—umph—*exact and oppress the weak in various ways, making violent contracts of purchase, of rent, &c.*"—"Where is it? Ah! here it is, listen, listen,"—"*who, whether matrimony follow or not.*"

"Ah! that's my case!" said Renzo.

"Listen, listen, here is more; now we will find the punishment." Umph—"*that they leave the place of their abode, &c. &c.—that if one pays a debt he must not be molested.*" "All this has nothing to do with us. Ah! here it is!" "*the priest refusing to do that to which he is obliged by his office,*"—"Eh?"

"It appears the proclamation was made purposely for me."

"Ah! is it not so? listen, listen." "*And other similar oppressions which flow from the vassals, nobility, middle and lower classes.*" "None escape, they are all here—it is like the valley of Jehoshaphat. Hear now the penalty." "*For all these and other similar evil deeds, which having been prohibited, it is nevertheless necessary to exact with rigour, &c.—His Excellency, not annulling, orders and commands, that whoever the offenders be, they shall be subjected to pecuniary and corporal punishment—to banishment, the galleys, or to death,*" "a mere trifle!" "*at the will of His Excellency, or of the Senate. And from this there is no escape, &c. &c.*" "And see here the signature," "*Gonsalez Fernandez de Cordova;*" "and lower down," "*Platonas;*" "and here again"—"*Videt Ferrar,*" "nothing is wanting." Whilst the doctor was reading, Renzo had kept his eyes on the paper, seeking to ascertain for himself its real meaning. The doctor, perceiving his new client more attentive than dismayed, marvelled greatly. "He must be enrolled as one of the bravoes," said he to himself; "Ah! ah!" exclaimed he, addressing Renzo, "you have shaved off the long lock! Well, well, it was prudent; but placing yourself in my hands, you need not have done so. The case is a serious one—you can have no idea how much resolution is required to conduct these matters wisely."

To understand this mistake of the doctor's, it should be known, that the bravoes by profession used to wear a long lock of hair, which they pulled over the face as a mask in enterprises that required prudence as well as strength. The proclamation had not been silent with regard to this custom.

"*His Excellency commands, that whosoever shall wear hair of such a length as to cover the forehead to the eyebrows, will incur the penalty of a fine of three hundred crowns; in case of incapability of payment, three years in the galleys for the first offence; and for the second, in addition to the aforesaid, greater punishments still, at the will of His Excellency.*" The long lock had become a distinctive mark of the loose and disorderly.

"Indeed, indeed," replied Renzo, "I have never worn a long lock in my life."

"I can do nothing," replied the doctor, shaking his head, with a knowing and rather impatient smile, "nothing, if you do not trust me. He who utters falsehoods to the doctor is a fool who will tell the truth to the judge. It is necessary to relate things plainly to the lawyer, but it rests with us to render them more intricate. If you wish me to help you, you must tell all from beginning to end, as to your confessor: you must name the person who commissioned you to do the deed; doubtless he is a person of consequence; and, considering this, I will go to his house to perform an act of duty. I will not betray you at all, be assured; I will tell him I come to implore his protection for a poor calumniated youth; and we will together use the necessary means to finish the affair in a satisfactory manner. You understand; in securing himself, he will likewise secure you. If, however, the business has been all your own, I will not withdraw my protection: I have extricated others from worse difficulties; provided you have not offended a person of consequence;—you understand—I engage to free you from all embarrassment, with a little expense—you understand. As to the curate, if he is a person of judgment, he will keep his own counsel; if he is a fool, we will take care of him. One may escape clear out of every trouble; but for this, a *man*, a *man* is necessary. Your case is a very, very serious one—the edict speaks plainly; and if the thing rested between you and the law, to be candid, it would go hard with you. If you wish to pass smoothly—money and obedience!"

Whilst the doctor poured forth this rhapsody, Renzo had been regarding him with mute astonishment, as the countryman watches the juggler, whom he sees cramming his mouth with handful after handful of tow; when, lo! he beholds immediately drawn forth from the same mouth a never-ending line of riband. When at last he perceived his meaning, he interrupted him with, "Oh! Signor Doctor, how you have misunderstood me! the matter is directly the reverse; I have threatened no one—not I—I never do such things; ask my companions, all of them, and they will tell you I never had any thing to do with the law. The injury is mine, and I have come to you to know how I can obtain justice, and am well satisfied to have seen this proclamation."

"The devil!" exclaimed the doctor, opening wide his eyes; "what a cock and a bull story you have made! So it is; you are all alike: is it possible you can't tell a plain fact?"

"But, Signor Doctor, you must pardon me, you have not given me time; now I will tell you all. Know, then, that I was to have been married to-day"—and here his voice trembled—"was to have been married to-day to a young person to whom I have been some time betrothed; to-day was the day fixed upon by the Signor Curate, and every thing was in readiness. The Signor Curate began to make excuses—and—not to weary you—I compelled him to tell me the cause; and he confessed that he had been forbidden, on pain of death, to perform the ceremony. This powerful Don Roderick—"

"Eh!" hastily interrupted the doctor, contracting his brow and wrinkling his red nose, "away with you; what have I to do with these idle stories? Tell them to your companions, and not to one of my condition. Begone; do you think I have nothing to do but listen to tales of this sort—"

"I protest—"

"Begone, I say; what have I to do with your protestations? I wash my hands from them!" and pacing the room, he rubbed his hands together, as if really performing that act. "Hereafter learn when to speak; and do not take a gentleman by surprise."

"But hear me, hear me," vainly repeated Renzo.

The doctor, still growling, pushed him towards the door, set it wide open, called the maid, and said to her, "Return this man immediately what he brought, I will have nothing to do with it." The woman had never before been required to execute a similar order, but she did not hesitate to obey; she took the fowls and gave them to Renzo with a compassionate look, as if she had said, "You certainly have made some very great blunder." Renzo wished to make apologies; but the doctor was immovable. Confounded, therefore, and more enraged than ever, he took back the fowls and departed, to render an account of the ill success of his expedition.

At his departure, Agnes and Lucy had exchanged their nuptial robes for their humble daily habits, and then, sorrowful and dejected, occupied themselves in suggesting fresh projects. Agnes expected great results from Renzo's visit to the doctor; Lucy thought that it would be well to let Father Christopher know what had happened, as he was a man who would not only advise, but assist whenever he could serve the unfortunate; Agnes assented, but how was it to be accomplished? the convent was two miles distant, and at this time *they* certainly could neither of them hazard a walk thither. Whilst they were weighing the difficulties, some one knocked at the door, and they heard a low but distinct *Deo Gracias*. Lucy, imagining who it was, hastened to open it; and, bowing low, there entered a capuchin collector of contributions, with his wallet swung over his left shoulder. "Oh! brother Galdino!" said Agnes. "The Lord be with you," said the brother; "I come for your contribution of nuts."

"Go, get the nuts for the fathers," said Agnes. Lucy obeyed; but before she quitted the room, she gave her mother a kind and impressive look, as much as to say, "Be secret."

The capuchin, looking significantly at Agnes, said, "And the wedding? It was to have taken place to-day; what has happened?"

"The curate is sick, and we are obliged to defer it," replied the dame, in haste; "but what success in the contributions?" continued she, anxious to change the subject, which she would willingly have prolonged, but for Lucy's earnest look.

"Very poor, good dame, very poor. This is all," said he, swinging the wallet from his shoulder—"this is all; and for this I have been obliged to knock at ten doors."

"But the year is a scarce one, brother Galdino, and when we have to struggle for bread, our alms are necessarily small."

"If we wish abundance to return, my good dame, we must give alms. Do you not know the miracle of the nuts, which happened many years ago in our convent of Romagna?"

"No, in truth; tell me."

"Well you must know, then, that in this convent there was one of our fathers who was a saint; he was called Father Macario. One winter's day, passing by a field of one of our patrons,—a worthy man he was,—he saw him standing near a large nut tree, and four peasants with their axes raised to level it to the ground. 'What are you doing to the poor tree?' demanded father Macario. 'Why, father, it is unfruitful, and I am about to cut it down.' 'Do not do so, do not do so,' said the father; 'I tell you that next year it will bear more nuts than leaves. The master ordered the workmen to throw at once the earth on the roots which had been already bared; and, calling after the Father Macario, said, 'Father Macario, the half of the crop shall be for the convent.' The prediction was noised about, and every one went to look at the tree. In fact, when spring arrived, there were flowers in abundance, and afterwards nuts in abundance! But there was a greater miracle yet, as you shall hear. The owner, who, before the nut season, was called hence to enjoy the fruits of his charity, left a son of a very different character from himself. Now, at the time of harvest, the collector went to receive his appointed portion; but the son affected entire ignorance, and presumptuously replied, he never had understood that the capuchins knew how to make nuts. Now guess what happened then. One day he had invited to dinner some friends, and, making merry, he amused them with the story of the nuts; they desired to visit his granary, to behold his abundance; he led the way, advanced towards the corner where they had been placed, looked—and what do you think he saw?—a heap of dry nut leaves! Was not this a miracle? And the convent gained, instead of suffering loss; the profusion of nuts bestowed upon it in consequence was so great, that one of our patrons, compassionating the poor collector, gave him a mule to assist in carrying them home. And so much oil was made, that it was freely given to the poor; like the sea, which receives waters from every part, and distributes abundantly to the rivers."

Lucy now reappeared with her apron so loaded with nuts, that she could with difficulty support the burthen. Whilst Friar Galdino untied his wallet to receive them, Agnes cast an astonished and displeased glance at her for her prodigality; she returned it with a look which seemed to say, "I will satisfy you." The friar was liberal of thanks, and, replacing his wallet, was about to depart, when Lucy called him back. "I wish you to do me a service," said she; "I wish you to say to Father Christopher that I have a great desire to speak with him, and request him to have the goodness to come hither immediately, as it is impossible for me to go to the convent."

"Willingly; an hour shall not elapse before Father Christopher shall be informed of your wish."

"I rely on you."

"Trust me," said he, "I will be faithful," and moved off, bending under the increased weight of his wallet. We must not suppose, from the readiness with which Lucy sent this request to Father Christopher, and the equal readiness of Father Galdino to carry it, that the father was a person of no consequence; on the contrary, he was a man of much authority amongst his companions, and throughout all the neighbourhood. To serve the feeble, and to be served by the powerful; to enter the palace and the hut; to be at one time a subject of pastime, and at another regarded with profound respect; to seek alms, and to bestow them;—to all these vicissitudes a capuchin was well accustomed. The name of *Friar*, at this period, was uttered with the greatest respect, and with the most bitter contempt; of both of which sentiments, perhaps, the capuchins were, more than any other order, the objects. They possessed no property, wore a coarser habit than others, and made a more open profession of humility; they therefore exposed themselves, in a greater degree, to the veneration or the scorn which might result from the various characters among men.

The Friar Galdino being gone, "Such a quantity of nuts!" exclaimed Agnes, "and in a year of scarcity!"—"I beg pardon," replied Lucy; "but if we had been as penurious as others in our charity, who can tell how long the friar would have been in reaching home, or, amongst all the gossipings, whether he would have remembered—"

"True, true, it was a good thought; and besides, charity always produces good fruit," said Agnes, who, with all her defects, was a kind-hearted woman, and would have sacrificed every thing she had in the world for the sake of her child, in whom she had reposed all her happiness.

Renzo entered at this moment, with an angry and mortified countenance. "Pretty advice you gave me!" said he to Agnes. "You sent me to a fine man, indeed! to one truly who aids the distressed!" And he briefly related his interview with the doctor. The dame, astonished at the issue, endeavoured to prove that the advice was good, and that the failure must have been owing to Renzo himself. Lucy interrupted the debate, by informing him of her message to Father Christopher: he seized with avidity the new hopes inspired by the expectation of assistance from so holy a man. "But if the father," said he, "should not extricate us from our difficulties, I will do it myself by some means or other." Both mother and daughter implored him to be patient and prudent.

"To-morrow," said Lucy, "Father Christopher will certainly be here, and he will no doubt suggest to us some plan of action which we ourselves would not have thought of in a year."

"I hope so," said Renzo; "but if not, I will obtain redress, or find another to do it for me; for surely there must be justice to be had in the world."

Their mournful conversation might have continued much longer, but approaching night warned him to depart.

"Good night!" said Lucy mournfully, to Renzo, who could hardly resolve to go.

"Good night!" replied he, yet more sadly.

"Some saint will watch over us," said she. "Be patient and prudent." The mother added some advice of the like nature. But the disappointed bridegroom, with a tempest in his heart, left them, repeating the strange proposition—"Surely, there's justice in the world." So true is it that, under the influence of great misfortune, men no longer know what they say.

Chapter IV.

The sun had not yet risen above the horizon, when Father Christopher left the convent of Pescarenico, to go to the cottage where he was so anxiously expected. Pescarenico is a small hamlet on the left bank of the Adda, or, rather, of the Lake, a few steps below the bridge; a group of houses, inhabited for the most part by fishermen, and adorned here and there with nets spread out to dry. The convent was situated (the building still subsists) at a short distance from them, half way between Lecco and Bergamo.

The sky was clear and serene. As the sun rose behind the mountain, its rays brightened the opposite summits, and thence rapidly spread themselves over the declivities and valleys; a light autumn breeze played through the leaves of the mulberry trees, and brought them to the ground. The vineyards were still brilliant with leaves of various hues; and the newly made nets appeared brown and distinct amid the fields of stubble, which were white and shining with the dew. The scene was beautiful; but the misery of the inhabitants formed a sad contrast to it. At every moment you met pale and ragged beggars, some grown old in the trade, others youthful, and induced to it from extreme necessity. They passed quietly by Father Christopher, and although they had nothing to hope from him, since a capuchin never touches money, they bowed low in thanks for the alms they had received, or might hereafter receive at the convent. The spectacle of the labourers scattered in the fields was still more mournful; some were sowing thinly and sparingly their seed, as if hazarding that which was too precious; others put the spade into the earth with difficulty, and wearily turned up the clods. The pale and sickly child was leading the meagre cattle to the pasture ground, and as he went along plucked carefully the herbs found in his path, as food for his family. This melancholy picture of human misery increased the sadness of Father Christopher, who, when he left the convent, had been filled with presentiments of evil.

But why did he feel so much for Lucy? And why, at the first notice, did he hasten to her with as much solicitude as if he had been sent for by the Father Provincial. And who was this Father Christopher? We must endeavour to satisfy all these enquiries.

Father Christopher, of —, was a man nearer sixty than fifty years of age. His head was shaven, with the exception of the band of hair allowed to grow round it like a crown, as was the custom of the capuchins; the expression of his countenance was habitually that of deep humility, although occasionally there passed over it flashes of pride and inquietude, which were, however, succeeded by a deeper shade of self-reproach and lowliness. His long grey beard gave more character to the shape of the upper part of his head, on which habitual abstinence had stamped a strong expression of gravity. His sunken eyes were for the most part bent to the earth, but brightened at times with unexpected vivacity, which he ever appeared to endeavour to repress. His name, before entering the convent, had been Ludovico; he was the son of a merchant of —, who, having accumulated great wealth, had renounced trade in the latter part of his life, and having resolved to live like a gentleman, he studied every means to cause his former mode of life to be forgotten by those around him. He could not, however, forget it himself; the shop, the goods, the day-book, the yard measure, rose to his memory, like the shade of Banquo to Macbeth, amidst the pomp of the table and the smiles of his parasites; whose continual effort it was to avoid any word which might appear to allude to the former condition of the host. Ludovico was his only child: he caused him to be nobly educated, as far as the laws and customs permitted him to do so; and died, bequeathing him a splendid fortune. Ludovico had contracted the habits and feelings of a gentleman, and the flatterers who had surrounded him from infancy had accustomed him to the greatest deference and respect. But he found the scene changed when he attempted to mingle with the nobility of the city; and that in order to live in their company he must school himself to patience and submission, and bear with contumely on every occasion. This agreed neither with his education nor his disposition. He retired from them in disgust, but unwillingly, feeling that such should naturally have been his companions; he then resolved to outdo them in pomp and magnificence, thereby increasing the enmity with which they had already regarded him. His open and violent nature soon engaged him in more serious contests: he sincerely abhorred the extortions and injuries committed by those to whom he had opposed himself; he therefore habitually took part with the weak against the powerful, so that by degrees he had constituted himself the defender of the oppressed, and the vindicator of their wrongs. The office was onerous; and fruitful in evil thoughts, quarrels, and enmities against himself. But, besides this external warfare, he perhaps suffered still more from inward conflicts; for often, in order to compass his objects, he was obliged to adopt measures of circumvention and violence, which his conscience disapproved. He was under the painful necessity of keeping in pay a band of ruffians for his own security, as well as to aid him in his enterprises; and for these purposes he was necessarily obliged to select the boldest, that is, the vilest, and to live with vagabonds from a love of justice; so that, disgusted with the world and its conflicts, he had many times seriously thought of entering some monastery, and retiring from it for ever. Such intentions were more strongly entertained on the failure of some of his enterprises, or the perception of his own danger, or the annoyance of his vicious associates, and would probably have still continued *intentions*, but for one of the most serious and terrible events of his hazardous mode of life.

He was walking one day through the streets of the city, accompanied by a former shopman, who had been transformed by his father into a steward, followed by two bravoes. The name of the shopman was Christopher; he was a man about fifty years of age, devoted to the master whom he had tended in infancy, and upon whose liberality he supported himself, his wife, and a large family of children. Ludovico saw a gentleman approaching at a distance, with whom he had never spoken in his life, but whom he hated for his arrogance and pride, which hatred the other cordially returned. He had in his train four bravoes; he advanced with a haughty step, and an expression of insolence and disdain on his countenance. It was Ludovico's right, being on the left side, to pass nearest the wall, according to the custom of the day, and every one was tenacious of this privilege. As they met they stopped face to face, like two figures on a bass relief, neither of them being disposed to yield to the other. The gentleman, eyeing Ludovico proudly and imperiously, said, with a corresponding tone of voice, "Pass on the outside."

"Pass there yourself," replied Ludovico, "the street is mine."

"With persons of your condition the street is always mine."

"Yes, if your arrogance were a law to others."

The attendants of each stood still, with their hands on their daggers, prepared for battle. The passers-by retreated to a distance to watch the event.

"Pass on, vile mechanic, or I will teach you the civility due to a gentleman."

"You lie; I am not vile."

"Ha! Do you give me the lie? If you were a gentleman I would soon settle matters with my sword."

"You are a coward also, or you would not hesitate to support by deeds the insolence of your words."

"Throw this rascal in the dirt," said the gentleman, turning to his followers.

"Let us see who will dare to do so," said Ludovico, stepping back and laying his hand on his sword.

"Rash man," cried the other, unsheathing his own, "I will break this in pieces when it shall have been stained with your base blood."

They rushed violently on each other; the servants of both sprang to the defence of their masters. The combat was unequal in numbers, and also unequal from Ludovico's desire to defend himself rather than to wound his enemy; whilst the latter intended nothing less than murder. Ludovico was warding off the dagger of one of the bravoes, after having received a slight scratch on the cheek, when his enemy thrust at him from behind; Christopher, seeing his master's peril, went to his assistance; upon this the anger of the enraged cavalier was turned against the shopman, and he thrust him through the heart with his sword. Ludovico, as if beside himself at the sight, buried his weapon in the breast of the murderer, who fell almost at the same instant with the poor Christopher! The attendants of the gentleman, beholding him on the ground, took to flight; and Ludovico found himself alone, in the midst of a crowd, with two bodies lying at his feet.

"What has happened? One—two—he has been thrust through the body. Who is killed? A nobleman.—Holy Virgin! what destruction! who seeks, finds.—A moment pays all.—What a wound!—It must have been a serious affair!—And this unfortunate man!—Mercy! what a spectacle!—Save, save him.—It will go hard with him also.—See how he is wounded—he is covered with blood!—Escape, poor man, escape; do not let yourself be taken." These words expressed the common suffrage, and with advice came also assistance; the affair had taken place near a church of the capuchins, an asylum impenetrable to the officers of justice. The murderer, bleeding and stupified, was carried thither by the crowd; the brotherhood received him from their hands with this recommendation, "He is an honest man who has made a proud rascal cold; but he did it in his own defence."

Ludovico had never before shed blood, and although in these times murder was a thing so common that all ceased to wonder at it, yet the impression which he received from the recollection of the dying (dying through his instrumentality,) was new and indescribable; a revelation of feelings hitherto unknown. The fall of his enemy, the alteration of those features, passing in a moment from angry threatenings to the solemn stillness of death; this was a spectacle which wrought an instantaneous change in the soul of the murderer. Whilst they were carrying him to the convent he had been insensible to what was passing; returning to his senses, he found himself in a bed of the infirmary, in the hands of a friar who was dressing his wounds. Another, whose particular duty it was to administer comfort to the dying, had been called to the scene of combat. He returned in a short time, and approaching Ludovico's bed, said, "Console yourself; he has died in peace, has forgiven you, and hoped for your forgiveness." At these words the soul of Ludovico was filled with remorse and sorrow. "And the other?" asked he anxiously.

"The other had expired before I arrived."

In the mean time the avenues and environs of the convent swarmed with people; the officers of justice arrived, dispersed the crowd, and placed themselves in ambush at a short distance from the gates, so that no one could pass through them unobserved. A brother of the deceased and some of his family appeared in full armour with a large attendance of bravoes, and surrounded the place, watching with a threatening aspect the bystanders, who did not dare say, he is safe, but they had it written on their faces.

Scarcely had Ludovico recalled his scattered thoughts, when he asked for a father confessor, prayed him to seek out the widow of Christopher, to ask forgiveness in his name for having been (however involuntarily) the cause of her affliction, and to assure her that he would take the care of her family on himself. Reflecting further on his own situation, his determination was made to become a friar. It seemed as if God himself had willed it, by placing him in a convent at such a conjuncture. He immediately sent for the superior of the monastery, and expressed to him his intention. He replied to him, that he should be careful not to form a resolution precipitately, but that, if he persisted, he would be accepted. Ludovico then sent for a notary, and made a donation of all his estate to the widow and family of Christopher.

The resolution of Ludovico happened opportunely for his hosts, who felt themselves embarrassed concerning him. To send him from the monastery, and thus expose him to justice and the vengeance of his enemies, was not to be thought of a moment; it would be the same as a renunciation of their privileges, a discrediting of the convent amongst the people; and they would draw upon themselves the animadversion of all the capuchins of the universe for this relinquishment of the rights of the order, this defiance of the ecclesiastical authorities, who then considered themselves the guardians of these rights. On the other hand, the family of the deceased, rich, and powerful in adherents, were determined on vengeance, and disposed to consider as enemies whoever should place obstacles to its accomplishment. History declares, not that they grieved much for the dead, or that a single tear was shed for him amongst his whole race, but that they were urged on by scenting the blood of his opponent. But Ludovico, by assuming the habit of a capuchin, removed all difficulties: to a certain degree he made atonement; imposed on himself penitence; confessed his fault; withdrew from the contest; he was, in short, an enemy who laid down his arms. The relations of the deceased could, if they pleased, believe and boast that he had become a friar through despair and dread of their revenge. And at all events, to reduce a man to dispossess himself of his wealth, to shave his head, to walk bare-footed, to sleep on straw, and to live on alms, might appear a punishment competent to the offence.

The superior presented himself before the brother of the deceased with an air of humility; after a thousand protestations of respect for his illustrious house, and of desire to comply with its wishes as far as was practicable, he spoke of the repentance and resolution of Ludovico, politely hoping that the family would grant their accordance; and then insinuating, mildly and dexterously, that, agreeable or not agreeable, the thing would take place. After some little vapouring, he agreed to it on one condition; that the murderer of his brother should depart immediately from the city. To this the capuchin assented, as if in obedience to the wishes of the family, although it had been already so determined. The affair was thus concluded to the satisfaction of the illustrious house, of the capuchin brotherhood, of the popular feeling, and, above all, of our generous penitent himself. Thus, at thirty years of age, Ludovico bade farewell to the world; and having, according to custom, to change his name, he took one which would continually recall to him his crime,—thus he became *Friar Christopher!*

Hardly was the ceremony of assuming the habit completed, when the superior informed him he must depart on the morrow to perform his noviciate at —, sixty miles' distance. The noviciate bowed submissively. "Permit me, father," said he, "before I leave the scene of my crime, to do all that rests with me now to repair the evil; permit me to go to the house of the brother of him whom I have murdered, to acknowledge my fault, and ask forgiveness; perhaps God will take away his but too just resentment."

It appeared to the superior that such an act, besides being praiseworthy in itself, would serve still more to reconcile the family to the monastery. He therefore bore the request himself to the brother of the murdered man; a proposal so unexpected was received with a mixture of scorn and complacency. "Let him come to-morrow," said he, and appointed the hour. The superior returned to Father Christopher with the desired permission.

The gentleman reflected that the more solemn and public the apology was, the more it would enhance his credit with the family and the world; he made known in haste to the members of the family, that on the following day they should assemble at his house to receive a common satisfaction. At mid-day the palace swarmed with nobility of either sex; there was a blending of veils, feathers, and jewels; a heavy motion of starched and crisped bands; a confused entangling of embroidered trains. The antechambers, the courts, and the street, were crowded with servants, pages, and bravoes.

Father Christopher experienced a momentary agitation at beholding all this preparation, but recovering himself, said, "It is well; the deed was committed in public, the reparation should be public." Then, with his eyes bent to the earth, and the father, his companion, at his elbow, he crossed the court, amidst a crowd who eyed him with unceremonious curiosity; he entered, ascended the stairs, and passing through another crowd of lords, who made way for him at his approach, he advanced towards the master of the mansion, who stood in the middle of the room waiting to receive him, with downcast looks, grasping with one hand the hilt of his sword, and with the other pressing the cape of his Spanish cloak on his breast. The countenance and deportment of Father Christopher made an immediate impression on the company; so that all were convinced that he had not submitted to this humiliation from fear of man. He threw himself on his knees before him whom he had most injured, crossed his hands on his breast, and bending his head, exclaimed, "I am the murderer of your brother! God knows, that to restore him to life I would sacrifice my own; but as this cannot be, I supplicate you to accept my useless and late apology, for the love of God!"

All eyes were fixed in breathless and mute attention on the novice, and on the person to whom he addressed himself; there was heard through the crowd a murmur of pity and respect; the angry scorn of the nobleman relaxed at this appeal, and bending towards the kneeling supplicant, "Rise," said he, with a troubled voice. "The offence—the deed truly—but the habit you wear—not only this—but on your own account—rise, father!—my brother—I cannot deny it—was a cavalier—of a hasty temper. Do not speak of it again. But, father, you must not remain in this posture." And he took him by the arm to raise him. Father Christopher, standing with his eyes still bent to the ground, continued, "I may, then, hope that you have granted me your pardon. And if I obtain it from you, from whom may I not expect it? Oh! if I could hear you utter the word!"

"Pardon!" said the nobleman; "I pardon you with all my heart, and all—" turning to the company—"All! all!" resounded at once through the room.

The countenance of the father expanded with joy, under which, however, was still visible an humble and profound compunction for the evil, which the remission of men could not repair. The nobleman, entirely vanquished, threw his arms around his neck, and the kiss of peace was given and received.

Loud exclamations of applause burst from the company; and all crowded eagerly around the father. In the meanwhile the servants entered, bearing refreshments; the master of the mansion, again addressing Father Christopher, said, "Father, afford me a proof of your friendship by accepting some of these trifles."

"Such things are no longer for me," replied the father; "but if you will allow me a loaf of bread, as a memorial of your charity and your forgiveness, I shall be thankful." The bread was brought, and with an air of humble gratitude he put it in his basket. He then took leave of the company; disentangled himself with difficulty from the crowd in the antechambers, who would have kissed the hem of his garment, and pursued his way to the gate of the city, whence he commenced his pedestrian journey towards the place of his noviciate.

It is not our design to write the history of his cloistral life; we will only say, he executed faithfully the offices ordinarily assigned to him, of preaching, and of comforting the dying; but beyond these, "the oppressor's wrongs, the proud man's contumely," aroused in him a spirit of resistance which humiliation and remorse had not been able entirely to extinguish. His countenance was habitually mild and humble, but occasionally there passed over it a shade of former impetuosity, which was with difficulty restrained by the high and holy motives which now predominated in his soul. His tone of voice was gentle as his countenance; but in the cause of justice and truth, his language assumed a character of solemnity and emphasis singularly impressive. One who knew him well, and admired his virtues, could often perceive, by the smothered utterance or the change of a single word, the inward conflict between the natural impetus and the resolved will, which latter never failed to gain the mastery.

If one unknown to him in the situation of Lucy had implored his assistance, he would have granted it immediately; with how much more solicitude, then, did he direct his steps to the cottage, knowing and admiring her innocence, trembling for her danger, and experiencing a lively indignation at the persecution of which she had become the object. Besides, he had advised her to remain quiet, and not make known the conduct of her persecutor, and he felt or feared that his advice might have been productive of bad consequences. His anxiety for her welfare, and his inadequate means to secure it, called up many painful feelings, which the good often experience.

But while we have been relating his history, he arrived at the dwelling; Agnes and her daughter advanced eagerly towards him, exclaiming in one breath, "Oh! Father Christopher, you are welcome."

Chapter V.

Father Christopher perceived immediately, from the countenances of Lucy and her mother, that some evil had occurred. "Is all well with you?" said he. Lucy replied by a flood of tears. "Quiet yourself, poor child," continued he; "and do you," turning to Agnes, "tell me what is the matter." Whilst the good dame proceeded with the melancholy relation, he experienced a variety of painful emotions. The story being done, he buried his face in his hands, and exclaimed, "Oh, blessed God! how long?"—He then turned to Lucy; "Poor child! God has, indeed, visited you," said he.

"You will not abandon us, father?" said Lucy, sobbing.

"Abandon you!" replied he. "How should I dare ask the protection of Almighty God for myself, if I abandoned *you*! You, so defenceless!—you, whom he has confided to me! Take courage! He will assist you—His eye beholds you—He can even make use of a feeble instrument like myself to confound a —. Let us think what can be done."

Thus saying, he grasped his beard and chin with his hand, as if to concentrate more completely the powers of his mind. But the more clearly he perceived the pressing nature of the case, the more uncertain and dangerous appeared every mode of meeting it. To endeavour to make Don Abbondio sensible of a failure in duty? This appeared hopeless; fear was more powerful with him than either shame or duty. To inform the cardinal archbishop, and invoke his authority? That would require time; and, in the meanwhile, what was to be done? To resist Don Roderick? How? Impossible! The affair being one of a private nature, he would not be sustained by the brethren of his order: he would, perhaps, be raising a storm against himself; and, what was worse, by a useless attempt render the condition of Lucy more hopeless and deplorable. After many reflections he came to the conclusion to go to Don Roderick himself, and to endeavour by prayers and representations of the punishments of the wicked in another state, to win him from his infamous purpose. At least he might at the interview discover something of his intentions, and determine his measures accordingly. At this moment Renzo, who, as the reader will readily imagine, could not long be absent at so interesting a crisis, appeared at the door of the room; the father raised his head and bowed to him affectionately, and with a look of intense pity.

"Have they told you, father?" enquired he, with a troubled voice.

"Yes, my son; and on that account I am here."

"What do you say of the villain?"

"What do I say of *him*? I say to *you*, dear Renzo, that you must confide in God, and He will not abandon you."

"Blessed words!" exclaimed the youth: "you are not one of those who wrong the poor. But the curate and this doctor—"

"Do not torment yourself uselessly: I am but a poor friar; but I repeat to you that which I have already said to Lucy and her mother—poor as I am, I will never abandon you."

"Oh! you are not like the friends of the world—rascals—when I was in prosperity, abundant in protestations; ready to shed their blood for me, to sustain me against the devil! Had I an enemy, they would soon put it out of his power to molest me! And now, to see them withdraw themselves!" He was interrupted in his vituperations by the dark shade which passed over the countenance of his auditor; he perceived the blunder he had made, and attempting to remedy it, became perplexed and confused. "I would say—I did not at all intend—that is, I meant to say—"

"What did you mean to say? You have already begun to mar my undertaking. It is well that thou art undeceived in time. What! thou didst seek friends! and what friends! they could not have aided thee, had they been willing. And thou didst not apply to the only friend who can and will protect thee;—dost thou not know that God is the friend of all who trust in Him? dost thou not know that to spread the talons does little good to the weak? and even if—" at these words he grasped forcibly Renzo's arm; his countenance, without losing his wonted authority, displayed an affecting remorse; his eyes were fixed on the ground; and his voice became slow and sepulchral: "and even if that little should be gained, how terribly awful! Renzo, will you confide in me?—that I should say in me! a worm of the dust! will you not confide in God?"

"Oh! yes!" replied Renzo; "He only is the Lord."

"Promise me, then, that you will not meet or provoke any one; that you will suffer yourself to be guided by me."

"I promise," said Renzo.

Lucy drew a long breath, as if relieved from a weight, and Agnes was loud in applauses.

"Listen, my children," resumed Father Christopher: "I will go myself to-day to speak to this man: if God touches his heart through my words, well; if not, *He* will provide some other remedy. In the mean time keep yourselves quiet and retired; this evening, or to-morrow at the latest, you shall see me again." Having said this, he departed amidst thanks and blessings.

He arrived at the convent in time to perform his daily duty in the choir, dined, and then pursued his way towards the den of the wild beast he had undertaken to tame.

The palace of Don Roderick stood by itself, on the summit of one of the promontories that skirt the coast; it was three or four miles distant from the village; at the foot of the promontory nearest the lake, there was a cluster of decayed cottages inhabited by peasantry belonging to Don Roderick. This was the little capital of his little kingdom. As you cast a glance within their walls, you beheld suspended to them various kinds of arms, with spades, mattocks, and pouches of powder, blended promiscuously. The persons within appeared robust and strong, with a daring and insulting expression of countenance, and wearing a long lock of hair on the head, which was covered with net-work. The aged, that had lost their teeth, seemed ready to show their gums at the slightest call: masculine women, with sinewy arms, seemed disposed to use them with as much indifference as their tongues; the very children exhibited the same daring recklessness as the parent stock. Friar Christopher passed through the hamlet, ascending a winding path which conducted him to the little esplanade in the front of the castle. The door was shut, which was a sign that the chief was dining and did not wish to be disturbed. The few windows that looked on the road were small and decayed by time; they were, however, secured by large iron bars; and the lowest of them were more than ten feet from the ground. A profound silence reigned within, and a traveller might have believed the mansion deserted, but for the appearance of four animals, two alive and two dead, in front of the castle. Two large vultures, with their wings expanded, were nailed each at the posts of the gate; and two bravoes, extended at full length on the benches on either side, were keeping guard until their master should have finished his repast. The father stopped, as if willing also to wait. "Father, father, come on," said one, "we do not make the capuchins wait here; we are the friends of the convent; I have been within its walls when the air on the outside of them was not very wholesome for me; it was well the fathers did not refuse me admittance." So saying, he gave two strokes with the knocker: at the sound, the howls of mastiffs were heard from within; and in a few moments there appeared an aged domestic. On seeing the father, he bowed reverently, quieted the animals with his voice, introduced the guest into a narrow court, and closed the gate. Then escorting him into a saloon, and regarding him with an astonished and respectful look, said, "Is not this—the Father Christopher of Pescarenico?"

"The same."

"And here!"

"As you see, good man."

"It must be to do good," continued he, murmuring between his teeth; "good can be done every where." He then guided him through two or three dark halls, and led the way to the banqueting room: here was heard a confused noise of plates, and knives and forks, and discordant voices. Whilst Father Christopher was urging the domestic to suffer him to remain in some other apartment until the dinner should be finished, the door opened. A certain Count Attilio, a cousin of the noble host, (of whom we have already spoken, without giving his name,) was seated opposite: when he saw the bald head and habit of the father, and perceived his motion to withdraw, "Ho! father," cried he, "you sha'n't escape us; reverend father, forward, forward!" Don Roderick seconded somewhat unwillingly this boisterous command, as he felt some presentiment of the object of his visit. "Come, father, come in," said he. Seeing there was no retreating, Father Christopher advanced, saluting the nobleman and his guests.

An honest man is generally fearless and undaunted in presence of the wicked; nevertheless, the father, with the testimony of a good conscience and a firm conviction of the justice of his cause, with a mixture of horror and compassion for Don Roderick, felt a degree of embarrassment in approaching him. He was seated at table, surrounded by guests; on his right was Count Attilio, his colleague in libertinism, who had come from Milan to visit him. To the left was seated, with respectful submissiveness, tempered, however, with conscious security, the *podestà* of the place,—he whose duty it was, according to the proclamation, to cause justice to be done to Renzo Tramaglino, and to inflict the allotted penalty on Don Roderick. Nearly opposite to the *podestà* sat our learned Doctor *Azzecca Garbugli*, with his black cap and his red nose; and over against him two obscure guests, of whom our story says nothing beyond a general mention of their toad-eating qualities.

"Give a seat to the father," said Don Roderick. A servant presented a chair, and the good father apologised for having come at so inopportune an hour. "I would speak with you alone on an affair of importance," added he, in a low tone, to Don Roderick.

"Very well, father, it shall be so," replied he; "but in the meanwhile bring the father something to drink."

Father Christopher would have refused, but Don Roderick, raising his voice above the tumult of the table, cried, "No, by Bacchus, you shall not do me this wrong; a capuchin shall never leave this house without having tasted my wine, nor an insolent creditor without having tasted the wood of my forests." These words produced a universal laugh, and interrupted for a moment the question which was hotly agitated between the guests. A servant brought the wine, of which Father Christopher partook, feeling the necessity of propitiating the host.

"The authority of Tasso is against you, respected Signor *Podestà*," resumed aloud the Count Attilio: "this great man was well acquainted with the laws of knighthood, and he makes the messenger of Argantes, before carrying the defiance of the Christian knights, ask permission from the pious Bouillon."

"But that," replied vociferously the *podestà*, "that is poetical licence merely: an ambassador is in his nature inviolable, by the law of nations, *jure gentium*; and moreover, the ambassador, not having spoken in his own name, but merely presented the challenge in writing—"

"But when will you comprehend that this ambassador was a daring fool, who did not know the first—"

"With the good leave of our guests," interrupted Don Roderick, who did not wish the argument to proceed farther, "we will refer it to the Father Christopher, and submit to his decision."

"Agreed," said Count Attilio, amused at submitting a question of knighthood to a capuchin; whilst the *podestà* muttered between his teeth, "Folly!"

"But, from what I have comprehended," said the father, "it is a subject of which I have no knowledge."

"As usual, modest excuses from the father," said Don Roderick; "but we will not accept them. Come, come, we know well that you came not into the world with a cowl on your head; you know something of its ways. Well, how stands the argument?"

"The facts are these," said the Count Attilio—

"Let me tell, who am neutral, cousin," resumed Don Roderick. "This is the story: a Spanish knight sent a challenge to a Milanese knight; the bearer, not finding him at home, presented it to his brother, who, having read it, struck the bearer many blows. The question is—"

"It was well done; he was perfectly right," cried Count Attilio.

"There was no right about it," exclaimed the *podestà*. "To beat an ambassador—a man whose person is sacred! Father, do *you* think this was an action becoming a knight?"

"Yes, sir; of a knight," cried the count, "I think I know what belongs to a knight. Oh! if it had been an affair of fists, that would have been quite another thing, but a cudgel soils no one's hands."

"I am not speaking of this, Sir Count; I am speaking of the *laws* of knighthood. But tell me, I pray you, if the messengers that the ancient Romans sent to bear defiance to other nations, asked permission to deliver the message; find, if you can, a writer who relates that such messenger was ever cudgelled."

"What have the ancient Romans to do with us? a people well enough in some things, but in others, far, far behind. But according to the laws of modern knighthood, I maintain that a messenger, who dared place in the hands of a knight a challenge without having previously asked permission, is a rash fool who deserves to be cudgelled."

"But answer me this question—"

"No, no, no."

"But hear me. To strike an unarmed person is an act of treachery. *Atqui* the messenger *de quo* was without arms. *Ergo*—"

"Gently, gently, Signor *Podestà*."

"How? gently."

"Gently, I tell you; I concede that under other circumstances this might have been called an act of treachery, but to strike a low fellow! It would have been a fine thing truly, to say to him, as you would to a gentleman, Be on your guard! And you, Sir Doctor, instead of sitting there grinning your approbation of my opinion, why do you not aid me to convince this gentleman?"

"I," replied the doctor in confusion; "I enjoy this learned dispute, and am thankful for the opportunity of listening to a war of wit so agreeable. And moreover, I am not competent to give an opinion; his most illustrious lordship has appointed a judge—the father."

"True," said Don Roderick; "but how can the judge speak when the disputants will not keep silence?"

"I am dumb," said the Count Attilio. The *podestà* made a sign that he would be quiet.

"Well! father! at last!" said Don Roderick, with comic gravity.

"I have already said, that I do not comprehend—"

"No excuses! we must have your opinion."

"If it must be so," replied the father, "I should humbly think there was no necessity for challenges, nor bearers, nor blows."

The guests looked in wonder at each other.

"Oh! how ridiculous!" said the Count Attilio. "Pardon me, father; but this is exceedingly ridiculous. It is plain you know nothing of the world."

"He?" said Don Roderick; "he knows as much of it as you do, cousin. Is it not so, father?"

Father Christopher made no reply; but to himself he said, "submit thyself to every insult for the sake of those for whom thou art here."

"It may be so," said the count; "but the father—how is the father called?"

"Father Christopher," replied more than one.

"But, Father Christopher, your reverend worship, with your maxims you would turn the world upside down—without challenges! without blows! Farewell, the point of honour! Impunity to ruffians! Happily, the thing is impossible."

"Stop, doctor," cried Don Roderick, wishing to divert the dispute from the original antagonists. "You are a good man for an argument; what have you to say to the father?"

"Indeed," replied the doctor, brandishing his fork in the air—"indeed I cannot understand how the Father Christopher should not remember that his judgment, though of just weight in the pulpit, is worth nothing—I speak with great submission—on a question of knighthood. But perhaps he has been merely jesting, to relieve himself from embarrassment."

The father not replying to this, Don Roderick made an effort to change the subject.

"Apropos," said he, "I understand there is a report at Milan of an accommodation."

There was at this time a contest regarding the succession to the dukedom of Mantua, of which, at the death of Vincenzo Gonzaga, who died without male issue, the Duke de Nevers, his nearest relation, had obtained possession. Louis XIII., or rather the Cardinal de Richelieu, wished to sustain him there; Philip IV., or rather the Count d'Olivares, commonly called the Count Duke, opposed him. The dukedom was then a fief of the empire, and the two parties employed intrigue and importunity at the court of the Emperor Ferdinand II. The object of one was to obtain the investiture of the new duke; of the other, the denial of his claim, and also assistance to oblige him to relinquish it.

"I rather think," said the Count Attilio, "that the thing will be arranged satisfactorily. I have reasons—"

"Do not believe it, count, do not believe it," added the *podestà*; "I have an opportunity of knowing, because the Spanish keeper of the castle, who is my friend, and who is the son of a dependant of the Count Duke, is informed of every thing."

"I tell you I have discoursed on the subject daily at Milan; and I know from good authority that the pope, exceedingly interested as he is for peace, has made propositions—"

"That may be, the thing is in order; his Holiness does his duty; a pope should always endeavour to make peace between Christian princes; but the Count Duke has his own policy, and—"

"And, and, and, do you know, Signor *Podestà*, how much thought the emperor now gives to it? Do you believe there is no place but Mantua in the world! There are many things to provide for, signor, mind. Do you know, for instance, how far the emperor can trust this Prince of Valdistano, or di Vallistai, as they call him; and if—"

"His name, in the German language," interrupted the magistrate, "is Wallenstein, as I have heard it uttered many times by the Spanish keeper of the castle. But be of good courage—"

"Do you dare teach me," replied the count. Here Don Roderick whispered to him to cease contradiction, as there would be no end to it. He obeyed; and the *podestà*, like a vessel unimpeded by shoals, continued with full sails the course of his eloquence. "Wallenstein gives me but little anxiety; because the Count Duke has his eye every where; and if Wallenstein carries matters with a high hand, he will soon set him right. He has his eye every where, I say, and unlimited power; and if it is his policy that the Signor Duke of Nevers should not take root in Mantua, he will never flourish there, he assured. It makes me laugh to see the Signor Cardinal de Richelieu contend with an Olivares. The Count Duke, gentlemen," pursued he, with the wind still in his favour, and much wondering at not meeting with opposition, "the Count Duke is an old fox—speaking with due respect—who would make any one lose his track: when he appears to go to the right, it would be safest to follow him to the left: no one can boast of knowing his designs; they who are to execute them, they who write the despatches, know nothing of them. I speak from authority, for the keeper of the castle deigns to confide in me. The Count Duke knows well enough how the pot boils in all the courts in Europe; and these politicians have hardly laid a plan, but he begins to frustrate it. That poor man, the Cardinal Richelieu, attempts and dissembles, toils and strives; and what does it all produce? When he has dug the mine, he finds a countermine already prepared by the Count Duke—"

None can tell when the magistrate would have cast anchor, if Don Roderick had not interrupted him. "Signor *Podestà*," said he, "and you, gentlemen, a bumper to the Count Duke, and you shall then judge if the wine is worthy of the personage." The *podestà* bowed low in gratitude for an honour he considered as paid to himself in part for his eloquent harangue.

"May Don Gaspero Guzman, Count de Olivares, Duke of St. Lucar, live a thousand years!" said he, raising his glass.

"May he live a thousand years!" exclaimed all the company.

"Help the father," said Don Roderick.

"Excuse me," replied he, "I could not—"

"How!" said Don Roderick; "will you not drink to the Count Duke? Would you have us believe that you hold to the Navarre party?"

This was the contemptuous term applied to the French interest at the time of Henry IV.

There was no reply to be made to this, and the father was obliged to taste the wine. All the guests were loud in its praise, except the doctor, who had kept silence. "Eh! doctor," asked Don Roderick, "what think *you* of it?"

"I think," replied the doctor, withdrawing his ruddy and shining nose from the glass, "that this is the Olivares of wines: there is not a liquor resembling it in all the twenty-two kingdoms of the king our master, whom God protect! I maintain that the dinners of the most illustrious Signor Don Roderick exceed the suppers of Heliogabalus, and that scarcity is banished for ever from this palace, where reigns a perpetual and splendid abundance."

"Well said! bravo! bravo!" exclaimed with one voice the guests; but the word *scarcity*, which the doctor had accidentally uttered, suggested a new and painful subject. All spoke at once:—"There is no famine," said one, "it is the speculators who—"

"And the bakers, who conceal the grain. Hang them!"

"That is right; hang them, without mercy."

"Upon fair trial," cried the magistrate.

"What trial?" cried Attilio, more loudly; "summary justice, I say. Take a few of them who are known to be the richest and most avaricious, and hang them."

"Yes, hang them! hang them! and there will be grain scattered in abundance."

Thus the party continued absorbing the wine, whose praises, mixed with sentences of economical jurisprudence, formed the burthen of the conversation; so that the loudest and most frequent words were, *Nectar, and hang 'em.*

Don Roderick had, from time to time, during this confusion, looked at the father: perceiving him calmly, but firmly, awaiting his leisure for the interview which had been promised him, he relinquished the hope of wearying him by its postponement. To send away a capuchin, without giving him an audience, was not according to his policy; and since it could not be avoided, he resolved to meet it at once: he rose from the table, excused himself to his guests, and saying proudly, "At your service, father," led the way to another room.

Chapter VI.

"In what can I serve you?" said Don Roderick, as soon as they entered into the room. Such were his words, but his manner said plainly, "Remember before whom thou standest, weigh well thy words, and be expeditious."

There were no means more certain to impart courage to Father Christopher than arrogance or pride. He had stood for a moment in some embarrassment, passing through his fingers the beads of the rosary that hung suspended from his girdle; but he soon "resumed new courage, and revived," at the haughty air of Don Roderick. He had, however, sufficient command over himself to reply with caution and humility. "I come to supplicate you to perform an act of justice: some wicked persons have, in the name of your lordship, frightened a poor curate, and have endeavoured to prevent his fulfilling his duty towards an innocent and unoffending couple. You can by a word confound their machinations, and impart consolation to the afflicted. You can—and having it in your power—conscience, honour—"

"Speak to me of conscience, when I ask your advice on the subject; and as to my honour, know that I only am the guardian of it, and that whoever dares to meddle with it is a rash man."

Friar Christopher, warned by these words that the intention of Don Roderick was to turn the conversation into a dispute, so as to win him from his original purpose, determined to bear whatever insult might be offered him, and meekly replied, "It was certainly not my intention to say any thing to displease you: correct me, reprove me; but deign to listen to me. By the love of Heaven, by that God before whom we must all appear, I charge thee, do not obstinately refuse to do justice to the innocent and oppressed! Think that God watches over them, that their imprecations are heard above, and—"

"Stop," interrupted Don Roderick, rudely. "The respect I bear to your habit is great; but if any thing could make me forget it, it would be to see it worn by one coming as a spy into my house."

These words spread an indignant glow over the face of the father; but swallowing them as a bitter medicine, he resumed: "You do not believe that I am such; you feel in your heart that I am here on no vile or contemptible errand. Listen to me, Signor Don Roderick; and Heaven grant that the day may never arrive, when you shall repent of not having listened to me! Listen to me, and perform this deed of justice and benevolence. Men will esteem you! God will esteem you! you have much in your power, but—"

"Do you know," again interrupted Don Roderick with warmth, but with something like remorse, "that when the whim takes me to hear a sermon, I can go to church? But, perhaps," continued he, with a forced smile of mockery, "you are putting regal dignity on me, and giving me a preacher in my own palace."

"And to God princes are responsible for the reception of his messages; to God you are responsible; he now sends into your palace a message by one of his ministers, the most unworthy—"

"In short, father," said Don Roderick, preparing to go, "I do not comprehend you: I suppose you have some affair of your own on hand; make a confidant of whom you please; but use not the freedom of troubling a gentleman any farther."

"Don Roderick, do not say *No* to me; do not keep in anguish the heart of an innocent child! a word from you would be sufficient."

"Well," said Don Roderick, "since you think I have so much in my power, and since you are so much interested—"

"Yes!" said Father Christopher, anxiously regarding him.

"Well, advise her to come, and place herself under my protection; she will want for nothing, and no one shall disturb her, as I am a gentleman."

At such a proposal, the indignation of the friar, which had hitherto been restrained with difficulty, loudly burst forth. All his prudence and patience forsook him: "Your protection!" exclaimed he, stepping back, and stretching forth both his hands towards Don Roderick, while he sternly fixed his eyes upon him, "your protection! You have filled the measure of your guilt by this wicked proposal, and I fear you no longer."

"Dare you speak thus to me?"

"I dare; I fear you no longer; God has abandoned you, and you are no longer an object of fear! Your protection! this innocent child is under the protection of God; you have, by your infamous offer, increased my assurance of her safety. Lucy, I say; see with what boldness I pronounce her name before you; Lucy—"

"How! in this house—"

"I compassionate this house; the wrath of God is upon it! You have acted in open defiance of the great God of heaven and earth; you have set at naught his counsel; you have oppressed the innocent; you have trampled on the rights of those whom you should have been the first to protect and defend. The wrath of God is upon you! A day will come!"

"Villain!" said Don Roderick, who at first was confounded between rage and astonishment; but when he heard the father thundering forth this prediction, a mysterious and unaccountable dread took possession of his soul. Hastily seizing his outstretched arm, and raising his voice in order to drown the maledictions of the monk, he cried aloud, "Depart from me, rash villain, cowled spy!"

These words instantly cooled the glowing enthusiasm of Father Christopher. The ideas of insult and injury in his mind had long been habitually associated with those of suffering and silence. His usual habits resumed their sway, and he became calm; he awaited what farther might be said, as, after the strength of the whirlwind has passed, an aged tree naturally recomposes its branches, and receives the hail as Heaven sends it.

"Villain! scoundrel! talk to your equals," said Don Roderick; "but thank the habit you bear for saving you from the chastisement which is your due. Begone this instant, and with unscathed limbs, or we shall see." So saying, he pointed imperiously to an opposite door. The friar bowed his head, and departed, leaving Don Roderick to measure with hasty and agitated steps the field of battle.

When he had closed the door behind him, the father perceived a man stealing softly away through another, and he recognised him as the aged domestic who had been his guide to the presence of Don Roderick. Before the birth of that nobleman, he had been in the service of his father, who was a man of a very different character. At his death, the new master expelled all the domestics, with the exception of this one, whom he retained on account of two valuable qualifications; a high conception of the dignity of the house, and a minute knowledge of the ceremonial required to support that dignity. The poor old man had never dared even to hint disapprobation of the daily proceedings at the castle before the signor, but he would sometimes venture to allow an exclamation of grief and disapproval to escape him before his fellow servants, who were infinitely diverted by his simple honesty, and his warm love of the good old times. His censures did not reach his master's ears unaccompanied by a relation of the raillery bestowed upon them, so that he became an object of general ridicule. On the days of formal entertainment, therefore, the old man was a person of great importance.

Father Christopher bowed to him as he passed by him, and pursued his way; but the old man approached him with a mysterious air, and made a sign that he should follow him into a dark passage, where, speaking in an under tone, he said, "Father! I have heard all, and I want to speak to you."

"Speak at once, then, good man."

"Here! oh no! Woe be to us if the master suspect it! But I shall be able to discover much, and I will endeavour to come to-morrow to the convent."

"Is there any base plot?"

"There is something hatching, certainly; I have long suspected it; but now I shall be on the look out, and I will come at the truth. These are strange doings—I live in a house where—But I wish to save my soul."

"God bless you!" said the friar, placing his hands on his head, as he bent reverently towards him; "God reward you! Do not forget then to come to-morrow."

"I will not," replied the domestic; "but go, now, for the love of Heaven, and do not betray me."

So saying, he looked cautiously on all sides, and led the way through the passage into a large hall, which fronted the court-yard, and pointing to the door, silently bade him "Farewell."

When once in the street, and freed from this den of depravity, the father breathed more freely; he hastened down the hill, pale in countenance, and agitated and distressed by the scene he had witnessed, and in which he had taken so leading a part. But the unlooked-for proffer of the servant came like a cordial. It seemed as if Heaven had sent a visible sign of its protection—a clue to guide him in his intricate undertaking—and in the very house where it was least likely to be found. Occupied with these thoughts, he raised his eyes towards the west, and beheld the sun declining behind the mountain, and felt that he had but a few minutes in which to reach the monastery, without violating the absolute law of the capuchins, that none of the brotherhood should remain beyond the walls after sunset.

Meanwhile, in the cottage of Lucy there had been plans agitated of which it is necessary to inform the reader. After the departure of the father, they had continued some time in silence; Lucy, with a heavy heart, prepared the dinner; Renzo, wavering and anxious, knew not how to depart; Agnes was apparently absorbed with her reel, but she was really maturing a thought, which she in a few moments thus declared:—

"Listen, my children. If you will have the necessary courage and dexterity; if you will confide in your mother; I pledge myself to free you from perplexity, sooner than Father Christopher could do, although he is the best man in the world." Lucy looked at her mother with an expression of astonishment rather than confidence, in a promise so magnificent. "Courage! dexterity!" cried Renzo, "say, say, what can I do?"

"Is it not true," said Agnes, "that if you were married, your chief difficulty would be removed, and that for the rest we would easily find a remedy!"

"Undoubtedly," said Renzo, "if we were married—The world is before us; and at a short distance from this, in Bergamo, a silk weaver is received with open arms. You know how often my cousin Bartolo has solicited me to go there, and enter into business with him; how many times he has told me that I should make a fortune, as he has done; and if I never listened to his request, it was—because my heart was here. Once married, we would all go together, and live happily far from the clutches of this villain, far from the temptation to do a rash deed. Is it not so, Lucy?"

"Yes," said Lucy, "but how—"

"As I said," resumed Agnes, "courage and dexterity, and the thing is easy."

"Easy!" exclaimed they, in wonder.

"Easy," replied Agnes, "if you are prudent. Hear me patiently, and I will endeavour to make you comprehend my project. I have heard it said by persons who knew, and moreover I have seen one instance of it myself, that a curate's *consent* is not necessary to render a marriage ceremony lawful, provided you have his presence."

"How so?" asked Renzo.

"You shall hear. There must be two witnesses, nimble and cunning. You go to the curate; the point is to catch him unexpectedly, that he may have no time to escape. You say, 'Signor Curate, this is my wife;' Lucy says, 'Signor Curate, this is my husband;' you must speak so distinctly that the curate and the witnesses hear you, and the marriage is as inviolable as if the pope himself had celebrated it. When the words are once uttered, the curate may fret, and fume, and scold; it will be of no use, you are man and wife."

"Is it possible?" exclaimed Lucy.

"Do you think," said Agnes, "that the thirty years I was in the world before you, I learned nothing? The thing is as I tell you."

The fact was truly such as Agnes represented it; marriages contracted in this manner were at that time held valid. Such an expedient was, however, not recurred to, but in cases of great necessity, and the priests made use of every precaution to avoid this compulsive co-operation.

"If it be true, Lucy!" said Renzo, regarding her attentively, with a supplicating expression.

"*If* it be true!" exclaimed Agnes. "Do you think I would say that which is *not* true? Well, well, get out of the difficulty as you can, I wash my hands from it."

"Ah, no! do not abandon us!" said Renzo; "I mean not to suggest a doubt of it. I place myself in your hands; I look to you as to a mother."

The momentary anger of Agnes vanished.

"But why, mamma," said Lucy, in her usual modest tone, "why did not Father Christopher think of this?"

"Think you that it did not come into his mind?" replied Agnes; "but he would not speak of it."

"Why?" exclaimed they, both at once.

"Why?—because, if you must know it, the friars do not approve of it."

"If it is not right," said Lucy, "we must not do it."

"What!" said Agnes, "do you think I would advise you to do that which is not right? If, against the advice of your parents, you were going to marry a rogue—but, on the contrary, I am rejoiced at your choice, and he who *causes* the disturbance is the only villain; and the curate—"

"It is as clear as the sun," said Renzo.

"It is not necessary to speak of it to Father Christopher," continued Agnes. "Once over, what do you think he will say to you? 'Ah! daughter, it was a great error; but it is done.' The friars must talk thus; but, believe me, in his heart he will be well content."

Lucy made no reply to an argument which did not appear to her very powerful; but Renzo, quite encouraged, said, "If it be thus, the thing is done."

"Softly," said Agnes; "there is need of caution. We must procure the witnesses; and find means to present ourselves to the curate unexpectedly. He has been two days concealed in his house; we must make him remain there.

If he suspects your intention, he will be as cunning as a cat, and flee as Satan from holy water."

Lucy here gained courage to offer her doubts of the propriety of such a course. "Until now we have lived with candour and sincerity," said she; "let us continue to do so; let us have faith in God, and God will aid us. Father Christopher said so: let us listen to his advice."

"Be guided by those who know better than you do," said Agnes gravely. "What need of advice? God tells us, 'Help thyself, and I will help thee.' We will tell the father all about it, when it is over."

"Lucy," said Renzo, "will you fail me now? Have we not done all that we could do, like good Christians? Had not the curate himself fixed the day and the hour? And whose is the blame if we are now obliged to use a little management? No, you will not fail me. I go at once to seek the witnesses, and will return to tell you my success." So saying, he hastily departed.

Disappointment sharpens the wit; and Renzo, who, in the straightforward path he had hitherto travelled, had not been required to subtilise much, now conceived a plan which would have done honour to a lawyer. He went directly to the house of one Anthony, and found him in his kitchen, employed in stirring a *polenta* of wheat, which was on the fire, whilst his mother, brother, and his wife, with three or four small children, were seated at the table, eagerly intent on the earthen pan, and awaiting the moment when it should be ready for their attack. But, on this occasion, the pleasure was wanting which the sight of dinner usually produces in the aspect of the labourer who has earned it by his industry. The size of the *polenta* was proportioned to the scantiness of the times, and not to the number and appetite of the assailants: and in casting a dissatisfied look on the common meal, each seemed to be considering the extent of appetite likely to survive it. Whilst Renzo was exchanging salutations with the family, Tony poured out the pudding on the pewter trencher prepared for its reception, and it appeared like a little moon within a large circumference of vapour. Nevertheless, the wife of Tony said courteously to Renzo, "Will you be helped to something?" This was a compliment that the peasants of Lombardy, however poor, paid to those who were, from any accident, present at their meals.

"I thank you," replied Renzo; "I only came to say a few words to Tony; and, Tony, not to disturb your family, we can go and dine at the inn, and we shall then have an opportunity to converse." The proposal was as agreeable as it was unexpected. Tony readily assented to it, and departed with Renzo, leaving to his family his portion of the *polenta*. They arrived at the inn, seated themselves at their ease in a perfect solitude, since the penury of the times had driven away the daily frequenters of the place. After having eaten, and emptied a bottle of wine, Renzo, with an air of mystery, said to Tony, "If you will do me a small service, I will do you a *great* one."

"Speak, speak, command me," said Tony, filling his glass; "I will go through fire to serve you."

"You are twenty-five livres in debt to the curate, for the rent of his field, that you worked last year."

"Ah! Renzo, Renzo! why do you mention it to me now? You've spoiled your kindness, and put to flight my good wishes."

"If I speak to you of your debt," said Renzo, "it is because I intend to give you the means of paying it."

"Do you really?"

"Really; would this content you?"

"Content me! that it would, indeed; if it were only to be freed from those infernal shakings of the head the curate makes me every time I meet him. And then always, '*Tony, remember; Tony, when shall we see each other for this business?*' When he preaches, he fixes his eyes on me in such a manner, I am almost afraid he will speak to me from the pulpit. I have wished the twenty-five livres to the devil a thousand times: and I was obliged to pawn my wife's gold necklace, which might be turned into so much *polenta*. But—"

"But, if you will do me a small favour, the twenty-five livres are ready."

"Agreed."

"But," said Renzo, "you must be silent and talk to no one about it."

"Need you tell me that?" said Tony; "you know me."

"The curate has some foolish reason for putting off my marriage, and I wish to hasten it. I am told that the parties going before him with two witnesses, and the one saying, *This is my wife*, and the other, *This is my husband*, that the marriage is lawful. Do you understand me?"

"You wish me to go as a witness?"

"Yes."

"And you will pay the twenty-five livres?"

"Yes."

"Done; I agree to it."

"But we must find another witness."

"I have found him already," said Tony. "My simpleton of a brother, Jervase, will do whatever I tell him; but you will pay him with something to drink?"

"And to eat," replied Renzo. "But will he be able?"

"I'll teach him; you know I was born with brains for both."

"To-morrow."

"Well."

"Towards evening."

"Very well."

"But be silent," said Renzo.

"Poh!" said Tony.

"But if thy wife should ask thee, as without doubt she will?"

"I am in debt to my wife for lies already; and for so much, that I don't know if we shall ever balance the account. I will tell her some idle story or other to set her heart at rest." With this good resolution he departed, leaving Renzo to pursue his way back to the cottage. In the meanwhile Agnes had in vain solicited Lucy's consent to the measure; she could not resolve to act without the approbation of Father Christopher. Renzo arrived, and triumphantly related his success. Lucy shook her head, but the two enthusiasts minded her not. They were now determined to pursue their plan, and by authority and entreaties induce her finally to accede to it.

"It is well," said Agnes, "it is well, but you have not thought of every thing."

"What have I not thought of?" replied Renzo.

"Perpetua! You have not thought of Perpetua. Do you believe that she would suffer Tony and his brother to enter? How then is it probable she would admit you and Lucy?"

"What shall we do?" said Renzo, pausing.

"I will tell you. I will go with you; I have a secret to tell her, which will engage her so that she will not see you. I will take her aside, and will touch such a chord—you shall see."

"Bless you!" exclaimed Renzo, "I have always said you were our best support."

"But all this will do no good," said Agnes, "if we cannot persuade Lucy, who obstinately persists that it is sinful."

Renzo made use of all his eloquence, but Lucy was not to be moved. "I know not what to say to your arguments," replied she. "I perceive that to do this, we shall degrade ourselves so far as to lie and deceive. Ah! Renzo, let us not so abase ourselves! I would be your wife" (and a blush diffused itself over her lovely countenance), "I would be your wife, but in the fear of God—at the altar. Let us trust in Him who is able to provide. Do you not think He will find a way to help us, far better than all this deception? And why make a mystery of it to Father Christopher?"

The contest still continued, when a trampling of sandals announced Father Christopher. Agnes had barely time to whisper in the ear of Lucy, "Be careful to tell him nothing," when the friar entered.

Chapter VII.

"Peace be with you!" said the friar as he entered. "There is nothing more to hope from man: so much the greater must be our confidence in God; and I've already had a pledge of his protection." None of the three entertained much hope from the visit of Father Christopher: for it would have been not only an unusual, but an absolutely unheard-of fact, for a nobleman to desist from his criminal designs at the mere prayer of his defenceless victim. Still, the sad certainty was a painful stroke.

The women bent down their heads; but in the mind of Renzo anger prevailed over disappointment. "I would know," cried he, gnashing his teeth, and raising his voice as he had never done before in the presence of Father Christopher, "I would know what reasons this dog has given, that my wife should not *be* my wife?"

"Poor Renzo!" said the father, with an accent of pity, and with a look which greatly enforced moderation; "poor Renzo! if those who commit injustice were always obliged to give a reason for it, things would not be as they are!"

"He has said, then, the dog! that he will not, because he will not?"

"He has not even said *so*, poor Renzo! There would be something gained, if he would make an open confession of his iniquity."

"But he has said something; *what* has this firebrand of hell said?"

"I could not repeat his words. He flew into a passion at me for my suspicions, and at the same time confirmed me in them: he insulted me, and then called himself offended; threatened, and complained. Ask no farther. He did not utter the name of Lucy, nor even pretend to know you: he affected to intend nothing. In short, I heard enough to feel that he is inexorable. But confidence in God! Poor children! be patient, be submissive! And thou, Renzo! believe that I sympathise with all that passes in thy heart.—But *patience*! It is a poor word, a bitter word to those who want faith; but, Renzo, will you not let God work? Will you not trust Him? Let Him work, Renzo; and, for your consolation, know that I hold in my hand a clue, by which I hope to extricate you from your distress. I cannot say more now. To-morrow I shall not be here; I shall be all day at the convent employed for you. Renzo, if thou canst, come there to me; but, if prevented by any accident, send some trusty messenger, by whom I can make known to you the success of my endeavours. Night approaches; I must return to the convent. Farewell! Faith and courage!" So saying, he departed, and hastened by the most abrupt but shortest road, to reach the convent in time, and escape the usual reprimand; or, what was worse, the imposition of some penance, which might disenable him, for the following day, from continuing his efforts in favour of his protégés.

"Did you hear him speak of a clue which he holds to aid us?" said Lucy; "it is best to trust in him; he is a man who does not make rash promises."

"He ought to have spoken more clearly," said Agnes; "or at least have taken me aside, and told me what it was."

"I'll put an end to the business; I'll put an end to it," said Renzo, pacing furiously up and down the room.

"Oh! Renzo!" exclaimed Lucy.

"What do you mean?" said Agnes.

"What do I mean? I mean to say that he may have a hundred thousand devils in his soul, but he is flesh and blood notwithstanding."

"No, no, for the love of Heaven!" said Lucy, but tears choked her voice.

"It is not a theme for jesting," said Agnes.

"For jesting?" cried Renzo, stopping before her, with his countenance inflamed by anger; "for jesting! you will see if I am in jest."

"Oh! Renzo!" said Lucy, sobbing, "I have never seen you thus before!"

"Hush, hush!" said Agnes, "speak not in this manner. Do you not fear the law, which is always to be had against the poor? And, besides, how many arms would be raised at a word!"

"I fear nothing," said Renzo; "the villain is well protected, dog that he is! but no matter. Patience and resolution! and the time will come. Yes! justice shall be done! I will free the country! People will bless me! Yes, yes."

The horror which Lucy felt at this explicit declaration of his purpose inspired her with new resolution. With a tearful countenance, but determined voice, she said to Renzo, "It can no longer be of any consequence to you, that I should become yours; I promised myself to a youth who had the fear of God in his heart; but a man who had once—were you safe from the law, were you secure from vengeance, were you the son of a king—"

"Well!" cried Renzo, in a voice of uncontrollable passion, "well! I shall not have you, then; but neither shall he; of *that* you may—"

"For pity's sake, do not talk thus; do not talk so fiercely!" said Lucy imploringly.

"You to implore me!" said he, somewhat appeased. "You! who will do nothing for *me*! What proof do you give me of your affection? Have I not supplicated in vain? Have I been able to obtain—"

"Yes, yes," replied Lucy, hastily, "I will go to the curate's to-morrow; now, if you wish it. Only be yourself again; I will go."

"Do you promise me?" said Renzo, softening immediately.

"I promise."

"Well, I am satisfied."

"God be praised!" said Agnes, much relieved.

"I have promised you," said Lucy, with an accent of timid reproach, "but you have also promised me to refer it to Father Christopher."

"Ha! will you now draw back?" said Renzo.

"No, no," said Lucy, again alarmed, "no, no, I have promised, and will perform. But you have compelled me to it by your own impetuosity. God forbid that—"

"Why will you prognosticate evil, Lucy? God knows we wrong no person."

"Well, well," said Lucy, "I will hope for the best."

Renzo would have wished to prolong the conversation, in order to allot to each their several parts for the morrow, but the night drew on, and he reluctantly felt himself compelled to depart.

The night was passed, by all three, in that state of agitation and trouble which always precedes an important enterprise whose issue is uncertain. Renzo returned early in the morning, and Agnes and he busied themselves in concerting the operations of the evening. Lucy was a mere spectator; but although she disapproved these measures in her heart, she still promised to do the best she could.

"Will you go to the convent, to speak to Father Christopher, as he desired you last night?" said Agnes to Renzo.

"Oh! no," replied he, "the father would soon read in my countenance that there was something on foot; and if he interrogated me, I should be obliged to tell him. You had better send some one."

"I will send Menico."

"Yes, that will do," replied Renzo, as he hurried off to make farther arrangements.

Agnes went to a neighbouring house to obtain Menico, a smart lad of twelve years of age, who, by the way of cousins and sisters-in-law, was a sort of nephew to the dame. She asked and obtained permission of his parents to keep him all day "for a particular service." She took him home, and after giving him breakfast, told him he must go to Pescarenico, and show himself to Father Christopher, who would send him back with a message.

" *Father Christopher*, you understand; that nice old man, with a white beard; him they call the Saint."

"I know him, I know him!" said Menico: "he speaks so kindly to the children, and often gives them pictures."

"Yes! that is he; and if, Menico, if he tells you to wait near the convent until he has an answer ready, don't stray away; don't go to the lake to throw stones in the water with the boys; nor to see them fish, nor—"

"Poh! aunt, I am no longer a baby."

"Well, behave well, and when you return with the answer, I will give you these new *parpagliole*."

During the remainder of this long morning, several strange things occurred, calculated to infuse suspicion into the already troubled minds of Lucy and her mother. A mendicant, but not in rags like others of his kind, and with a dark and sinister countenance, narrowly observing every object around him, entered to ask alms. A piece of bread was presented to him, which he received with ill-dissembled indifference. Then, with a mixture of impudence and hesitation, he made many enquiries, to which Agnes endeavoured to return evasive replies. When about to depart, he pretended to mistake the door, and went through the one that led to the stairs. They called to him, "Stay, stay! where are you going, good man? this way." He returned, excusing himself with an affectation of humility, to which he felt it difficult to compose his hard and stern features. After him, they saw pass, from time to time, other strange people. One entered the house, under pretence of asking the road; another stopped before the gate, and glanced furtively into the room, as if to avoid suspicion. Agnes went often to the door of the house during the remainder of the day, with an undefined dread of seeing some one approach who might cause them alarm. These mysterious visitations, however, ceased towards noon, but they had left an impression of impending evil on their minds, which they felt it impossible altogether to suppress.

To explain to the reader the true character of these suspicious wanderers, we must recur to Don Roderick, whom we left alone, in the hall of his palace, at the departure of Father Christopher. The more he reflected on his interview with the friar, the more was he enraged and ashamed, that he should have dared to come to him with the rebuke of Nathan to David on his lips. He paced with hurried steps through the apartment, and as he gazed at the portraits of his ancestors, warriors, senators, and abbots, which hung against its walls, he felt his indignation at the insult which had been offered him increase. A base-born friar to speak thus to one of noble birth! He formed plans of vengeance, and discarded them, without his being willing to acknowledge it to himself. The prediction of the father again sounded in his ears, and caused an unaccustomed perplexity. Restless and undetermined, he rang the bell, and ordered a servant to excuse him to the company, and to say to them, that urgent business prevented his seeing them again. The servant returned with the intelligence that the guests had departed. "And the Count Attilio?" asked Don Roderick.

"He has gone with the gentlemen, my lord."

"Well; six followers to accompany me; quickly. My sword, cloak, and hat. Be quick."

The servant left the room, and returned in a few moments with a rich sword, which his master girded on; he then threw the cloak around his shoulders, and donned his hat with its waving plumes with an air of proud defiance. He then passed into the street, followed by six armed ruffians, taking the road to Lecco. The peasantry and tradesmen shrunk from his approach; their profound and timid salutations received no notice from him; indeed, he acknowledged but by a slight inclination of the head those of the neighbouring gentry, whose rank, however, was incontestably inferior to his own. Indeed, the only man whose salutations he condescended to return upon an equal footing was the Spanish governor. In order to get rid of his *ennui*, and banish the idea of the monk and his imprecations, he entered the house of a gentleman, where a party was met together, and was received with that apparent cordiality which it is a necessary policy to manifest towards the powerful who are held in fear. On his return at night to his palace, he found

Count Attilio seated at supper. Don Roderick, full of thought, took a chair, but said little.

Scarcely was the table cleared, and the servants departed, when the count, beginning to rally his dull companion, said, "Cousin, when will you pay me my wager?"

"San Martin's day has not yet passed."

"Well, you will have to pay it; for all the saints in the calendar may pass, before you—"

"We will see about that!" said Don Roderick.

"Cousin, you would play the politician, but you cannot deceive me; I am so certain that I have won the wager, that I stand ready for another."

"Why!"

"Why? because the father—the father—in short, this friar has converted you."

"One of your fine imaginations, truly!"

"Converted, cousin, converted, I tell you; I rejoice at it; it will be a fine spectacle to see you penitent, with your eyes cast down! And how flattering to the father! he don't catch such fish every day. Be assured, he will bring you forward as an example to others; your actions will be trumpeted from the pulpit!"

"Enough, enough!" interrupted Don Roderick, half annoyed, and half disposed to laugh. "I will double the wager with you, if you please."

"The devil! perhaps *you* have converted the father!"

"Do not speak of him; but as to the wager, San Martin will decide." The curiosity of the count was aroused; he made many enquiries, which Don Roderick evaded, referring him to the day of decision.

The following morning, when he awoke, Don Roderick was "himself again." The various emotions that had agitated him after his interview with the father, had now resolved themselves into the simple desire of revenge. Hardly risen, he sent for Griso.—"Something serious," muttered the servant to whom the order was given; as this *Griso* was nothing less than the leader of the *bravoes* to whom was intrusted the most dangerous and daring enterprises, who was the most trusted by the master, and the most devoted to him, from gratitude and interest. This man had been guilty of murder; he had fled from the pursuit of justice to the palace of Don Roderick, who took him under his protection, and thus sheltered him from the pursuit of the law. He, therefore, stood pledged to the performance of any deed of villany that should be imposed on him.

"Griso," said Don Roderick, "you must show your skill in this emergency. Before to-morrow, this Lucy must be in this palace."

"It shall never be said that Griso failed to execute a command from his illustrious protector."

"Take as many men as are necessary, and dispose of them as appears to you best; only let the thing succeed. But be careful that no harm be done to her."

"Signor, a little fright—we cannot do less."

"Fright—may be unavoidable. But touch not a hair of her head; and, above all, treat her with the greatest respect. Do you hear?"

"Signor, I could not take a flower from the bush, and carry it to your Highness, without touching it; but I will do only what is absolutely necessary."

"Well; I trust thee. And—how wilt thou do it?"

"I was thinking, signor. It is fortunate that her cottage is at the extremity of the village; we have need of some place of concealment; and not far from her house there is that old uninhabited building in the middle of the fields, that one—but, your Highness knows nothing of these matters—which was burnt a few years ago, and, not having been repaired, is now deserted, except by the witches, who keep all cowardly rascals away from it; so that we may take safe possession."

"Well; what then?"

Here Griso went on to propose, and Don Roderick to approve, until they had agreed upon the manner of conducting the enterprise to the desired conclusion, without leaving a trace of the authors of it: and also upon the manner of imposing silence, not only upon poor Agnes, but also upon the more impatient and fiery Renzo.

"If this rash fellow fall in your way by chance," added Don Roderick, "you had best give him, on his shoulders, something he will remember; so that he will be more likely to obey the order to remain quiet, which he will receive to-morrow. Do you hear?"

"Yes, yes, leave it to me," said Griso, as, with an air of importance, he took his leave.

The morning was spent in reconnoitring,—the mendicant of whom we have spoken was Griso; the others were the villains whom he employed, to gain a more perfect knowledge of the scene of action. They returned to the palace to arrange and mature the enterprise;—all these mysterious movements were not effected without rousing the suspicions of the old domestic, who, partly by listening, and partly by conjecture, came to the knowledge of the concerted attempt of the evening. This knowledge came a little too late, for already a body of ruffians were laying in wait in the old house. However, the poor old man, although well aware of the dangerous game he played, did not fail to perform his promise; he left the palace on some slight pretence, and hurried to the convent. Griso and his band left shortly after, and met at the old building,—the former had previously left orders at the palace, that, at the approach of night, there should be a litter brought thither,—he then despatched three of the bravoes to the village inn; one to remain at its entrance to observe the movements on the road, and to give notice when the inhabitants should have retired to rest; the other two to occupy themselves within as idlers, gaming and drinking. Griso, with the rest of the troop, continued in ambush, on the watch.

All this was going forward, and the sun was about to set, when Renzo entered the cottage, and said to Lucy and her mother, "Tony and Jervase are ready; I am going with them to sup at the inn; at the sound of the 'Ave Maria,' we will come for you; take courage, Lucy, all depends on a moment."

"Oh, yes," said Lucy, "courage;" with a voice that contradicted her words.

When Renzo and his companions arrived at the inn, they found the door blockaded by a sentinel, who, leaning on one side of it, with his arms folded on his breast, occupied half its width; at the same time rolling his eagle eyes first to the right and then to the left, displaying alternately their blacks and their whites. A flat cap of crimson velvet, placed sideways, covered the half of the *long lock*, which, parted on a dark forehead, was fastened behind with a comb. He held in his hand a club; his arms, properly speaking, were concealed beneath his garments. When Renzo evinced a desire to enter, he looked at him fixedly without moving; of this, the young man, wishing to decline all conversation, took no notice, but, beckoning to his companions to follow his example, slid between the figure and the door-post. Having gained an entrance, he beheld the other two bravoes with a large mug between them, seated at play; they stared at him with a look of enquiry, making signs to each other, and then to their comrade at the door. This was not unobserved by Renzo, and his mind was filled with a vague sentiment of suspicion and alarm. The innkeeper came for his orders; which were, "a private room, and supper for three."

"Who are those strangers?" asked he of the landlord, when he came in to set the table.

"I do not know them," replied he.

"How! neither of them?"

"The first rule of our trade," said he, spreading the cloth, "is, not to meddle with the affairs of others; and, what is wonderful, even our women are not curious. It is enough for us that customers pay well; who they are, or who they are not, matters nothing. And now, I will bring you a dish of polpette, the like of which you have never eaten."

When he returned to the kitchen, and was employed in taking the polpette from the fire, one of the bravoes approached, and said, in an under tone, "Who are those men?"

"Good people of this village," replied the host, pouring the mince-meat into a dish.

"Well; but what are their names? Who are they?" insisted he, in a rough voice.

"One is called Renzo," replied the host; "esteemed a good youth, and an excellent weaver of silk. The other is a peasant, whose name is Tony; a jovial fellow,—it is a pity he has no more money, for he would spend it all here. The other is a simpleton, who eats when they feed him. By your leave—" So saying, he slipped past him, with the dish in his hand, and carried it to the place of its destination.

"How do you know?" said Renzo, continuing the conversation from the point at which it had been dropped, "how do you know that they are honest men, when you are not acquainted with them?"

"From their actions, my good fellow; men are known by their actions. He who drinks wine without criticising it; he who shows the face of the king on the counter without prattling; he who does not quarrel with other customers, and, if he has a blow or two to give, goes away from the inn, so that the poor host need not suffer from it; he is an honest man. But what the devil makes you so inquisitive, when you are engaged to be married, and should have other things in your head? And with this mince-meat before you, which would make the dead revive?" So saying, he returned to the kitchen.

The supper was not very agreeable; the two guests would have lingered over the unusual luxury; but Renzo, preoccupied, and troubled and uneasy at the singular appearance of the strangers, longed for the hour of departure. He conversed in brief sentences, and in an under tone, so that he might not be overheard by them.

"What an odd thing it is," blundered Jervase, "that Renzo wishes to be married, and has needed—" Renzo looked sternly at him. "Keep silence, you beast!" said Tony to him, accompanying the epithet with a cuff. Jervase obeyed, and the remainder of the repast was consumed in silence. Renzo observed a strict sobriety, in order to keep his companions under some restraint. Supper being over, he paid the reckoning, and prepared to depart: they were obliged to pass the three men again, and encounter a repetition of their eager gaze. When a few steps distant from the inn, Renzo, looking back, perceived that he was followed by the two whom he had left seated in the kitchen. He stopped; observing this, they stopped also, and retraced their steps.

If he had been near enough, he would have heard a few words of strange import; "It would be a glorious thing," said one of the scoundrels, "without reckoning the cash, if we could tell at the palace how we had flattened their ribs,—without the direction, too, of Signor Griso."

"And spoil the whole work," added the other; "but see! he stops to look at us! Oh! if it were only later! But let us turn back, not to create suspicion. People are coming on all sides; let us wait till they go to their rests."

Then was heard in the village the busy hum of the evening, which precedes the solemn stillness of the night; then were seen women returning from their daily labour, with their infants on their backs, and leading by the hand the older children, to whom they were repeating the evening prayers; men with their spades, and other instruments of culture, thrown over their shoulders. At the opening of the cottage doors, was discerned the bright light of the fires, kindled in order to prepare their meagre suppers; in the street there were salutations given and returned, brief and mournful observations on the poverty of the harvest, and the scarcity of the year; and at intervals was heard the measured strokes of the bell which announced the departure of the day.

When Renzo saw that the two men no longer followed him, he continued his way, giving instructions, in a low voice, from time to time, to his two companions. It was dark night when they arrived at the cottage of Lucy.

"Between the acting of a dreadful thing   And the first motion, all the
interim is   Like a phantasma, or a hideous dream."

Lucy endured many hours the anguish of such a dream; and Agnes, even
Agnes, the author of the plot, was thoughtful and silent. But, in the moment
of action, new and various emotions pass swiftly through the mind: at one
instant, that which had appeared difficult becomes perfectly easy; at another,
obstacles present themselves which were never before thought of, the
imagination is filled with alarm, the limbs refuse their office, and the heart
fails at the promise it had given with such security. At the gentle knock of
Renzo, Lucy was seized with such terror, that, at the moment, she resolved to
suffer any thing, to endure a separation from him for ever, rather than
execute her resolution; but when, with an assured and encouraging air, he
said, "All is ready; let us begone," she had neither heart nor time to suggest
difficulties. Agnes and Renzo placed her between them, and the adventurous
company set forward. Slowly and quietly they took the path that led around
the village,—it would have been nearer to pass directly through it, to Don
Abbondio's house, but their object was to avoid observation. Upon reaching
the house, the lovers remained concealed on one side of it, Agnes a little in
advance, so as to be prepared to speak to Perpetua as soon as she should make
her appearance. Tony, with Jervase, who did nothing, but *without* whom
nothing could be done, courageously knocked at the door.

"Who is there, at this hour?" cried a voice from the window, which they
recognised to be that of Perpetua. "No one is sick, that I know of. What is the
matter?"

"It is I," replied Tony, "with my brother; we want to speak with the curate."

"Is this an hour for Christians?" replied Perpetua, briskly. "Come
to-morrow."

"Hear me; I will come, or not, as I choose; I have received I can't tell how
much money, and I have come to balance the small account that you know
of. I have here twenty-five fine new pieces; but if he cannot see me,—well—I
know how and where to spend them."

"Wait, wait. I will speak to you in a moment. But why come at this hour?"

"If you can change the hour, I am willing; as for me, I am here, and, if you
don't want me to stay, I'll go away."

"No, no, wait a moment; I will give you an answer." So saying, she closed
the window. As soon as she disappeared, Agnes separated herself from the

lovers, saying to Lucy, in a low voice, "Courage, it is but a moment." She then entered into conversation with Tony at the door, that Perpetua, on opening it, might suppose she had been accidentally passing by, and that Tony had detained her.

Chapter VIII.

"Carneades! who was he?" said Don Abbondio to himself, seated in his large chair, with a book open before him. "Carneades! this name I have either heard or read of; he must have been a man of study, a scholar of antiquity; but who the devil *was* he?" Now, it should be known, that it was Don Abbondio's custom to read a little every day, and that a curate, his neighbour, who had a small library, furnished him with books, one after the other, as they came to hand. That with which he was at this moment engaged, was a panegyric on St. Carlos, delivered many years before in the cathedral of Milan. The saint was there compared for his love of study to Archimedes; which comparison the poor curate well understood, inasmuch as this did not require, from the various anecdotes related of him, an erudition very extensive. But the author went on to liken him also to Carneades, and here the poor reader was at fault. At this moment, Perpetua announced the visit of Tony.

"At such an hour?" said Don Abbondio.

"What do you expect? They have no discretion. But if you do not shoot the bird flying—"

"Who knows if I shall ever be able to do it?" continued he. "Let him come in. But are you very sure that it is Tony?"

"The devil!" said Perpetua, as she descended, and, opening the door, demanded, "Where are you?"

Tony appeared, in company with Agnes, who accosted Perpetua by name.

"Good evening, Agnes," said she; "whence come you at this hour?"

"I come from—," naming a neighbouring village. "And do you know," she continued, "that I have been delayed on your account?"

"On my account!" exclaimed she; and turning to the two brothers, said, "Go in, and I will follow you."

"Because," resumed Agnes, "a gossiping woman of the company said—would you believe it?—obstinately persisted in saying, that you were never engaged to Beppo Suolavecchia, nor to Anselmo Lunghigna, because they would not have you. I maintained that you had refused them both—"

"Certainly I did. Oh! what a liar! oh! what a great liar! Who was it?"

"Don't ask me; I don't wish to make mischief."

"You must tell me; you must tell me. Oh! what a lie!"

"So it was; but you can't believe how sorry I felt not to know all the story, that I might have confuted her."

"It is an infamous lie," said Perpetua. "As to Beppo, every one knows—"

In front of Don Abbondio's house, there was a short and narrow lane, between two old cottages, which opened at the farther end into the fields. Agnes drew Perpetua thither, as if for the purpose of talking with her more freely. When they were at a spot, from which they could not see what passed before the curate's house, Agnes coughed loudly.

This was the concerted signal, which, being heard by Renzo, he, with Lucy on his arm, crept quietly along the wall, approached the door, opened it softly, and entered the passage, where the two brothers were waiting their approach. They all ascended the stairs on tiptoe; the brothers advanced towards the door of the chamber; the lovers remained concealed on the landing.

"*Deo gratias*," said Tony, in a clear voice.

"Tony, eh? come in," replied the voice from within. Tony obeyed, opening the door just enough to admit himself and brother, one at a time. The rays of light, which shone unexpectedly through this opening on the darkness by which Renzo and Lucy were protected, made the latter tremble as if already discovered. The brothers entered, and Tony closed the door; the lovers remained motionless without; the beating of poor Lucy's heart might be heard in the stillness.

Don Abbondio was, as we have said, seated in his arm chair, wrapped in a morning-gown, with an old cap on his head, in the fashion of a tiara, which formed a sort of cornice around his face, and shaded it from the dim light of a little lamp. Two thick curls which escaped from beneath the cap, two thick eyebrows, two thick mustachios, a dense tuft along his chin, all quite grey, and studding his sun-burnt and wrinkled visage, might be compared to snowy bushes projecting from a rock by moonlight.

"Ah! ah!" was his salutation, as he took off his spectacles and placed them on his book.

"Does the curate think I have come at too late an hour?" said Tony, bowing: Jervase awkwardly followed his example.

"Certainly, it is late; late on all accounts. Do you know that I am ill?"

"Oh! I am sorry."

"Did you not hear that I was sick, and could not be seen? But why is this boy with you?"

"For company, Signor Curate."

"Well; let us see."

"Here are twenty-five new pieces, with the image of St. Ambrose on horseback," said Tony, drawing forth a little bundle from his pocket.

"Give here," said Don Abbondio; and taking the bundle, he opened it, counted the money, and found it correct.

"Now, sir, you will give me the necklace of my Teela."

"Certainly," replied Don Abbondio; and going to an old press, he drew forth the pledge, and carefully returned it.

"Now," said Tony, "you will please to put it in black and white?"

"Eh!" said Don Abbondio, "how suspicious the world has become! Do you not trust me?"

"How! Sir. If I trust you! you do me wrong. But since my name is on your book on the side of debtor—"

"Well, well," interrupted Don Abbondio; and seating himself at the table, he began to write, repeating, with a loud voice, the words as they came from his pen. In the meanwhile, Tony, and, at a sign from him, Jervase, placed themselves before the table, in such a manner as to deprive the writer of a view of the door; and, as if from heedlessness, moved their feet about on the floor, as a signal to those without, and also for the purpose of drowning the noise of their footsteps; of this Don Abbondio, occupied in writing, took no notice. At the grating sounds of the feet Renzo drew Lucy trembling into the room, and stood with her behind the brothers. Don Abbondio, having finished writing, read it over attentively, folded the paper, and reaching it to Tony, said, "Will you be satisfied now?" Tony, on receiving it, retired on one side, Jervase on the other, and, behold, in the midst, Renzo and Lucy! Don Abbondio, affrighted, astonished, and enraged, took an immediate resolution; and while Renzo was uttering the words, "Sir Curate, in the presence of these witnesses, this is my wife," and the poor Lucy had begun, "And this is—" he had snatched from the table the cloth which covered it, throwing on the ground books, pen, ink, and paper, and in haste letting fall the light, he threw it over and held it wrapped around the face of Lucy, at the same time roaring out, "Perpetua! Perpetua! treachery! help!" The wick, dying in the socket, sent a feeble and flickering light over the figure of Lucy, who, entirely overcome, stood like a statue, making no effort to free herself. The light died away, and left them in darkness; Don Abbondio quitted the poor girl, and felt cautiously along the wall for a door that led to an inner chamber; having found it, he entered, and locked himself in, crying out, "Perpetua! treachery! help! out of the house! out of the house!" All was confusion in the apartment he had quitted; Renzo, groping in the dark to find the curate, had followed the sound of his voice, and was knocking at the door of the room, crying, "Open, open; don't make such an outcry;" Lucy calling to Renzo, in a supplicating voice, "Let us go, let us go, for the love of God!" Tony, creeping on all fours, and feeling along the floor for his receipt, which had been dropped in the tumult; the poor Jervase, crying and jumping, and endeavouring to find the door on the stairs, so as to escape with whole bones.

In the midst of this turmoil, we cannot stop to make reflections; but Renzo, causing disturbance at night in another person's house, and holding the master of it besieged in an inner room, has all the appearance of an oppressor; when in fact he was the oppressed. Don Abbondio, assaulted in his own house, while he was tranquilly attending to his affairs, appeared the victim; when, in fact, it was he who had inflicted the injury. Thus goes the world, or rather, thus it went in the seventeenth century.

The besieged, seeing that the enemy gave no signs of retreat, opened a window which looked out upon the churchyard, and cried, "Help, help!" The moon shone brightly—every object could be clearly discerned as in the day; but a deep repose rested over all—there was no indication of a living soul. Contiguous to the church, and on that side of it which fronted the parsonage, was a small habitation in which slept the sexton. Aroused by this strange outcry, he jumped from his bed, opened the small window, with his eyelids glued together all the time, and cried, "What is the matter?"

"Run, Ambrose, run! help! people in the house!" cried Don Abbondio. "I come in a moment," replied he, drawing in his head; he closed his curtain, and half stupid, and half affrighted, thought of an expedient to bring more help than had been required of him, without risking his own life in the contest, whatever it might be. He hastily took his breeches from the bed, and putting them under his arm, like an opera hat, ran to the belfry and pulled away lustily.

Ton, Ton, Ton; the peasant aroused, sat up in his bed; the boy, sleeping in the hay-loft, listened eagerly, and sprang on his feet; "What is the matter? What is it? Fire! Robbers!" Each woman entreated her husband not to stir, but to leave it to others: such as were cowards obeyed, whilst the inquisitive and courageous took their arms, and ran towards the noise.

Long before this, however, the alarm had been given to other personages of our story; the bravoes in one place; and Agnes and Perpetua in another. It is necessary to relate briefly how the former had been occupied, since we last took leave of them; those at the old house, and those at the inn. The latter, when they ascertained that the inhabitants of the village had retired to rest, and that the road was clear, went to the cottage of Lucy, and found that a perfect stillness reigned within. They then returned to the old house to give in their report to Signor Griso. He immediately put on a slouched hat, with a pilgrim's habit, and staff, saying, "Let us act as becometh soldiers; cautious, quiet, and attentive to orders." Then leading the way, he, with his company, arrived at the cottage, by a route different from that taken by our poor cottagers. Griso kept the band a few steps off, went forward alone to explore, and seeing all deserted and quiet on the outside, he beckoned to two of them, ordered them to mount very carefully and quietly the wall which enclosed the court-yard, and to conceal themselves on the other side behind a thick fig-tree, which he had observed in the morning. That being done, he knocked gently at the door, with the intention to call himself a pilgrim, who had wandered from his way, and request shelter until the morning. No answer; he knocked again, louder; not a sound! He then called a third robber, made him also descend into the yard, with orders to unfasten the bolt on the inside, so that they might have free entrance. All was performed with the utmost caution, and the most complete success. Griso then called the rest, and made some of them conceal themselves by the side of those behind the fig-tree; he then opened the door very softly, placed two centinels on the inside of it, and advanced to the lower chamber. He knocked; he waited—and well might wait; he raised the latch; no one from within said, "Who is there?" Nothing could go on better. He then called the robbers from the fig-tree, and with them entered the room where he had in the morning so villanously received the loaf of bread. He drew out his flint, tinder-box, and matches, and striking a light, proceeded to the inner chamber; it was empty! He returned to the stairs, and listened; solitude and silence! He left two to keep watch below, and with the others carefully ascended the stairs, cursing in his heart the creaking of the steps. He reached the summit, pushed softly open the door of the first room, and listened if any one breathed or moved: no one! He advanced, shading his face with the lamp, and perceived a bed; it was made, and perfectly smooth, with the covering arranged in order on the bolster! He shrugged his shoulders, and returning to the company, made a sign to them, that he was going into the other room, and that they should remain quietly behind,—he did so, and had the same success; all deserted and quiet.

"What the devil's this?" said he aloud; "some traitorous dog has played the spy!" They then searched with less ceremony the rest of the house, putting every thing out of its place. Meanwhile those at the doorway heard a light step approaching in the street,—they kept very quiet, thinking it would pass on; but, behold! it stopped exactly in front of the cottage! It was Menico, who had come in haste from the convent, to warn Agnes and her daughter to escape from the house, and take refuge *there*, because—the *because* is already known. He was surprised to find the door unbolted, and entering with a vague sentiment of alarm, found himself seized by two ruffians, who said in a menacing tone, "Hush! be quiet, or you die!" He uttered a cry, at which one struck him a blow on the mouth, the other placed his hand on his sword to inspire him with fear. The boy trembled like a leaf, and did not attempt to stir; but all at once was heard the first sound of the bell, and immediately after, a thundering peel burst forth. "The wicked are always cowards," says a Milanese proverb; alarmed at the sound, the bravoes let go in haste the arms of Menico, and fled away hastily to the old house, to join the main body of their comrades. Menico, finding himself free, also fled, by the way of the fields, towards the belfry, naturally supposing he would find some one there. As to the other villains above stairs, the terrible sound made the same impression on them; amazed and perplexed, they hit one against the other, in striving to find the nearest way to the door. Nevertheless, they were brave, and accustomed to confront any known danger; but here was something unusual, an undetermined peril, and they became panic-struck. It now required all the superiority of Griso to keep them together, so that there should be a retreat, and not a flight. He succeeded, however, in assembling them in the middle of the court-yard. "Halt, halt," cried he, "pistols in hand, knives ready, all in order, and then we will march. Cowards! for shame! fall behind me, and keep together." Reduced to order, they followed him in silence.

We will leave them, in order to give an account of Agnes and Perpetua, whom we left at the end of the little lane, engaged in conversation. Agnes had managed to draw the latter off to some distance, by dint of appearing to give great heed to her story, which she urged on by an occasional "Certainly; now I comprehend; that is plain; and then? and he? and you?" In the midst of an important part of her narrative, the deep silence of the night was broken by the cry of Don Abbondio for "*help!*" "Mercy! what is the matter?" cried Perpetua, and prepared to run.

"What is the matter? what is the matter?" cried Agnes, holding her by the gown.

"Mercy! did you not hear?" replied she, struggling to get free.

"What is the matter? what is the matter?" repeated Agnes, holding her firmly by the arm.

"Devil of a woman!" exclaimed Perpetua, still struggling. Then was heard at a distance the light scream of Menico.

"Mercy!" cried Agnes also, and they both ran at full speed; the sound of the bell, which now succeeded, spurred them on. Perpetua arrived first, and, behold, at the door, Tony, Jervase, Renzo, and Lucy, who had found the stairs, and, at the terrible sound of the bell, were flying to some place of safety.

"What is the matter? What is the matter?" demanded Perpetua, out of breath, of the brothers. They answered her with a violent push, and fled away. "And you! what are you here for?" said she then to Renzo and Lucy. They made no reply. She then ascended the stairs in haste, to seek her master. The two lovers (still lovers) stood before Agnes, who, alarmed and grieved, said, "Ah! you are here! How has it gone? Why did the bell ring?"

"Home, home!" said Renzo, "before the people gather." But Menico now appeared running to meet them. He was out of breath, and hardly able to cry out, "Back! back! by the way of the convent. There is the devil at the house," continued he, panting; "I saw him, I did; he was going to kill me. The Father Christopher says you must come quickly.—I saw him, I did.—I am glad I found you all here,—I will tell you all when we are safe off."

Renzo, who was the most self-possessed of the party, thought it best to follow his advice. "Let us follow him," said he, to the females. They silently obeyed, and the little company moved on. They hastily crossed the churchyard, passing through a private street, into the fields. They were not many paces distant, before the people began to collect, each one asking of his neighbour what was the matter, and no one being able to answer the question. The first that arrived ran to the door of the church: it was fastened. They then looked through a little window into the belfry, and demanded the cause of the alarm. When Ambrose heard a known voice, and knew, by the hum, that there was an assemblage of people without, he hastily slipped on that part of his dress which he had carried under his arm, and opened the church door.

"What is all this tumult? What is the matter? Where is it?"

"Where is it? Do you not know? Why, in the curate's house. Run, run." They rushed in a crowd thither; looked,—listened. All was quiet. The street door was fastened; not a window open; not a sound within.

"Who is within there? Holla! holla! Signor Curate, Signor Curate!"

Don Abbondio, who, as soon as he was relieved by the flight of the invaders, had retired from the window, and closed it, was now quarrelling with Perpetua for leaving him to bear the brunt of the battle alone. When he heard himself called by name, by the people outside, he repented of the rashness which had produced this undesired result.

"What has happened? Who are they? Where are they? What have they done to you?" cried a hundred voices at a time.

"There is no one here now; I am much obliged to you.—Return to your houses."

"But who *has* been here? Where have they gone? What has happened?"

"Bad people, bad people, who wander about in the night; but they have all fled.—Return to your houses. I thank you for your kindness." So saying, he retired and shut the window. There was a general murmur of disappointment through the crowd. Some laughed, some swore, some shrugged up their shoulders and went home; but at this moment a person came running towards them, panting and breathless. He lived at the house opposite to the cottage of Lucy, and had witnessed from the window the alarm of the bravoes, when Griso endeavoured to collect them in the court-yard. When he recovered breath, he cried, "What do you do here, friends? The devil is not here, he is down at the house of Agnes Mondella. Armed people are in it. It seems they wish to murder a pilgrim; but who knows what the devil it is?"

"What! what! what!" And then began a tumultuous conversation. "Let us go. How many are there? How many are we? Who are they?—The constable! the constable!"

"I am here," replied the constable, from the midst of the crowd, "I am here, but you must assist me; you must obey.—Quick;—where is the sexton? To the bell, to the bell. Quick; some one run to Lecco to ask for succour.—Come this way." The tumult was great, and as they were about to depart for the cottage of Agnes, another messenger came flying, and exclaimed, "Run, friends;—robbers who are carrying off a pilgrim. They are already out of the village! On! on! this way."

In obedience to this command they moved in a mass, without waiting the orders of their leader, towards the cottage of Lucy. While the army advances, many of those at the head of the column, slacken their pace, not unwilling to leave the post of honour to their more adventurous friends in the rear. The confused multitude at length reach the scene of action. The traces of recent invasion were manifest,—the door open, the bolts loosened, but the invaders, where were they? They entered the court, advanced into the house, and called loudly, "Agnes! Lucy! Pilgrim! Where is the pilgrim! Did Stephano dream that he saw him? No, no, Carlandrea saw him also. Hallo! Pilgrim! Agnes! Lucy! No reply! They have killed them! they have killed them!" There was then a proposition to follow the murderers, which would have been acceded to, had not a voice from the crowd cried out, that Agnes and Lucy were in safety in some house. Satisfied with this, they soon dispersed to their homes, to relate to their wives that which had happened. The next day, however, the constable being in his field, and, with his foot resting on his spade, meditating on the mysteries of the past night, was accosted by two men, much resembling, in their appearance, those whom Don Abbondio had encountered a few days before. They very unceremoniously forbade him to make a deposition of the events of the night before the magistrate, and, if questioned by any of the gossips of the villagers, to maintain a perfect silence on pain of death.

Our fugitives for a while continued their flight, rapidly and silently, utterly overwhelmed by the fatigue of their flight, by their late anxiety, by vexation and disappointment at their failure, and a confused apprehension of some future danger. As the sound of the bell died away on the ear, they slackened their pace. Agnes, gathering breath and courage, first broke the silence, by asking Renzo what had been done at the curate's? He related briefly his melancholy story. "And who," said she to Menico, "was the devil in the house? What did you mean by that?" The boy narrated that of which he had been an eye-witness, and which imparted a mingled feeling of alarm and gratitude to the minds of his auditors,—alarm at the obstinacy of Don Roderick in pursuing his purpose, and gratitude that they had thus escaped his snares. They caressed affectionately the boy who had been placed in so great danger on their account: Renzo gave him a piece of money in addition to the new coin already promised, and desired him to say nothing of the message given him by Father Christopher. "Now, return home," said Agnes, "because thy family will be anxious about thee: you have been a good boy; go home, and pray the Lord that we may soon meet again." The boy obeyed, and our travellers advanced in silence. Lucy kept close to her mother, dexterously but gently declining the arm of her lover. She felt abashed, even in the midst of all this confusion, at having been so long and so familiarly alone with him, while expecting that a few moments longer would have seen her his wife: but this dream had vanished, and she felt most sensitively the apparent indelicacy of their situation. They at length reached the open space before the church of the convent. Renzo advanced towards the door, and pushed it gently. It opened, and they beheld, by the light of the moon, which then fell upon his pallid face and silvery beard, the form of Father Christopher, who was there in anxious expectation of their arrival. "God be thanked!" said he, as they entered. By his side stood a capuchin, whose office was that of sexton to the church, whom he had persuaded to leave the door half open, and to watch with him. He had been very unwilling to submit to this inconvenient and dangerous condescension, which it required all the authority of the holy father to overcome; but, perceiving who the company were, he could endure no longer. Taking the father aside, he whispered, to him, "But Father—Father—at night—in the church—with women—shut—the rules—but Father!—" "Omnia munda mundis," replied he, turning meekly to Friar Fazio, and forgetting that he did not understand Latin. But this forgetfulness was exactly the most fortunate thing in the world. If the father had produced arguments, Friar Fazio would not have failed to oppose them; but these mysterious words, he concluded, must contain a solution of all his doubts. He acquiesced, saying, "Very well; you know more than I do."

Father Christopher then turned to our little company, who were standing in suspense, by the light of a lamp which was flickering before the altar.

"Children," said he, "thank the Lord, who has preserved you from great peril. Perhaps at this moment—" and he entered into an explanation of the reasons which had induced him to send for them to the convent, little suspecting that they knew more than he did, and supposing that Menico had found them tranquil at their home, before the arrival of the robbers. No one undeceived him, not even Lucy, although suffering the keenest anguish at practising dissimulation with such a man; but it was a night of confusion and duplicity.

"Now," continued he, "you perceive, my children, that this country is no longer safe for you. It is your country, I know; you were born here; you have wronged no one: but such is the will of God! It is a trial, children, support it with patience, with faith, without murmuring; and be assured, there will come a day, in which you will see the wisdom of all that now befalls you. I have procured you a refuge for a season, and I hope you will soon be able to return safely to your home; at all events, God will provide, and I his minister will faithfully exert myself to serve you, my poor persecuted children. You," continued he, turning to the females, "can remain at —. There you will be beyond danger, and yet not far from home; go to our convent in that place, ask for the superior, give him this letter, he will be to you another Friar Christopher. And thou, my Renzo, thou must place thyself in safety from the impetuosity of others, and your own. Carry this letter to Father Bonaventura, of Lodi, in our convent at the eastern gate of Milan; he will be to you a father, will advise you, and find you work, until you can return to live here tranquilly. Now, go to the border of the lake, near the mouth of the Bione" (a stream a short distance from the convent); "you will see there a small boat fastened; you must say, 'A boat;' you will be asked for whom, answer, 'Saint Francis.' The boatman will receive you, will take you to the other side, where you will find a carriage, which will conduct you to —. If any one should ask how Father Christopher came to have at his disposal such means of transport by land and by water, he would show little knowledge of the power possessed by a capuchin who held the reputation of a saint."

The charge of the houses remained to be thought of; the father received the keys of them; Agnes, on consigning hers, thought with a sigh, that there was no need of keys, the house was open, the devil had been there, and it was doubtful if there remained any thing to be cared for.

"Before you go," said the father, "let us pray together to the Lord, that he may be with you in this journey, and always, and above all, that he may give you strength to submit cheerfully to that which he has ordained." So saying, he knelt down; all did the same. Having prayed a few moments in silence, he pronounced with a low but distinct voice the following words: "We pray thee also for the wretched man who has brought us to this state. We should be unworthy of thy mercy if we did not earnestly solicit it for him: he has most need of it. We, in our sorrow, have the consolation of trusting in thee; we can still offer thee our supplications, with thankfulness. But he—he is an enemy to thee! Oh wretched man! He dares to strive against thee: have pity on him, O Lord! touch his heart, soften his rebellious will, and bestow on him all the good we would desire for ourselves."

Rising hastily, he then said, "Away, my children, there is no time to lose; God will go with you, his angel protect you: away." They kept silence from emotion, and as they departed, the father added, "My heart tells me we shall soon meet again." Without waiting for a reply, he retired; the travellers pursued their way to the appointed spot, found the boat, gave and received the watchword, and entered into it. The boatmen made silently for the opposite shore: there was not a breath of wind; the lake lay polished and smooth in the moonlight, agitated only by the dipping of the oars, which quivered in its gleam. The waves breaking on the sands of the shore, were heard deadly and slowly at a distance, mingled with the rippling of the waters between the pillars of the bridge.

The silent passengers cast a melancholy look behind at the mountains and the landscape, illumined by the moon, and varied by multitudes of shadows. They discerned villages, houses, cottages; the palace of Don Roderick, raised above the huts that crowded the base of the promontory, like a savage prowling in the dark over his slumbering prey. Lucy beheld it, and shuddered; then cast a glance beyond the declivity, towards her own little home, and beheld the top of the fig-tree which towered in the court-yard; moved at the sight, she buried her face in her hands, and wept in silence.

Farewell, ye mountains, source of waters! farewell to your varied summits, familiar as the faces of friends! ye torrents, whose voices have been heard from infancy! Farewell! how melancholy the destiny of one, who, bred up amid your scenes, bids you farewell! If voluntarily departing with the hope of future gain at this moment, the dream of wealth loses its attraction, his resolution falters, and he would fain remain with you, were it not for the hope of benefiting you by his prosperity. The more he advances into the level country, the more his view becomes wearied with its uniform extent; the air appears heavy and lifeless: he proceeds sorrowfully and thoughtfully into the tumultuous city; houses crowded against houses, street uniting with street, appears to deprive him of the power to breathe; and in front of edifices admired by strangers, he stops to recall, with restless desire, the image of the field and the cottage which had long been the object of his wishes, and which, on his return to his mountains, he will make his own, should he acquire the wealth of which he is in pursuit.

But how much more sorrowful the moment of separation to him, who, having never sent a transient wish beyond the mountains, feels that they comprise the limit of his earthly hopes, and yet is driven from them by an adverse fate; who is compelled to quit them to go into a foreign land, with scarcely a hope of return! Then he breaks forth into mournful exclamations. "Farewell native cottage! where, many a time and oft, I have listened with eager ear, to distinguish, amidst the rumour of footsteps, the well-known sound of those long expected and anxiously desired. Farewell, ye scenes, where I had hoped to pass, tranquil and content, the remnant of my days! Farewell, thou sanctuary of God, where my soul has been filled with admiring thoughts of him, and my voice has united with others to sing his praise! Farewell! He, whom I worshipped within your walls, is not confined to temples made with hands; heaven is his dwelling place, and the earth his footstool; he watches over his children, and, if he chastises them, it is in love, to prepare them for higher and holier enjoyments."

Of such a nature, if not precisely the same, were the reflections of Lucy and her companions, as the bark carried them to the right bank of the Adda.

Chapter IX.

The shock which the boat received, as it struck against the shore, aroused Lucy from her reverie; they quitted the bark, and Renzo turned to thank and reward the boatman. "I will take nothing—nothing," said he: "we are placed on earth to aid one another." The carriage was ready, the driver seated; its expected occupants took their places, and the horses moved briskly on. Our travellers arrived then at Monza, which we believe to have been the name of the place to which Father Christopher had directed Renzo, a little after sunrise. The driver turned to an inn, where he appeared to be well acquainted, and demanded for them a separate room. He, as well as the boatman, refused the offered recompence of Renzo; like the boatman, he had in view a reward, more distant indeed, but more abundant; he withdrew his hand, and hastened to look after his beast.

After an evening such as we have described, and a night passed in painful thoughts both in regard to recent events and future anticipations—disturbed, indeed, by the frequent joltings of their incommodious vehicle,—our travellers felt a little rest in their retired apartment at the inn highly necessary. They partook of a small meal together, not more in proportion to the prevailing want, than to their own slender appetites; and recurred with a sigh to the delightful festivities, which, two days before, were to have accompanied their happy union. Renzo would willingly have remained with his companions all the day, to secure their lodging and perform other little offices. But they strongly alleged the injunctions of Father Christopher, together with the gossiping to which their continuing together would give rise, so that he at length acquiesced. Lucy could not conceal her tears; Renzo with difficulty restrained his; and, warmly pressing the hand of Agnes, he pronounced with a voice almost choked, "Till we meet again."

The mother and daughter would have been in great perplexity, had it not been for the kind driver, who had orders to conduct them to the convent, which was at a little distance from the village. Upon their arrival there, the guide requested the porter to call the superior: he appeared, and the letter of Father Christopher was delivered to him. "Oh, from Father Christopher!" said he, recognising the handwriting. His voice and manner told evidently that he uttered the name of one whom he regarded as a particular friend. During the perusal of the letter, he manifested much surprise and indignation, and, raising his eyes, fixed them on Lucy and her mother with an expression of pity and interest. When he had finished reading, he remained for a moment thoughtful, and then exclaimed, "There is no one but the signora; if the signora would take upon herself this obligation—" and then addressing them, "My friends," said he, "I will make the effort, and I hope to find you a shelter, more than secure, more than honourable; so that God has provided for you in the best manner. Will you come with me?"

The females bowed reverently in assent; the friar continued, "Come with me, then, to the monastery of the signora. But keep yourselves a few steps distant, because there are people who delight to speak evil of others, and God knows how many fine stories might be told, if the superior of the convent was seen walking with a beautiful young woman—with women, I mean."

So saying, he went on before: Lucy blushed; the guide looked at Agnes, who could not conceal a momentary smile; and they all three obeyed the command of the friar, and followed him at a distance. "Who is the signora?" said Agnes, addressing their conductor.

"The signora," replied he, "is not a nun; that is, not a nun like the others. She is not the abbess, nor the prioress; for they say that *she* is one of the youngest of them; but she is from Adam's rib, and her ancestors were great people, who came from Spain; and they call her the *signora*, to signify that she is a great lady,—every one calls her so, because they say that in this monastery they have never had so noble a person; and her relations down at Milan are very powerful, and in Monza still more so; because her father is the first lord in the country; for which reason she can do as she pleases in the convent,—and moreover people abroad bear her a great respect, and if she undertakes a thing, she makes it succeed; and if this good father induces her to take you under her protection, you will be as safe as at the foot of the altar."

When the superior arrived at the gate of the town, which was defended at that time by an old tower, and part of a dismantled castle, he stopped and looked back to see if they followed him—then advanced towards the monastery, and, remaining on the threshold, awaited their approach. The guide then took his leave, not without many thanks from Agnes and her daughter for his kindness and faithfulness. The superior led them to the portress's chamber, and went alone to make the request of the signora. After a few moments he re-appeared, and with a joyful countenance told them that she would grant them an interview: on their way, he gave them much advice concerning their deportment in her presence. "She is well disposed towards you," said he, "and has the power to protect you. Be humble, and respectful; reply with frankness to the questions she will ask you, and when not questioned, be silent."

They passed through a lower chamber, and advanced towards the parlour. Lucy, who had never been in a monastery before, looked around as she entered it for the signora; but there was no one there; in a few moments, however, she observed the friar approach a small window or grating, behind which she beheld a nun standing. She appeared about twenty-five years of age; her countenance at first sight produced an impression of beauty, but of beauty prematurely faded. A black veil hung in folds on either side of her face; below the veil a band of white linen encircled a forehead of different, but not inferior whiteness; another plaited band encompassed the face, and terminated under the chin in a neck handkerchief, or cape, which, extending over the shoulders, covered to the waist the folds of her black robe. But her forehead was contracted from time to time, as if by some painful emotion; now, her large black eye was fixed steadfastly on your face with an expression of haughty curiosity, then hastily bent down as if to discover some hidden thought; in certain moments an attentive observer would have deemed that they solicited affection, sympathy, and pity; at others, he would have received a transient revelation of hatred, matured by a cruel disposition; when motionless and inattentive, some would have imagined them to express haughty aversion, others would have suspected the labouring of concealed thought, the effort to overcome some secret feeling of her soul, which had more power over it than all surrounding objects. Her cheeks were delicately formed, but extremely pale and thin; her lips, hardly suffused with a feeble tinge of the rose, seemed to soften into the pallid hue of the cheeks; their movements, like those of her eyes, were sudden, animated, and full of expression and mystery. Her loftiness of stature was not apparent, owing to an habitual stoop; as well as to her rapid and irregular movements, little becoming a nun, or even a lady. In her dress itself there was an appearance of studied neglect, which announced a singular character; and from the band around her temples was suffered to escape, through forgetfulness or contempt of the rules which prohibited it, a curl of glossy black hair.

These things made no impression on the minds of Agnes and Lucy, unaccustomed as they were to the sight of a nun; and to the superior it was no novelty—he, as well as many others, had become familiarised to her habit and manners.

She was, as we have said, standing near the grate, against which she leaned languidly, to observe those who were approaching. "Reverend mother, and most illustrious lady," said the superior, bending low, "this is the poor young woman for whom I have solicited your protection, and this is her mother."

Both mother and daughter bowed reverently. "It is fortunate that I have it in my power," said she, turning to the father, "to do some little service to our good friends the capuchin fathers. But tell me a little more particularly, the situation of this young woman, that I may be better prepared to act for her advantage."

Lucy blushed, and held down her head. "You must know, reverend mother," said Agnes—but the father interrupted her;—"This young person, most illustrious lady," continued he, "has been recommended to me, as I have told you, by one of my brethren. She has been obliged to depart secretly from her native place, in order to escape heavy perils; and she has need for some time of an asylum, where she can remain unknown, and where no one will dare to molest her."

"What perils?" demanded the lady. "Pray, father, do not talk so enigmatically: you know, we nuns like to hear stories minutely."

"They are perils," replied the father, "that should not be told to the pure ears of the reverend mother."—"Oh, certainly," said the lady, hastily, and slightly blushing. Was this the blush of modesty? He would have doubted it, who should have observed the rapid expression of disdain which accompanied it, or have compared it with that which from time to time diffused itself over the cheek of Lucy.

"It is sufficient to say," resumed the friar, "that a powerful lord—it is not all the rich and noble who make use of the gifts of God for the promotion of his glory, as you do, most illustrious lady—a powerful lord, after having persecuted for a long time this innocent creature with wicked allurements, finding them unavailing, has had recourse to open force, so that she has been obliged to fly from her home."

"Approach, young woman," said the signora. "I know that the father is truth itself; but no one can be better informed than you with regard to this affair. To you it belongs to tell us if this lord was an odious persecutor." Lucy obeyed the first command, and approached the grating; but the second, accompanied as it was with a certain malicious air of doubt, brought a blush over her countenance, and a sense of painful embarrassment, which she found it impossible to overcome. "Lady—mother—reverend—" stammered she. Agnes now felt herself authorised to come to her assistance. "Most illustrious lady," said she, "I can bear testimony that my daughter hates this lord as the devil hates holy water. I would call him the devil, were it not for your reverend presence. The case is this: this poor maiden was promised to a good and industrious youth; and if the curate had done his duty—"

"You are very ready to speak without being interrogated," interrupted the lady, with an expression of anger on her countenance, which changed it almost to deformity. "Silence; I have not to be informed that parents have always an answer prepared in the name of their children."

Agnes drew back mortified, and the father guardian signified to Lucy by a look, as well as by a movement of the head, that now was the time to rouse her courage, and not leave her poor mother in the dilemma. "Reverend lady," said she, "what my mother has told you is the truth. I willingly engaged myself to the poor youth (and here she became covered with blushes)— Pardon me this boldness; but I would not have you think ill of my mother. And as to this lord (God forgive him!) I would rather die than fall into his hands. And if you do this deed of charity, be certain, signora, none will pray for you more heartily than those whom you have thus sheltered."

"I believe you," said the lady, with a softened voice; "but we will see you alone. Not that I need farther explanation, nor other motives to accede to the wishes of the father superior," added she, turning to him with studied politeness. "Nay," continued she, "I have been thinking, and this is what has occurred to me. The portress of the monastery has bestowed in marriage, a few days since, her last daughter; these females can occupy her room, and supply her place in the little services which it was her office to perform."

The father would have expressed his thanks, but the lady interrupted him. "There is no need of ceremony; in case of need, I would not hesitate to ask assistance of the capuchin fathers. In short," continued she, with a smile, in which appeared a degree of bitter irony, "are we not brothers and sisters?"

So saying, she called a nun, her attendant (by a singular distinction she had two assigned for her private service), and sent her to inform the abbess; she then called the portress, and made with her and Agnes the necessary arrangements. Then taking leave of the superior, she dismissed Agnes to her room, but retained Lucy. The signora, who, in presence of a capuchin, had studied her actions and her words, thought no longer of putting a restraint on them before an inexperienced country girl. Her discourse became by degrees so strange, that, in order to account for it, we will relate the previous history of this unhappy and misguided person.

She was the youngest daughter of the Prince, a great Milanese nobleman, who was among the wealthiest of the city. The magnificent ideas he entertained of his rank, made him suppose his wealth hardly sufficient to support it properly; he therefore determined to preserve his riches with the greatest care. How many children he had does not clearly appear; it is only known that he had destined to the cloister all the youngest of both sexes, in order to preserve his fortune for the eldest son. The condition of the unhappy signora had been settled even before her birth; it remained only to be decided whether she were to be a monk or a nun. At her birth, the prince her father, wishing to give her a name which could recall at every moment the idea of a cloister, and which had been borne by a saint of a noble family, called her Gertrude. Dolls, clothed like nuns, were the first toys that were put into her hands; then pictures of nuns; and these gifts were accompanied with many injunctions to be careful of them, for they were precious things. When the prince or princess, or the young prince, who was the only one of the children brought up at home, wished to praise the beauty of the infant, they found no way of expressing their ideas, except in exclamations of this sort, "What a mother abbess!" But no one ever said directly to her, "Thou must be a nun;" such an intention, however, was understood, and included in every conversation regarding her future destiny. If, sometimes, the little Gertrude betrayed perversity and impetuosity of temper, they would say to her, "Thou art but a child, and these manners are not becoming: wait till thou art the mother abbess, and then thou shalt command with a rod; thou shalt do whatever pleases thee." At other times, reprehending her for the freedom and familiarity of her manners, the prince would say, "Such should not be the deportment of one like you; if you wish at some future day to have the respect of all around you, learn now to have more gravity; remember that you will be the first in the monastery, because noble blood bears sway every where."

By such conversations as these the implicit idea was produced in the mind of the child, that she was to be a nun. The manners of the prince were habitually austere and repulsive; and, with respect to the destination of the child, his resolution appeared fixed as fate. At six years of age she was placed for her education in the monastery where we find her: her father, being the most powerful noble in Monza, enjoyed there great authority; and his daughter, consequently, would receive those distinctions, with those allurements, which might lead her to select it for her perpetual abode. The abbess and nuns, rejoicing at the acquisition of such powerful friendship, received with great gratitude the honour conferred in preference on them, and entered with avidity into the views of the prince; Gertrude experienced all sorts of favours and indulgences, and, child as she was, the respectful attention of the nuns towards her was exercised with the same deference as if she had been the abbess herself! Not that they were all pledged to draw the poor child into the snare; many acted with simplicity, and through tenderness, merely following the example of those around them; if the suspicions of others were excited, they kept silence, so as not to cause useless disturbance; some, indeed, more discriminating and compassionate, pitied the poor child as being the object of artifices, to the like of which they themselves had been the victims.

Things would have proceeded agreeably to the wishes of all concerned, had Gertrude been the only child in the monastery; but this was not the case; and there were some among her school companions who were destined for the matrimonial state. The little Gertrude, filled with the idea of her superiority, spoke proudly of her future destiny, expecting thereby to excite their envy at her peculiar honours: with scorn and wonder she perceived that their estimation of them was very different. To the majestic but circumscribed and cold images of the power of an abbess, they opposed the varied and bright pictures of husband, guests, cities, tournaments, courts, dress, and equipage. New and strange emotions arose in the mind of Gertrude: her vanity had been cultivated in order to make the cloister desirable to her; and now, easily assimilating itself with the ideas thus presented, she entered into them with all the ardour of her soul. She replied, that no one could oblige her to take the veil, without her own consent; that she could also marry, inhabit a palace, and enjoy the world; that she could if she wished it; that she *would* wish it, and *did* wish it. The necessity of her own consent, hitherto little considered, became henceforth the ruling thought of her mind; she called it to her aid, at all times, when she desired to luxuriate in the pleasing images of future felicity.

But her fancied enjoyment was impaired by the reflection, which at such moments intruded itself, that her father had irrevocably decided her destiny; and she shuddered at the recollection of his austere manners, which impressed upon all around him the sentiments of a fatal necessity as being necessarily conjoined with whatever he should command. Then would she compare her condition to that of her more fortunate companions; and envy soon grew into hatred. This would manifest itself by a display of present superiority, and sometimes of ill-nature, sarcasm, and spite; at other times her more amiable and gentle qualities would obtain a transitory ascendency. Thus she passed the period allotted for her education, in dreams of future bliss, mingled with the dread of future misery. That which she anticipated most distinctly, was external pomp and splendour; and her fancy would often luxuriate in imaginary scenes of grandeur, constructed out of such materials as her memory could faintly and confusedly furnish forth, and the descriptions of her companions supply. There were moments when these brilliant imaginings were disturbed by the idea of religion; but the religion which had been inculcated to the poor girl did not proscribe pride, but, on the contrary, sanctified it, and proposed it as a means of obtaining terrestrial felicity. Thus despoiled of its essence, it was no longer religion, but a phantom, which, assuming at times a power over her mind, the unhappy girl was tormented with superstitious dread, and, filled with a confused idea of duties, imagined her repugnance to the cloister to be a crime, which could only be expiated by her voluntary dedication.

There was a law, that no young person could be accepted for the monastic life, without being examined by an ecclesiastic, called the vicar of the nuns, so that it should be made manifest that it was the result of her free election; and this examination could not take place until a year after she had presented her petition for admission, in writing, to the vicar. The nuns, therefore, who were aware of the projects of her father, undertook to draw from her such a petition; encountering her in one of those moments, when she was assailed by her superstitious fears, they suggested to her the propriety of such a course, and assured her, nevertheless, that it was a mere formality (which was true), and would be without efficacy, unless sanctioned by some after-act of her own. The petition, however, had scarcely been sent to its destination, when Gertrude repented of having written it; she then repented of this repentance, passing months in incessant vicissitude of feeling. There was another law, that, at this examination, a young person should not be received, without having remained at least a month at her paternal home. A year had nearly passed since the petition had been sent, and Gertrude had been warned that she would soon be removed from the monastery, and conducted to her father's house, to take the final steps towards the consummation of that which they held certain. Not so the poor girl; her mind was busied with plans of escape: in her perplexity, she unbosomed herself to one of her companions, who counselled her to inform her father by letter of the change in her views. The letter was written and sent; Gertrude remained in great anxiety, expecting a reply, which never came. A few days after, the abbess took her aside, and, with a mixed expression of contempt and compassion, hinted to her the anger of the prince, and the error she had committed; but that, if she conducted herself well for the future, all would be forgotten. The poor girl heard, and dared not ask farther explanation.

The day, so ardently desired and so greatly feared, came at last. The anticipation of the trials that awaited her was forgotten in her tumultuous joy at the sight of the open country, the city, and the houses. She might well feel thus, after having been for eight years enclosed within the walls of the monastery! She had previously arranged with her new confidant the part she was to act. Oh! they will try to force me, thought she: but I will persist, humbly and respectfully; the point is, not to say *Yes*; and I will *not* say it. Or, perhaps they will endeavour to shake my purpose by kindness: but I will weep, I will implore, I will excite their compassion, I will beseech them not to sacrifice me. But none of her anticipations were verified: her parents and family, with the usual artful policy in such cases, maintained a perfect silence with regard to the subject of her meditations; they regarded her with looks of contemptuous pity, and appeared to avoid all conversation with her, as if she had rendered herself unworthy of it. A mysterious anathema appeared to hang over her, and to keep at a distance every member of the household. If, wearied with this proscription, she endeavoured to enter into conversation, they made her understand indirectly, that by obedience alone could she regain the affections of the family. But this was precisely the condition to which she could not assent: she therefore continued in her state of excommunication, which unhappily appeared to be, at least partially, the consequence of her own conduct.

Such a state of things formed a sad contrast to the radiant visions which had occupied her imagination. Her confinement was as strict at home as it had been in the monastery; and she, who had fancied she should enjoy, at least for this brief period, the pleasures of the world, found herself an exile from all society. At every announcement of a visiter, she was compelled to retire with the elderly persons of the family; and always dined apart whenever a guest was present. Even the servants of the family appeared to concur with the designs of their master, and to treat her with carelessness, ill concealed by an awkward attempt at formality. There was one among them, however, who seemed to feel towards her respect and compassion. This was a handsome page, who equalled, in her imagination, the ideal images of loveliness she had so often fondly cherished. There was soon apparent a change in her manner, a love of reverie and abstraction, and she no longer appeared to covet the favour of her family; some engrossing thought had taken possession of her mind. To be brief, she was detected one day in folding a letter, which it had been better she had not written, and which she was obliged to relinquish to her female attendant, who carried it to the prince, her father. He came immediately to her apartment with the letter in his hand, and in few but terrible words told her, that for the present she should be confined to her chamber, with the society only of the woman who had made the discovery; and intimated for the future still darker punishments. The page was dismissed, with an imperative command of silence, and solemn threatenings of punishment should he presume to violate it. Gertrude was then left alone, with her shame, her remorse, and her terror; and the sole company of this woman, whom she hated, as the witness of her fault, and the cause of her disgrace. The hatred was cordially returned, inasmuch as the attendant found herself reduced to the annoying duty of a jailer, and was made the guardian of a perilous secret for life. The first confused tumult of her feelings having in some measure subsided, she recalled to mind the dark intimations of her father with regard to some future punishment: what could this be? It most probably was a return to the monastery at Monza, not as the signorina, but as a guilty wretch, who, loaded with shame, was to be inclosed within its walls for ever! Now, indeed, her fancy no longer dwelt on the bright visions with which it had been so often busied; they were too much opposed to the sad reality of her present condition. Such an act would repair all her errors, and change (could she doubt it) in an instant her condition. The only castle in which Gertrude could imagine a tranquil and honourable asylum, and which was not in the *air*, was the monastery, in which she now resolved to place herself for ever! Opposed to this resolution rose up the contemplations of many years past: but times were changed, and to the depth in which Gertrude had fallen, the condition of a nun, revered, obeyed, and feared, formed a bright contrast. She was perpetually tormented also by her jailer, who, to revenge herself for the confinement imposed on her, failed not to taunt her for her misdemeanor, and to repeat the menaces of her father; or whenever she seemed disposed to relent, and to show something like pity, her tone of protection was still more intolerable. The predominant desire of Gertrude was to escape from her clutches, and to raise herself to a condition above her anger or her pity. At the end of four or five long days, with her patience exhausted by the bitter railings of her keeper, she sat herself down in a corner of the chamber, and covering her face with her hands, wept in bitterness of soul. She experienced an absolute craving for other faces and other sounds than those of her tormentor; and a sudden joy imparted itself to her mind, from the reflection, that it depended only on herself to be restored to the good-will and attentions of the family. Mingled with this joy, came repentance for her fault, and a desire to expiate it. She arose, went to a small table, and taking a pen, wrote to her father, expressing her penitence and her hope, imploring his pardon, and promising to do all that might be required of her.

Chapter X.

There are moments in which the mind, particularly of the young, is so disposed, that a little importunity suffices to obtain from it any thing that has the appearance of virtuous sacrifice; as a flower scarcely budded abandons itself on its fragile stem, ready to yield its sweets to the first breeze which plays around it. These moments, which ought to be regarded by others with timid respect, are exactly those of which interested cunning makes use, to insnare the unguarded will.

On the perusal of this letter, the prince saw the way opened to the furtherance of his views. He sent for Gertrude; she obeyed the command, and, in his presence, threw herself at his feet, and had scarcely power to exclaim, "Pardon!" He made a sign to her to rise, and in a grave voice answered, that it was not enough merely to confess her fault, and ask forgiveness, but that it was necessary to merit it. Gertrude asked submissively, "what he would have her do?" To this the prince did not reply directly, but spoke at length of the fault of Gertrude: the poor girl shuddered as at the touch of a hand on a severe wound. He continued, that even if he had entertained the project of settling her in the world, she had herself placed an insuperable obstacle to it; since he could never, as a gentleman of honour, permit her to marry, after having given such a specimen of herself. The miserable listener was completely humbled!

The prince, then, by degrees softened his voice and manner to say, that for all faults there was a remedy, and that the remedy for hers was clearly indicated; that she might perceive, in this fatal accident, a warning that the world was too full of dangers for her—

"Oh, yes!" exclaimed Gertrude, overwhelmed with shame and remorse.

"Ah, you perceive it yourself!" resumed the prince. "Well, we will speak no more of the past; all is forgotten. You have taken the only honourable way that remains for you; and because you *have* taken it voluntarily, it rests with me to make it turn to your advantage, and to make the merit of the sacrifice all your own." So saying, he rang the bell, and said to the servant who appeared, "The princess and the prince immediately." He continued to Gertrude, "I wish to make them the sharers of my joy; I wish that they should begin at once to treat you as you deserve. You have hitherto found me a severe judge; you shall now prove that I am a loving father."

At these words Gertrude remained stupified; she thought of the "yes" she had so precipitately suffered to escape from her lips, and would have recalled it; but she did not dare; the satisfaction of the prince appeared so entire, his condescension so conditional, that she could not presume to utter a word to disturb it.

The princess and prince came into the room. On seeing Gertrude there, they appeared full of doubt and surprise; but the prince, with a joyful countenance, said to them, "Behold here the lost sheep! and let these be the last words that shall recall painful recollections. Behold the consolation of the family! Gertrude has no longer need of advice; she has voluntarily chosen her own good. She has resolved, she has signified to me that she has resolved—" She raised to him a look of supplication, but he continued more plainly, "that she has resolved to take the veil."

"Well done, well done," exclaimed they both, overwhelming her with embraces, which Gertrude received with tears, which they chose to interpret as tears of joy. Then the prince enlarged on the splendid destiny of his daughter, on the distinction she would enjoy in the monastery and in the country, as the representative of the family. Her mother and her brother renewed their congratulations and praises. Gertrude stood as if possessed by a dream.

It was then necessary to fix the day for the journey to Monza, for the purpose of making the request of the abbess. "How rejoiced she will be!" said the prince; "I am sure all the nuns will appreciate the honour Gertrude does them. But why not go there to-day? Gertrude will willingly take the air."

"Let us go, then," said the princess.

"I will order the carriage," said the young prince.

"But—" said Gertrude submissively.

"Softly, softly," said the prince, "let her decide; perhaps she does not feel disposed to go to-day, and would rather wait until to-morrow. Say, do you wish to go to-day or to-morrow?"

"To-morrow," said Gertrude, in a feeble voice, glad of a short reprieve.

"To-morrow," said the prince, solemnly; "she has decided to go to-morrow. Meanwhile I will see the vicar of the nuns, to have him to appoint a day for the examination." He did so, and the vicar named the day after the next. In the interval Gertrude was not left a moment to herself. She would have desired some repose for her mind after so many contending emotions; to have reflected on the step she had already taken, and what remained to be done—but the machine once in motion at her direction, it was no longer in her power to arrest its progress; occupations succeeded each other without interruption. The princess herself assisted at her toilette, which was completed by her own maid. This effected, dinner was announced, and poor Gertrude was made to pass through the crowd of servants, who nodded their congratulations to each other. She found at the table a few relations of the family, who had been invited in haste to participate in the general joy. The young bride—thus they called young persons about to enter the monastic life—the young bride had enough to do to reply to the compliments which were paid to her; she felt that each reply was a confirmation of her destiny; but how act differently? After dinner came the hour of riding, and Gertrude was placed in a carriage with her mother and two uncles, who had been among the guests. They entered the street Marina, which then crossed the space now occupied by the public gardens, and was the public promenade, where the nobility refreshed themselves after the fatigues of the day. The uncles conversed much with Gertrude, and one of them in particular, who appeared to know every body, every carriage, and every livery, had something to tell of signor such an one, and signora such an one; but checking himself, he said to his niece, "Ah! you little rogue! you turn your back upon all these follies; you are the righteous person; you leave us worldlings far behind; you are going to lead a happy life, and take yourself to paradise in a coach."

They returned home in the dusk of the evening, and the servants, appearing with torches, announced to them that numerous visiters had arrived. The report had spread, and a multitude of relations and friends had come to offer their congratulations. The young bride was the idol, the amusement, the victim of the evening. Finally, Gertrude was left alone with the family. "At last," said the prince, "I have had the consolation of seeing my daughter in society becoming her rank and station. She has conducted herself admirably, and has evinced that there will be no preventive to her obtaining the highest honours, and supporting the dignity of the family." They supped hastily, so as to be ready early in the morning.

At the request of Gertrude, her attendant, of whose insolence she bitterly complained to her father, was removed, and another placed in her stead. This was an old woman, who had been nurse to the young prince, in whom was centred all her hopes and her pride. She was overjoyed at the decision of Gertrude, who, as a climax to her trials, was obliged to listen to her congratulations and praises. She talked of her numerous aunts and relatives, who were so happy as nuns; of the many visits she would doubtless receive. She further spoke of the young prince, and the lady who was to be his wife, and the visit which they would doubtless pay to Gertrude at the monastery, until, wearied out with the conflicts of the day, the poor girl fell asleep. She was aroused in the morning by the harsh voice of the old woman, "Up, up, signora, young bride! it is day; the princess is up, and waiting for you. The young prince is impatient. He is as brisk as a hare, the young devil; he was so from an infant. But when he is ready, you must not make him wait; he is the best temper in the world, but that always makes him impatient and noisy. Poor fellow, we must pity him, it is the effect of temperament; in such moments he has respect to no one but the head of the household; however, one day he will be the head; may that day be far off! Quick, quick, signorina! You should have been out of your nest before this."

The idea of the young prince, risen and impatient, recalled the scattered thoughts of Gertrude, and hastily she suffered herself to be dressed, and descended to the saloon, where her parents and brother were assembled. A cup of chocolate was brought her, and the carriage was announced. Before their departure, the prince took his daughter aside, and said to her, "Courage, Gertrude; yesterday you did well, to-day you must excel yourself; the point is now to make a suitable appearance in the country and in the monastery, where you are destined to hold the first station. They expect you, and all eyes will be on you. Dignity and ease. The abbess will ask you what is your request; it is a mere form, but you must reply that you wish to be admitted to take the veil in this monastery, where you have been educated, and treated so kindly; which is the truth. Speak these words with a free unembarrassed air, so as not to give occasion for scandal. These good mothers know nothing of the unhappy occurrence; that must remain buried with the family. However, an anxious countenance might excite suspicion; show whose is the blood in your veins; be polite and modest; but remember also, that in this country, out of the family, there is none your superior."

During their ride, the troubles and the trials of the world, and the blessed life of the cloister, were the principal subjects of conversation. As they approached the monastery, the crowd collected from all parts; as the carriage stopped before the walls, the heart of Gertrude beat more rapidly: they alighted amidst the concourse; all eyes were fastened on her, and compelled her to study the movements of her countenance; and, above all, those of her father, upon whom she could not help fixing her regards, notwithstanding the fear he inspired. They crossed the first court, entered the second, and here appeared the interior cloister, wide open, and occupied by nuns. In front was the abbess, surrounded by the most aged of the sisterhood; behind these the others, raised promiscuously on tiptoe, and farther back the lay sisters, standing on benches and overlooking the scene; whilst here and there were seen, peeping between the cowls, some youthful faces, which Gertrude recognised as those of her school companions. As she stood fronting the abbess, the latter demanded, with grave solemnity, "What she desired to have in this place, where nothing could be denied her?"

"I am here," began Gertrude; but, about to utter the words which were to decide her destiny irrevocably, she felt her heart fail, and hesitating, she fixed her eyes on the crowd before her. She beheld there the well-known face of one of her companions, who regarded her with looks of compassion and malice, as if to say, "They have caught the brave one." This sight required all her courage, and she was about to give a reply very different from that which was expected from her, when, glancing at her father, she caught from his eye such an anxious and threatening expression, that, overcome by terror, she proceeded, "I am here to ask admittance into this monastery, where I have been instructed so kindly." The abbess immediately expressed her regret, that the regulations were such as to prohibit an immediate answer, which must be given by the common suffrage of the sisterhood; but that Gertrude knew well the sentiments they entertained towards her; and might judge what that answer would be. In the mean time nothing prevented them from manifesting their joy at her request. There was then heard a confused murmur of congratulations and rejoicing.

Whilst the nuns were surrounding their new companion, and offering their congratulations to all the party, the abbess expressed her wish to address a few words to the prince at the parlour grating.

"Signor," said she, "in obedience to our rules—to fulfil a necessary form—I must inform you—that whenever a young person desires to assume—the superior, which I am, though unworthily, is obliged to make known to the parents that if—they have forced the will of their daughter, they will incur the pains of excommunication. You will excuse—"

"Oh! yes, yes, reverend mother. Your exactitude is very praiseworthy, very just. But you cannot doubt—"

"Oh! imagine, prince, if—but I merely speak by order; besides—"

"True—true, reverend mother."

After these few words, and a renewal of compliments and thanks, they departed.

Gertrude was silent during their ride; overcome and occupied by conflicting thoughts, ashamed of her own want of resolution, vexed with others as well as herself, she was still meditating some way of escape, but every time she looked at her father, she felt her destiny to be irrevocable. After the various engagements of the day were over,—the dinner, the visits, the drive, the *conversazione*, the supper,—the prince brought another subject under discussion, which was the choice of a godmother (so they called the lady who is selected as chaperone to the young candidate in the interval between the request for admission, and the putting on of the habit); the duty of this person was to visit, with her charge, the churches, public palaces, the *conversazioni*, in short, every thing of note in the city and its environs; so as to afford a peep at that world they were about to quit for ever. "We must think of a godmother," said the prince, "because to-morrow the vicar of the nuns will be here for the examination, and soon after that, Gertrude will be finally accepted. Now the choice shall come from Gertrude herself, although contrary to usage; but she deserves to be made an exception, and we may confidently trust to her judgment in the selection." And then, turning to her, as if bestowing a singular favour, he continued, "Any one of the ladies who were at the *conversazione* this evening, possesses the necessary qualifications for a godmother; any one of them will consider it an honour; make your selection." Gertrude instantly felt that the choice would be a renewal of consent; but the proposal was made with such an air of condescension, that a refusal would have appeared to spring from contempt or ingratitude. Thus she took another step, and named a lady who had been forward in attentions to her during the whole evening. "A perfectly wise choice," said the prince, who had expected no less. The affair had all been previously arranged; this lady had been so much with Gertrude at the *conversazione*, and had displayed such kindness of manner, that it would have been an effort for her to think of another. The attentions, however, of this lady were not without their object: she had also for a long time contemplated making the young prince her son; she, therefore, naturally interested herself in all that concerned the family, and felt the deepest interest in her dear Gertrude.

On the morrow, the imagination of Gertrude was occupied with the expected examination, and with a vague hope of some opportunity to retract. At an early hour she was sent for by the prince, who addressed her in these words:—"Courage, my daughter; you have as yet conducted yourself admirably; to-day you must crown the work. All that has been done, has been done with your consent. If, in the meanwhile, you had any doubts, any misgivings, you should have expressed them; but at the point to which things have now arrived, it will no longer do to play the child. The worthy man who is to come this morning, will put a hundred questions to you, concerning your vocation; such as, whether you go voluntarily, and the why and the wherefore. If you falter in your replies, he will continue to urge you; this will produce pain to yourself, but might become the source of a more serious evil. After all the public demonstrations that we have made, the slightest hesitation on your part might place my honour in danger, by conveying the idea that I had taken a mere youthful whim for a confirmed resolution, and that I had thus acted precipitately; in this case, I should feel myself under the necessity, in order to preserve my character inviolate, to reveal the true motive—" But, seeing the countenance of Gertrude all on flame, and contracting itself like the leaves of a flower in the heat which precedes a tempest, he stopped a moment, and then resumed, "Well, well, all depends on yourself. I know you will not show yourself a child; but recollect, you must reply with freedom, so as not to create suspicion in the mind of this worthy man." He then suggested the answers to be made to the probable questions that would be put, and concluded with various remarks upon the happiness that awaited Gertrude at the convent. At this moment the servant announced the arrival of the vicar, and the prince was obliged to leave his daughter alone to receive him.

The good man had come with a preconceived opinion that Gertrude went voluntarily to the cloister, because the prince had told him so. It was one of his maxims, however, to preserve himself unprejudiced, and to depend only on the assertions of the candidates themselves. "Signorina," said he, "I come to play the part of the tempter; I come to suggest doubts where you have affirmed certainties; I come to place before your eyes difficulties, and ascertain if you have well considered them. You will allow me to trouble you with some interrogatories?"

"Say on," replied Gertrude.

The good priest then began to interrogate her in the form prescribed. "Do you feel in your heart a free spontaneous resolution to become a nun? Have menaces, or allurements, or authority been made use of? Speak without reserve to one whose duty it is to ascertain the true state of your feelings, and to prevent violence being done to them."

The true reply to such a question presented itself suddenly to the mind of Gertrude, with terrible reality. But to come to an explanation, to say she was threatened, to relate the unfortunate story—from this her spirit shrank, and she brought herself to the resolution of saying, "I become a nun, freely, from inclination."

"How long have you had this intention?" asked the good priest.

"I have always had it," said Gertrude, finding it easier after the first step to proceed in falsehood.

"But what is the principal motive which has induced you?"

The interrogator was not aware of the chord he touched; and Gertrude, making a great effort to preserve the tranquillity of her countenance, amid the tumult of her soul, replied. "The motive is, to serve God, and to fly the perils of the world."

"Has there never been any disgust? any—excuse me—caprice? Often trifling causes make impressions which we deem will be perpetual, but the causes cease—"

"No, no," replied Gertrude, hastily; "the cause is that which I have said."

The vicar, in order to execute his duty fully, persisted in his enquiries, but Gertrude was determined to deceive him. She could not for a moment think of rendering the good man acquainted with her weakness; she knew, indeed, that he could prevent her being a nun, but that this would be the extent of his authority and his protection. When he should be gone, she would still be left alone, to endure fresh trials from her father and the family. Finding, therefore, a uniform answer to all his questions, he became somewhat wearied of putting them, and, concluding that all was as it should be, with many prayers for her welfare, he took his leave. As he crossed the hall he met the prince, and congratulated him on the good dispositions of his daughter. This put an end to a very painful state of suspense and anxiety on the part of the prince; who, forgetting his usual gravity, ran to his daughter, and loaded her with praises, caresses, and promises, and with a tenderness of affection in great measure sincere: such is the inconsistency of the human heart.

Then ensued a round of spectacles and diversions, during which we cannot attempt to describe minutely or in order the emotions to which the heart of Gertrude was subjected. The perpetual change of objects, the freedom enjoyed by this change, rendered more odious to her the idea of her prison; still more pungent were the impressions she received in the festivals and assemblies of the city. The pomp of the palaces, the splendour of their furniture, the buzzing and festal clamour of the *conversazione*, communicated to her such an intoxication, such an eager desire for happiness, that she thought she could encounter all the consequences of a recantation, or even suffer death, rather than return to the cold shades of the cloister. But all such resolutions instantly fled as her eyes rested on the austere countenance of the prince.

Meanwhile, the vicar of the nuns had made the necessary deposition, and liberty was given to hold a chapter for the acceptation of Gertrude. The chapter was held, and she was received! Wearied out with her long conflicts, she requested immediate admittance, which was readily granted. After a noviciate of twelve days, full of resolves and counter-resolves, the moment arrived when she finally pronounced the fatal "yes," which was to exclude her from the world for ever. But even in the depths of the monastery she found no repose; she had not the wisdom to make a virtue of necessity, but was continually and uselessly recurring to the past. She could not call religion to her aid, for religion had no share in the sacrifice she had made; and heavily and bitterly she bore the yoke of bondage. She hated the nuns, because she remembered their artifices, and regarded them in some measure as the authors of her misfortune; she tyrannised over them with impunity, because they dared not rebel against her authority, and incur the resentment of the powerful lord, her father. Those nuns who were really pious and harmless, she hated for their piety itself, as it seemed to cast a tacit reproach on her weakness; and she suffered no occasion to escape without railing at them as bigots and hypocrites. It might, however, have mitigated her asperity towards them, had she known that the black balls to oppose her entrance had been cast into the urn by their sympathetic generosity. She found, however, one consolation, in the unlimited power she possessed, in being courted and flattered, and in hearing herself called the "signora." But what a consolation! Her soul felt its insufficiency, but had not the courage nor the virtue to seek happiness from the only source where it could be found. Thus she lived many years, tyrannising over and feared by all around her, till an occasion presented itself for a further developement of her habitual, but secret feelings. Among other privileges which had been accorded to her in the monastery, was that of having her apartments on a side of the building little frequented by the other nuns. Opposite to this quarter of the convent was a house, inhabited by a young man, a villain by profession, one of those who, at this period, by their mutual combinations were enabled to set at nought the public laws. His name was Egidio. From his small window, which overlooked the court-yard, he had often seen Gertrude wandering there from listlessness and melancholy. Allured rather than intimidated by the danger and iniquity of the act, he dared one day to speak to her. The wretched girl replied!

Then was experienced a new but not unmixed satisfaction; into the painful void of her soul was infused a powerful stimulus, a fresh principle of vitality: but this enjoyment resembled the restoring beverage which the ingenious cruelty of the ancients presented to the criminal, in order to strengthen him to sustain his martyrdom. A change came also over her whole deportment; she was regular, tranquil, endearing, and affable; in such a degree, that the sisters congratulated themselves upon the circumstance, little imagining the true motive, and that the alteration was none other than hypocrisy added to her other defects. This outward improvement, however, did not last long; she soon returned to her customary caprices, and, moreover, was heard to utter bitter imprecations against the cloistral prison, in unusual and unbecoming language. The sisters bore these vicissitudes as well as they could, and attributed them to the light and capricious nature of the signora. For some time it did not appear that the suspicions of any one of them were excited; but one day the signora had been speaking with one of the sisters, her attendant, and reviling her beyond measure for some trifling matter: the sister suffered a while, and gnawed the bit in silence; but finally, becoming impatient, declared that she was mistress of a secret, and could advise the signora in her turn. From this time forward her peace was lost. Not many days after, however, this very sister was missing from her accustomed offices; they sought her in her cell, and did not find her; they called, and she answered not; they searched diligently in every place, but without success. And who knows what conjectures might have arisen, if there had not been found a great opening in the wall of the orchard, through which she had probably made her escape. They sent messengers in various directions to pursue, and restore her, but they never heard of her more! Perhaps they would not have been so unfortunate in their search, if they had dug near the garden wall! Finally, the nuns concluded that she must have gone to a great distance, and because one of them happened to say, she has taken refuge in Holland, "O yes," said they, "she has, without doubt, taken refuge in Holland." The signora did not believe this, but she had certain reasons for encouraging the opinion, and this she did not fail to do. Thus the minds of the nuns became satisfied; but who can tell the torments of the signora's soul? Who can tell how many times a day the image of this sister came unbidden into her mind, and fastened itself there with terrible tenacity? Who can tell how many times she desired to behold the real and living person, for the company of this empty, impassible, terrible shade? Who can tell with what delight she would have heard the very words of the threat repeated in her mental ear, rather than this continual and fantastic murmur of those very words, sounding with a pertinacity of which no living voice could have been capable.

It was about a year after this event, that we find Lucy at the monastery, and under the protection of the signora. The reader may remember, that after Agnes and the portress had left the room, the signora and Lucy had entered into conversation alone; the former continued her questions concerning Don Roderick, with a fearlessness which filled the mind of Lucy with astonishment, little supposing that the curiosity of the nuns ever exercised itself upon such subjects. The opinions which were blended with these enquiries, were not less strange; she laughed at the dread which Lucy expressed herself to have of Don Roderick, asking her if he was not handsome; and surmising that Lucy would have liked him very well, if it had not been for her preference of Renzo. When again with her mother, the poor girl expressed her astonishment at such observations from such a source, but Agnes, as more experienced, solved the mystery. "Do not be surprised," said she; "when you have known the world as I have, you will cease to wonder at any thing. The nobility, some more, some less, some one way, some another, have all a little oddity. We must let them talk, especially when we have need of them; we must appear to listen to them seriously, as if they were talking very wisely. Did you not hear how she interrupted me, as if I had uttered some absurdity? I did not wonder at it; they are all so. Notwithstanding that, Heaven be thanked, she seems to have taken a liking to you, and is willing to protect us; and if we would retain her favour, we must let her say that which it shall please her to say."

A desire to oblige the superior, the complacency experienced in protecting, the thought of the good opinions which would be the result of a protection thus piously extended, a certain inclination towards Lucy, and also a degree of self-satisfaction in doing good to an innocent creature, in succouring and consoling the oppressed, had really disposed the signora to take to heart the fate of our poor fugitives. The mother and daughter congratulated themselves on their safe and honourable asylum. They would have wished to remain unknown to all; but this, in a convent, was impossible; and one there was, besides, too far interested in obtaining an account of one of the two, stimulated as his passion had been by the opposition he had encountered. We will leave them for the present in their safe retreat, and return to the palace of Don Roderick, at the hour in which he was anxiously expecting the result of his wicked and villanous enterprise.

Chapter XI.

As a pack of blood-hounds, after having in vain tracked the hare, return desponding towards their master, with their ears down, and tails hanging, so, in this night of confusion, returned the bravoes to the palace of Don Roderick, who was pacing, in the dark, the floor of an upper uninhabited chamber. Full of impatience and uncertainty as to the issue of the expedition, and not without anxiety for the possible consequences, his ear was attentive to every sound, and his eye to every movement on the esplanade. This was the most daring piece of villany he had ever undertaken; but he felt that the precautions he had used would preserve him from suspicion. "And who will dare to come here, and ask if she is not in this palace? Should this young fellow do so, he will be well received, I promise him. Let the friar come! yea, let him come. If the old woman presumes so far, she shall be sent to Bergamo. As for the law, I do fear it not; the *podestà* is neither a boy nor a fool! Pshaw! there's nothing to fear. How will Attilio be surprised to-morrow morning; he will find I am not a mere boaster. But if any difficulty should arise, he'll assist—the honour of all my relatives will be pledged." But these anxious thoughts subsided as he reverted to Lucy.—"She will be frightened to find herself alone, surrounded only by these rough visages: by Bacchus, the most human face here is my own, and she will be obliged to have recourse to me—to entreaty." In the midst of these calculations he heard a trampling of feet, approached the window, and looking out exclaimed, "It is they! But the litter! the devil! where is the litter? Three, five, eight, they are all there; but where is the litter? The devil! Griso shall render me an account of this." He then advanced to the head of the stairs to meet Griso. "Well," cried he, "Signor Bully, Signor Captain, Signor 'Leave it to me!'"

"It is hard," said Griso,—"it is hard to meet with reproach, when one has hazarded one's life to perform his duty."

"How has it happened? Let us hear, let us hear," said he, as he advanced towards the room, followed by Griso, who related, as clearly as he could, the occurrences of the night.

"Thou hast done well," said Don Roderick; "thou hast done all that thou couldst—but to think that this roof harbours a spy! If I discover him I will settle matters for him; and I tell thee, Griso, I suspect the information was given the day of the dinner."

"I have had the same suspicion," said Griso; "and if my master discovers the scoundrel, he has only to trust him to me. He has made me pass a troublesome night, and I wish to pay him for it. But there must be, I think, some other cause, which we cannot at present fathom; to-morrow, Signor, to-morrow we will see clear water."

"Have you been recognised by any one?"

Griso thought not; and after having given him many orders for the morrow, and wishing to make amends for the impetuosity with which he had at first greeted him, Don Roderick said, "Go to rest, poor Griso! you must indeed require it. Labouring all day, and half the night, and then to be received in this manner! Go to rest now; for we may yet be obliged to put your friendship to a severer test. Good night."

The next morning Don Roderick sought the Count Attilio, who, receiving him with a laugh, said, "San Martin!"

"I will pay the wager," said Don Roderick. "I thought indeed to have surprised you this morning, and therefore have kept from you some circumstances. I will now tell you all."

"The friar's hand is in this business," said his cousin, after having heard him through: "this friar, with his playing at bo-peep, and giving advice; I know him for a busybody and a rascal! And you did not confide in me, and tell me what brought him here the other day to trifle with you. If I had been in your place he should not have gone out as he came in, of that be assured."

"What! would you wish me to incur the resentment of all the capuchins in Italy?"

"In such a moment," said the count, "I should have forgotten there was any other capuchin in the world than this daring rascal; but the means are not wanting, within the pale of prudence, to take satisfaction even of a capuchin. It is well for him that he has escaped the punishment best suited to him; but I take him henceforth under my protection, and will teach him how to speak to his superiors."

"Do not make matters worse."

"Trust me for once; I will serve you as a relation and a friend."

"What do you mean to do?"

"I don't know yet; but I will certainly pay the friar. Let me see—the count my uncle, who is one of the secret council, will do the service; dear uncle! How pleased I am when I can make him work for me, a politician of his stamp! The day after to-morrow I will be at Milan, and in some way or other the friar shall have his due."

Meanwhile breakfast was brought in, which however did not interrupt the important discussion. Count Attilio interested himself in the cause from his friendship for his cousin, and the honour of the name, according to his notions of friendship and honour; yet he could hardly help laughing every now and then at the ridiculous issue of the adventure. But Don Roderick, who had calculated upon making a master-stroke, was vexed at his signal failure, and agitated by various passions. "Fine stories will be circulated," said he, "of last night's affair, but no matter; as to justice, I defy it: it does not exist; and if it did, I should equally defy it. Apropos, I have sent word this morning to the constable, to make no deposition respecting the affair, and he will be sure to follow my advice; but tattling always annoys me,—it is enough that *you* have it in your power to laugh at me."

"It is well you have given the constable his message," said the count; "this great empty-headed, obstinate proser of a *podestà* is however a man who knows his duty, and we must be careful not to place him in difficulty. If a fellow of a constable makes a deposition, the *podestà*, however well intentioned, is obliged to—"

"But you," interrupted Don Roderick, with a little warmth,—"you spoil my affairs, by contradicting him, and laughing at him on every occasion. Why the devil can't you suffer a magistrate to be an obstinate beast, while in other things that suit our convenience he is an honest man?"

"Do you know, cousin," said the count, regarding him with an expression of affected surprise, "do you know that I begin to think you capable of fear? You take the *podestà* and myself to be in earnest."

"Well, well, have not you yourself said that we should be careful?"

"Certainly; and when the question is serious, I will show you I am not a boy. Shall I tell you what I will do for you? I will go in person to make the *podestà* a visit; do you not think he will be pleased with the honour? And I will let him talk by the half hour of the count duke, and the Spanish keeper of the castle, and then I will throw in some remarks about the signor count of the secret council, my uncle; you know what effect this will have. Finally, he has more need of our protection, than you have of his condescension. He knows this well enough, and I shall leave him better disposed than I find him, that you may depend upon." So saying, he took his departure, leaving Don Roderick alone to wait the return of Griso, who had been, in obedience to his orders, reconnoitring the ground, and ascertaining the state of the public mind with regard to the events of the preceding night. He came at last, at the hour of dinner, to give in his relation. The tumult of this night had been so loud, and the disappearance of three persons from the village so mysterious, that strict and indefatigable search would naturally be made for them; and on the other hand, those who were possessed of partial information on the subject were too numerous to preserve an entire silence. Perpetua was assailed every where to tell what had caused her master such a fright, and she, perceiving how she had been deceived by Agnes, and feeling exasperated at her perfidy, had need of a little self-restraint; not that she complained of the deception practised on herself, of that she did not breathe a syllable; but the injury done to her poor master could not pass in silence, and that such an injury should have been attempted by such worthy people! Don Abbondio could command and entreat her to be silent, and she could reply that there was no necessity for inculcating a thing so obvious and proper, but certain it is that the secret remained in the heart of the poor woman as new wine in an old cask, which ferments and bubbles, and if it does not send the bung into the air, works out in foam between the staves, and drops here and there, so that one can drink it, and tell what sort of wine it is. Jervase, who could scarcely believe that for once he knew a little more than others, and who felt himself a man, since he had been an accomplice in a criminal affair, was dying to communicate it. And Tony, however alarmed at the thoughts of further enquiries and investigation, was bursting, in spite of all his prudence, till he had told the whole secret to his wife, who was not dumb. The one who spoke least was Menico, because his parents, alarmed at his coming into collision with Don Roderick, had kept him in the house for several days; they themselves, however, without wishing to appear to know more than others, insinuated that the fugitives had taken refuge at Pescarenico. This report, then, became current among the villagers. But no one could account for the attack of the bravoes: all agreed in suspecting Don Roderick; but the rest was total obscurity. The presence of the three bravoes at the inn was discussed, and the landlord was interrogated; but his memory was, on this point, as defective as ever. His inn, he concluded as usual, was just like a sea-port. Who was this pilgrim, seen by Stefano and Carlandrea, and whom the robbers wished to murder, and had carried off? For what purpose had he been at the cottage? Some said it was a good spirit, come to the assistance of the inmates; others, that it was the spirit of a wicked pilgrim, who came at night to join such companions, and perform such deeds, as he had been accustomed to while living; others, again, went so far as to conjecture that it was one of these very robbers, clothed like a pilgrim; so that Griso, with all his experience, would have been at a loss to discover who it was, if he had expected to acquire this information from others. But, as the reader knows, that which was perplexity to them, was perfect clearness to Griso. He was enabled, therefore, from these various sources, to obtain a sufficiently distinct account for the ear of Don Roderick. He related the attempt upon Don Abbondio, which accounted for the desertion of the cottage, without the necessity of imagining a spy in the palace: he told of their flight, which might be accounted for by the fear of the discovery of their trick upon Don Abbondio, or by the intelligence that their cottage had been broken into, and that they had probably gone together to Pescarenico. "Fled together!" cried Don Roderick, hoarse with rage: "together! and this rascal friar! this friar shall answer it! Griso, this night I must know where they are. I shall have no peace; ascertain if they are at Pescarenico; quick; fly; four crowns immediately, and my protection for ever! this rascal! this friar!"

Griso was once more in the field; and on the evening of this very day reported to his worthy master the desired intelligence, and by the following means. The good man by whom the little party had been conducted to Monza, returning with his carriage to Pescarenico at the hour of vespers, chanced to meet, before he reached his home, a particular friend, to whom he related, in great confidence, the good work he had accomplished; so that Griso could, two hours after, inform Don Roderick that Lucy and her mother had taken refuge in a convent of Monza, and that Renzo had proceeded on his way to Milan. Don Roderick felt his hopes revive at this separation; and having, during great part of the night, revolved in his mind the measures for effecting his wicked purpose, he aroused Griso early in the morning, and gave him the orders he had premeditated.

"Signor?" said Griso, hesitating.

"Well, have I have not spoken clearly?"

"If you would send some other—"

"How?"

"Most illustrious signor, I am ready to sacrifice my life for my master, and it is my duty to do so; but you, you would not desire me to place it in peril?"

"Well?"

"Your illustrious lordship knows well these few murders that are laid to my account, and—Here I am under the protection of your lordship, and in Milan the livery of your lordship is known, but in Monza I am known. And, your lordship knows, I do not say it boastingly, he who should deliver me up to justice would be well rewarded, a hundred good crowns, and permission to liberate two banditti."

"What, the devil!" said Don Roderick, "you are like a vile cur, who has scarce courage to rush at the legs of such as pass by the door; and, not daring to leave the house, keeps himself within the protection of his master."

"I think I have given proof, signor," said Griso.

"Well?"

"Well," resumed Griso, boldly, thus put on his mettle, "your lordship must forget my hesitation; heart of a lion, legs of a hare, I am ready to go."

"But you shall not go alone; take with you two of the best; *Cut-face* and *Aim-well*, and go boldly, and show yourself to be still Griso. The devil! people will be well content to let such faces as yours pass without molestation! And as to the bailiffs of Monza, they must have become weary of life to place it in such danger, for the chance of a hundred crowns! But I do not believe that I am so far unknown there, that the stamp of my service should pass for nothing."

Griso, having received ample and minute instructions, took his departure, accompanied by the two bravoes; cursing in his heart the whims of his master.

It now became the design of Don Roderick to contrive some way, by which Renzo, separated as he was from Lucy, should be prevented from attempting to return. He thought that the most certain means would be to have him sent out of the state, but this required the sanction of the law; he could, for example, give a colouring to the attempt at the curate's house, and represent it as a seditious act, and through Doctor Azzecca Garbugli give the *podestà* to understand that it was his duty to apprehend Renzo. But while he thought of the doctor as the man the most suitable for this service, Renzo himself put an end to much further deliberation on the subject by withdrawing himself.

Like the boy who drives his little Indian pigs to the fold, whose obstinacy impels them divers ways, and thus obliges him first to apply to one and then to another till he can succeed in penning them all, so are we obliged to play the same game with the personages of our story. Having secured Lucy, we ran to Don Roderick. Him we now quit to give an account of Renzo.

After the mournful parting which we have related, he set out, discouraged and disheartened, on his way to Milan. To bid farewell to his home and his country, and what was more, to Lucy! to find himself among strangers, not knowing where to rest his head, and all on account of this villain! When these thoughts presented themselves to the mind of Renzo, he was, for the moment, absorbed by rage and the desire of revenge; but when he recollected the prayer that he had uttered with the good friar in the convent of Pescarenico, his better feelings prevailed, and he was enabled to acquire some degree of resignation to the chastisements of which he stood so much in need. The road lay between two high banks; it was muddy, stony, and furrowed by deep wheel tracks, which, after a rain, became rivulets, overflowing the road, and rendering it nearly impassable. In such places small raised footpaths indicated that others had found a way by the fields. Renzo ascended one of these paths to the high ground, whence he beheld, as if rising from a desert, and not in the midst of a city, the noble structure of the cathedral, and he forgot all his misfortunes in contemplating, even at a distance, this eighth wonder of the world, of which he had heard so much from his infancy. But looking back, he saw in the horizon the notched ridge of mountains, and distinctly perceiving, among them, his own *Resegone*, he gazed at it mournfully a while, and then with a beating heart went on his way; steeples, towers, cupolas, and roofs soon appeared: he descended into the road, and when he perceived that he was very near the city, he accosted a traveller, with the civility which was natural to him, "Will you be so good, sir—"

"What do you want, my good young man?"

"Will you be so good as to direct me by the shortest way to the convent of the capuchins, where Father Bonaventura resides?"

He replied, very affably, "My good lad, there is more than one convent; you must tell me more clearly what and whom you seek."

Renzo then took from his bosom the letter of Father Christopher, and presented it to the gentleman, who, after having read it, returned it, saying, "The eastern gate; you are fortunate, young man—the convent you seek is but a short distance from this. Take this path to the left; it is a by-way, and in a little while you will find yourself by the side of a long and low building; that is the *lazaretto*; keep along the ditch that encircles it, and you will soon be at the eastern gate. Enter, and a few steps further on you will see before you an open square with fine elm trees; the convent is there—you cannot mistake it. God be with you!" And accompanying his last words with a kind wave of his hand, he proceeded on his way. Renzo was astonished at the good manners of the citizens to countrymen, not knowing that it was an extraordinary day, a day in which cloaks humbled themselves to doublets. He followed the path which had been pointed out to him, and arrived at the eastern entrance, which consisted of two pilasters, with a roofing above to secure the gates, and on one side was a small house for the toll-gatherer. The openings of the rampart descended irregularly, and their surface was filled with rubbish. The street of the suburb which led from this gate was not unlike the one which now opens from the Tosa gate. A small ditch ran in the midst of it, until within a few steps of the gate, and divided it into two small crooked streets, covered with dust or mud, according to the season. At the place where was, and is still, the collection of houses called the Borghetto, the ditch empties itself into a common sewer, and thence into another ditch which runs along the walls. At this point was a column with a cross oh it, dedicated to *San Dionigi*; to the right and left were gardens enclosed by hedges, and at intervals, small houses inhabited for the most part by washerwomen. Renzo passed through the gate, without being stopped by the toll-gatherer, which appeared to him very remarkable, as he had heard those few of his townsmen, who could boast of having been at Milan, relate wonderful stories of the strict search and close enquiries to which those were subjected who entered its gates. The street was deserted, and if he had not heard the humming of a crowd at a distance, he might have thought he was entering a city which had been abandoned by its inhabitants. As he advanced, he saw on the pavement something scattered here and there, which was as white as snow, but snow at this season it could not be; he touched it, and found that it was flour. "There must be a great plenty in Milan," said he, "if they thus throw away the gifts of God. They give out that famine is every where; this they do to keep poor people abroad quiet." But in a few moments he arrived in front of the column, and saw on the steps of the pedestal certain things scattered, which were not assuredly stones, and which, if they had been on a baker's counter, he would not have hesitated to call loaves of bread. But Renzo dared not so easily trust his eyes, because truly this was not a place for bread. "Let us see what this is," said he, and approaching the column, he took one in his hand; it was, indeed, a very white loaf of bread, such as Renzo was accustomed to eat only on festival days. "It is really bread!" said he, in wonder. "Do they scatter it thus here? And in a year like this? And do they suffer it to lie here, and not take the trouble to gather it? This must be a fine place to live in!" After ten miles of travel, in the fresh air of the morning, the sight of the bread awaked his appetite. "Shall I take it?" said he again. "Poh! they have left it to the dogs; surely, a Christian may take advantage of it; and if the owner should come, I can pay him at any rate." So saying, he put in one pocket that which he had in his hand, took a second, and put it in the other, and a third, which he began to eat, and resumed his way, full of wonder at the strangeness of the incident. As he moved on he saw people approaching from the interior of the city; and his attention was drawn to those who appeared first; a man, a woman, and a boy, each with a load which seemed beyond their strength, and exhibiting each a grotesque appearance. Their clothes, or rather their rags, powdered with meal, their faces the same, and excessively heated; they walked, not only as if overcome by the weight, but as if their limbs had been beaten and bruised. The man supported with difficulty a great bag of flour, which having holes here and there, scattered its contents at every unequal movement. But the figure of the woman was still more remarkable: she had her petticoat turned up, filled with as much flour as it could hold, and a little more; so that from time to time it flew over the pavement. She was, indeed, a grotesque picture, with her arms stretched out to encompass her burden, and staggering under its weight, her bare legs were seen beneath it. The boy held with both hands a basket full of bread on his head, but he was detained behind his parents to pick up the loaves which were constantly falling from it.

"If you let another fall, you ugly little dog—" said the mother, in a rage.

"I don't let them fall; they fall of themselves. How can I help it?" replied he.

"Eh! it's well for thee that my hands are full," resumed the woman.

"Come, come," said the man, "now that we have a little plenty, let us enjoy it in peace."

Meanwhile there had arrived a company of strangers, and one of them addressed the woman, "Where are we to go for bread?"—"On, on," replied she, and added, muttering, "These rascal countrymen will sweep all the shops and warehouses, and leave none for us."

"There is a share for every one, chatterer," said her husband; "plenty, plenty."

From all that Renzo saw and heard, he gathered that there was an insurrection in the city, and that each one provided for himself, in proportion to his will and strength. Although we would desire to make our poor mountaineer appear to the most advantage, historical truth obliges us to say that his first sentiment was that of complacency. He had so little to rejoice at, in the ordinary course of affairs, that he congratulated himself on a change, of whatever nature it might be. And for the rest, he, who was not a man superior to the age in which he lived, held the common opinion that the scarcity of bread had been caused by the speculators and bakers, and that any method would be justifiable, of wresting from them the aliment which they cruelly denied to the people. However, he determined to keep away from the tumult, and congratulated himself on the good fortune of having for his friend a capuchin, who would afford him shelter and good advice. Occupied with such reflections, and noticing from time to time as more people came up loaded with plunder, he proceeded to the convent.

The church and convent of the capuchins was situated in the centre of a small square, shaded by elm trees; Renzo placed in his bosom his remaining half loaf, and with his letter in his hand, approached the gate and rung the bell. At a small grated window appeared the face of a friar, porter to the convent, to ask "who was there?"

"One from the country, who brings a letter to Father Bonaventura, from Father Christopher."

"Give here," said the friar, thrusting his hand through the grate.

"No, no," said Renzo, "I must give it into his own hands."

"He is not in the convent."

"Suffer me to enter and wait for him," replied Renzo.

"You had best wait in the church," said the friar; "perhaps that may be of service to you. Into the convent you do not enter at present." So saying, he hastily closed the window, leaving Renzo to receive the repulse with the best grace he could. He was about to follow the advice of the porter, when he was seized with the desire to give a glance at the tumult. He crossed the square, and advanced towards the middle of the city, where the disturbance was greatest. Whilst he is proceeding thither, we will relate, as briefly as possible, the causes of this commotion.

Chapter XII.

This was the second year of the scarcity; in the preceding one, the provisions, remaining from past years, had supplied in some measure the deficiency, and we find the population neither altogether satisfied, nor yet starved; but certainly unprovided for in the year 1628, the period of our story. Now this harvest, so anxiously desired, was still more deficient than that of the past year, partly from the character of the season itself (and that not only in the Milanese but also in the surrounding country), and partly from the instrumentality of men. The havoc of the war, of which we have before made mention, had so devastated the state, that a greater number of farms than ordinary remained uncultivated and deserted by the peasants, who, instead of providing, by their labour, bread for their families, were obliged to beg it from door to door. We say a greater number of farms than ordinary, because the insupportable taxes, levied with a cupidity and folly unequalled; the habitual conduct, even in time of peace, of the standing troops (conduct which the mournful documents of the age compare to that of an invading army), and other causes which we cannot enumerate, had for some time slowly operated to produce these sad effects in all the Milanese,—the particular circumstances of which we now speak were, therefore, like the unexpected exasperation of a chronic disease. Hardly had this harvest been gathered, when the supplies for the army, and the waste which always accompanies them, caused an excessive scarcity, and with it its painful but profitable concomitant, a high price upon provisions; but this, attaining a certain point, always creates in the mind of the multitude a suspicion that scarcity is not in reality the cause of it. They forget that they had both feared and predicted it: they imagine all at once that there must be grain sufficient, and that the evil lies in an unwillingness to sell it for consumption. Preposterous as these suppositions were, they were governed by them, so that the speculators in grain, real or imaginary, the farmers, the bakers, became the object of their universal dislike. They could tell certainly where there were magazines overflowing with grain, and could even enumerate the number of sacks: they spoke with assurance of the immense quantity of corn which had been despatched to other places, where probably the people were deluded with a similar story, and made to believe that the grain raised among *them* had been sent to Milan! They implored from the magistrate those precautions, which always appear equitable and simple to the populace. The magistrates complied, and fixed the price on each commodity, threatening punishment to such as should refuse to sell; notwithstanding this, the evil continued to increase. This the people attributed to the feebleness of the remedies, and loudly called for some of a more decided character; unhappily they found a man that was willing to grant them all they should ask.

In the absence of the Governor Don Gonzalo Fernandez de Cordova, who was encamped beyond Casale, in Montferrat, the High Chancellor Antonio Ferrer, also a Spaniard, supplied his place in Milan. He considered the low price of bread to be in itself desirable, and vainly imagined that an order from him would be sufficient to accomplish it. He fixed the limit, therefore, at the price the bread would have had when corn was thirty-three livres the bushel; whereas it was now as high as eighty.

Over the execution of these laws the people themselves watched, and were determined to receive the benefit of them quickly. They assembled in crowds before the bakers' houses to demand bread at the price fixed; there was no remedy; the bakers were employed night and day in supplying their wants, inasmuch as the people, having a confused idea that the privilege would be transient, ceased not to besiege their houses, in order to enjoy to the utmost their temporary good fortune. The magistrates threatened punishment—the multitude murmured at every delay of the bakers in furnishing them. These remonstrated incessantly against the iniquitous and insupportable weight of the burden imposed on them; but Antonio Ferrer replied, that they had possessed great advantages in times past, and now owed the public some reparation. Finally, the council of ten (a municipal magistracy composed of nobles, which lasted until the ninety-seventh year of the century just elapsed,) informed the governor of the state in which things were, hoping that he would find some remedy. Don Gonzalo, immersed in the business of war, named a council, upon whom he conferred authority to fix a reasonable price upon bread, so that both parties should be satisfied. The deputies assembled, and after much deliberation felt themselves compelled to augment the price of it: the bakers breathed, but the people became furious.

The evening preceding the day on which Renzo arrived at Milan, the streets swarmed with people, who, governed by one common feeling, strangers or friends, had intuitively united themselves in companies throughout the city. Every observation tended to increase their rage and their resentment; various opinions were given, and many exclamations uttered; here, one declaimed aloud to a circle of bystanders, who applauded vehemently; there, another more cautious, but not less dangerous, was whispering in the ear of a neighbour or two, that something must and would be done: in short, there was an incessant and discordant din from the medley of men, women, and children, which composed the various assemblages. There was now only required an impetus to set the machine in motion, and reduce words to deeds; and an opportunity soon presented itself. At the break of day little boys were seen issuing from the bakers' shops with baskets on their heads, loaded with bread, which they were about to carry to their usual customers. The appearance of one of these unlucky boys in an assembly of people was like a squib thrown into a gunpowder mill. "Here is bread!" cried a hundred voices at once. "Yes, for our tyrants, who swim in abundance, and wish to make us die in hunger," said one, who drew near the boy, and seizing the basket, cried out, "Let us see." The boy coloured, grew pale, trembled, and would have entreated them to let him pass on, but the words died on his lips; he then endeavoured to free himself from the basket. "Down with the basket" was heard on all sides; it was seized by many hands, and placed on the earth: they raised the napkin which covered it, and a tepid fragrance diffused itself around. "We are Christians also," said one; "and have a right to eat bread as well as other people:" so saying, he took a loaf and bit it; the rest followed his example; and it is unnecessary to add, that in a few moments the contents of the basket had disappeared. Those who had not been able to secure any for themselves were irritated at the sight of their neighbours' gains, and animated by the facility of the enterprise, went in search of other boys with baskets; as many, therefore, as they met were stopped and plundered. Still the number who remained unsatisfied was beyond comparison the greatest, and even the gainers were only stimulated by their success to ampler enterprises; so that simultaneously there was a shout from the crowd of "To the bake-house! to the bake-house!"

In the street called the *Corsia de' Servi* there was, and is still, a bakery of the same name,—a name that signifies in Tuscan the *Shop of the Crutches*, and in Milanese is composed of such barbarous words, that it is impossible to discover their sound from any rule of the language. To this place the throng approached: the shopkeepers were listening to the sad relation of the boys, who had but just escaped with their lives, when they heard a distant murmur, and beheld the crowd advancing.

"Shut, shut! quick, quick!" some ran to ask aid from the sheriff; others in haste closed the shop, and barricadoed and secured the doors from within. The throng thickened in front, and cries of "Bread, bread! open, open!" were heard from every quarter. The sheriff arrived with a troop of halberdiers. "Make way, make way, friends! home, home! make way for the sheriff," cried they. The people gave way a little, so that they could draw themselves up in front of the door of the shop. "But, friends," cried the sheriff from this place, "what do you do here? Home, home! have you no fear of God? What will our lord the king say? We do not wish you harm; but go home. There is no good to be gained here for soul or body. Home, home!" The crowd, regardless of his expostulations, pressed forward, themselves being urged on by increasing multitudes behind. "Make them draw back, that I may recover breath," continued he to the halberdiers, "but harm no one—we will endeavour to get into the shop—make them keep back, and knock at the door."—"Back, back," cried the halberdiers, presenting the but-ends of their arms; the throng retreated a little; the sheriff knocked, crying to those within to open; they obeyed, and he and his guard contrived to intrench themselves within the house; then, appearing at a window above, "Friends," cried he, "go home. A general pardon to whoever shall return immediately to their houses."

"Bread, bread! open, open!" vociferated the crowd in reply.

"You shall have justice, friends; but return to your houses. You shall have bread; but this is not the way to obtain it. Eh! what are you doing below there? At the door of the house! hah! hah! Take care; it is a criminal act. Eh! away with those tools! take down those hands! hah! hah! You Milanese, who are famous throughout the world for your benevolence, who have always been accounted good citi— Ah! rascals!"

This rapid change of style was occasioned by a stone thrown by one of these good citizens at the sheriff's head. "Rascals! rascals!" continued he, closing the window in a rage. The confusion below increased; stones were thrown at the doors and windows, and they had nearly opened a way into the shop. Meanwhile the master and boys of the shop, who were at the windows of the story above, with a supply of stones (obtained probably from the court-yard), threatened to throw them upon the crowd if they did not disperse. Perceiving their threats to be of no avail, they commenced putting them in execution.

"Ah! villains! ah! rogues! Is this the bread you give to the poor?" was screamed from below. Many were wounded, two were killed; the fury of the multitude increased; the doors were broken open, and the torrent rushed through all the passages. At this, those within took refuge under the shop floor; the sheriff and the halberdiers hid themselves beneath the tiles; others escaped by the skylights, and wandered upon the roofs like cats.

The sight of their prey made the conquerors forget their designs of sanguinary vengeance; some rushed to the chests, and plundered them of bread; others hastened to force the locks of the counter, and took from thence handfulls of money, which they pocketed, and then returned to take more bread, if there should remain any. Others, again, entered the interior magazines, and, throwing out part of the flour, reduced the bags to a portable size; some attacked a kneading trough, and made a booty of the dough; a few had made a prize of a bolting cloth, which they raised in the air as in triumph, and, in addition to all, men, women, and children were covered with a cloud of white powder.

While this shop was so ransacked, none of the others in the city remained quiet, or free from danger. But at none had the people assembled in such numbers as to be very daring; in some, the owners had provided auxiliaries, and were on the defensive; in others, the owners less strong in numbers, and more affrighted, endeavoured to compromise matters; they distributed bread to those who crowded around their shops, and thus got rid of them. And these did not depart so much because they were content with the acquisition, as from fear of the halberdiers and officers of justice, who were now scattered throughout the city, in companies sufficient to keep these little bands of mutineers in subjection. In the mean time the tumult and the crowd increased in front of the unfortunate bakery, as the strength of the populace had here the advantage. Things were in this situation, when Renzo, coming from the eastern gate, approached, without knowing it, the scene of tumult. Hurried along by the crowd, he endeavoured to extract from the confused shouting of the throng some more positive information of the real state of affairs.

"Now the infamous imposition of these rascals is discovered," said one; "they said there was neither bread, flour, nor corn. Now we know things just as they are, and they can no longer deceive us."

"I tell you that all this answers no purpose," said another; "it will do no good unless justice be done to us. Bread will be cheap enough, 'tis true, but they will put poison in it to make the poor die like flies. They have already said we are too numerous, I know they have; I heard it from one of my acquaintances, who is a friend of a relation of a scullion of one of the lords."

"Make way, make way, gentlemen, I beseech you; make way for a poor father of a family who is carrying bread to five children!" This was said by one who came staggering under the weight of a bag of flour.

"I," said another, in an under tone, to one of his companions, "I am going away. I am a man of the world, and I know how these things go. These clowns, who now make so much noise, will prove themselves cowards to-morrow. I have already perceived some among the crowd who are taking note of those who are present, and when all is over, they will make up the account, and the guilty will pay the penalty."

"He who protects the bakers," cried a sonorous voice, which attracted the attention of Renzo, "is the superintendent of provisions."

"They are all rogues," said a neighbour.

"Yes, but he is the chief," replied the one who had first spoken.

The superintendent of provisions, elected every year by the governor from a list of seven nobles formed from the council of ten, was the president of the court of provision, which, composed of twelve nobles, had, with other duties, that of superintending the corn for the citizens. Persons in such a station would naturally, in times of starvation and ignorance, be considered as the authors of all the evil.

"Cheats!" exclaimed another; "can they do worse? They have had the audacity to say that the high chancellor is a childish old man, and they wish to take the government into their own hands. We ought to make a great coop, and put them in, to feed upon dry peas and cockleweed, as they would fain have us do."

While listening to such observations as the above, Renzo continued to make his way through the crowd, and at last arrived in front of the bakery. On viewing its dilapidated and ruinous state, after the assault just sustained, "This cannot be a good deed," thought he: "if they treat all the bake-houses in this manner, where will they make bread?"

From time to time, some were seen issuing from the house, loaded with pieces of chests, or troughs, or a bench, basket, or some other relic of the poor building, and crying, "Make way, make way!" passed through the crowd. These were all carried in the same direction, and it appeared to a place agreed upon. Renzo's curiosity being excited, he followed one who carried a bundle of pieces of board and chips on his shoulder, and found that he took the direction of the cathedral. On passing it, the mountaineer could not avoid stopping a moment to gaze with admiring eyes on the magnificent structure. He then quickened his steps to rejoin him whom he had taken as a guide, and, keeping behind him, they drew near the middle of the square. The crowd was here more dense, but they opened a way for the carrier, and Renzo, skilfully introducing himself in the void left by him, arrived with him in the very midst of the multitude. Here there was an open space, in the centre of which was a bonfire, a heap of embers, the remains of the tools mentioned above; surrounding it was heard a clapping of hands and stamping of feet, the tumult of a thousand cries of triumph and imprecation.

He of the boards threw them on the embers, and some, with pieces of half-burnt shovel, stirred them until the flame ascended, upon which their shouts were renewed louder than before. The flame sank again, and the company, for want of more combustibles, began to be weary, when a report spread, that at the Cordusio (a square or cross-way not far from there) they were besieging a bakery: then was heard on all sides, "Let us go, let us go;" and the crowd moved on. Renzo was drawn along with the current, but in the mean while held counsel with himself, whether he had not best withdraw from the fray, and return to the convent in search of Father Bonaventura; but curiosity again prevailed, and he suffered himself to be carried forward, with the determination, however, of remaining a mere spectator of the scene.

The multitude passed through the short and narrow street of Pescheria, and thence by the crooked arch to the square de' Mercanti. Here there were very few, who, in passing before the niche that divides towards the centre the terrace of the edifice then called the College of Doctors, did not give a slight glance at the great statue contained in it of Philip II., who even from the marble imposed respect, and who, with his arm extended, appeared to be menacing the populace for their rebellion.

This niche is now empty, and from a singular circumstance. About one hundred and sixty years after the events we are now relating, the head of the statue was changed, the sceptre taken from its hand, and a dagger substituted in its place, and beneath it was written *Marcus Brutus*. Thus inserted it remained perhaps a couple of years, until one day, some persons, who had no sympathies with Marcus Brutus, but rather an aversion to him, threw a rope around the statue, pulled it down, and, reducing it to a shapeless mass, dragged it, with many insulting gestures, beyond the walls of the city. Who would have foretold this to Andrea Biffi when he sculptured it?

From the square de' Mercanti, the clamorous troop at length arrived at the Cordusio. Each one immediately looked towards the shop; but, instead of the crowd of friends which they expected to find engaged on its demolition, there were but a few, at a distance from the shop, which was shut, and defended from the windows by armed people. They fell back, and there was a murmur through the crowd of unwillingness to risk the hazard of proceeding, when a voice was heard to cry aloud, "Near by is the house of the superintendent of provision; let us do justice, and plunder it." There was a universal acceptance of the proposal, and "To the superintendent's! to the superintendent's!" was the only sound that could be heard. The crowd moved with unanimous fury towards the street where the house, named in such an evil moment, was situated.

Chapter XIII.

The unfortunate superintendent was at this moment painfully digesting his miserable dinner, whilst awaiting anxiously the termination of this hurricane; he was, however, far from suspecting that its greatest fury was to be spent on himself. Some benevolent persons hastened forward to inform him of his urgent peril. The servants, drawn to the door by the uproar, beheld, in affright, the dense mass advancing. While they listened to the friendly notice, the vanguard appeared; one hastily informed his master; and while he, for a moment, deliberated upon flight, another came to say there was no longer time for it; in hurry and confusion they closed and barricadoed the windows and the doors. The howling without increased; each corner of the house resounded with it; and in the midst of the vast and mingled noise was heard, fearfully and distinctly, the blows of stones upon the door. "The tyrant! the tyrant! the causer of famine! we must have him, living or dead!"

The poor man wandered from room to room in a state of insupportable alarm, commending himself to God, and beseeching his servants to be firm, and to find for him some way of escape! He ascended to the highest floor, and, from an opening between the garret and the roof, he looked anxiously out upon the street, and beheld it filled with the enraged populace; more appalled than ever, he withdrew to seek the most secure and secret hiding-place. Here, concealed, he listened intently to ascertain if at any time the importunate transport of passion should weaken, if the tumult should in any degree subside; but his heart died within him to hear the uproar continue with aggravated and savage ferocity.

Renzo at this time found himself in the thickest of the confusion, not now carried there by the press, but by his own inclination. At the first proposal of blood-shedding, he felt his own curdle in his veins; as to the plundering, he was not quite certain whether it was right or wrong; but the idea of murder caused him unmixed horror. And although he was greatly persuaded that the vicar was the primary cause of the famine, the grand criminal, still, having, at the first movement of the crowd, heard, by chance, some expressions which indicated a willingness to make any effort to save him, he had suddenly determined to aid such a work, and had therefore pressed near the door, which was assailed in a thousand ways. Some were pounding the lock to break it in pieces; others assisted with stakes, and chisels, and hammers; others, again, tore away the plastering, and beat in pieces the wall, in order to effect a breach. The rest, who were unable to get near the house, encouraged by their shouts those who were at the work of destruction; though, fortunately, through the eagerness with which they pressed forward, they impeded its progress.

The magistrates, who were the first to have notice of the fray, despatched a messenger to ask military aid of the commander of the castle, which was then called, from the gate, Giovia; and he forthwith detached a troop, which arrived when the house was encompassed with the throng, and undergoing its tremendous assault; and was therefore obliged to halt at a distance from it, and at the extremity of the crowd. The officer who commanded it did not know what course to pursue; at the order to disperse and make way, the people replied by a deep and continued murmur, but no one moved. To fire on the crowd appeared not only savage, but perilous, inasmuch as the most harmless might be injured, and the most ferocious only irritated, and prepared for further mischief; and moreover his instructions did not authorise it. To break the crowd, and go forward with his band to the house, would have been the best, if success could have been certain; but who could tell if the soldiers could proceed united and in order? The irresolution of the commander seemed to proceed from fear: the populace were unmoved by the appearance of the soldiers, and continued their attacks on the house. At a little distance there stood an ill-looking, half-starved old man, who, contracting an angry countenance to a smile of diabolical complacency, brandished above his hoary head a hammer, with which he said he meant to nail the vicar to the posts of his door, alive as he was.

"Oh, shame! shame!" exclaimed Renzo. "Shame! would you take the hangman's business out of his hand? to assassinate a Christian? How can you expect God will give us bread, if we commit such iniquity? He will send us his thunders, and not bread!"

"Ah! dog! ah! traitor to the country!" cried one who had heard these words, turning to Renzo with the countenance of a demon. "It is a servant of the vicar's disguised like a countryman; it is a spy!" A hundred voices were heard exclaiming, "Who is it? where is he?"—"A servant of the vicar's—a spy—the vicar himself, escaping in the disguise of a peasant!"—"Where is he? where is he?"

Renzo would have shrunk into nothingness,—some of the more benevolent contrived to help him to disappear through the crowd; but that which preserved him most effectually was a cry of "Make way, here comes our help, make way!" which attracted the attention of the throng.

This was a long scaling ladder, supported by a few persons who were endeavouring to penetrate the living mass, and by which they meant to gain entrance to the house. But, happily, this was not easy of execution; the length of the machine precluded the possibility of its being carried easily through such a multitude; it came, however, just in time for Renzo, who profited by the confusion, and escaped to a distance, with the intention of making his way, as soon as he could, to the convent, in search of Father Bonaventura.

Suddenly a new movement began at one extremity, and diffused itself through the crowd:—"Ferrer, Ferrer!" resounded from every side. Some were surprised, some rejoiced, some were exasperated, some applauded, some affirmed, some denied, some blessed, some cursed!

"Is he here? It is not true; it is not true. Yes, yes, long live Ferrer, he who makes bread cheap.—No, no! He is here—here in a carriage! Why does he come?—we don't want him.—Ferrer! long live Ferrer! the friend of the poor! he comes to take the vicar prisoner.—No, no, we would revenge *ourselves*, we would fight our own battles; back, back.—Yes, yes, Ferrer! Let him come! to prison with the vicar!"

At the extremity of the crowd, on the side opposite to that where the soldiers were, Antonio Ferrer, the high chancellor, was approaching in his carriage, who, probably condemning himself as the cause of this commotion, had come to avert at least its most terrific and irreparable effects, to spend worthily a popularity unworthily acquired.

In popular tumults there are always some who, from heated passion, or fanaticism, or wicked design, do what they can to push things to the worst; proposing and promoting the most barbarous counsels, and assisting to stir the fire whenever it appears to slacken. But, on the other hand, there are always those who, perhaps with equal ardour, and equal perseverance, employ their efforts for the production of contrary effects; some led by friendship or partiality for the persons in danger, others without other impulse than that of horror of bloodshed and atrocity. The mass, then, is ever composed of a mixed assemblage, who, by indefinite gradations, hold to one or the other extreme; prompt to rage or compassion, to adoration or execration, according as the occasion presents itself for the developement of either of these sentiments: *life* and *death* are the words involuntarily uttered, and with equal facility; and he who succeeds in persuading them that such an one does not deserve to be quartered, has but little more to do, to convince them that he ought to be carried in triumph.

While these various interests were contending for superiority in the mob, before the house of the vicar, the appearance of Antonio Ferrer gave instantly a great advantage to the humane, who were manifestly yielding to the greater strength of the ferocious and blood-thirsty. The man himself was acceptable to the multitude, from his having previously favoured their cause, and from his heroic resistance to any arguments against it. Those already favourably inclined towards him were now much more affected by the courageous confidence of an old man, who, without guards or retinue, came thus to confront an angry and stormy multitude. The announcement that his purpose was to take the vicar prisoner, produced at once a wonderful effect; and the fury against that unhappy person, which would have been aggravated by any attempt at defiance, or refusal of concession, now, with the promise of satisfaction, and, to speak in the Milanese fashion, with this bone in the mouth, became in a degree appeased, and gave place to other opposite sentiments, which began to prevail over their minds.

The partisans of peace, having recovered breath, aided Ferrer in various ways; those who were near him, while endeavouring by their own to perpetuate the general applause, sought at the same time to keep off the crowd, so as to open a passage for the carriage; others applauded and repeated his words, or such as appeared appropriate to his undertaking and his peril; imposed silence on the obstinately furious, or contrived to turn against *them* the anger of the fickle assembly. "Who is it that will not say, Long live Ferrer? You don't wish bread to be cheap, then, eh? They are rogues who are not willing to receive justice at the hands of a Christian, and there are some among them who cry louder than the rest, to allow the vicar to escape. To prison with the superintendent! Long live Ferrer! Make way for Ferrer!" The numbers of those who spoke in this manner increasing continually, the numbers of the opposite party diminished in proportion; so that the former, from admonishing, had recourse to blows, in order to silence those who were still disposed to pursue the work of destruction. The menaces and threatenings of the weaker party were of no longer avail; the cause of blood had ceased to predominate, and in its place were heard only the cries of "Prison, justice, Ferrer!" The rebellious spirits were finally silenced: the remainder took possession of the door, in order to defend it from fresh attacks, and also to prepare a passage for Ferrer; and some among them called to those within (openings were not wanting) that succour had arrived, and that the vicar must get ready "to go quickly—to prison—hem! do you hear?"

"Is this the Ferrer who helps in making the proclamations?" asked our Renzo of one of his new neighbours, remembering the *vidit Ferrera* that the doctor had shown him appended to the famous proclamation, and which he had reiterated in his ears with so great a degree of pertinacity.

"The same, the high chancellor," replied he.

"He is a worthy man, is he not?"

"He is more than worthy; it is he who has lowered the price of bread, against the wishes of others in power, and now he comes to carry the vicar to prison, because he has not acted justly."

It is unnecessary to say, that Renzo's feelings were immediately enlisted on the side of Ferrer. He was desirous to approach near him, but the undertaking was no easy one; however, with the decision and strength of a mountaineer, he continued to elbow himself through the crowd, and finally reached the side of the carriage.

The carriage had already penetrated into the midst of the crowd, but was here suddenly stopped by one of those obstructions, the unavoidable consequence of a journey like this. The aged Ferrer presented, now at one window of his carriage, now at the other, a countenance full of humility, of sweetness, and benevolence; a countenance which he had always kept in reserve for the day in which he should appear before Don Philip IV.; but he was constrained to make use of it on this occasion. He spoke; but the noise and buzzing of so many voices, and the shouts of applause which they bestowed on him, allowed but little of his discourse to be heard. He had recourse also to gestures; now placing his fingers on his lips, to take from thence a kiss, which his enclosed hands distributed to right and left, as if to render thanks for the favour with which the public regarded him; then he extended them, waving them slowly beyond the window as if to entreat a little space; and now again lowering them politely, as if to request a little silence.

When he had succeeded in obtaining, in some measure, his last request, those who were nearest to him heard and repeated his words:—"Bread, abundance. I come to do justice; a little space, if you please." Then, as if stifled and suffocated with the press, and the continual buzzing of so many voices, he threw himself back in the carriage, and with difficulty drawing a long breath, said to himself, "*Por mi vida, que de gente.*"

"Long live Ferrer; there is no occasion for fear; you are a brave man. Bread! bread!"

"Yes, bread, bread," replied Ferrer, "in abundance! *I* promise you, I do," placing his hand on his heart. "Clear a passage for me," added he, then, in the loudest voice he could command; "I come to carry him to prison, to inflict on him a just punishment;" and he added, in a very low tone, "*Si esta culpable.*" Then leaning forward to the coachman, he said hastily, "*Adelante, Pedro, si puedes.*"

The coachman smiled also on the people with an affected politeness, as if he were some great personage; and, with ineffable grace, he waved the whip slowly from right to left, as if requesting his inconvenient neighbours to retire a little on either side. "Be so kind, gentlemen," said he, "a little space, ever so little, just enough to let us pass."

Meanwhile the most active and officious employed themselves in preparing the passage so politely requested. Some made the crowd retire from before the horses with good words, placing their hands on their breast, and pushing them gently, "There, there, a little space, gentlemen." Others pursued the same plan at the sides of the carriage, so that it might pass on without damage to those who surrounded it; which would have subjected the popularity of Antonio Ferrer to great hazard. Renzo, after having been occupied for a few moments in admiring the respectable old man, a little disturbed by vexation, overwhelmed with fatigue, but animated by solicitude, embellished, so to speak, by the hope of wresting a fellow-creature from the pains of death,—Renzo, I say, threw away all idea of retreat. He resolved to assist Ferrer in every way that lay in his power, and not to abandon him until he had accomplished his designs. He united with the others to free the way, and he was certainly not one of the least active or industrious. A passage was opened. "Come on, come on," said a number of them to the coachman, retiring in front of the crowd to maintain the passage clear. "*Adelante, presto, con juicio,*" said his master also to him, and the carriage moved forward. In the midst of the salutes which he lavished promiscuously on the public, Ferrer, with a smile of intelligence, bestowed particular thanks upon those whom he beheld busily employed for him; more than one of these smiles was directed to Renzo, who, in truth, deserved them richly, serving the high chancellor on this day with more devoted zeal than the most intrepid of his secretaries. The young mountaineer was delighted with his condescension, and proud of the honour of having, as he thought, formed a friendship with Antonio Ferrer.

The carriage, once in motion, continued its way with more or less slowness, and not without being frequently brought to a full stop. The space to be traversed was short, but, with respect to the time it occupied, it would have appeared interminable, even to one not governed by the holy motive of Ferrer. The people thronged around the carriage, to right and left, as dolphins around a vessel, hurried forward by a tempest. The noise was more piercing and discordant than that of a tempest itself. Ferrer continued to speak to the populace the whole length of the way. "Yes, gentlemen, bread in abundance. I will conduct him to prison; he shall be punished—*si esta culpable*. Yes, yes, I will order it so; bread shall be cheap. *Asi es*. So it shall, I mean. The king our master does not wish his faithful subjects to suffer from hunger. *Oh, oh! guardaos*. Take care that we do not hurt you, gentlemen, *Pedro, adelante, con juicio*. Abundance! abundance! a little space, for the love of Heaven! Bread, bread! To prison! to prison! What do you want?" demanded he of a man who had thrust himself partly within the window to howl at him some advice, or petition, or applause, no matter what; but he, without having heard the question, had been drawn back by another, who saw him in danger of being crushed by the wheel. Amidst all this clamour, Ferrer at last gained the house, thanks to his kind auxiliaries.

Those who had stationed themselves there had equally laboured to procure the desired result, and had succeeded in dividing the crowd in two, and keeping them back, so that between the door and the carriage there should be an empty space, however small. Renzo, who in acting as a scout and a guide had arrived with the carriage, was able to find a place, whence he could, by making a rampart of his powerful shoulders, see distinctly all that passed.

Ferrer breathed again on seeing the place free, and the door still shut, or, to speak more correctly, not yet open. However, the hinges were nearly torn from their fastenings, and the panels shivered in many pieces; so that an opening was made, through which it could be seen that what held it together was the bolt, which, however, was almost twisted from its socket. Through this breach some one cried to those within to open the door, another ran to let down the steps of the carriage, and the old man descended from it, leaning on the arm of this benevolent person.

The crowd pressed forward to behold him: curiosity and general attention caused a moment's silence. Ferrer stopped an instant on the steps, turned towards them, and putting his hand to his heart, said, "Bread and justice." Clothed in his toga, with head erect, and step assured, he continued to descend, amid the loud applause that rent the skies.

In the mean while the people of the house had opened the door, so as to permit the entrance of so desired a guest; taking care, however, to contract the opening to the space his body would occupy. "Quick, quick!" said he, "open, so that I may enter; and you, brave men, keep back the people, do not let them come behind me—for the love of Heaven! Open a way for us, presently.—Eh! eh! gentlemen, one moment," said he to the people of the house; "softly with this door; let me pass. Oh, my ribs, take care of my ribs. Shut now—no, my gown, my gown!" It would have remained caught within the door if Ferrer had not hastily withdrawn it.

The doors, closed in the best manner they could be, were nevertheless supported with bars from within. On the outside, those who had constituted themselves the bodyguard of Ferrer worked with their shoulders, their arms, and their voice to keep the place empty, praying from the bottom of their hearts that they would be expeditious.

"Quick, quick!" said Ferrer, as he reached the portico, to the servants who surrounded him, crying, "May your excellency be rewarded! What goodness! Great God, what goodness!"

"Quick, quick," repeated Ferrer, "where is this poor man?"

The superintendent descended the stairs half led, half carried by his domestics, and pale as death. When he saw who had come to his assistance, he sighed deeply, his pulse returned, and a slight colour tinged his cheek. He hastened to meet Ferrer, saying, "I am in the hands of God and your excellency; but how go hence? we are surrounded on all sides by people who desire my death."

"*Venga con migo usted*, and take courage. My carriage is at the door; quick, quick!" He took him by the hand, and, continuing to encourage him, led him towards the door, saying in his heart, however, *Aqui esta el busilis! Dios nos valga!*

The door, opened; Ferrer appeared first; the superintendent followed, shrinking with fear, and clinging to the protecting toga, as an infant to the gown of its mother. Those who had maintained the space free raised their hands and waved their hats; making in this manner a sort of cloud to conceal the superintendent from the view of the people, and to enable him to enter the carriage, and place himself out of sight. Ferrer followed, and the carriage was closed. The people drew their own conclusions as to what had taken place, and there arose, in consequence, a mingled sound of applauses and imprecations.

The return of the carriage might seem to be even more difficult and dangerous; but the willingness of the public to suffer the superintendent to be carried to prison was sufficiently manifest; and the friends of Ferrer had been busy in keeping the way open whilst he was at the house, so that he could return with a little more speed than he went. As it advanced, the crowd, ranged on either side, closed and united their ranks behind it.

Ferrer, as soon as he was seated, whispered the superintendent to keep himself concealed in the bottom of the carriage, and not to let himself be seen, for the love of Heaven; there was, however, no need of this advice. It was the policy of the high chancellor, on the contrary, to attract as much of the attention of the populace as possible, and during all this passage, as in the former, he harangued his changeable auditory with a great quantity of sound, and very little sense; interrupting himself continually to breathe into the ear of his invisible companion a few hurried words of Spanish. "Yes, gentlemen, bread and justice. To the castle, to prison under my care. Thanks, thanks, a thousand thanks! No, no, he shall not escape! *Por ablanderlos.* It is too just, we will examine, we will see. I wish you well. A severe punishment. *Esto lo digo por su bien.* A just and moderate price, and punishment to those who oppose it. Keep off a little, I pray you. Yes, yes; I am the friend of the people. He shall be punished; it is true; he is a villain, a rascal. *Perdone usted.* He shall be punished, he shall be punished—*si esta culpable.* Yes, yes; we will make the bakers do that which is just. Long live the king! long live the good Milanese, his faithful subjects! *Animo estamos ya quasi afuera.*"

They had, in fact, passed through the thickest of the throng, and were rapidly advancing to a place of safety; and now Ferrer gave his lungs a little repose, and looking forward, beheld the succours from Pisa, those Spanish soldiers, who had at last rendered themselves of service, by persuading some of the people to retire to their homes, and by keeping the passage free for the final escape. Upon the arrival of the carriage, they made room, and presented arms to the high chancellor, who bowed to right and left; and to the officer who approached the nearest to salute him he said, accompanying his words with a wave of his hand, "*Beso à usted las manos,*" which the officer interpreted to signify, You have given me much assistance!

He might have appropriately added, *Cedant arma togæ*; but the imagination of Ferrer was not at this moment at liberty to occupy itself with quotations, and, moreover, they would have been addressed to the wind, as the officer did not understand Latin.

Pedro felt his accustomed courage revive at the sight of these files of muskets, so respectfully raised; and recovering entirely from his amazement, he urged on his horses, without deigning to take further notice of the few, who were now harmless from their numbers.

"*Levantese, levantese, estamos afueras,*" said Ferrer to the superintendent, who, re-assured by the cessation of the tumult, the rapid motion of the carriage, and these words of encouragement, drew himself from his corner, and overwhelmed his liberator with thanks. The latter, after having condoled with him on account of his peril, and rejoiced at his deliverance, exclaimed, "*Ah! que dira de esto su excelencia,* who is already weary of this cursed Casale, because it will not surrender? *que dira el conde duque?* who trembles if a leaf makes more noise than usual? *Que dira el rey nuestro señor?* who must necessarily be informed of so great a tumult? And is it at an end? *Dios lo sabe.*"—"Ah, as for me, I will have nothing more to do with it," said the superintendent. "I wash my hands of it. I resign my office into the hands of your excellency, and I will go and live in a cavern on a mountain, as a hermit, far, very far from this savage people."

"*Usted* will do that which is best *por el servicio de su majestad,*" replied the high chancellor, gravely.

"His majesty does not desire my death," replied the superintendent. "Yes, yes, in a cavern, in a cavern far from these cruel people."

It is not known what became of this project, as, after conducting the poor man in safety to his castle, our author makes no farther mention of him.

Chapter XIV.

The crowd began to disperse; some went home to take care of their families, some wandered off from the desire to breathe more freely, after such a squeeze, and others sought their acquaintances, to chat with them over the deeds of the day. The other end of the street was also thinning, so that the detachment of Spanish soldiers could without resistance advance near the superintendent's house. In front of it there still remained, so to speak, the dregs of the commotion; a company of the seditious, who, discontented with "so lame and impotent a conclusion," of that which promised so much, muttered curses at the disappointment, and united themselves in knots to consult with each other on the possibility of yet attempting something; and, to afford themselves proof that this was in their power, they attacked and pounded the poor door, which had been propped up anew from within. At the arrival of the troop, however, their valour diminished, and without further consultation they dispersed, leaving the place free to the soldiers, who took possession, in order to serve as a guard to the house and road. But the streets and small squares of the vicinity were full of little gatherings; where three or four individuals stopped, twenty were soon added to them; there was a confused and constant babbling; one narrated with emphasis the peculiar incidents of which he had been the witness, another related his own feats, another rejoiced that the affair had ended so happily, loaded Ferrer with praises, and predicted serious consequences to the superintendent; to which another still replied, that there was no danger of it, because wolves do not eat wolves; others, in anger, muttered that they had been duped, and that they were fools to allow themselves to be deceived in this manner.

Meanwhile the sun had set, and twilight threw the same indistinct hue over every object. Many, fatigued with the day, and wearied with conversing in the dark, returned to their houses. Our hero, after having assisted the carriage as far as was necessary, rejoiced when he beheld it in safety, and as soon as it was in his power left the crowd, so that he might, once more, breathe freely. Hardly had he taken a few steps in the open air, when he experienced a re-action after such excitement, and began to feel the need of food and repose; he therefore looked upward on either side, in search of a sign, which might hold out to him the prospect of satisfying his wants, as it was too late to think of going to the convent. Thus, walking with his eyes directed upward, he stumbled on one of these groups, and his attention was attracted by hearing them speak of designs and projects for the morrow; it appeared to him that he, who had been such a labourer in the field, had a right to give his opinion. Persuaded from all he had witnessed during the day, that, in order to secure the success of an enterprise, it was only necessary to gain the co-operation of the populace, "Gentlemen," cried he, in a tone of exordium, "allow me to offer my humble opinion. My humble opinion is this; it is not only in the matter of bread that iniquity is practised: and since we have discovered to-day, that we have only to make ourselves heard, to obtain justice, we must go on, until we obtain redress for all their other knavish tricks—until we compel them to act like Christians. Is it not true, gentlemen, that there is a band of tyrants who reverse the tenth commandment; who commit injuries on the peaceful and the poor, and in the end make it out that they act justly? And even when they have committed a greater villany than usual, they carry their heads higher then ever. There are some such even in Milan."

"Too many," said a voice.

"I say it, I do," resumed Renzo; "it has even reached our ears. And then the thing speaks for itself. By way of illustration, let us suppose one of those to whom I allude to have one foot in Milan, and the other elsewhere; if he is a devil there, will he be an angel here? Tell me, gentlemen, have you ever seen one of these people with a countenance like Ferrer's? But what renders their practices more wicked, I assure you that there are printed proclamations against them, in which their evil deeds are clearly pointed out, and a punishment assigned to each, and it is written, 'Whoever he be, ignoble and plebeian, &c. &c.' But go now to the doctors, scribes, and pharisees, and demand justice according to the proclamation; they listen to you as the pope does to rogues: it is enough to make an honest man turn rascal! It is evident, that the king and those who govern would willingly punish the villains, but they can do nothing, because there is a league among them. We must break it up, then; we must go to-morrow to Ferrer, who is a good worthy man; it was plain how delighted he was to-day to find himself among the poor; how he tried to hear what was said to him, and how kindly he answered them. We must go, then, to Ferrer, and inform him how things are situated; and I, for my part, can tell him something that will astonish him; I, who have seen with my own eyes a proclamation, with ever so many coats of arms at the head of it, and which had been made by three of the rulers; their names were printed at the bottom, and one of these names was Ferrer; this I saw with my own eyes! Now this proclamation was exactly suited to my case; so that I demanded justice from the doctor, since it was the desire of these three lords, among whom was Ferrer; but in the eyes of this very doctor, who had himself shown me this fine proclamation, I appeared to be a madman. I am sure that when this dear old man shall hear these doings, especially in the country, he will not let the world go on in this manner, but will quickly find some remedy. And then, they themselves, if they issue proclamations, they should wish to see them obeyed; for it is an insult, an epitaph, with their *name*, if counted for nothing. And if the nobility will not lower their pretensions, and cease their evil doings, we must compel them as we have done to-day. I do not say that he should go in his carriage to take all the rascals to gaol—it would need Noah's ark for that; he must give orders to those whose business it is, not only at Milan but elsewhere, to put the proclamations in force, to enter an action against such as have been guilty of those iniquities, and where the edict says, 'Prison,' then prison; where it says, 'The galleys,' the galleys; and to say to the various *podestà* that they must conduct themselves uprightly, or they shall be dismissed and others put in their place, and then, as I say, we will be there also to lend a helping hand, and to command the doctors to listen to the poor, and talk reasonably. Am I not right, gentlemen?"

Renzo had spoken so vehemently, that he had attracted the attention of the assembly, and, dropping by degrees all other discourse, they had all become his listeners. A confused clamour of applause, a "bravo! certainly! assuredly! he is right, it is but too true," followed his harangue. Critics, however, were not wanting. "It is a pretty thing, indeed," said one, "to listen to a mountaineer! they are all lawyers!" and he turned on his heel.

"Now," muttered another, "every barefooted fellow will give his opinion, and with this rage for meddling, we shall at last not have bread at a low price, and that is all that disturbs us." Compliments, however, were all that reached the ears of Renzo; they seized his hands, and exclaimed,—

"We will see you again to-morrow."

"Where?"

"On the square of the cathedral."

"Yes, very well. And something shall be done, something shall be done."

"Which of these good gentlemen will show me an inn, where I may obtain refreshment and repose for the night?" said Renzo.

"I am the one for your service, worthy youth," said one, who had listened to the sermon very attentively, but had not yet opened his mouth; "I know an inn, that will suit you exactly; I will recommend you to the keeper, who is my friend, and moreover a very honest man."

"Near by?"

"Not very far off."

The assembly dissolved; and Renzo, after many shakes of the hand, from persons unknown, followed his guide, adding many thanks for his courtesy.

"It is nothing, it is nothing," said he; "one hand washes the other, and both the face. We ought to oblige our neighbour." As they walked along, he put many questions to Renzo, by way of discourse.

"It is not from curiosity, nor to meddle with your affairs, but you appear to be fatigued. From what country do you come?"

"All the way from Lecco, all the way from Lecco."

"All the way from Lecco! Are you from Lecco?"

"From Lecco; that is to say, from the province."

"Poor youth! From what I have understood of your discourse, it appears you have been hardly treated."

"Ah! my dear and worthy man, I have been obliged to use much skill in speaking, not to make the public acquainted with my affairs; but—it is enough that they will one day be known, and then— But I see here a sign, and, by my faith, I don't wish to go farther."

"No, no; come to the place I told you of, it is but a short distance off. You will not be well accommodated here."

"Oh yes. I am not a gentleman accustomed to delicacies; any thing to satisfy my hunger; and a little straw will answer my purpose: that which I have most at heart is to find them both very soon, under Providence!" And he entered a large gate, from which hung a sign of the *Full Moon*.

"Well, I will conduct you here, since you desire it," said the unknown; and Renzo followed him.

"There is no necessity for troubling you longer," replied Renzo; "but," he added, "do me the favour to go in, and take a glass with me."

"I accept your obliging offer," said he; and preceding Renzo as being more accustomed to the house, he entered a little court-yard, approached a glass door, and opening it, advanced into the kitchen with his companion.

It was lighted by two lamps suspended from the beam of the ceiling. Many people, all busy, were seated on benches which surrounded a narrow table, occupying almost all one side of the apartment; at intervals napkins were spread, and dishes of meat; cards played, and dice thrown; and bottles and wine-glasses amid them all. *Berlinghe, reali,* and *parpagliole,* were also scattered in profusion over the table, which, could they have spoken, would probably have said, "We were this morning in a baker's counter, or in the pocket of some spectator of the tumult, who, occupied with public affairs, neglected the care of private affairs." The confusion was great; a boy ran to and fro busily engaged in attending to the dinner and gaming tables; the host was seated on a low bench under the mantle-tree of the chimney, apparently occupied in tracing figures in the ashes with the tongs, but in reality deeply attentive to all that passed around him. He raised his head at the sound of the latch, and turned towards the new comers. When he saw the guide, "Curse the fellow," said he to himself, "he must always be under my feet, when I wish him at the devil!" Casting a rapid glance towards Renzo, he continued, "I know you not; but if you come with such a hunter, you are either a dog or a hare. When you shall have spoken a few words, I shall know which of the two you are."

Nothing of this mute soliloquy could be traced, however, in the countenance of the host, who was motionless as a statue: his eyes were small and without expression, his face fat and shining, and his short and thick beard of a reddish hue.

"What are your orders, gentlemen?" said he.

"First, a good flagon of wine," said Renzo, "and then something to eat." So saying, he threw himself on a bench at one end of the table, and uttered a loud and sonorous *Ah!* as if to say, "It is a good thing to sit down after having been so long on one's feet." But recollecting the table at which he had been seated the evening before with Agnes and Lucy, he sighed deeply. The host brought the wine; his companion had seated himself opposite to him; Renzo filled a glass for him, saying, "To wet your lips," and another for himself, which he swallowed at a draught.

"What can you give me to eat?" said he, addressing the host.

"A good piece of stewed meat," replied he.

"Well, sir, a good piece of stewed meat."

"You shall be served immediately," said the host, and calling to the boy, "Serve this gentleman. But," resumed he, turning again to Renzo, "I have no bread to-day."

"As for bread," said Renzo, in a loud voice, and laughing, "Providence has provided that." And he drew forth the third and last loaf, picked up under the cross of St. *Dionigi*, and holding it up, cried, "Here is the bread of Providence!"

At this exclamation many of the company turned round, and seeing this trophy in the air, one of them cried, "Bread for ever at a low price!"

"At a low price!" said Renzo; "*gratis et amore.*"

"Better still, better still."

"But," added he, "I do not wish these gentlemen to think evil of me. I have not stolen it—I found it on the ground; and if I could find the owner, I am ready to pay him."

"Bravo, bravo!" cried they, laughing louder still, not imagining that he was in earnest.

"They think that I jest, but it is really so," said Renzo to his guide, and turning the bread in his hand; "see how they have formed it—you would call it a cake, but they were so packed one on the other. If there were any with the crust a little tender, one might know they were fresh." Then devouring three or four mouthfulls of the bread, he washed them down with another glass of wine, adding, "The bread will not go down alone—my throat was never so dry—a glorious uproar we made!"

"Prepare a good bed for this young man," said the guide; "he is going to pass the night here."

"Do you wish to sleep here?" said the host to Renzo, approaching the table.

"Certainly; I shall be content with any bed, provided the sheets are white; for although poor, I am accustomed to cleanliness."

"Oh, as to that—" said the host. So saying, he went to his counter, which was in a corner of the kitchen, and returned, bringing in his hand paper, pen, and ink.

"What does this mean?" swallowing a piece of the stew which had been placed before him, and smiling with an air of surprise; "is that the white sheet?"

The host, without replying, placed the paper on the table, and himself in an attitude to write, and with the pen in his hand, leaning towards Renzo, he said, "Do me the favour to tell me your name and country."

"What!" said Renzo, "what has this to do with the bed?"

"I do my duty," said the host, looking at the guide. "We are obliged to give an exact account of all who lodge at our house. *Name and surname, and from what country they are; why they are here; if they have arms; and how long they expect to remain in the city.* These are the very words of the proclamation."

Before answering, Renzo emptied another glass; it was the third, but I fear for the future we shall not find it possible to count them. "Ah, ah!" exclaimed he, "you have the proclamation. Well, I pride myself on being a doctor of laws, and I know what importance is attached to proclamations."

"I speak in earnest," said the host, looking again at the mute companion of Renzo; and returning to his desk, he drew from it a large sheet of paper, which he unfolded before Renzo, as an exact copy of the proclamation.

"Ah! there it is!" cried he, quickly emptying the contents of the glass which he held in his hand. "Ah! there it is! the fine sheet! I rejoice to see it. I know these arms; I know what this pagan head means with a noose around its neck." (The proclamations of that time were headed by the arms of the governor, and in those of Don Gonzalo Fernandez de Cordova was seen a Moorish king, chained by the throat.) "This face means, Command who can, and obey who will. When the Signor Don—shall have been sent to the galleys—well, well, I know what I would say—I have seen another leaf just like this. When he shall have so taken measures that an honest young man can, without molestation, marry her to whom he is betrothed, and by whom he is beloved, then I will tell my name to this face, and will give him a kiss in the bargain. I may have very good reasons for not telling my name; it's a fine thing, truly! And if a robber, who might have under his command a band of villains, because if he were alone—" He hesitated a moment, finishing the phrase with a gesture, and then proceeded, "If a robber wished to know who I was, in order to do me some evil turn, I ask you if that face would move from the paper to help me. Am I obliged to tell my business? Truly, this is something new. Suppose, for instance, that I have come to Milan to confess—I would wish to do it to a capuchin father, and not to the landlord of an inn."

The host kept silence, looking at the guide, who appeared not to notice any thing that passed. Renzo, it grieves us to say, swallowed another glass, and continued, "I will give you reasons enough to satisfy you, my dear host; if those proclamations which speak favourably of good Christians are worth nothing, those which speak unfavourably are worth less than nothing. Take away, then, all these encumbrances, and bring in exchange another flagon, because this one is broken." So saying, he struck it lightly with his hand, adding, "Don't you hear how it is cracked?"

The discourse of Renzo had again attracted the general attention of the company, and when he concluded, there was a general murmur of applause.

"What must I do?" said the host, looking at the strange companion, who was, however, no stranger to him.

"Yes, yes," cried many of the company, "this countryman is right; they are vexatious impositions. New laws to-day! new laws to-day!"

The stranger took advantage of the noise to say to the host, in a tone of reproach for his too abrupt demand, "Leave him to his own way a little; do not raise a disturbance."

"I have done my duty," said the host aloud, "and secured myself," continued he, lowering his voice; "and that is all I care for." He removed the pen, ink, and paper, and gave the empty flagon to the boy.

"Bring the same kind of wine," said Renzo, "for it suits my taste exactly; and we will send it to sleep with the other, without asking its name, surname, nor what is its business, nor whether it is going to remain long in this city."

"Of the same kind," said the host to the boy, giving him the flagon, and returning to his seat by the chimney. "He is no other than a hare," thought he, raking in the ashes. "And in what hands art thou fallen, poor silly youth! If you will drown, drown; but the host of the *Full Moon* will not go halves with thy folly."

Renzo returned thanks to his guide, and to all those who had taken his side. "Worthy friends," said he, "I know that honest people support each other." Then striking the table, and placing himself in the attitude of an orator, "Is it not an unheard of thing," cried he, "that those who govern must always introduce paper, pen, and ink? Always the pen in hand! Such a passion for the pen!"

"Eh! young and worthy stranger! would you know the reason?" said one of the gamesters, laughing.

"Let us hear it," replied Renzo.

"The reason is, as these lords eat geese, they have so many quills, they know not what to do with them."

"Oh, oh!" said Renzo, "you are a poet! You have poets here, then? I have also a vein for poetry, and I sometimes make verses—but it is when things go on well."

To comprehend this witticism of poor Renzo, it is necessary to be informed, that in the eyes of the vulgar of Milan, and more particularly in its environs, the name of poet did not signify, as among cultivated people, a sublime genius, an inhabitant of Pindus, a pupil of the muses, but a whimsicality and eccentricity in discourse and conduct, which had more of singularity than sense; and an absurd wresting of words from their legitimate signification.

"But I will tell the true reason," added Renzo, "it is because they themselves hold the pen, and, therefore, they do not record their own words; but let a poor man speak, they are very attentive, and in a moment, *there* it is, in black and white for some future occasion. They are cunning, also; and when they want to perplex a poor youth, who does not know how to read, but who has a little—I know well—" beating his forehead with his hand, and pointing to it with his finger, to make himself understood; "and when they perceive that he begins to comprehend the difficulty, they throw into the conversation some Latin, to make him lose the thread of their argument, to put him at his wits' end, to confuse his brains. This custom must be broken up: to-day, every thing has been done after the people's fashion, without paper, pen, and ink. To-morrow, if they know how to conduct themselves, we shall do still better, without hurting a hair of any one's head; all in the way of justice."

In the mean while some of the company had engaged again in play, and some in eating; some went away, others came in their place. The unknown guide continued to remain; and without appearing to have any business to detain him, lingered to talk a little more with Renzo, and resumed the conversation about bread.

"If I had the control, I would order things better," said he.

"What would you do?" said Renzo, endeavouring to exhibit every appearance of attention.

"What would I do? Every one should have bread—the poor as well as the rich."

"Ah! that is right."

"See how I would do. I would fix a reasonable rate within the ability of every one; then bread should be distributed according to the number of mouths, because there are gluttons who seize all they can get for themselves, and leave the poor still in want. We must then divide it. And how shall we do this? Why in this way. Give a ticket to every family in proportion to the mouths, to authorise them to get bread from the bakers. For example: they give me a ticket expressed in this manner; Ambrose Fusella, by trade a sword cutler, with a wife and four children, all old enough to eat bread (mind that); he must be furnished with so much bread at such a price. But the thing must be done in order, always with regard to the number of mouths. For instance, they should give you a ticket for—your name?"

"Lorenzo Tramaglino," said the young man, who, enchanted with the project, did not reflect that it all depended on pen, ink, and paper; and that the first point towards its success was to collect the names of the persons to be served.

"Very well," said the unknown; "but have you a wife and children?"

"I ought to have—children, no—not yet—but a wife—if people had acted as their duty required—"

"Ah, you are single! then have patience; they will only give you a smaller portion."

"That is but just. But if soon, as I hope—by the help of God—enough; suppose I have a wife."

"Then the ticket must be changed, and the portion increased, as I have said, according to the mouths," replied the unknown, rising.

"That would be very good," cried Renzo, thumping the table with his fist; "and why don't they make such a law?"

"How can I tell you? meanwhile I wish you a good night, as my wife and children must have been expecting me this long while."

"Another drop, another drop," filling his glass, and endeavouring to force him to sit down again; "another drop!"

But his friend contrived to disengage himself; and leaving Renzo, pouring forth a torrent of entreaties and reproaches, he departed. Renzo continued to talk until he was in the street, and then fell back on his seat. He looked at the glass which he had filled to the brim; and seeing the boy pass before the table, he beckoned to him, as if he had something particular to communicate. He pointed to the glass, and with a tone of solemnity said, "See there! I prepared it for that worthy man; you see it is full, as it should be for a friend; but he would not have it. Sometimes people have singular ideas; however, I have shown my good will; but now, since the thing is done, it must not be lost." So saying, he emptied it at one draught.

"I understand," said the boy, moving off.

"You understand too, do you? It is true, when the reasons are sufficient—"

Here we have need of all our love of truth to induce us to pursue faithfully our hero's history; at the same time this same impartiality leads us to inform the reader, that this was his first error of a similar character; and precisely because he was so unaccustomed to merry-making did this prove so fatal. The few glasses of wine which he swallowed so rapidly, contrary to his custom, partly to cool his throat, and partly from an exaltation of spirits, which deprived him of the power of reflection, went immediately to his head. Upon an habitual drinker it would have produced no visible effect; our author observes this, that "temperate and moderate habits have this advantage, that the more a man practises them, the more he finds a departure from them to be disagreeable and inconvenient; so that his fault itself serves as a lesson to him for the future."

However this may be, when these first fumes had mounted to the brain of Renzo, wine and words continued to flow without rule or reason. He felt a great desire to speak, and for a while his words were arranged with some degree of order, but by little and little he found it difficult to form a connected sentence. The thoughts which presented themselves to his mind were cloudy and indistinct, and his expressions, in consequence, unconnected and obscure: to relieve his perplexity, by one of those false instincts which, under similar circumstances, lead men to the accomplishment of their own ruin, he had recourse to the flagon.

We will relate only a few of the words which he continued to ejaculate, during the remainder of this miserable evening. "Ah! host, host," resumed he, following him with his eye around the table, or gazing at him where he was not, and taking no notice of the noise of the company, "host that thou art! I cannot swallow it—this request of name, surname, and business. To a peaceable youth like me! you have not behaved well! what satisfaction, what advantage, what pleasure—to put a poor youth on paper? Am I not right—speak, gentlemen? Hosts should stand by good fellows. Listen, listen, host, I wish to make a comparison for you—for the reason—They laugh, do they? I am a little gay, I know; but the reasons, I say, are just. Tell me, if you please, who is it that brings custom to your house? Poor young men, is it not? Do these lords, they of the proclamations, ever come here to wet their lips?"

"They are all water-drinkers," said one who sat near Renzo.

"They wish to keep possession of their understandings, so as to tell lies skilfully," added another.

"Ah!" cried Renzo, "that is the poet who spoke. Then hear my reasons. Answer me, host. Ferrer, who is the best of all of them, has he ever been here to drink the health of any one, and to spend so much as a farthing? And this dog of an assassin, this Don —? I must be silent, because I am too much in the humour for babbling. Ferrer, and Father Crr—, I know, are two honest men. But there are few honest men. The old are worse than the young; and the young—are much worse than the old. I am glad there was no blood shed, these are things we must leave to the hangman. Bread! Oh yes, for that I have had many a thrust, but I have also given some. Make way! Abundance! *vivat!* And Ferrer too—some words in Latin,—*Si es baraos trapolorum.* Cursed fault! *vivat!* justice! bread! Ah, those are good words! We had need of them. When we heard that cursed ton, ton, ton, and then again, ton, ton, ton, the question was not of flight; but hold the signor curate to—I, I know what I am thinking of."

At these words he hung down his head, and remained for a time as if absorbed by some new imagination; then, sighing deeply, he raised it again, and looked up with such a mournful and silly expression, as excited the amusement of all around. In short, he became the laughingstock of the whole company. Not that they were all perfectly sober, but, to say truth, they were so in comparison with poor Renzo. They provoked and angered him with silly questions, and with mock civilities; sometimes he pretended to be offended, then, without noticing them at all, spoke of other things; then replied, then interrogated, and always wide of the mark. By good fortune, in his folly, he seemed from instinct to avoid pronouncing the names of persons; so that the one most deeply graven in his memory was not uttered. We should have been sorry ourselves if this name, for which we feel so much love and respect, had passed from mouth to mouth, and been made a theme of jesting by these vulgar and degraded wretches.

Chapter XV.

The host, seeing that the game was about to be carried too far, approached Renzo, and entreating the others to be quiet, endeavoured to make him understand that he had best go to bed. But our mountaineer could think of nothing but _name, surname, and *proclamations*; yet the words *bed* and *sleep*, repeated frequently in his ear, made at last some impression, and producing a sort of lucid interval, made him feel that he really had need of both. The little sense that remained to him enabled him to perceive that the greater part of the company had departed; and with his hands resting on the table before him, he endeavoured to stand on his feet; his efforts would have been, however, unavailing, without the assistance of the host, who led him from between the table and the bench, and taking a lantern in one hand, managed partly to lead and partly to drag him to the stairs, and thence up the narrow staircase to the room designed for him. At the sight of the bed, he endeavoured to look kindly upon the host; but his eyes at one time sparkled, at another disappeared, like two fireflies: he endeavoured to stand erect, and stretched out his hand to pat the shoulder of his host in testimony of his gratitude; but in this he failed: however he did succeed in saying, "Worthy host, I see now that you are an honest man; but I don't like your rage for *name* and *surname*. Happily I am also—"

The host, who did not expect to hear him utter one connected idea, and who knew from experience how prone men in his situation were to sudden changes of feeling, wishing to profit by this lucid interval, made another attempt. "My dear fellow," said he, in a tone of persuasion, "I have not intended to vex you, nor to pry into your affairs. What would you have had me do? There is a law, and if we innkeepers do not obey it, we shall be the first to be punished; therefore it is better to conform. And after all, as regards yourself, what is it? A hard thing, indeed! just to say two words. It is not for them, but to do me a favour. Now, here, between ourselves, tell me your *name*, and then you shall go to bed in peace."

"Ah, rascal! knave!" cried Renzo, "do you dare to bring up this cursed *name* and *surname* and *business* again?"

"Hush! you fool! and go to bed," said the host.

But Renzo continued to bellow, "I understand it, you belong to the league. Wait, wait, till I settle matters for you;" and turning to the door, he bellowed down the stairs, "Friends! the host is of the——"

"I spoke in jest," cried the host, pushing him towards the bed, "in jest; did you not perceive I spoke in jest?"

"Ah, in jest; now you talk reasonably. Since you said it in jest—they are just the thing to make a jest of——." And he fell on the bed. "Undress yourself quickly," said the host; and adding his assistance to his advice, the thought occurred to him, to ascertain if there were any money in Renzo's pockets, as on the morrow it would fall into hands from which an innkeeper would have but little chance of recovering it; he therefore hazarded another attempt, saying to Renzo, "You are an honest youth, are you not?"

"Yes, an honest youth," replied Renzo, still endeavouring to rid himself of his clothes.

"Well, settle this little account with me now, because to-morrow I am obliged to leave home on business."

"That's right," said Renzo "I am honest. But the money—we must find the money—!"

"Here it is," said the host; and calling up all his patience and skill, he succeeded in obtaining the reckoning.

"Lend me your hand to finish undressing, host," said Renzo; "I begin to comprehend, do you see, that—I am very sleepy."

The host rendered him the desired service, and covering him with the quilt, bade him "Good night."

The words were scarcely uttered before poor Renzo snored. The host stopped to contemplate him a moment by the light of his lantern; "Mad blockhead!" said he to the poor sleeper, "thou hast accomplished thy own ruin! dunces, who want to travel over the world, without knowing where the sun rises, to entangle themselves with affairs they know nothing of, to their own injury and that of their neighbour!"

So saying, he left the apartment, having locked the door outside, and calling to his wife, told her to take his place in the kitchen, "Because," said he, "I must go out for a while, thanks to a stranger who is here, unhappily for me;" he then briefly related the annoying circumstance, adding, "And now keep an eye on all, and above all be prudent. There is below a company of dissolute fellows, who, between drink and their natural disposition, are very very free of speech. Enough—if any of them should dare—"

"Oh! I am not a child! I know what I ought to do. It could never be said—"

"Well, well. Be careful to make them pay. If they talk of the superintendant of provision, the governor, Ferrer, and the council of ten, and the gentry, and Spain and France, and other follies, pretend not to hear them, because, if you contradict them, it may go ill with you now, and if you argue with them, it may go ill with you hereafter; and take care, when you hear any dangerous remarks, turn away your head, and call out 'Coming, sir.' I will endeavour to return as soon as possible."

So saying, he descended with her into the kitchen, put on his hat and cloak, and taking a cudgel in his hand, departed. As he walked along the road, he resumed the thread of his apostrophe to poor Renzo. "Headstrong mountaineer!"—for that Renzo was such, had been manifest from his pronunciation, countenance, and manners, although he vainly tried to conceal it,—"on a day like this, when by dint of skill and prudence I had kept my hands clean, you must come at the end of it to spoil all I have done! Are there not inns enough in Milan, that you must come to mine! at least, if you had been alone, I would have winked at it for to-night, and made you understand matters to-morrow. But no; my gentleman must come in company, and, to do the thing better, in company with an informer."

At this moment he perceived a patrole of soldiers approaching; drawing on one side to let them pass, and eyeing them askance, he continued, "There go the fool-punishers. And thou, great booby, because thou saw'st a few people making a little noise, thou must think the world was turned upside down; and on this fine foundation thou hast ruined thyself and would have ruined me; I have done all I could to save thee, now thou must get thyself out of trouble. As if I wanted to know thy name from curiosity! What was it to me whether it were Thaddeus or Bartholomew? I have truly great satisfaction in taking a pen in my hand! I know well enough that there are proclamations which are disregarded; just as if we had need of a mountaineer to tell us that! And dost thou not know, thou fool! what would be done to a poor innkeeper, who should be of thy opinion (since upon them the proclamation bear hardest), and should not inform himself of the name of any one who did him the favour to lodge at his house. *Under penalty of whoever of the above-said hosts, tavern keepers, and others, of three hundred crowns,*—behold three hundred crowns hatched; and now to spend them well,—*two thirds to be applied to the royal chamber, and the other third to the accuser or informer. And in case of inability, five years in the galleys, and greater pecuniary and corporal punishments, at the discretion of his Excellency.* Very much obliged for such favours, indeed!" He ended his soliloquy, finding himself at his destined point, the palace of the *Capitano di Giustizia.*

There, as in all the offices of the secretaries, there was a great deal of business going on; on all sides, persons were employed in issuing orders to ensure the peace of the following day, to take from rebellion every pretext, to cool the audacity of those who were desirous of fresh disorders, and to concentrate power in the hands of those accustomed to exercise it. The number of the soldiers who protected the house of the superintendant was increased; the ends of the streets were defended by large pieces of timber thrown across them; the bakers were ordered to bake bread without intermission; expresses were sent to all the surrounding villages, with orders to send corn into the city; and at every baker's some of the nobility were stationed, to watch over the distribution, and to restrain the discontented by fair words and the authority of their presence. But to give, as they said, a blow to the hoop, and another to the cask, and increase the efficacy of their caresses by a little awe, they took measures to seize some of the seditious, and this was the principal duty of the *Capitano di Giustizia.* His blood-hounds had been in the field since the commencement of the tumult; and this self-styled Ambrose Fusella was a police officer in disguise, who, having listened to the famous sermon of Renzo, concluded him to be fair game. Finding that he had but newly arrived from his village, he would have conducted him immediately to prison, as the safest inn in the city; but in this, as we have seen, he did not succeed. He could, however, carry to the police certain information of his *name, surname,* and *country,* besides many other conjectures; so that when the host arrived to tell what he knew of Renzo, their knowledge was already more precise than his. He entered the accustomed hall, and gave in his deposition, that a stranger had come to lodge at his house, who would not tell his name.

"You have done your duty in giving us the information," said a notary, laying down his pen; "but we know it already."

"That is very singular!" thought the host; "you must have a great deal of cunning."

"And we know also," continued the notary, "this famous name."

"The devil! the name also. How do they know that?" thought the host again.

"But," resumed the notary, with a serious air, "you do not tell all."

"What is there more to tell?"

"Ah! ah! we know well that this man carried to your house a quantity of stolen bread—bread acquired by theft and sedition."

"A man comes with bread in his pocket; am I to know where he got it? if it was on my death-bed, I can say, I only saw him have one loaf."

"Thus it is! you are always excusing and defending yourselves! If we were to take your word for it, you are all honest people. How can you prove that this bread was honestly acquired?"

"Why need I prove it? it is nothing to me. I am an innkeeper."

"You cannot, however, deny, that this, your customer, had the audacity to complain of the proclamations, and make indecent jokes on the arms of his Excellency."

"Pardon me, signor; how could he be my customer, when I never saw him before? It was the devil, saving your presence, who sent him to my house. If I had known him, there would have been no need of asking his name, as your honour knows."

"However, in your inn, and in your presence, seditious and inflammatory conversation has been held; your customers have been riotous, clamorous, and complaining."

"How would your honour expect me to pay attention to the absurdities uttered by a parcel of brawlers. I attend only to my own affairs, for I am a poor man. And then your honour knows, that those who are lavish of their tongue, are often lavish of their fists, especially when there are many together."

"Yes, yes, they may have their way now; to-morrow—to-morrow, we will see if the heat is dislodged from their brains. What do you think?"

"I don't know."

"That the mob will become masters in Milan?"

"Certainly!"

"You shall see, you shall see."

"I understand—I know the king will be always the king; but he who has taken any thing will keep it. Naturally a poor father of a family has no desire to give back; your honours have the power; that belongs to you."

"Have you still some people at your house?"

"A number."

"And this your customer, what is he about? Is he still labouring to excite the people to sedition?"

"This stranger, your honour means; he is gone to sleep."

"Then you have a number? Well, be careful not to let them go away."

"Am I to play the constable?" thought the host, but said nothing.

"Return to your house, and be prudent," resumed the notary.

"I have always been prudent. Your honour can say that I have never made any disturbance."

"Well, well; but do not think that justice has lost its power."

"I! Good heavens! I think nothing. I am an innkeeper."

"The same old tune. Have you nothing more to say?"

"What else would your honour have me say? Truth is one."

"Well; you have done enough for to-day: but to-morrow, we will see; you must give more full information, and answer all questions that shall be put to you."

"What information have I to give? I know nothing; I have hardly brains enough to attend to my own affairs."

"Take care not to let him go away."

"I hope your honour will remember that I have done my duty. Your honour's humble servant."

On the following morning, Renzo was still in a sound and deep sleep, when he was suddenly roused by a shaking of the arms, and by a voice at the foot of the bed, crying, "Lorenzo Tramaglino!" He sat up, and rubbing his eyes, perceived a man clothed in black standing at the foot of his bed, and two others, one on each side of the bolster. Between surprise, sleep, and the fumes of the wine, he remained a moment stupified, believing himself to be still dreaming.

"Ah! you have heard at last! Lorenzo Tramaglino," said the man in black, the notary of the preceding evening. "Up, up; get up, and come with us."

"Lorenzo Tramaglino!" said Renzo Tramaglino. "What does this mean? What do you want with me? Who has told you my name?"

"Few words, and get up quickly," said one of the men at his side, seizing him by the arm.

"Oh! oh! what violence is this?" cried Renzo, drawing away his arm. "Host! oh! host!"

"Shall we carry him off in his shirt?" said one of the officers; turning to the notary.

"Did you hear what he said?" said he to Renzo; "we will do so, if you do not rise quickly, and come with us!"

"Why?" demanded Renzo.

"You will hear that from the *Capitano di Giustizia*."

"I! I am an honest man; I have done nothing; I am astonished—"

"So much the better for you! so much the better for you! In two words you will be dismissed, and then go about your affairs."

"Let me go now, then; there is no reason why I should go before the *capitano*."

"Come, let us finish the business," said an officer.

"We shall be obliged to carry him off!" said the other.

"Lorenzo Tramaglino!" said the notary.

"How does your honour know my name?"

"Do your duty," said he to the men, who attempted to draw Renzo from the bed.

"Oh! don't touch me! I can dress *myself*."

"Dress yourself, then, and get up," said the notary.

"I will," said Renzo, and he gathered his clothes, scattered here and there on the bed, like the fragments of a shipwreck on the coast. Whilst engaged in the act of dressing, he continued, "but I will not go to the *Capitano di Giustizia*; I have nothing to do with him: since you put this affront on me, I wish to be conducted to Ferrer; I am acquainted with him; I know he is an honest man, and he is under obligations to me."

"Yes, yes, my good fellow, you shall be conducted to Ferrer," replied the notary.

In other circumstances he would have laughed heartily at the absurdity of such a proposition, but he felt that this was not a moment for merriment. On his way to the inn, he had perceived so many people abroad, such a stirring—some collecting in small quantities, others gathering in crowds—that he was not able to determine whether they were the remnants of the old insurrection not entirely suppressed, or the beginnings of a new one. And now, without appearing to do so, he listened, and thought the buzzing increased. He felt haste to be of importance; but he did not dare to take Renzo against his will, lest, finding himself in the street, he might take advantage of public sympathy, and endeavour to escape from his hands. He made a sign to his officers to be patient, and not exasperate the youth; whilst he himself sought to appease him with fair words.

Renzo meanwhile began to have a confused recollection of the events of the preceding day, and to comprehend that the *proclamations, name,* and *surname,* were the cause of all this trouble; but how the devil did this man know his name? And what the devil had happened during the night, that they should come to lay hands on one, who, the day before, had such a voice in the assembly, which could not be yet dispersed, because he also heard a growing murmur in the street. He perceived also the agitation which the notary vainly endeavoured to conceal; therefore, to feel his pulse, and clear up his own conjectures, as well as to gain time, he said, "I comprehend the cause of all this, it is on account of the *name* and *surname.* Last night, 'tis true, I was a little merry; these hosts have such treacherous wine and, you know, often when wine passes through the channel of speech, it will have its say too. But if that is all the difficulty, I am ready to give you every satisfaction. Besides, you know my name already. Who the devil told it to you?"

"Bravo! my good fellow, bravo!" replied the notary in a tone of encouragement. "I see you are in the right, and you must believe that I am also. I am only following my trade. You are more tractable than others. It is the easiest way to get out of the difficulty quickly. With such an accommodating spirit, you will soon be set at liberty; but my hands are tied, and I cannot release you now, although I would wish to do so. Be of good courage, and come on boldly. When they see who you are—and I will tell—Leave it to me—quick, quick, my good fellow!"

"Ah! you cannot! I understand," said Renzo. "Shall we pass by the square of the cathedral?"

"Where you choose. We will go the shortest road, that you may be the sooner at liberty," said he, inwardly cursing his stars at being unable to follow up this mysterious demand of Renzo's, which might have been made the subject of a hundred interrogatories. "Miserable that I am!" thought he, "here is a fellow fallen into my hands, who likes no better fun than to prate. Were there but a little time, he would confess all in the way of friendly discourse, without the aid of rope. Ay! and without perceiving it too. But that he should fall into my hands at such an unlucky moment.—Well, it can't be helped," thought he, while turning his head and listening to the noise without, "there is no remedy: this will be a hotter day than yesterday!"

That which gave rise to this last thought was an extraordinary uproar in the street, which tempted him to open the window and reconnoitre. There was a concourse of citizens, who, at the order given them by the patrole to separate, had resisted for a while, and then moved off, on all sides, in evident discontent. It was a fatal sign to the eyes of the notary, that the soldiers treated them with much politeness. He closed the window, and remained for a moment undecided, whether he should conduct the enterprise to an end, or, leaving Renzo in the care of the bailiffs, go himself to the *Capitano di Giustizia*, and relate the whole difficulty. "But," thought he, "he will tell me I am a poltroon, a coward, and that it was my business to execute orders. We are at the ball; we must dance, it seems. Cursed crowd! what a damned business!" He, however addressed Renzo in a tone of kind entreaty, "Come, my worthy fellow, do let us be off, and make haste."

Renzo, however, was not without his thoughts. He was almost dressed, with the exception of his doublet, into the pockets of which he was fumbling. "Oh!" said he, regarding the notary significantly, "Oh! I had a letter, and some money here, once, sir!"

"When these formalities are over, all shall be faithfully restored to you. Come, come, let us be off."

"No, no, no!" said Renzo, shaking his head, "that won't do: I must have what belongs to me, sir. I will render an account of my actions, but I must have what belongs to me."

"I will show you that I have confidence in you; here they are. And now make haste," said the notary, drawing from his bosom the sequestered goods, and consigning them, with something like a sigh, to Renzo, who muttered between his teeth, as he put them in his pocket, "You have so much to do with thieves, that you have learned the trade!"

"If I get you once safe out of the house, you shall pay this with interest," thought the notary.

As Renzo was putting on his hat, the notary made a sign to the officers, that one of them should go before, and the other follow the prisoner; and as they passed through the kitchen, and whilst Renzo was saying, "And this blessed host, where has he fled?" they seized, one his right hand, the other the left, and skilfully slipped over his wrists, hand-fetters, as they were called, which, according to the customs of the times, consisted of a cord, a little longer than the usual size of the fist, which had at the two ends two small pieces of wood. The cord encircled the wrist of the patient; the captor held the pegs in his hand, so that he could, by twisting them, tighten the cord at will, and this enabled him, not only to secure the prisoner, but also to torment him, if restless; and, to ensure this more effectually, the cord was full of knots.

Renzo struggled and exclaimed, "What treachery is this? to an honest man!" But the notary, who had fair words prepared for every occasion, said, "Be patient, they only do their duty. What would you have? It is a mere ceremony. We cannot treat people as we would wish. If we did not obey orders, we should be worse off than you. Be patient."

As he spoke, the two operators twisted the pegs; Renzo plunged like a skittish horse upon the bit, and cried, "Patience, indeed!"

"But, worthy young man," said the notary, "it is the only way to come off well in these affairs. It is troublesome, I confess, but it will soon be over; and since I see you so well disposed, I feel an inclination to serve you, and will give you another piece of advice for your good, which is, to pass on quietly, looking neither to right nor left, so as to attract notice. If you do this, no one will pay any attention to you, and you will preserve your honour. In one hour you will be at liberty. There are so many other things to be done, that your business will soon be despatched; and then I will tell them——. You shall have your liberty, and no one will know you have been in the hands of the law. And you," pursued he, addressing his followers in a tone of severity, "do him no harm, because I take him under my protection. You must do your duty, I know; but remember that this is a worthy and honest youth, who in a little while will be at liberty, and who has a regard for his honour. Let nothing appear but that you are three peaceable men, walking together. You understand me!" and smoothing his brow, and twisting his face into a gracious smile, he said to Renzo, "A little prudence,—do as I tell you; do not look about; trust to one who has your interest at heart! And now let us begone." And the convoy moved forward.

But of all these fine speeches Renzo believed not a word. He understood very well the fears that prevailed over the mind of the notary, and his exhortations only served to confirm him in his purpose to escape; and to this end to act directly contrary to the advice given him. No one must conclude from this that the notary was an inexperienced knave. On the contrary, he was master of his trade, but at the present moment his spirits were agitated. At another time he would have ridiculed any one for pursuing the measures he had now himself employed, but his agitation had deprived him of his accustomed cunning and self-possession. We would recommend, therefore, to all knaves by trade, to maintain on all occasions their *sang froid*, or, what is better, never to place themselves in difficult circumstances.

Renzo, then, hardly found himself in the street, when he began to look around, and listen eagerly. There was not, however, an extraordinary concourse of people; and although on the countenance of more than one passer-by you could read an expression of discontent and sedition, yet each one pursued his way in quietness.

"Prudence! prudence!" murmured the notary behind him. "Your honour, young man, your honour."

But when Renzo heard three men, who were approaching, talk of a bakery, of flour concealed, of justice, he began to make signs to them, and cough in such a manner, as indicated any thing but a cold. They looked attentively at the convoy, and stopped; others who had passed by, turned back, and kept themselves a short distance off.

"Take care; be prudent, my good fellow; do not spoil all; your honour, your reputation," said the notary in a low voice, but unheeded by Renzo. The men again twisted the pegs.

"Ah! ah! ah!" cried the prisoner. At this cry the crowd thickened around; they gathered from all parts of the street. The convoy was stopped! "He is a wicked fellow," said the notary in a whisper to those nearest him; "he is a thief taken in the fact. Draw back, and let justice have its way." But Renzo perceived that the occasion was favourable: he saw the officers pale and almost dead with fright. "If I do not help myself now," thought he, "so much the worse for me;" and raising his voice, he cried, "My friends; they are carrying me off, because I cried, 'Bread! and justice!' yesterday. I have done nothing; I am an honest man! Help me, do not abandon me, my friends."

He was answered by a light murmur, which soon changed to an unanimous cry in his favour. The officers ordered, requested, and entreated those nearest them to go off, and leave their passage free; but the crowd continued to press around. The officers, at the sight of the danger, left their prisoner, and endeavoured to lose themselves in the throng, for the purpose of escaping without being observed; and the notary desired heartily to do the same, but found it more difficult on account of his black cloak. Pale as death, he endeavoured, by twisting his body to work his way through the crowd. He studied to appear a stranger, who, passing accidentally, had found himself in the crowd like a bit of straw in the ice; and finding himself face to face with a man who looked at him more intently and sternly than the rest, he composed his countenance to a smile, and asked, "What is this confusion?"

"Oh! you ugly raven!" replied he. "A raven! a raven!" resounded from all sides. To the cries they added threats, so that, finally, partly with his own legs, partly with the elbows of others, he succeeded in obtaining a release from the squabble.

Chapter XVI.

"Fly, fly, honest man! Here is a convent, there is a church; this way! this way!" was shouted to Renzo from every side. The advice was not necessary; from the moment that he conceived the hope of extricating himself from the talons of the police, he had determined, if he succeeded, to depart immediately, not only from the city, but the dukedom. "Because," thought he, "however they may have procured it, they have my name on their books; and with name and surname, they will take me again if they choose to do so." As to an asylum, he was determined not to have recourse to it, but in the last extremity. "Because," thought he, "if I can be a bird of the woods, I will not be a bird of the cage." He then determined to seek his cousin Bartolo in the territory of Bergamo, who had often urged him to establish himself there; but to find the road was the difficulty! In a part of the city entirely unknown to him, he did not know which gate led to Bergamo; nor if he had known it, would he have been able to find it. He thought a moment of asking directions from his liberators, but he had for some time had strange suspicions with regard to the obliging sword-cutler, father of four children; so that he did not dare openly declare his design, lest, amidst the crowd, there might be another of the same stamp. He determined therefore to hasten from this spot, and ask the way when he should arrive at a place where there would be nothing to fear from the curiosity or the character of others. He said to his liberators, "Thanks, a thousand thanks! friends! may Heaven reward you!" and quitting the crowd through a passage made for him, he ran down lanes and narrow streets, without knowing whither.

When he thought himself sufficiently removed from the scene of peril, he slackened his steps, and began to look around for some countenance which might inspire him with confidence enough to make his enquiries. But the enquiry would of itself be suspicious; time pressed; the police, recovering from their fright, would, without doubt, pursue their fugitive; the noise of his escape might have reached even there; and in so great a multitude Renzo might pass many judgments in physiognomy before he should find one which seemed favourable. After suffering many to pass whose appearance was unpropitious, he at last summoned courage to address a man, who seemed in such haste, that Renzo deemed he would not hesitate to answer his questions, in order to get rid of him. "Will you be so good, sir, as to tell me through which gate to go to Bergamo?"

"To Bergamo? through the eastern gate. Take this street to the left; you will come to the square of the cathedral; then—"

"That is enough, sir; I know the way after that; God reward you!" And he went on hastily by the way pointed out to him, and arrived at the square of the cathedral. He crossed it, passed by the remains of the extinguished bonfire, at which he had assisted the day before; the bake-house of the Crutches half demolished, and still guarded by soldiers; and finally, reaching the convent of the capuchins, and looking at the door of the church, he said to himself, sighing, "The friar gave me good advice yesterday, when he told me it would be best for me to wait patiently in the church." He stopped a moment, and seeing that many persons guarded the gate through which he had to pass, he felt a repugnance to confront them; and hesitated whether it would not be his wisest plan to seek this asylum and deliver his letter. But he soon resumed courage, saying, "A bird of the woods as long as I can be. Who knows me? Certainly the police cannot be waiting for me at all the gates." He looked around, therefore, and perceiving that no one appeared to notice him, and, whistling as he went, as if from carelessness, he approached the gate. A company of custom-house officers, with a reinforcement of Spanish soldiers, were stationed precisely at its entrance, to keep out persons from abroad, who might be attracted, by the noise of the tumult, to rush into the city; their attention was therefore directed beyond the gate, and Renzo, taking advantage of this, contrived, with a quiet and demure look, to pass through, as if he were some peaceful traveller; but his heart beat violently. He pursued a path on the right, to avoid the high road, and for some distance did not dare to look behind him.

On! on! he passed hamlets and villages, without asking the name of them; hoping that, whilst he was removing from Milan, he was approaching Bergamo. He looked behind him from time to time, while pressing onwards, and rubbing first one wrist, then the other, which bore the red marks from the painful pressure of the manacles. His thoughts were a confused medley of repentance, anxiety, and resentment; and he wearily retraced the circumstances of the preceding night, to ascertain what had plunged him into these difficulties, and above all, how they came to know his name. His suspicions rested on the cutler, whose curiosity he well remembered, and he had also a confused recollection that after his departure he had continued to talk, but with whom, his memory did not serve to inform him. The poor fellow was lost in these speculations; the past was a chaos.

He then endeavoured to form some plan for the future; but all other considerations were soon swallowed up in the necessity which he was under of ascertaining the road; and to do this, he was obliged to address himself to some one. He was reluctant to name Bergamo, lest it might excite suspicion: why it should, he knew not; but his mind was a prey to vague apprehensions of evil. However, he could not do otherwise; and, as at Milan, he accosted the first passenger whose appearance promised favourably.

"You are out of the road," replied the traveller; and directed him to a path by which he might regain the high road. Renzo thanked him, and followed the direction, with the intention, however, of keeping the high road in sight, without exposing himself to hazard by travelling on it. The project was more easily conceived than executed; in pursuing a zigzag course, from right to left, and left to right, and endeavouring still to keep the general direction of the way, he had probably traversed twelve miles, when he was only six miles from Milan; and as to Bergamo, it was a chance if he was not farther from it, than when he began his journey. He reflected that this would never do, and he must seek some other expedient; that which occurred to him, was to inform himself of the name of some village near the frontier, which he would reach by crossroads, and asking the way to that, be enabled to avoid the mention of this dreaded Bergamo, which seemed to him so likely to cause distrust and suspicion.

Whilst he was reflecting on the best method of pursuing this plan without awakening conjectures, he saw a green branch hanging from the door of a lonely cottage, some distance beyond a village; and as he had for some time felt the need of refreshment, he thought he could now kill two birds with one stone, and therefore entered the humble dwelling. There was no one within, but an old woman, with her distaff by her side, and spindle in her hand. He asked for a mouthful to eat; she offered him some *stracchino*, and some wine. He accepted the food, but refused the wine; of which he felt an intuitive horror since the events of the preceding night. The old woman then began to assail her guest with enquiries of his trade, his journey, and of the news from Milan, of the disturbances of which she had heard some rumours. To her question, "Where are you going?" he replied, "I am obliged to go to many places, but if I find a moment of time, I should like to stop awhile at the village on the road to Bergamo, near the frontier, but in the territory of Milan—what do they call it?—There must be some village there," thought he.

"Gorgonzola, you mean," replied the old woman.

"Gorgonzola," repeated Renzo, as if to fix it in his memory, "is it far from here?"

"I don't know for certain; perhaps ten or twelve miles. If one of my children were here, they could tell you."

"And do you think I could reach there by keeping on these pleasant paths, without taking the high road, where there is so much dust? such a quantity of dust! It is so long since we have had any rain!"

"I think you can. You can ask at the first village to the right,"—naming it.

"Thank you," said Renzo, carrying off the remains of his bread, which was much coarser than what he had lately eaten from the foot of the Cross of St. Dionysius; and paying the bill, departed. He took the road to the right, and with the name of Gorgonzola in his mouth, from village to village, he succeeded in reaching it an hour before sunset.

He had on his way intended to halt here for some more substantial refreshment; he felt also the need of sleep; but rather than indulge himself in this, he would have dropped dead on the road. His design was to inform himself, at the inn, of the distance from the Adda, to contrive to obtain some direction to the cross paths which led to it, and after having eaten, to go on his way. Born at the second source of this river, he had often heard that at a certain point, and for some distance, its waters marked the confines of the Milanese and Venetian states. He had no precise idea of the spot where this boundary commenced, but, at this time, the principal matter was to reach the river. Provided he could not accomplish it by daylight, he decided to travel as long as the darkness and his strength would permit, and then to wait the approach of day in a field, among brambles, or any where, where it should please God, an inn excepted. After advancing a few steps in Gorgonzola, he saw a sign, and entering the house, asked the host for a mouthful to eat, and a half-pint of wine, his horror of which had been subdued by his excessive fatigue. "I pray you to be in haste," added he, "for I must continue my journey immediately." And he said this, not only because it was the truth, but from fear that the host, imagining he was going to lodge there, might ask him his *name, surname,* and *whence he came,* and *what was his business!*

The host replied that he should have what he requested, and Renzo seated himself at the end of a bench near the door.

There were in the room some idle people of the neighbourhood, who, after having discussed the great news from Milan of the preceding day, wondered how affairs were going on; as the circumstances of the rebellion had left their curiosity unsatisfied as to its termination; a sedition neither suppressed nor successful; suspended rather than terminated; an unfinished work; the end of an act rather than of a drama. One of them detached himself from the company, and, approaching the new-comer, asked him, "If he came from Milan?"

"I?" said Renzo, endeavouring to collect his thoughts for a reply.

"You; if the enquiry be lawful."

Renzo, contracting his mouth, made a sort of inarticulate sound, "Milan, from what I hear—from what they say—is not a place where one would go now, unless necessity required it."

"The tumult continues, then?" asked he, with eagerness.

"One must have been on the spot, to know if it were so," said Renzo.

"But do you not come from Milan?"

"I come from Liscate," replied the youth, who, in the mean while had prepared his answer. He had, indeed, come from that place, as he had passed through it. He had learned its name from a traveller who had mentioned it, as the first village on his road to Gorgonzola.

"Oh!" said his interrogator, "I wish you had come from Milan. But patience—and did you hear nothing from Milan at Liscate?"

"It is very possible that others knew something," replied our mountaineer; "but I have heard nothing."

The inquisitive person rejoined his companions.

"How far is it from this to the Adda?" said Renzo to the host, in a low careless tone, as he set before him something to eat.

"To the Adda? to cross the river?"

"That is—yes—to the Adda."

"Would you cross the bridge of Cassano, or the ferry of Canonica?"

"Where are they?—I ask simply from curiosity."

"Ah! I name them because they are the places chosen by honest people, who are willing to give an account of themselves."

"That is right. And how far are they?"

"It must be about six miles."

"Six miles! I did not know that," said he. "But," resuming an air of indifference, "if one wished to shorten the distance, are there not other places, where one might cross?"

"Certainly," replied the host, looking at him with an expression of malignant curiosity, which restrained Renzo from any further enquiry. He drew the dish towards him, and looking at the decanter the host had put on the table, said, "Is this wine pure?"

"As gold. Ask all the inhabitants of the village, and hereabouts. But you can judge yourself." So saying, he joined the other customers.

"Curse the hosts!" said Renzo, in his heart. "The more I know of them, the worse I find them."

He began to eat, listening at the same time to the conversation, to learn what was thought, in this place, of the events in which he had acted so principal a part; and also to discover if there were not some honest man among the company, of whom a poor youth might ask his way without fear of being compelled in return to tell his business.

"But," said one, "to-morrow, at the latest, we shall know something from Milan."

"I am sorry I did not go to Milan this morning," said another.

"If you will go to-morrow, I will go with you," said two or three.

"That which I wish to know," replied the first speaker, "is, if these gentlemen of Milan will think of poor people abroad, or if they will only think of obtaining advantages for themselves. You know how they are. The citizens are proud—they think only of themselves; the villagers are treated as if they were not Christians."

"We have mouths also, to eat, and to give our reasons," said another in a voice as timid as the remark was daring, "and since the thing has begun—" But he did not think to finish his sentence.

"It is not only in Milan, that they conceal grain," said another, with a mysterious air—when suddenly they heard approaching the trampling of a horse. They ran to the door, and recognising the person who arrived, they went out to receive him. It was a merchant of Milan, who, going frequently to Bergamo on business, was accustomed to pass the night at this inn, and as he had almost always found there the same company, he had formed an acquaintance with all of them. They crowded around him—one held the bridle, another the stirrup. "You are welcome."

"And I am glad to find you all here."

"Have you made a good journey?"

"Very good. And you all, how do you do?"

"Well, well. What news from Milan?"

"Ah! there is great news truly," said the merchant, dismounting, and leaving his horse in the care of a boy. "But," continued he, entering the house with the company, "perhaps you know by this time better than I do."

"Truly, we know nothing."

"Is it possible?—Well, you will hear fine news, or rather bad news. Eh! host! is my bed unoccupied? It is well. A glass of wine, and my usual dish. Quick, quick! because I must go to bed early, in order to rise early, as I must be at Bergamo to dinner. And you," pursued he, seating himself at the table opposite to Renzo, who continued silent and attentive, "you know nothing of the mischief of yesterday!"

"We heard about yesterday."

"I knew that you must have heard it, being here always on guard to watch travellers."

"But to-day? What has been done to-day?"

"Ah! to-day! Then you know nothing of to-day?"

"Nothing at all. No one has passed."

"Then let me wet my lips, and I will tell you what has happened to-day." He filled the glass, swallowed its contents, and continued: "To-day, my dear friends, little was wanting to make the tumult worse than yesterday. And I can hardly believe that I am here to tell you, for I had nearly given up all thoughts of coming, that I might stay to guard my shop."

"What was the matter, then?" said one of his auditors.

"What was the matter? I will tell you." And beginning to eat, he at the same time pursued his relation; the company standing on his right and left, listened with open mouths and ears. Renzo, without appearing to hear him, was, in fact, the most attentive of all; and ate his last mouthful very, very slowly. "This morning, then, those vagabonds who made such a hurly-burly yesterday, met at the points agreed on, and began to run from street to street, sending forth cries in order to collect a crowd. You know it is with such people, as when one sweeps a house; the more you sweep, the more dirt you have. When they thought there were people enough, they approached the house of the superintendant of provision, as if the atrocities they committed yesterday were not enough, to a gentleman of his character. Oh! the rascals! And the abuse they bestowed on him! All invention and falsehood: he is a worthy punctual man; I can say it, for I know; and I furnish him cloth for his liveries. They hurried then towards his house—such a mob! such faces! They passed before my shop. Such faces—the Jews of the *Via Crucis* are nothing to them. And the blasphemies they uttered! enough to make one stop one's ears, had it not been for fear of observation. Their intention was to plunder, but—"

"But?" said they all.

"But they found the street barricadoed, and a company of musketeers on guard. When they saw this ceremony—what would you have done?"

"Turn back."

"Certainly; and that is precisely what they did. But see if the devil did not carry them there. When they came on the Cordusio, they saw the baker that they had wanted to plunder the day before; and what do you think they were doing at this baker's? They were distributing bread to purchasers; the first gentlemen of the land were there, watching over its distribution. The mob, instigated by the devil, rushed upon them furiously, and, in the twinkling of an eye, gentlemen, bakers, purchasers, bread, counters, benches, loaves, bags, flour, all topsy-turvy."

"And the musketeers?"

"The musketeers had the vicar's house to guard. One can't sing and carry the cross too. It was done in the twinkling of an eye, I say. Plunder, plunder; every thing was carried off. And then they proposed the amusement of yesterday, to burn what remained, in the square, and make a bonfire. And immediately they began, the rascals! to drag every thing out of the house, when one among them—Guess what fine proposal he made!"

"What?"

"What! to gather every thing in the shop in a heap, and set fire to it and the shop at the same time. No sooner said than done—"

"Did they set fire to it?"

"Wait a bit. An honest man in the neighbourhood had an inspiration from Heaven. He ran into the house, ascended the stairs, took a crucifix, and hung it in front of a window; took from the head of the bed two wax candles which had been blessed, lit them, and placed them right and left of the crucifix. The crowd looked up; there is a little fear of God yet, in Milan, it must be confessed; the crowd retired—a few would have been sacrilegious enough to set fire to paradise itself; but seeing the rest not of their opinion, they were obliged to be quiet. Guess what happened then! All the lords of the cathedral in procession, with the cross elevated, and in pontifical robes; and my lord the arch-priest began to preach on one side, and my lord the *penitenziere* on the other, and then others here and there: '*But, honest people, what would you do? Is this the example you set to your children? Return to your homes; you shall have bread at a fair price; you can see, yourselves, the rate is affixed at every corner!*'"

"Was it true?"

"Can you doubt it? Do you think the lords of the cathedral would come in their robes and declare falsehoods?"

"And what did the people do?"

"By little and little they dispersed; they ran to the corners of the streets; the rate was there for those who knew how to read. Eight ounces of bread for a penny!"

"What good fortune."

"The vine is fine, if its fruitfulness continues. Do you know how much flour has been consumed since yesterday? As much as would supply the dukedom two months."

"And have they made no good law for us country people?"

"What they have done at Milan is for the city alone. I know not what to tell you; for you, it must be as God shall direct. The tumult has entirely ceased for the present; I have not told you all yet. Here is the best—"

"What! is there any thing more?"

"Yesterday evening, or this morning, they have arrested some of the leaders, and they have been told that four will be hung. Hardly was this known, when every one betook himself home by the shortest road, so as not to be the fifth. Milan, when I left it, resembled a convent of monks."

"But will they really hang them?"

"Undoubtedly, and very soon," replied the merchant.

"And what will the people do?"

"The people will go to see them," said the merchant. "They desired so much to see a man hung, that the rascals were about to satisfy their curiosity on the superintendent of provision. They will see instead, four rogues, accompanied by capuchins and friars of the *buona morte;* well, they have richly deserved it. It is a providence, you see; it was a necessary thing. They had begun to enter the shops, and take what they wanted, without putting their hand to their purse. If they had been suffered to go on their own way, after bread, it would have been wine, and then something else—and I assure you, as an honest man, keeping a shop, it was not a very agreeable idea."

"Assuredly not," said one of his auditors.

"Assuredly not," repeated the others in chorus.

"And," continued the merchant, "it had been in preparation a long while. There was a league, you know?"

"A league!"

"A league. Cabals instigated by the Navarrese, by that cardinal of France, you know, who has a half-barbarous name, and who every day offers some new affront to the crown of Spain. But he aims chiefly at Milan, because he knows, the knave, that the strength of the king lies there."

"Indeed!"

"Would you have a proof of it? Those who made the most noise were strangers; people who were never seen before in Milan. I have forgotten, after all, to tell you something I heard; one of these had been caught in an inn—"

When this chord was touched, poor Renzo felt a cold shiver, and could with difficulty conceal his agitation. No one however perceived it, and the orator proceeded:—

"They do not yet know whence he came, by whom he was sent, nor what kind of man he was; but he was certainly one of the leaders. Yesterday, in the height of the tumult, he played the devil; then, not content with that, he began to exhort, and propose a fine thing truly! to murder all the lords! Rascal! how would poor people live, if the lords were killed? He was taken, however, and they found on him an enormous packet of letters, after which they were taking him to prison. But what do you think? his companions, who were keeping watch round the inn, came in great force, and delivered him. The rogue!"

"And what has become of him?"

"It is not known. He has escaped, or is concealed in Milan. These people find lodging and concealment any where, although they have neither house nor home of their own. The devil helps them; but they are sometimes taken in the snare, when they least expect it. When the pear is ripe, it must fall. It is well known that these letters are in the hands of government, that they contain an account of the whole plot, that many people are implicated, that they have turned the city upside down, and would have done much worse. Some say the bakers are rogues, and so say I: but they ought to be hanged at least in a legal manner. There certainly is corn concealed; and the government ought to have spies and find it out, and hang up all that keep it back in company with the bakers; and if they don't, all the city ought to remonstrate again and again, but never allow the villainous practice of entering shops and warehouses for plunder."

The little that Renzo had eaten had become poison. It appeared like an age before he dared rise to quit. He felt nailed to the spot. To have moved from the inn and the village, in the midst of the conversation, would have incurred suspicion. He determined to wait till the babbler should cease to speak of him and apply to some other subject.

"And I," said one of the company, "who have some experience, know that a tumult like this is no place for an honest man; therefore I have not suffered my curiosity to conquer me, and have remained quietly at home."

"And did I move?" said another.

"And I," added a third, "if by any chance I had been at Milan, I would have left my business unfinished, and returned home."

At this moment the host approached the corner of the table, to see how the stranger came on. Renzo gathered courage to speak, asked for his bill, settled it, and rapidly crossed the threshold, trusting himself to the guardian care of a kind Providence.

Chapter XVII.

The discourse of the merchant had plunged our poor Renzo into inexpressible agitation and alarm; there was no doubt that his adventure was noised abroad—that people were in search of him? Who could tell how many bailiffs were in pursuit of him? Who could tell what orders had been given to watch at the villages, inns, and along the roads? True it was, that two only of the officers were acquainted with his person, and he didn't bear his name stamped on his forehead. Yet he had heard strange stories of fugitives being discovered by their suspicious air, or some unexpected mark; in short, he was alarmed at every shadow.

Although at the moment he quitted Gorgonzola, the bells struck the *Ave Maria*, and the increasing darkness diminished his danger, he unwillingly took the high road, with the intention, however, of entering the first path which should appear to him to lead in the right direction. He met some travellers, but, his imagination filled with apprehensions, he dared not interrogate them. "The host called it six miles," said he; "if, in travelling through by-paths, I make it eight or ten, these good limbs will not fail me, I know. I am certainly not going towards Milan, and must therefore be approaching the Adda. If I keep on, sooner or later I must arrive there; the Adda has a voice sufficiently loud to be heard at some distance, and when I hear it, there will be no longer any need of direction. If there is a boat there, I shall cross immediately; if not, I will wait until morning in a field, upon the ground, like the sparrows, which will be far better than a prison."

He saw a cross-road open to the left, and he pursued it: "I play the devil!" continued he, "I assassinate the lords! A packet of letters! My companions keeping watch! I would give something to meet this merchant face to face, on the other side of the Adda; (Oh! when shall I reach the beautiful stream?) I would ask him politely where he picked up that fine story. Know, my good sir, that, devil as I am, it was I who aided Ferrer, and like a good Christian saved your superintendent of provisions from a rough joke that those ruffians, my friends, were about to play on him. Ay, while you were keeping watch over your shop—and that enormous packet of letters—in the hands of the government. See, sir, here it is; a single letter, written by a worthy man, a monk; a hair of whose beard is worth—but in future learn to speak with more charity of your neighbours." However, after a while, these thoughts of the poor traveller gave way to more urgent considerations of his present difficulties; he no longer feared pursuit or discovery; but darkness, solitude, and fatigue combined to distress him and retard his progress. A chill north wind penetrated his light clothing, his wedding suit; and, uncomfortable and disheartened, he wandered on, in hopes of finding some place where he might obtain concealment and repose for the night.

He passed through villages, but did not dare ask shelter; the dogs howled at his approach, and induced him to quicken his steps. At single houses near the road-side his fatigue tempted him to knock for shelter; but the apprehension of being saluted with the cry of "Help, thieves! robbers!" banished the idea from his mind. Leaving the cultivated country, he found himself in a plain, covered with fern and broom; and thinking this a favourable symptom of the near vicinity of the river, he followed the path across it. When he had advanced a few steps, he listened, but in vain. The desolation of the place increased the depression of his spirits. Strange forms and apparitions, the birth of former tales and legends, began to haunt his imagination; and to drive them away he began to chant the prayers for the dead. He passed through a thicket of plum-trees and oaks, and found himself on the borders of a wood; he conquered his repugnance to enter it, but as he proceeded into its depths, every object excited his apprehensions. Strange forms appeared beneath the bushes; and the shade of the trees, trembling on his moon-lit path, with the crackling of the dead leaves between his footsteps, inspired him with dread. He would have hastened through the perilous passage, but his limbs refused their office; the wind blew cold and sharp, and penetrating his weakened frame, almost subdued its small remains of vigour. His senses, affected by undefined horrors, appeared to be leaving him; aroused to his danger, he made a violent effort to regain some degree of resolution, in order to return through the wood, and seek shelter in the last village he had passed through, even if it should be in an inn! As he stopped for a moment, before putting his design in execution, the wind brought a new sound to his ear—the murmur of running water. Intently listening, to ascertain if his senses did not deceive him, he cried out, "It is the Adda!" His fatigue vanished, his pulse returned, his blood flowed freely through his veins, his fears disappeared; and guided by the friendly sound, he went forward. He soon reached the extremity of the plain, and found himself on the edge of a steep precipice, whence looking downward, he discovered, through the bushes, the long-desired river, and, on the other side of it, villages scattered here and there, with hills in the distance; and on the summit of one of these a whitish spot, which in the dimness he took to be a city; Bergamo certainly! He descended the declivity, and throwing aside the bushes with his hands, looked beyond them, to spy if some friendly bark were moving on the flood, or if he could not, by listening, hear the sound of oars cleaving the water; but he saw, he heard nothing. If it had been any stream less than the Adda, he would have attempted to ford it, but this he well knew to be impracticable.

He was uncertain what plan to pursue: to lie down on the grass for the next six hours, and wait until morning, exposed to the north wind and the damps of the night; or to continue walking to and fro, to protect himself from the cold, until the day should dawn: neither of these held out much prospect of comfort. He suddenly recollected to have seen, in a neighbouring part of the uncultivated heath, a *cascinotto*;—this was the name given by the peasants of the Milanese to cabins covered with straw, constructed with the trunks and branches of trees, and the crevices filled with mud, where they were in the habit of placing the crop, gathered during the day, until a more convenient opportunity for removing it; they were therefore abandoned except at such seasons. Renzo found his way thither, pushed open the door, and perceiving a bundle of straw on the ground, thought that sleep, even in such a place, would be very welcome. Before, however, throwing himself on the bed Providence had provided for him, he kneeled, and returned thanks for the blessing, and for all the assistance which had been this day afforded him, and then implored forgiveness for the errors of the previous day; then gathering the straw around him as some defence against the cold, he closed his eyes to sleep; but sleep was not so soon to visit our poor traveller. Confused images began to throng his fancy; the merchant, the notary, the bailiffs, the cutler, the host, Ferrer, the superintendent, the company at the inn, the crowds in the streets, assailed his imagination by turns; then came the thought of Don Abbondio, Roderick, Lucy, Agnes, and the good friar. He remembered the paternal counsels of the latter, and reflected with shame and remorse on his neglect of them; and what bitter retrospection did the image of Lucy produce! and Agnes! poor Agnes! how ill had she been repaid for her motherly solicitude on his behalf! an outcast from her home, solitary, uncertain of the future, reaping misery from what seemed to promise the happiness of her declining years! Poor Renzo! what a night didst thou pass! what an apartment! what a bed for a matrimonial couch! tormented, too, with apprehensions of the future! "I submit to the will of God," said he, speaking aloud, "to the will of God! He does only that which is right; I accept it all as a just chastisement for my sins. Lucy, however, is so good! the Lord will not long afflict her with suffering."

In the mean time he despaired of obtaining any repose; the cold was insupportable; his teeth chattered; he ardently wished for day, and measured with impatience the slow progress of the hours; this he was enabled to do, as he heard, every half hour, in the deep silence, the heavy sound of some distant clock, probably that of Trezzo. When the time arrived which he had fixed on for his departure, half benumbed with exposure to the night air, he stretched his stiffened limbs, and opening the door of the *cascinotto*, looked out, to ascertain if any one were near, and finding all silent around, he resumed his journey along the path he had quitted.

The sky announced a beautiful day; the setting moon shone pale in an immense field of azure, which, towards the east, mingled itself lightly with the rosy dawn. Near the horizon were scattered clouds of various hues and forms; it was, in fact, the sky of Lombardy, beautiful, brilliant, and calm. If Renzo had had a mind at ease, he would no doubt have stopped to contemplate this splendid ushering in of day, so different from that which he had been accustomed to witness amidst his mountains; but his thoughts were otherwise occupied. He reached the brow of the precipice where he had stood the preceding night, and looking below, perceived, through the bushes, a fisherman's bark, which was slowly stemming the current, near the shore. He descended the precipice, and standing on the bank, made a sign to the fisherman to approach. He intended to do this with a careless air, as if it were of little importance, but in spite of himself, his manner was half supplicatory. The fisherman, after having for a moment surveyed the course of the water, as if to ascertain the practicability of reaching the shore, directed the boat towards it; before it touched the bank, Renzo, who was standing on the water's edge, awaiting its approach, seized the prow, and jumped into it.

"Do me a service, and I will pay you for it," said he; "I wish to cross to the other shore."

The fisherman having divined his object, had already turned his boat in that direction. Renzo, perceiving another oar in the bottom of the bark, stooped to take it.

"Softly, softly," said the fisherman. But seeing with what skill the young man managed the oar, "Ah! ah!" added he, "you know the trade."

"A very little," replied Renzo, and he continued to row with a vigour and skill beyond that of a mere amateur in the art. With all his efforts, however, the bark moved slowly; the current, setting strong against it, drove it continually from the line of its direction, and impeded the rapidity of its course. New perplexities presented themselves to the mind of Renzo; now that the Adda was almost passed, he began to fear that it might not, at this place, serve for the boundary between the states, and that, this obstacle surmounted, there would yet be others remaining. He spoke to the fisherman, and pointing to the white spot he had noticed the night before, and which was now much more distinct, "Is that Bergamo?" said he.

"The city of Bergamo," replied the fisherman.

"And the other shore, does it belong to Bergamo?"

"It is the territory of St. Mark."

"Long live St. Mark!" cried Renzo. The fisherman made no reply.

The boat reached the shore, at last; Renzo thanked God in his heart, as he stepped upon it; and turning to the fisherman took from his pocket a *berlinga* and gave it to him. The man took it in silence, and with a significant look, placed his forefinger on his lip; and saying, "A good journey to you," returned to his employment.

In order to account for the prompt and discreet civility of this man towards a perfect stranger, we must inform the reader, that he was accustomed to render similar favours to smugglers and outlaws, not so much for the sake of the little gain which accrued to him thereby, as not to create enemies among these classes of people. He rendered these services, therefore, when he was sure of not being seen by the custom-house officers, bailiffs, or spies. Thus he endeavoured to act with an impartiality, which should give offence to neither party.

Renzo stopped a moment to contemplate the shore he had quitted, and where he had suffered so much; "I am at last safely beyond it," was his first thought; then the remembrance of those he had left behind rushed over his mind, overwhelming it with regret and shame; for, with the calm and virtuous image of Lucy, came the recollection of his extravagances in Milan.

He shook off, however, these oppressive thoughts, and went on, taking the direction of the whitish mass on the declivity of the mountain, until he should meet some one who could direct him on his way. And now with what a different and careless air he accosted travellers! he hesitated no more, he pronounced boldly the name of the place where his cousin lived, to ask the way to it; from the information given him by the first traveller he met, he found that he had still nine miles to travel.

His journey was not agreeable. Without referring to his own causes of trouble, Renzo was affected every moment by the sight of painful and distressing objects; so that he foresaw, that he should find in this country the poverty he had left in his own. All along the way he was assailed by mendicants,—mendicants of necessity, not of choice,—peasants, mountaineers, tradesmen, whole families reduced to poverty, and to the necessity of begging their bread. This sight, besides the compassion it excited, made him naturally recur to his own prospects.

"Who knows," thought he, mournfully, "if I shall find work to do? perhaps things are not as they were in preceding years. Bartolo wishes me well, I know; he is a good fellow; he has made money; he has invited me many times to come to him; I am sure he will not abandon me. And then Providence has aided me until now; and will continue to do so."

Meanwhile, the walk had sharpened his appetite; he could indeed have well waited to the end of his journey, which was only two miles farther, but he did not like to make his first appearance before his cousin as a hungry beggar; he therefore drew all his wealth from his pocket, and counting it on the palm of his hand, found that he had more than sufficient to procure a slight repast; after paying for which, he would still have a few pence remaining.

As he came out of the inn at which he had rested, to proceed on his journey, he saw, lying near the door, two women: the one was elderly, and the other more youthful, with an infant in her arms, which was in vain seeking sustenance from its exhausted mother; both were of the complexion of death: by them stood a man, whose countenance and limbs gave signs of former vigour; now lost from long inanition. All three stretched forth their hands, but spoke not—what prayer could be so moving as their appearance. Renzo sighed; "There is a Providence," said he, as he placed in the nearest hand the last remnant of his wealth.

The slight repast he had made, and the good deed he had performed (for we are composed of body and soul), had equally tended to refresh and invigorate him. If, to afford relief to these unhappy persons, Providence had kept in reserve the last farthing of a fugitive stranger, would he leave the wants of that stranger unsupplied? He looked with renewed hope to the future; he pictured to himself the return of abundant harvests, and in the mean time he had his cousin Bartolo and his own industry to depend on, and moreover he had left at home a small sum of money, the fruit of his economy, which he could send for, if needed. "Then," said he, "plenty will eventually return, and trade will be profitable again; the Milanese workmen will be in demand, and can set a high price on their labour; I shall have more than enough to satisfy my wants, and can lay by money, and can furnish my nice house, and then write to Agnes and Lucy to come—and then—But why wait for this? We should have been obliged to live, had we remained at home; we should have been obliged to live during this winter, upon my little savings, and we can do the same here. There are curates every where, and they can come shortly. Oh! what joy will it be to walk together on this same road; to go to the borders of the Adda, where I will point out to them the place where I embarked, the woods through which I passed, the spot where I stood watching for a boat."

He reached at last the village of his cousin; at its entrance, he saw a very high house, with numerous windows, and perceived it to be a silk manufactory; he entered, and amidst the noise of the water and machinery loudly demanded, "if Bartolo Castagneri was within?"

"Signor Bartolo? there he is."

"Signor! that's a good sign," thought Renzo. He perceived his cousin, and ran towards him, exclaiming, "I am come at last!" Bartolo made an exclamation of surprise, and embraced him; he then took him into another chamber, apart from the noise of the machinery and the notice of the inquisitive, and said, "I am glad to see you, but you are a droll fellow. I have invited you many times to come hither; you have always refused, and now choose a most unfavourable moment."

"What shall I say to you? I have not now come of my own free will," said Renzo; and he briefly, and with much emotion, related the mournful story.

"That's another affair truly," said Bartolo. "Poor Renzo! you have relied on me, and I will not abandon you. To say truth, workmen are not in much demand at present; and it is with difficulty that those already engaged are kept by their employers. But my master regards me, and he has money; and besides, without boasting, we are equally dependent on each other—he has the capital, and I the skill, such as it is! I am his first workman, his *factotum*! Poor Lucy Mondella! I remember her as if it was but yesterday that I last saw her! An excellent girl! always so modest at church; and if you passed by her cottage—I see it now, the little cottage beyond the village, with a large fig-tree against the wall—"

"No, no," said Renzo, "do not speak of it."

"I meant to say, that if you passed it, you always heard the noise of her reel. And Don Roderick! even before I left, showed symptoms of his character; but now, it seems, he plays the devil outright, until God shall put a bridle on his neck. Well, as I said, we suffer here also the consequences of scarce harvests.—But, apropos, are you not hungry?"

"It is not long since I have eaten," said Renzo.

"And how are you off for money?" Renzo extended the palm of his hand and shook his head. "No matter," said Bartolo: "I have plenty. Cheer up; things will change for the better soon, and then you can repay me."

"I have a small sum at home, and I will send for it."

"Well, in the mean while, depend on me. God has given me wealth to spend for others, and above all, for my relations and friends."

"I knew that you would befriend me," said Renzo, affectionately pressing his cousin's hand.

"Well, what a fuss they have made at Milan," continued Bartolo; "the people seem to me to be mad. The report has reached us, but I shall be glad to know the particulars from you. I think we shall have enough to talk about, shall we not? Here, however, things are conducted with more judgment. The city purchased two thousand loads of corn from a merchant of Venice; the corn comes from Turkey. Now, what do you think happened? The governors of Verona and Brescia forbade the transit of the corn. What did the people of Bergamo do then, do you think? They sent to Venice a man that knew how to talk, I can tell you: he went to the doge, and made a speech which they say deserves to be printed! Immediately an order was sent to let the corn pass: the governors were obliged to obey. The country, too, has been thought of.

Another good man informed the senate that the people here were famishing, and the senate granted us four thousand bushels of millet, which makes very good bread. And then, if there is no bread, you and I can eat meat; God has given me wealth I tell you. Now I will conduct you to my patron. I have often spoken of you to him; he will make you welcome. He is a native of Bergamo, a man of an excellent disposition. 'Tis true, he did not expect you at this time, but when he learns your story—And then he knows how to value skilful workmen, because scarcity lasts but a little while, and business must finally go on.—But I must hint to you one thing; do you know what name they give to us Milanese in this country?"

"What name they give us?"

"They call us simpletons."

"That is certainly not a very agreeable name."

"What matters it? Whoever is born in the territory of Milan, and would gain his living in that of Bergamo, must put up with it. As to the people here, they call a Milanese a simpleton as freely as they call a gentleman *sir*."

"They say so, I suppose, to those who will suffer it."

"My good fellow, if you are not disposed to submit to be called simpleton, till it becomes familiar to your taste, you must not expect to live in Bergamo. You would always be obliged to carry your knife in hand; and when you had killed three or four, you might be killed yourself, and have to appear before the bar of God with three or four murders to answer for?"

"And a Milanese who understands his trade?"

"It is all the same; he would still be a simpleton. Do you know how my master expresses himself when he talks of me to his friends? *Heaven has sent me this simpleton to carry on my business. If it were not for this simpleton I should never get on.* It is the custom."

"It is a silly custom, to say the least of it; and especially as it is we who have brought the art hither, and who carry it on. Is it possible that there is no remedy?"

"None. Time may accomplish it. The next generation may be different, but at present we must submit. And after all, what is it?"

"Why, if there is no other evil—"

"Ah! now that you are convinced, all will be well. Let us go to my master. Be of good courage."

In fact, the promises of Bartolo were realised, and all *was* well. It was truly a kind Providence; for we shall see how little dependence Renzo could place on the treasure he had left at home,—the savings of his labour.

Chapter XVIII.

On this same day, the 13th of November, there arrived a courier extraordinary to the signor *podestà* of Lecco. The courier brought an express from the head of the police, containing an order to make every possible search for a young man of the name of Lorenzo Tramaglino, silk weaver, who, having escaped from the hands "*of the illustrious head above cited,*" had probably returned to the territory of Lecco. That, in case of his discovery, he should be committed to prison, and an account rendered to the police of his wicked practices, his ostensible means of procuring subsistence, and his accomplices. And furthermore, that an execution should be put into the house of the above-said Lorenzo Tramaglino, and every thing taken from thence that might aid in throwing light on his nefarious deeds.

The signor podestà, after ascertaining as well as he could, that Renzo had not returned to the village, took with him the constable of the place, and obeyed these injunctions, accompanied by a large escort of notary, constable, and officers. The key of the house was not to be found; the door was accordingly forced. The report of this transaction spread around, and soon reached the ears of Father Christopher. The good man was surprised and afflicted; and not being able to gain satisfactory information with regard to Renzo, he wrote to the Father Bonaventura for intelligence concerning him. In the mean while the relations and friends of Renzo were summoned to give in their testimony, with regard to his depravity of character. To bear the name of Tramaglino became a disgrace; the village was all in commotion. By little and little, it was understood that Renzo had escaped from the hands of justice, even in the heart of Milan, and had disappeared: it was whispered that he had committed some enormous crime, the nature of which remained unknown. The more enormous, however, the less it was believed, for Renzo was known by every body to be a worthy youth; the greatest number thought, therefore, that it was a machination of Don Roderick to ruin his poor rival. Thus it is true, that judging from inference, and without the indispensable knowledge of facts, we often wrongfully suspect even the wicked.

But we, who have the facts in our hands, can affirm, that if Don Roderick had no share in creating these misfortunes, he rejoiced in them as if they had been his own work; and made them a subject of merriment with his friends, and above all with Count Attilio, who had been deterred from prosecuting his intended journey to Milan by the account received of the disturbances there: but this order from the police gave him to understand that things had resumed their usual course. He then determined to depart immediately, and, exhorting his cousin to persist in his undertaking, and to surmount every obstacle, he promised to use his efforts to rid him of the friar. Attilio had hardly taken his departure, when Griso arrived, safe and sound, from Monza, and gave in his report to his master of all he had been able to collect. He told him that Lucy had been taken into the convent under the protection of the signora; that she lived there as secluded as if she were a nun, never putting her foot without the walls; that she assisted at the ceremonies of the church behind a grated window; and that it was impossible to obtain a view of her.

This relation put the devil into Roderick, or rather rendered the one more uncontrollable that sojourned there already. So many favourable circumstances concurring to forward his designs, inflamed the medley of spleen, rage, and infamous desire, which he dignified by the name of love. Renzo absent, expelled, banished, every measure against him became lawful; his betrothed herself might be considered in some sort as the property of a rebel. The only man who could and would take her under his protection, the friar, would soon be deprived of the power to do so; but, amidst so many unlooked-for facilities, one obstacle appeared to render them unavailable. A monastery of Monza, even if there were no *signora* there, was an obstacle not to be surmounted even by Don Roderick. He in vain wandered, in his imagination, around this asylum, not being able to devise any means of violating it, either by force or intrigue. He was upon the point of renouncing the enterprise, of going to Milan, of mixing in its pleasures, and thus drowning all remembrance of Lucy; but, in place of relief, would he not find there fresh food for vexation? Attilio had certainly told the story, and every one would ask him about the mountain girl! What reply would he be obliged to give? He had been outwitted by a capuchin and a clown; and, moreover, when a happy unexpected chance had rid him of the one, and a skilful friend removed the other, then he, like a simpleton, abandoned the undertaking! There was enough in this to prevent his ever lifting up his head in the society of his equals; or else to compel him to go among them sword in hand! And on the other hand, how could he return and remain in this spot, where he would be tormented by the remembrance of his passion, and the disgrace of its failure. How resolve? What do? Shall he go forward? Shall he draw back? A means presented itself to his mind, by which his enterprise might succeed. This was to call to his aid the assistance of a man whose power could accomplish whatever he thought fit to undertake, and for whom the difficulty of an enterprise would be only an additional motive for engaging in it. But this project had nevertheless its inconveniences and dangers, the consequences of which it was impossible to calculate. No one could foresee the termination of an affair, when they had once embarked in it with this man; a powerful auxiliary, assuredly, but a guide not less absolute than dangerous. Such reflections kept Don Roderick many days in a state of painful irresolution: he received, in the meanwhile, a letter from his cousin, informing him that the intrigue was prospering. After the lightning came the thunder. One fine morning he heard that Father Christopher had left the convent of Pescarenico! Such complete and prompt success, and the letter of Attilio, who encouraged him by his advice and vexed him by his jokes, inclined him to hazard every thing; and what above all confirmed him in his intention, was the unexpected intelligence that Agnes had returned to the village, and was at her own house! We will relate these two events for the information of the reader.

Lucy and her mother had hardly entered their asylum, when the news of the terrible insurrection at Milan spread through Monza, and even penetrated the walls of the convent. The accounts were various and contradictory.

The portress, who from necessity went much abroad, heard all the news, and related them to her guests. "They have put several in prison," said she; "some were taken before the bakers of the Crutches, others in front of the house inhabited by the superintendant of provision—But listen to this; there was one who escaped, who was from Lecco, or thereabouts. I don't know his name, but I will ascertain it from some one; perhaps you may know him."

This intelligence, joined to the circumstance that Renzo must have arrived in Milan precisely on this fatal day, gave some uneasiness to Lucy and her mother; judge what must have been their feelings, when the portress came again to tell them, "He that fled to avoid hanging is from your village, a silk weaver, one Tramaglino. Do you know him?"

Lucy was seated, busy at her work; it fell from her hands; she turned pale, and her emotion must certainly have attracted the attention of the portress, had she not been too eagerly engaged in delivering her report to Agnes, who was standing by the door at some distance from the poor girl. Agnes, notwithstanding she was much agitated, avoided any exhibition of her feelings. She made an effort to reply, that in a small village every one was known, but she could hardly believe this to be true of Tramaglino, as he was a quiet worthy youth. She asked if it was true that he had escaped, and if it was known where he was?

"Escaped, he certainly has, for every one knows it; but where, no one knows. Perhaps they may take him again, perhaps he is in safety; but if your peaceful youth falls into their hands—"

Here very fortunately the portress was called away; you may imagine the feelings of Agnes and her daughter! The poor woman and the desolate Lucy remained more than a day in cruel uncertainty, imagining the details and the probable consequences of this unhappy event. Tormented with vain hopes and anxious fears, their only relief was in each other's sympathy.

At length, a man arrived at the convent, and asked to see Agnes; he was a fishmonger of Pescarenico, who was going, according to custom, to Milan, to sell his fish; the good Christopher had desired him to stop at the convent, to relate what he knew of the unhappy affair of Renzo to Lucy and her mother, and exhort them, in his name, to have patience and to confide in God. As for him, he should certainly not forget them, and would seize every possible opportunity to aid them; in the meanwhile he would not fail to send them news every week, by this or some other means. All that the messenger could tell them further of Renzo was, that it was considered certain that he had taken refuge in Bergamo. Such a certainty was a great balm to the affliction of Lucy; her tears flowed less bitterly, and she experienced some comfort in discoursing upon it with her mother; and they united in heartfelt thanks to the Great Being who had saved them from so many dangers.

Gertrude made Lucy often visit her in her private parlour, and conversed much with her, finding a charm in the ingenuousness and sweetness of the poor girl, and delighted with listening to expressions of gratitude from her mouth. She changed insensibly the suspicions of Lucy with regard to her into a sentiment of the deepest compassion, by relating to her, in confidence, a part of her history, that part of it which she dared avow. Lucy found in the relation reasons more than sufficient to explain what had appeared strange in the manners of her benefactress. She was very careful, however, not to return the confidence Gertrude placed in her, by speaking of her new fears and misfortunes, lest she should thereby extend the knowledge of Renzo's supposed crime and disgrace. She avoided as much as possible replying to the repeated enquiries of the signora on that part of her history, which preceded the promise of marriage; to her modesty and innocence it appeared an impossible thing to converse freely on such a subject. Gertrude was often tempted to quarrel with her shyness, but how could she? Lucy was nevertheless so respectful, so grateful, so trusting! Sometimes her shrinking and susceptible modesty might displease her, from other motives; but all was lost in the sweetness of the thought that to Lucy, if to no other human being, she was doing good. And this was true; for besides the asylum she afforded her, her conversation and endearments encouraged the timid mind of the maiden; whose only other resource was constant employment. The nuns, at her solicitation, furnished her with occupation; and, as from morning till night she plied her needle, her reel, her beloved but now forsaken reel, recurred to her memory, bringing with it a throng of painful recollections.

The following week another message was received from Father Christopher, confirming the flight of Renzo, but with regard to the extent or nature of his misdemeanor, there was no further information. The friar had hoped for satisfaction on this point from his brother at Milan, to whom he had recommended him; but had received for answer that he had neither seen the young man, nor received the letter; that some one from abroad had been at the convent to ask for him, and not finding him there, had gone away.

The third week there was no messenger, which not only deprived them of a desired and expected consolation, but also produced a thousand uneasy suspicions. Before this, Agnes had thought of taking a journey home, and this disappointment confirmed her resolution. Lucy was unwilling to be separated from her mother, but her anxiety to gain more satisfactory intelligence of Renzo, and the security she felt in her sacred asylum, reconciled her. It was therefore agreed between them, that Agnes should wait on the road the following day for the return of the fishmonger from Milan, and should ask the favour of a seat in his cart, in order to go to her mountains. Upon seeing him approach, therefore, she asked him if Father Christopher had not sent any message by him. The fishmonger had been occupied the whole day before his departure in fishing, and had received no message from the friar! She then preferred her request, and having obtained a compliance with it, bade farewell to her daughter and the signora, promising a speedy return.

The journey was without accident; early in the morning they arrived at Pescarenico. Here Agnes took leave of her conductor, with many thanks for the obligation he had conferred on her; and as she was before the convent gates, she determined to speak with the good friar before she proceeded homeward. She pulled the bell—the friar Galdino, whom we may remember as the nut collector, appeared to answer it.

"Oh! good dame, what good wind brings you here?"

"I come to see Father Christopher!"

"Father Christopher? He is not here!"

"No? will it be long before he returns? Where is he gone?"

"To Rimini."

"To—?"

"To Rimini."

"Where is that?"

"Eh! eh! eh!" replied the friar, extending his arms, as if to indicate a great distance.

"Miserable that I am! But why did he go so suddenly?"

"Because the father provincial would have it so."

"And why did they send away one who did so much good here? Oh! unhappy me!"

"If our superiors were obliged to give reasons for what they do, where would be our obedience, my good woman?"

"But this is such a loss!"

"Shall I tell you how it has happened? they have probably wanted a good preacher at Rimini; (we have them in every place to be sure, but sometimes a particular man is needed;) the father provincial of that place has written to the father provincial of this, to know if there were such a person in this convent; the father provincial returned for answer, that there was none but Father Christopher who corresponded to the description."

"Oh! unfortunate! When did he go?"

"The day before yesterday."

"Oh! if I had only come a few days sooner, as I wished to do! And do they not know when he will return?"

"Why! my dear woman! the father provincial knows, if any one does; but when one of our preachers has taken his flight, it is impossible to say on what branch he will rest. They want him here; they want him there; for we have convents in the four quarters of the world. Father Christopher will make a great noise at Rimini, with his Lent sermon; the fame of this great preacher will resound every where, and it is our duty to give him up, because we live on the charity of others, and it is but right we should serve all the world."

"Oh! misery! misery!" cried Agnes, weeping; "what shall I do without this good man? He was a father to us; what a loss! what a loss!"

"Hear me, good woman—Father Christopher was truly a good man, but we have others equally so; there is Father Antanasio, Father Girolamo, Father Zaccaria! Father Zaccaria is a worthy man! And you must not wonder, as some ignorant people do, at his shrill voice and his little beard; I do not say that he is a preacher, because every one has his talent; but to give advice, he is the man."

"Oh! holy patience!" cried Agnes, with a mixture of gratitude and vexation one feels at an offer containing more good-will than suitableness; "What is it to me what another man is, when he who is gone knew our affairs, and had every thing prepared to help us!"

"Then you must have patience."

"I know that. Excuse the trouble I have given you."

"That is of no consequence, my good woman; I pity you; if you decide upon asking advice of one of the fathers, you will find the convent still in its place. But let me see you soon, when I collect the oil."

"God preserve you," said Agnes; and she proceeded homeward, confused and disconcerted as a blind man who had lost his staff.

Having more information than Friar Galdino, we are enabled to relate the truth of this affair. Attilio, immediately on his arrival at Milan, performed his promise to Don Roderick, and visited his uncle of the secret council; (this was a committee composed of thirteen members, whose sanction was necessary to the proceedings of government; in case of the absence or death of the governor, the council assumed temporarily the control.) The count, one of the oldest members of the council, enjoyed in it some authority, which he did not fail to make known on all occasions. His language was ambiguous; his silence significant; he had the art of flattering, without absolutely promising; of menacing, without perhaps the power to perform; but these flatteries and menaces produced in the minds of others an impression of his unlimited power, which was the end and purpose of all his actions. Towards this point he lately made a great stride on an extraordinary occasion. He had been sent on an embassy to Madrid! And to hear him describe his reception there! Among other honours, the count-duke had treated him with particular attention, had admitted him to his confidence, so far as to ask him in the presence of the whole court, *if he were pleased with Madrid?* and to tell him on another occasion, at a window, that *the cathedral of Milan was the most magnificent church in the king's dominions.*

After having paid his duty to the count, and presented the compliments of his cousin, Attilio, with a seriousness which he knew well how to assume, said, "I believe it to be my duty to inform the signor, my uncle, of an affair in which Roderick is concerned, and which requires the interference of your lordship to avert the serious consequences that—"

"Ah! one of his pranks, I suppose."

"In truth, I must say that the injury has not been committed by Roderick, but he is exasperated, and none but my uncle can—"

"What is it? what is it?"

"There is in his neighbourhood a capuchin friar who sets himself in array against my cousin, who hates him, and the matter stands thus—"

"How often have I told you both to let the friars manage their own affairs? It is enough for those to whom it belongs—but you, you can avoid having any thing to do with them—"

"Signor uncle, it is my duty to inform you that Roderick would have avoided it, if it had been possible. It is the friar who has quarrelled with him, and he has used every means—"

"What the devil can the friar have in common with my nephew?"

"First of all, he is known to be a quarrelsome fellow; he protects a peasant girl of the village, and regards her with a benevolence, to say the least of it, very suspicious."

"I comprehend," said his uncle; and a ray of malice passed over the depth of dulness which nature had stamped on his countenance.

"For some time," continued Attilio, "the friar has suspected Roderick of designs on this young girl—"

"*He* has suspected, indeed! I know the signor Roderick too well myself, not to need to be told that he is incorrigible in such matters!"

"That Roderick, signor uncle, may have had some trifling conversation with this girl, I can very well believe; he is young, and, moreover, not a capuchin,—but these are idle tales, not worth engaging your attention. The serious part of the affair is, that the friar speaks of Roderick as if he were a villain, and instigates all the country against him—"

"And the other friars?"

"They do not meddle with it, because they know him to be hot-headed, though they have great respect for Roderick; but then, on the other hand, the friar passes for a saint with the villagers, and—"

"I imagine he does not know Roderick is my nephew."

"Does he not know it? it is that, precisely, which animates him to this course of conduct."

"How? how?"

"He takes pleasure, and he tells it to every one, he takes the more pleasure in vexing Roderick, because he has a protector as powerful as your lordship; he laughs at the nobility, and at diplomatists, and exults at the thought, that the girdle of Saint Francis can tie up all the swords, and that—"

"Oh! the presumptuous man! what is his name?"

"Friar Christopher, of ," said Attilio. The count drew his portfolio towards him, and inscribed the name.

Meanwhile, Attilio proceeded: "He has always had this character; his life is well known; he was a plebeian, and having some wealth, wished to associate with gentlemen, and not being able to succeed, killed one of them for rage; and to escape the gallows he assumed the habit of a friar."

"Bravo! well done! we will see, we will see," said the count in a fume.

"Now," continued Attilio, "he is more enraged than ever, because he has failed in a project he had much at heart. It is by this that your lordship can see what kind of a man he is. He wished to have this girl married, to remove her from the dangers of the world, you understand; and he had found his man, a fellow whose name you have doubtless heard, because I have understood that the secret council has been obliged to take notice of the worthy youth."

"Who is he?"

"A silk weaver, Lorenzo Tramaglino, he who—"

"Lorenzo Tramaglino!" cried the count. "Well done, friar! Truly—now I remember—he had a letter for a—it is a pity that—but no matter. And pray, why did Don Roderick say nothing of all this? why did he suffer things to go so far, before he acquainted one who has the power and the will to support him?"

"I will tell you also the truth with respect to that: knowing the multitude of cases which you have to perplex you, he has not been willing to add to them; and, besides, since I must say it, he is beside himself on account of the insults offered him by the friar, and would wish to wreak summary justice on him himself, rather than obtain it from prudence and the power of your lordship. I have tried to cool his ardour, but finding it impossible, I thought it my duty to inform your lordship, who, after all, is the prop and chief column of the house."

"You ought to have spoken sooner."

"That is true. But I hoped the affair would finish of itself, or that the friar would regain his reason, or that he would leave the convent, as often happens to these friars, who are sometimes here, sometimes there; and then all would have been settled. But—"

"The arrangement of the business now rests with me."

"That is what I thought; I said to myself, the signor our uncle is the only one who can save the honour of Don Roderick; he has a thousand means that I know not of: I know that the father provincial has a great respect for him, and if our uncle should think that the best thing for this friar would be a change of air, he can in a few words—"

"Will your lordship leave the care of the business to him to whom it appertains?" said the count, sharply.

"Ah! that is true," cried Attilio; "am I the man to give advice to your lordship? But the regard I have for the honour of the family made me speak. And I am afraid I have committed another folly," added he, affecting a pensive air: "I am afraid I have injured Don Roderick in your opinion; I should have no rest if you doubted Roderick's confidence in you, and submission to your will. I hope the signor our uncle will believe, that in this case, it is truly—"

"Well, well, you two will be always friends, until one of you become prudent. Ever in fault, and relying on me to repair it! You give me more trouble than all the affairs of state!" continued he, with an expression of grave importance.

Attilio proffered a few more excuses, promises, and compliments, and took his leave, with a parting injunction from his uncle *to be prudent!*

Chapter XIX.

The signor count formed the resolution to make use of the father provincial to cut the knot of these perplexities; whether he would have thought of this, had it not been suggested by Attilio, it is impossible to determine, inasmuch as he would never have acknowledged this to be the case. It was important that one of his family, his nephew, should not be obliged to yield in an open controversy; it was a point essential to the reputation of his power, which he had so much at heart. The satisfaction which his nephew might himself take of his adversary would be a remedy worse than the disease. Should he order him to leave his castle, when obedience would seem like flying from the field of battle? Legal force could have no power over the capuchin; the clergy were entirely exempt from secular jurisdiction. All that he could attempt against such an adversary was to endeavour to have him removed and the power to do this rested with the father provincial.

Now the count and the father provincial were old acquaintances; they saw each other rarely, but always with great demonstrations of friendship, and reiterated offers of service.

When all was matured in his mind, the count invited the father provincial to a dinner, where he found a company of choice guests; noblemen, who, by their deportment, their native boldness, and lordly disdain, impressed those around them with the idea of their superiority and power. There were also present some clients, who, attached to the house by hereditary devotion, and the service of a life, sat at their lord's table, in a spirit of implicit submission, "devouring his discourse" and his dinner with unqualified and equal approbation.

At table, the count led the conversation to Madrid; he spoke of the court, the count-duke, the ministers, the family of the governor; of the bull-fights, which he could well describe, having seen them from a distinguished place; of the escurial, of which he could speak in its most minute details, because a page of the count-duke had conducted him into every nook of it. For some time all the company were attentive to him alone; then they divided into separate parties. He continued for a while to relate a number of anecdotes, as in confidence, to the father provincial, who was seated near him. But suddenly he gave a turn to the conversation, and spoke of Cardinal Barberini, who was a capuchin, and brother to the reigning pope, Urban VIII. As they left the table, the count invited the father provincial to go with him into another apartment.

The noble lord gave a seat to the reverend father, and taking one himself, said, "Considering the friendship that exists between us, I thought I was authorised to speak to your reverence of an affair equally interesting to us both, and which had best be concluded between us without going farther, which might—and I will tell you frankly what it is, as I am certain we shall have the same opinion on the subject. Tell me, in your convent of Pescarenico, is there not a Father Christopher of ?"

The father provincial bowed assent.

"I pray your reverence to tell me, frankly, as a friend,—this man—this father—I have no personal acquaintance with him, 'tis true; I know many fervent, prudent, humble capuchins, who are worth their weight in gold; I have been the friend of the order from infancy; but in a numerous family there is always some individual—And I have reason to think that Friar Christopher is a man—a little fond of quarrelling—who has not all the prudence he might have: I imagine he has caused your reverence much anxiety."

"I perceive there is some intrigue," thought the father provincial; "it is my fault; I knew that this holy man should have been sent from pulpit to pulpit, and not have been suffered to remain six months in a convent in the country.—Oh," said he, aloud, "I am truly sorry that your excellency has conceived such an opinion of Father Christopher; for I know that his conduct in the convent is exemplary, and that he is esteemed by every body."

"I understand very well; your reverence ought—However, I would as a friend inform you of a matter which it is necessary you should know. This Father Christopher has taken under his protection a young man of that country, one of whom your reverence must have heard; him who recently escaped from the hands of justice, on the terrible day of San Martin—Lorenzo Tramaglino!"

"I had not heard of this," said the father provincial; "but your excellency knows that it is the duty of our order to seek those who have gone astray, for the purpose of leading them back."

"That is true; but I thought it best to give you this information, because, if ever his holiness—the intelligence of it may have been sent to Rome."

"I am much obliged to your excellency for the information. However, I am certain, that if the affair is enquired into, it will be found that Father Christopher has had no connection with this man but for the purpose of doing him good. I know the father well."

"Your reverence knows, then, better than I, what he was in the world, and the pranks of his youth."

"It is the glory of our habit, signor count, that whatever a man may have been in the world, once clothed with that, he is quite another person; and since the Father Christopher has belonged to our order—"

"I believe it from the bottom of my heart, I believe it; but sometimes—as the proverb says—The habit does not make the monk."

The proverb was not much to the purpose, but the count had cited it, in place of another which occurred to him,—"The wolf may change his skin, but he does not become a dog."

"I have certain information," pursued he.

"If your excellency knows positively that the father has committed a fault (we are all liable to err), I wish you would inform me of it. I am his superior—unworthily, 'tis true; but it is my duty to watch over, and, if necessary, correct—"

"Besides the circumstance of his granting protection to the man I have mentioned, this same Father Christopher has undertaken to contend—but we can settle it together with my nephew, Don Roderick."

"Oh, I am sorry for that, I am sorry for that, truly."

"My nephew is young, rash, and not accustomed to provocation."

"It becomes my duty to obtain the best information on the subject. Your excellency, with your experience of the world, knows better than I, that we are all frail, liable to error—some one way, some another; and if our Father Christopher has failed—"

"But these are things which had better be settled between ourselves; to spread them abroad would only increase the evil. These trifles are often the cause of numerous embarrassments and difficulties, which might have been prevented by some decisive act in the commencement. That is now our business; my nephew is young; the monk, from what I hear, has still the spirit, the inclinations of a young man; but we, who are advanced in years, (too true, is it not, reverend father?) must have prudence to act for the young, and apply a remedy to their follies. Happily there is yet time; we must remove the fire from the straw. An individual who does not do well in one place may in another; your reverence might see to his being removed, might find a suitable station for the friar at a sufficient distance—all may be easily arranged—or rather, there's no harm done."

The father provincial had expected this conclusion from the commencement of the conversation. "I perceive," thought he, "where you would lead me; when a poor friar gives one of you the least umbrage, the superior must make him march, right or wrong."

When the count had finished, the provincial said aloud, "I understand what the signor count would say; but before taking a step—"

"It is a step, and it is not a step, very reverend father: it is only a natural event, such as might happen in the ordinary course of affairs; and if we do not do it quickly, I foresee a deluge of disorders, a mountain of grievances. If we do not put a stop to the affair between ourselves, it is not possible it should remain a secret. And then it is not only my nephew—you raise a wasp's nest, very reverend father. We are a powerful house—we have adherents."

The father bowed in assent. The count proceeded. "You understand me; they are all people who have blood in their veins, and who in the world—count as something. They are proud of their honour; the affair will become theirs, and then— Even those who are the friends of peace— It would be a grief of heart to me to be obliged— I, who have always had such a friendship for the capuchins! The fathers, for their ministry to be efficient, should be in harmony with all men—no misunderstandings: besides, they have relations abroad—and these affairs of punctilio extend, ramify— I, too, have a certain dignity to maintain— His excellency—my noble colleagues— It becomes a party matter—"

"It is true," said the provincial, "that Father Christopher is a preacher; I had already the intention—I have even been solicited to do it—but under these circumstances, and just at this time, it might be considered as a punishment; and to punish without being well acquainted—"

"But it is not a punishment; it is a prudent precaution, an honest means of preventing evils that might—I have explained myself."

"The signor count and myself understand each other very well; but the facts being those which your excellency has adduced, it is impossible but that they should in part be known through the country: there are every where firebrands, or idle spirits, who find pleasure in the contests of the monks and the nobility, and love to make malignant observations. Each one has his own dignity to preserve; and I, in the character of a superior, have an express duty—the honour of the habit—it is not my own affair—it is a deposit which—and since the signor your nephew is so irritated, as your excellency has said, he might take it as a satisfaction offered to him, and—I do not say boast of it, but—"

"You jest, reverend father, surely; my nephew is a cavalier of consideration in the world, as he should be; but in his relations with me, he is but a child, and will do neither more nor less than I prescribe to him. And, moreover, he shall never know it. The thing is done between ourselves; there is no necessity for rendering an account to him. Let not that give you any uneasiness; I am accustomed to keep silence on important subjects. As to the idle talk of others, what can be said? It is a very common thing to see a friar leave one place to go and preach at another."

"However, in order to prevent malicious observations, it would be necessary, on this occasion, that the nephew of your excellency should give some demonstration of friendship, of deference,—not for us, but for the order."

"Certainly, certainly, that is but right; it is not necessary, however; I know that the capuchins are highly esteemed by my nephew, as well as by our whole family. But, in this case, something more signal is very proper. Leave it to me, very reverend father: I will give such orders to my nephew—that is to say, it shall be prudently suggested to him, that he may not suspect what has passed between us, because we need not apply a plaster where there is no wound. As to that which we have agreed on, the sooner it is done the better; and if you had a place at some distance—to remove every occasion—"

"They want a preacher at Rimini; and perhaps without this motive I should have thought—"

"That is very opportune, very opportune. And when?"

"Since the thing is to be done, it shall be quickly."

"Certainly, certainly; better to-day than to-morrow. And," continued he, rising, "if I or my adherents can render any service to the good father capuchins—"

"We have often experienced the kindness of the house," said the father provincial, also rising, and following his vanquisher to the door of the apartment.

"We have extinguished a spark," said the count,—"a spark, very reverend father, which might have excited a great conflagration. Between good friends, things are easily arranged."

They then entered the next apartment, and mixed with the rest of the company.

The count obtained his end: Friar Christopher was made to travel on foot from Pescarenico to Rimini, as we shall see.

One evening a capuchin from Milan arrived at Pescarenico, with a packet for the superior: it was an order for Father Christopher to repair to Rimini for the purpose of preaching the Lent sermons. The letter contained instructions to the superior, to insinuate to the friar, that he should give up every attention to any business he might have on hand in the country he must leave, and that he should not maintain any correspondence there. The friar, who was the bearer of the order, was to be the companion of his journey. The superior said nothing that night, but in the morning he sent for Father Christopher, showed him the order, and told him to take his basket, staff, and girdle, and with the friar, whom he presented to him, commence his journey.

Imagine what a blow this was for our good father. Renzo, Lucy, Agnes, passed rapidly over his mind, and he thought, "Great God! what will these unfortunate people do, when I am no longer here?" but raising his eyes to heaven, he placed his hope and confidence there. He crossed his hands on his breast, and bowed his head in token of obedience; he then went to his cell, took his basket, his staff, and his breviary, and after having bid farewell to his brethren, and obtained the benediction of his superior, took, with his companion, the route prescribed.

We have said that Don Roderick, more than ever determined on the accomplishment of his infamous enterprise, had resolved to seek the assistance of a powerful man. We cannot give his name, nor even hazard a conjecture with regard to it; this is the more astonishing, inasmuch as we find notices of this personage in several histories of the time. The identity of the facts does not leave a doubt of the identity of the man; but there is evidently an extreme care to avoid the mention of his name. Francesco Rivola, in his life of the Cardinal Federigo Borromeo, speaking of him, says, "He was a lord as powerful from his wealth as illustrious from his birth," and nothing further. Giuseppe Ripamonti makes farther mention of him, as a *man*, this *man*, a *person*, this *person*. "I will relate," says he, "the case of a man, who, belonging to the most powerful family in the city, chose the country for his residence; and there, assuring himself of impunity by the force of crime, he set at nought the law and the magistrates, the king and the nobles. Placed on the extreme confines of the state, he led an independent life; he offered an asylum to the outlaw; he was outlawed himself, and then absolved from the sentence which had led—" We will hereafter quote from this author other passages, which will confirm the history we are about to relate.

To do that which was forbidden by the laws; to be the arbiter, the supreme judge in the affairs of others, without other interest than a thirst for power; to be feared by all, even by those who were the objects of fear to all men; these had ever been the controlling principles which actuated the conduct of this man. From his youth he had been filled with impatient envy at the power and authority of others; superior to the greater number in riches and retinue, and to all perhaps in birth and audacity, he constrained them to renounce all competition with him; he took some into his friendship, but was far from admitting any equality between himself and them; his proud and disdainful spirit could only be content with those who were willing to acknowledge their inferiority, and to yield to him on all occasions. When, however, they found themselves in any difficulty, they did not fail to solicit the aid of so powerful an auxiliary; and a refusal from him would have been the destruction of his reputation, and of the high station which he had assumed. So that, for himself and others, he had performed such deeds that not all his own power and that of his family could prevent his banishment and outlawry; and he was obliged to leave the state. I believe that it is to this circumstance Ripamonti alludes:—

"He was obliged to leave the country: but his audacity was unsubdued; he went through the city on horseback, followed by a pack of hounds, and with the sound of the trumpet; passing by the court of the palace, he sent an abusive message to the governor by one of the guards."

In his absence he did not desist from his evil practices; he maintained a correspondence with his friends, "who were united to him," says Ripamonti, "in a secret league of atrocious deeds."

It appears that he even contracted new habits, of which the same historian speaks with mysterious brevity. "Foreign princes had recourse to him for important murders, and they even sent him reinforcements of soldiers to act under his orders."

At last, whether the proclamation of his outlawry was withdrawn from some powerful intercession, or that the audacity of the man outweighed all authority, he resolved to return home; not exactly to Milan, but to a castle on the frontier of the Bergamascan territory, which then belonged to the Venetian state. "This house," says Ripamonti, "was a focus of sanguinary mandates. The household was composed of such as had been guilty of great crimes; the cooks, and the scullions even, were not free from the stain of murder." Besides this notable household, he had men resembling them, stationed in different places of the two states, on the confines of which he lived.

All, however tyrannical themselves, had been obliged to choose between the friendship or enmity of this tyrannical man, and it fared ill with those who dared resist him. It was in vain to hope to preserve neutrality or independence; his orders to do such or such a thing, or to refrain, were arbitrary, and resistance was useless. Recourse was had to him on all occasions, and by all sorts of people, good as well as bad, for the arrangements of their difficulties; so that he occasionally became the protector of the oppressed, who could not have obtained redress in any other way, public or private. He was almost always the minister of wickedness, revenge, and caprice; but the various ways in which he had employed his power impressed upon all minds a great idea of his capability to devise and perform his acts in defiance of every obstruction, whether lawful or unlawful. The fame of ordinary tyrants was confined to their own districts, and every district had its tyrant; but the fame of this extraordinary man was spread throughout the Milanese; his life was the subject of popular tales, and his name carried with it something powerful and mysterious. Every tyrant was suspected of alliance with him, every assassin of acting under his orders; at every extraordinary crime, of the author of which they were ignorant, the name of this man was uttered, whom, thanks to the circumspection of our historians, we are obliged to call the Unknown.

The distance between his castle and that of Don Roderick was not more than six miles. The latter had long felt the necessity of keeping on good terms with such a neighbour, and had proffered his services, and entitled himself to the same sort of friendship, as the rest; he was however, careful to conceal the nature and strictness of the union between them. Don Roderick liked to play the tyrant, but not openly; tyranny was with him a means, not an end; he wished to live at ease in the city, and enjoy the advantages, pleasures, and honours of civilised life. To insure this, he was obliged to exhibit management, to testify a great esteem for his relations, to cultivate the friendship of persons in place, in order to sway the balance of justice for his own peculiar purposes. Now, an intimacy with such a man would not have advanced his interests in such points, and especially with his uncle; but a slight acquaintance with him might be considered unavoidable under the circumstances, and therefore in some degree excusable. One morning Don Roderick, equipped for the chase, with an escort of retainers, among whom was Griso, took the road to the castle of the Unknown.

Chapter XX.

The castle of the Unknown was situated above a narrow and shady valley, on the summit of a cliff, which, belonging to a rugged chain of mountains, was nevertheless separated from them by banks, caverns, and precipices. It was only accessible on the side which overlooked the valley. This was a declivity rather steep, but equal, and continued towards the summit: it was occupied as pasture ground, and its lower borders were cultivated, having habitations scattered here and there. The bottom was a bed of stones, through which flowed, according to the season, a small brook, or a large torrent, which served for a boundary between the two territories. The opposite chain of mountains, which formed, as it were, the other wall of the valley, was slightly cultivated towards its base; the rest was composed of precipitous rocks without verdure, and thrown together irregularly and wildly. The scene altogether was one of savage grandeur.

From this castle, as the eagle from his eyrie, its lawless owner overlooked his domain, and heard no human sound above him. He could embrace at a view all the environs, the declivities, the abyss, the practicable approaches. To the eyes of one viewing it from above, the winding path which ascended towards the terrible habitation could be perceived throughout its whole course, and from the windows and loopholes, the signor could leisurely count the steps of the person ascending, and examine him with the closest scrutiny. With the garrison of bravoes which he kept at the castle he could defy an army, which he would have crushed in the valley beneath, before an individual could reach the summit. But none, except such as were friends with the master of the castle, dared set foot even in the valley. Tragical stories were related of some who had attempted the dangerous enterprise, but these stories were already of times long past, and none of the young vassals could remember to have encountered a human being in this place, except under his lord's authority.

Don Roderick arrived in the middle of the valley, at the foot of the cliff, at the commencement of the rugged and winding path; at this point was a tavern, which might have been called a guard-house; an old sign, with a rising sun painted on both sides, was suspended before the door; but the people gave the place the more appropriate name of *Malanotte*.

At the noise of the approaching cavalcade a young boy, well furnished with swords and pistols, appeared on the threshold of the door; and casting a rapid glance at the party, informed three ruffians, who were playing at cards within the house, of its approach. He who appeared to be the chief among them arose, and recognising a friend of his master, saluted him respectfully; Don Roderick returned the salutation with much politeness, and asked if the signor was at the castle. The man replied in the affirmative; and he, dismounting, threw his horse's bridle to Aimwell, one of his retinue. Then, taking his musket from his shoulder, he gave it to *Montanarolo*, as if to relieve himself from an useless encumbrance, but in reality because he knew that on this cliff none were permitted to bear arms. Drawing from his pocket some *berlinghe*, he gave them to *Tanabuso*, saying, "Wait here till my return; and in the mean time amuse yourselves with these honest people." Then presenting to the chief of the band some crowns of gold for himself and his companions, he ascended the path with Griso.

Another bravo belonging to the Unknown, who was on his way to the castle, bore him company; thus sparing him the trouble of declaring his name to whomsoever he should meet. When he arrived at the castle (Griso was left at the gate) he was conducted through a long succession of dark galleries, and various halls hung with muskets, sabres, and other weapons of warfare; each of these halls was guarded by a bravo. After having waited some time, he was admitted to the presence of the Unknown, who advanced to meet him, replying to his salutation, and at the same time, as was his custom, even with his oldest friends, eying him from head to foot. He was tall in stature; and from the baldness of his head, and the deep furrows of his countenance, appeared to be much older than sixty, which was his real age; his countenance and movements, the firmness of his features, and the fire which sparkled from his eyes, indicated a vigour of body as well as of mind which would have been remarkable even in a young man.

Don Roderick told him he had come for advice and assistance; that, having embarked in a difficult enterprise, from which his honour did not suffer him to withdraw, he had remembered the promises of one who never promised in vain; and he then related his abominable intrigue. The Unknown, who had already heard something of it, listened with much attention to the recital, both because he naturally loved such relations, and because Friar Christopher, that avowed enemy of tyrants, was concerned in it. Don Roderick spoke of the difficulty of the undertaking, the distance of the place, a monastery, the *signora*,—but the Unknown, as if prompted by the demon in his heart, interrupted him, saying, that he took the charge of the affair on himself. He wrote down the name of the poor Lucy, and dismissed Don Roderick, saying, "In a little while you will receive news from me."

The reader may remember the villain Egidio, who lived near the walls of the monastery into which Lucy had been received; now, he was one of the most intimate colleagues in crime of the Unknown; and this accounts for the promptness with which this lord assumed the charge of the undertaking. However, no sooner was he left alone than he repented of his precipitation. He had for some time experienced, not remorse, but a vague uneasiness on account of his crimes; at every new addition to them, the remembrance of those he had previously committed pressed upon his memory, if not upon his conscience, and loaded it with an intolerable weight. An undefinable repugnance to the commission of crime, such as he had experienced and subdued at the outset of his career, returned with all its force to overwhelm his spirit. The thoughts of the future contributed to render the past more painful. "To grow old! to die! and then?" And the image of death, which he had so often met undaunted, in face of an enemy, and which seemed to inflame his courage and double his energy—this same image now, in the midnight silence of his castle, quelled his spirit, and impressed him with an awe which he in vain endeavoured to resist. Formerly, the frequent spectacle of violence and murder, inspiring him with a ferocious emulation, had served as a kind of authority against his conscience; now the confused but terrible idea arose in his mind of individual responsibility at the bar of God. The idea of having risen above the crowd of vulgar criminals, and of having left them far behind, an idea which once flattered his pride, now impressed him with a sentiment of fearful solitude; and experiencing at certain moments of despondence the power and presence of that God whose existence he had hitherto neither admitted nor denied, having been wholly immersed in himself, his accumulated crimes rose up, to justify the sentence which was about to condemn him to eternal banishment from the divine presence. But this uneasiness was not suffered to appear, either in his words or his actions; he carefully concealed it under the appearance of more profound and intense ferocity. Regretting the time when he was accustomed to commit iniquity without remorse, without any other solicitude than for its success, he made every effort to recall these habits and feelings; to take pleasure in wickedness; and glory in his shame, in order to convince himself that he was still the same man.

This accounts for the promptitude of his promise to Don Roderick: he wished to deprive himself of the chance of hesitation; but, scarcely alone, he felt his resolution fail, and thoughts arose in his mind which almost tempted him to break his word, and expose his weakness to an inferior accomplice. But with a violent effort he put an end to the painful conflict. He sent for Nibbio, one of the most skilful and resolute ministers of his atrocities, and of whom he had made use in his correspondence with Egidio, and ordered him to mount his horse, to go to Monza, to inform Egidio of the affair he had undertaken, and to require his assistance for its accomplishment.

The messenger returned sooner than his master expected him with the reply of Egidio; the enterprise was easy and safe; the Unknown had only to send a carriage with two or three bravoes, well disguised; Egidio took charge of the rest. The Unknown, whatever passed in his mind, gave orders to Nibbio to arrange every thing, and to set out immediately on the expedition.

If, to perform the horrible service which had been required of him, Egidio had depended only on his ordinary means, he would not certainly have sent back so explicit an answer. But in the asylum of the convent, where every thing appeared as an obstacle, the villain had a means known to himself alone; and that which would have been an insurmountable difficulty to others was to him an instrument of success. We have related how the unhappy signora once lent an ear to his discourse, and the reader may have surmised that this was not the last time; it was only the first step in the path of abomination and blood. The same voice which then addressed her, become imperious through crime, now imposed on her the sacrifice of the innocent girl who had been intrusted to her care.

The proposition appeared frightful to Gertrude; to lose Lucy in any manner would have seemed to her a misfortune, a punishment; and to deprive herself of her with criminal perfidy, to add to her crimes by dealing treacherously with the confiding girl, was to take away the only gleam of virtuous enjoyment which had shone upon her mysterious and wicked career. She tried every method to avoid obedience; every method, except the only infallible one, that was in her power. Crime is a severe and inflexible master, against whom we are strong only when we entirely rebel. Gertrude could not resolve on that, and obeyed.

The day agreed on came; the hour approached; Gertrude, alone with Lucy, bestowed on her more caresses than ordinary, which the poor girl returned with increasing tenderness, as the lamb licks the hand of the shepherd who entices it without the fold into the murderous power of the butcher who there awaits it.

"I want you to do me a great favour; many are ready to obey me, but there is none but yourself whom I can trust. I must speak immediately on an affair of great importance, which I will relate to you some other time, to the superior of the capuchins, who brought you hither, my dear Lucy; but no one must know that I have sent for him. I rely on you to carry a secret message—"

Lucy was astonished at such a request, and alleged her reasons for declining to perform it; without her mother! without a companion! in a solitary road! in a strange country! But Gertrude, instructed in an infernal school, showed great astonishment and displeasure at her refusal, after having been loaded with so many benefits; she affected to treat her excuses as frivolous. "In open day! a short distance! a road that Lucy had travelled a few days before!" She said so much, that the poor girl, touched with gratitude and shame, enquired, "What was to be done?"

"Go to the convent of the capuchins; ask for the superior, tell him to come here immediately, but to let no one suspect that he comes at my request."

"But what shall I say to the portress, who has never seen me go out, and will ask me where I am going?"

"Endeavour to pass without being seen; and if you cannot, say you are going to some church to perform your orisons."

A new difficulty for Lucy! to tell a falsehood! but the signora was so offended at her refusal, and so ridiculed her for preferring a vain scruple to her gratitude, that the unhappy girl, alarmed rather than convinced, replied, "Well, I will go; may God be my guide and protector."

Gertrude, from her grated window, followed her with anxious looks, and when she saw her about to cross the threshold, overcome by irresistible emotion, she cried, "Stop, Lucy."

Lucy returned to the window; but another idea, the one accustomed to predominate, had resumed its sway over the mind of the unhappy Gertrude.

She affected dissatisfaction at the directions she had given; described the road again to Lucy, and dismissed her: "Do exactly as I have told you, and return quickly."

Lucy passed the door of the cloister unobserved, and proceeding on her way with downcast eyes, found, with the aid of the directions given, and her own recollections, the gate of the suburb; timid and trembling, she continued on the high road, until she arrived at that which led to the convent. This road was buried, like the bed of a river, between two high banks, bordered with trees, whose branches united to form an arch above it. On finding it entirely deserted, she felt her fears revive; she hurried on, but gained courage from the sight of a travelling carriage which had stopped a short distance before her; before the door of it, which was open, there stood two travellers looking about, as if uncertain of their way. As she approached, she heard one of them say, "Here is a good girl, who will tell us the way." As she came on a line with the carriage, this same man addressed her: "My good girl, can you tell us the way to Monza?"

"You are going in the wrong direction," replied the poor girl; "Monza lies there." As she turned to point it out, his companion (it was Nibbio) seized her by the waist, and lifted her from the ground. Lucy screamed from surprise and terror; the ruffian threw her into the carriage; a third, who was seated in the bottom of it, seized her, and compelled her to sit down before him; another put a handkerchief over her mouth, and stifled her cries. Nibbio then entered the carriage, the door was closed, and the horses set off on a gallop. He who had asked her the perfidious question remained behind; he was an emissary of Egidio, who had watched Lucy when she quitted the convent, and had hastened by a shorter road to inform his colleagues, and wait for her at the place agreed on.

But who can describe the terror and anguish of the unfortunate girl? Who can tell what passed in her heart? Cruelly anxious to ascertain her horrible situation, she wildly opened her eyes, but closed them again at the sight of those frightful faces. She struggled in vain. The men held her down in the bottom of the carriage: if she attempted to cry, they drew the handkerchief tightly over her mouth. In the mean while, three gruff voices, endeavouring to assume a tone of humanity, said to her, "Be quiet, be quiet: do not be afraid; we do not wish to harm you." After a while her struggles ceased, she languidly opened her eyes, and the horrible faces before her appeared to blend themselves into one monstrous image; her colour fled, and she fell lifeless into their arms.

"Courage, courage," said Nibbio; but Lucy was now beyond the reach of his horrible voice.

"The devil! she appears to be dead," said one of them. "If she should really be dead!"

"Poh!" said the other, "these fainting fits are common to women; they don't die in this way."

"Hush," said Nibbio, "be attentive to your duty, and do not meddle with other affairs. Keep your muskets ready, because this wood we are entering is a nest for robbers. Don't keep them in your hands—the devil! put them behind you. Do you not see that this girl is a tender chicken, who faints at nothing? If she sees that you have arms, she may die in reality. When she comes to her senses, be careful not to frighten her. Touch her not, unless I tell you to do so. I can hold her. Keep quiet, and let me talk to her."

Meanwhile the carriage entered the wood. Poor Lucy awoke as from a profound and painful slumber. She opened her eyes, and her horrible situation rushed with full force upon her mind. She struggled again in vain, she attempted to scream, but Nibbio said to her, holding up the handkerchief, "Be tranquil; it is the best thing you can do. We do not wish to harm you; but if you do not keep silence, we must make you."

"Let me go. Who are you? Where are you taking me? Why am I here? Let me go, let me go."

"I tell you, don't be frightened. You are not a child, and you ought to know that we will not harm you. We might have murdered you before this, if such had been our intention. Be quiet, then."

"No, no, let me go; I know you not."

"We know you well enough, however."

"Oh, holy Virgin! Let me go, for charity's sake. Who are you? Why have you brought me here?"

"Because we have been ordered to do so."

"Who? who? who ordered you to do it?"

"Hush!" said Nibbio, in a severe tone. "Such questions must not be answered."

Lucy attempted to throw herself from the door of the carriage, but finding the effort vain, she had recourse again to entreaties, and with her cheeks bathed in tears, and her voice broken by sobs, she continued, "Oh, for the love of heaven, and the holy Virgin, let me go! What harm have I done you? I am a poor creature, who have never injured you; I forgive you all that you have done, and will pray to God for you. If you have a daughter, a wife, or a mother, think what they would suffer in my situation. Remember that we must all die, and that one day you will hope that God will show mercy to you. Let me go, let me go; the Lord will guide me on my way."

"We cannot."

"You cannot? Great God! why can you not? Where are you taking me?"

"We cannot; your supplications are useless. Do not be frightened; we will not harm you. Be quiet; no one shall harm you."

More than ever alarmed to perceive that her words produced no effect, Lucy turned to Him who holds in his powerful hand the hearts of men, and can, if he sees fit, soften the most ferocious. She crossed her arms on her breast, and prayed from the depth of her heart, fervently; then again vainly implored to be set free: but we have not the heart to relate more at length this painful journey, which lasted four hours, and which was to be succeeded by many hours of still deeper anguish.

At the castle, the Unknown was waiting her arrival with extraordinary solicitude and agitation of mind. Strange, that he who had coldly and calmly disposed of so many lives, and had regarded as nothing the torments he inflicted, should now feel an impression of remorse, almost of terror, at the tyranny he exercised over an unknown girl, an humble peasant! From a high window of his castle, he had for some time looked down upon the valley beneath; at last he saw the carriage approaching slowly at a distance, as if the horses were wearied with their rapid journey. He perceived it, and felt his heart beat violently.

"Is she there?" thought he. "What trouble this girl gives me! I must free myself from it." And he prepared himself to send one of his ruffians to meet the carriage, and tell Nibbio to conduct the girl immediately to the castle of Don Roderick; but an imperious *No*, which made itself heard by his conscience, caused him to relinquish his design. Tormented, however, by the necessity of ordering something to be done, and insupportably weary of waiting the slow approach of the carriage, he sent for an old woman who was attached to his service.

This woman had been born in the castle, and had passed her life in it. She had been impressed from infancy with an opinion of the unlimited power of its masters; and her principal maxim was implicit obedience towards them. To the ideas of duty were united sentiments of respect, fear, and servile devotion. When the Unknown became lord of the castle, and began to make such horrible use of his power, she experienced a degree of pain, and at the same time a more profound sentiment of subjection. In time she became habituated to what was daily acting before her: the powerful and unbridled will of such a lord she viewed as an exercise of fated justice. When somewhat advanced in years, she had espoused a servant of the house, who being sent on a hazardous expedition, left his body on the high road, and his wife a widow in the castle. The revenge that her lord took for his death imparted to her a savage consolation, and increased her pride at being under his protection. From that day she rarely set foot beyond the castle walls, and by degrees there remained to her no other idea of human beings, than that of those by whom she was daily surrounded. She was not employed in any particular service, but each one gave her something to do as it pleased him. She had sometimes clothes to mend, food to prepare, and wounds to dress. Commands, reproaches, and thanks were equally mingled with abusive raillery: she went by the appellation of the *old woman*, and the tone with which the name was uttered varied according to the circumstances and humour of the speaker. Disturbed in her idleness and irritated in her self-love, which were her two ruling passions, she returned these compliments with language in which Satan might have recognised more of his own genius than in that of her persecutors.

"You see that carriage below there," said the Unknown.

"I do," said she.

"Have a litter prepared immediately, and let it carry you to *Malanotte*. Quick, quick; you must arrive before the carriage; it approaches with the slow step of death. In this carriage there is—there ought to be—a young girl. If she is there, tell Nibbio from me, that he must place her in the litter, and that he must come at once to me. You will get into the litter with her; and when you arrive here, you must take her to your room. If she asks you where you are leading her, whose is this castle, be careful—"

"Oh, do not doubt me," said the old woman.

"But," pursued the Unknown, "comfort her, encourage her."

"What can I say to her?"

"What can you say to her? Comfort her, I tell you. Have you arrived at this age, and know not how to administer consolation to the afflicted? Have you never had any sorrow? Have you never been visited by fear? Do you not know the language that consoles in such moments? Speak this language to *her* then; find it in the remembrance of your own misfortunes. Go directly."

When she was gone, he remained some time at the window, gazing at the approaching carriage; he then looked at the setting sun, and the glorious display of clouds about the horizon. He soon withdrew, closed the window, and kept pacing the apartment in a state of uneasy excitement.

Chapter XXI.

The old woman hastened to obey, and gave orders, under authority of that name which, by whomsoever pronounced, set the whole castle in motion, as no one imagined that any one would dare to use it unauthorised. She reached *Malanotte* a little before the carriage: when it was near at hand, she left the litter; and making a sign to the coachman to stop, approached the window, and whispered in the ear of Nibbio the will of her master.

Lucy, sensible that the motion of the carriage had ceased, shook off the lethargy into which she had for some time been plunged, and in an agony of terror looked around her. Nibbio had drawn himself back on the seat, and the old woman, resting her chin on the window, said to Lucy, "Come, my child; come, poor girl; come with me. I have orders to treat you kindly, and to offer you every consolation."

At the sound of a female voice the unfortunate girl felt a momentary relief, which was, however, succeeded by deeper terror as she looked at the person from whom it proceeded. "Who are you?" said she, anxiously fixing her eyes upon her.

"Come, come, poor girl," repeated the old woman.

Nibbio and his two companions, inferring the designs of their master from the extraordinary deportment of the old woman, endeavoured to persuade the poor girl to obey; but Lucy kept gazing at the wild and savage solitude around, which left her no ray of hope. However, she attempted to cry out; but seeing Nibbio give a look to the handkerchief, she stopped, trembled, was seized, and then placed in the litter. The old woman was placed beside her; and Nibbio left the two villains for their escort, and hastened forward at the call of his master. Lucy, aroused to momentary energy by the near approach of the deformed and withered features of her companion, cried, "Where am I? Where are you taking me?"

"To one who wishes you well; to a great—you are a lucky girl; be happy, do not be afraid; be happy. He has told me to encourage you; you will tell him that I have done so, will you not?"

"Who is this man? What is he? What does he want with me? I do not belong to him. Tell me where I am. Let me go. Tell these men to let me go, to take me to some church. Oh, you, who are a woman, in the name of the holy Virgin, I entreat you."

This holy and tender name, so often pronounced with respect in her early years, and for so long a time neglected and forgotten, produced on the mind of the wretched woman, who had not heard it for so long a time, a confused impression, like the remembrance of lights and shadows on the mind of one blind from infancy.

Meanwhile the Unknown, standing at the door of the castle, looked below, and saw the litter slowly ascending, and Nibbio walking a few steps in advance of it. At the sight of his master, he hurried forward. "Come here," said the signor to him, and led the way to an inner hall. "Well?" said he, stopping.—"All has been done according to your wishes," replied Nibbio, bowing. "The order in time, the young girl in time, no one near the place, a single cry, no one alarmed, the coachman diligent, the horses swift; but—"

"But what?"

"But, to say truth, I would rather have received orders to plunge a dagger in her heart at once, than to have been obliged to look at her, and hear her entreaties."

"What is this? What is this? What do you mean?"

"I would say that during the whole journey—yes, during the whole journey—she has excited my compassion."

"Compassion! What dost thou know of compassion? What is compassion?"

"I have never understood what it is until to-day; it is something like fear; if it takes possession of one, one is no longer a man."

"Let me hear, then, what she has done to excite your compassion."

"Oh, most illustrious signor, she wept, implored, and looked so piteously; then turned pale, pale as death; then wept, and prayed again, and said such words—"

"I will not have this girl in the castle," thought the Unknown. "I was wrong to embark in this business; but I have promised, I have promised: when she is far away—" And looking imperiously at Nibbio, "Now," said he, "put an end to your compassion; mount a horse, take with you two or three companions, if you wish; go to the castle of Don Roderick, thou knowest it. Tell him to send immediately, immediately—or otherwise—"

But another No, more imperious than the first, whose sound was heard in the depth of his soul, prevented his proceeding. "No," said he in a determined tone, as if expressing the command of this secret voice,—"*no*; go to bed; and to-morrow morning you shall do what I shall then order."

"This girl must have some demon who protects her," thought he, as he remained alone, with his arms crossed on his breast, regarding the fitful shadows cast by the rays of the moon on the floor, which darted through the grating of the lofty windows. "She must have some demon or an angel who protects her. Compassion in Nibbio! To-morrow morning, to-morrow morning at the latest, she shall be sent away; she must submit to her destiny, that is certain. And," continued he, with the tone of one who gives a command to a wayward child, under the conviction that he will not obey it, "we will think of it no more. This animal Don Roderick must not come to torment me with thanks, for—I do not wish to hear her spoken of. I have served him—because I promised to do so; and I promised, because it was my destiny. But Don Roderick shall pay me with usury. Let us see—"

And he endeavoured to imagine some difficult enterprise in which to engage Don Roderick as a punishment; but his thoughts involuntarily recurred to another subject. "Compassion in Nibbio! What has she done? I must see her. No! Yes! I must see her."

He passed through several halls, and arriving at the apartment of the old woman, knocked with his foot at the door.

"Who is there?"

"Open."

At the sound of this voice, the old woman quickly obeyed, and flung the door wide open. The Unknown threw a glance around the chamber, and by the light of the lantern, which stood on the table, saw Lucy on the floor in one corner of it.

"Why did you place her there?" said he, with a frowning brow.

"She placed herself there," replied she, timidly. "I have done all I could to encourage her; but she will not listen to me."

"Rise," said he to Lucy, who, at the noise of his step, and at the sound of his voice, had been seized with new terror. She buried her face in her hands, and remained silent and trembling before him.

"Rise; I will not harm you; I can befriend you," said the signor. "Rise!" repeated he, in a voice of thunder, irritated at having spoken in vain.

As if alarm had restored her exhausted strength, the unfortunate girl fell on her knees, clasped her hands on her breast, as if before a sacred image, then with her eyes fixed on the earth, exclaimed, "Here I am, murder me if you will."

"I have already told you that I will not harm you," replied the Unknown, in a more gentle tone, gazing at her agonised and altered features.

"Courage, courage," said the old woman. "He tells you himself that he will not harm you."

"And why," resumed Lucy, in a voice in which indignation and despair were mingled with alarm and dismay,—"why make me suffer the torments of hell? What have I done to you?"

"Perhaps they have not treated you kindly? Speak!"

"Oh, kindly treated! They have brought me hither by treachery and force. Why, why did they bring me? Why am I here? Where am I? I am a poor creature. What have I done to you? In the name of God—"

"God! God! always God!" said the Unknown. "Those who are too weak to defend themselves, always make use of the name of God, as if they knew something concerning him! What! do you mean by this word to make me—" and he left the sentence unfinished.

"Oh, signor, what could I mean, a poor girl like me, except that you should have pity on me? God pardons so many deeds for one act of mercy! Let me go; for pity, for charity, let me go. Do not make a poor creature suffer thus! Oh, you, who have it in your power, tell them to let me go. They brought me hither by force. Put me again in the carriage with this woman, and let it carry me to my mother. O holy Virgin! My mother! my mother! Perhaps she is not far from here—I thought I saw my mountains! Why do you make me suffer? Carry me to a church; I will pray for you all my life. Does it cost you so much to say one word? Oh, I see that you are touched! Say but the word, say it. God pardons so many deeds for one act of mercy."

"Oh, why is she not the daughter of one of the cowards who outlawed me?" thought the Unknown. "I should then enjoy her sufferings; but now—"

"Do not stifle so good an inspiration," pursued Lucy, on seeing hesitation in the countenance of her persecutor. "If you do not grant me mercy, the Lord will; he will send death to relieve me, and all will be over. But you—one day, perhaps, you also—but no, no—I will pray the Lord to preserve you from evil. What would it cost you to say one word? If ever you experience these torments—"

"Well, well, take courage," said the Unknown, with a gentleness that astonished the old woman. "Have I done you any harm? Have I menaced you?"

"Oh, no. I see that you have a good heart, and that you pity a poor creature. If you chose, you could alarm me more than any of them, you could make me die with fear; and on the contrary, you have—you have given me some consolation. God reward you! Accomplish the work you have begun; save me, save me."

"To-morrow morning."

"Oh, save me now, now!"

"To-morrow morning I will see you again, I tell you. Be of good courage. Rest yourself. You must need food; it shall be brought to you."

"No, no, I shall die if any one comes into this room, I shall die. Take me away, God will reward you."

"A servant will bring you something to eat," said the Unknown; "and you," continued he, turning to the old woman, "persuade her to eat, and to repose on the bed. If she consents to have you sleep with her, well; if not, you can sleep very well on the floor. Be kind to her, I say; and take care that she makes no complaint of you."

He hastily quitted the room, before Lucy could renew her entreaties.

"Oh, miserable that I am! Shut, shut the door!" said Lucy, returning to seat herself in her corner. "Oh, miserable that I am! Who shall I implore now? Where am I? Tell me, tell me, for charity, who is this signor? Who has been talking to me? who is he?"

"Who is he? Do you wish me to tell you? you must wait awhile first. You are proud, because he protects you; provided you are satisfied, no matter what becomes of me. Ask *him* his name. If I should tell you, he would not speak to me so gently as he did to you. I am an old woman, I am an old woman," continued she, grumbling: but hearing the sobs of Lucy, she remembered the threat of her master; and addressing her in a less bitter tone, "Well! I have said no harm. Be cheerful. Do not ask me what I cannot tell you, but have courage. How satisfied most people would be, should he speak to them as he has spoken to you! Be cheerful! Directly, you shall have something to eat; and from what he said, I know it will be something good. And then, you must lie down, and you will leave a little room for me," added she, with an accent of suppressed rancour.

"I cannot eat; I cannot sleep. Leave me, approach me not. You will not go away?"

"No, no," said the old woman, seating herself on a large arm-chair, and regarding her with a mingled expression of alarm and rage. She looked at the bed, and did not very well relish the idea of being banished from it for the night, as it was very cold; but she hoped at least for a good supper. Lucy felt neither cold nor hunger; she remained stupified with grief and terror; her ideas became vague and confused as in the delirium of a fever.

She shuddered at hearing a knock at the door. "Who is there?" cried she, "who is there? Don't let any one come in."

"It is only Martha, bringing something to eat."

"Shut, shut the door!" cried Lucy.

"Certainly," replied the old woman. Taking a basket from the hands of Martha, she placed it on the table, and closed the door. She invited Lucy to taste the delicious food, bestowing on it profuse praises, and on the wine too, which was such as the signor himself drank with his friends; but seeing that they were useless she said, "It is your own fault, you *must* not forget to tell him that I asked you. I will eat, however, and leave enough for you, if you should come to your senses." When her supper was finished she approached Lucy again, and renewed her solicitations.

"No, no, I wish nothing," replied she, in a faint and exhausted voice. "Is the door shut?" she exclaimed, with momentary energy; "is it well secured?"

The old woman approached the door, and showed her that it was firmly bolted. "You see," said she, "it is well fastened. Are you satisfied now?"

"Oh! satisfied! satisfied! in this place!" said Lucy, sinking into her corner. "But God knows that I am here."

"Come to bed. What would you do there, lying like a dog? How silly to refuse comforts when you can have them!"

"No, no, leave me to myself."

"Well, remember it is your own fault; if you wish to come to bed, you can—I have left room enough for you; remember I have asked you very often." Thus saying, she drew the clothes over her, and soon all was profound silence.

Lucy remained motionless, with her face buried in her hands, which rested on her knees; she was neither awake nor asleep, but in a dreamy state of the imagination, painful, vague, and changeful. At first, she recalled with something of self-possession the minutest circumstances of this horrible day; then her reason for a moment forsook its throne, vainly struggling against the phantoms conjured by uncertainty and terror; at last, weary and exhausted, she sunk on the floor, in a state approaching to, and resembling, sleep. But suddenly she awoke, as at an internal call, and strove to recall her scattered senses, to know where she was, and why she had been brought thither. She heard a noise, and listened; it was the heavy breathing of the old woman, in a deep slumber; she opened her eyes on the objects around her, which the flickering of the lamp, now dying in its socket, rendered confused and indistinct. But soon her recent impressions returned distinctly to her mind, and the unfortunate girl recognised her prison; and with the knowledge came associated all the terrors of this horrible day; and, overcome anew by anxiety and terror, she wished earnestly for death. She could only pray, and as the words fell from her trembling lips, she felt her confidence revive. Suddenly a thought presented itself to her mind; that her prayer would be more acceptable if united with an offering of something dear to her; she remembered the object to which she had clung for her happiness, and resolved to sacrifice it; then clasping her hands over her chaplet, which hung upon her neck, and raising her tearful eyes to heaven, she cried, "O most holy Virgin! thou to whom I have so often prayed, and who hast so often consoled me—thou who hast suffered so much sorrow, and art now so glorious—thou who hast performed so many miracles for the afflicted—holy Virgin! succour me, take me from this peril, mother of God! return me safely to my mother, and I pledge myself to remain devoted to thy service; I renounce for ever the unfortunate youth, and from this time devote myself to thee!" After this consecration of herself, she felt her confidence and faith increase; she remembered the "to-morrow morning" uttered by the Unknown, and took it as a promise of safety. Her wearied senses yielded to this new sentiment, and she slept profoundly and peacefully with the name of her protectress on her lips.

But in this same castle was one who could not sleep: after having quitted Lucy, and given orders for her supper, he had visited the posts of his fortress; but her image remained stamped on his mind, her words still resounded in his ears. He retired to his chamber, and threw himself on his bed; but in the stillness around this same image of Lucy in her desolation and anguish took possession still more absolutely of his thoughts, and rendered sleep hopeless. "What new feelings are these?" thought he. "Nibbio was right; but what is there in a woman's tears to unman me thus? Did I never see a woman weep before? Ay, and how often have I beheld their deepest agonies unmoved? But now—"

And here he recalled, without much difficulty, many an instance when neither prayers nor tears were able to make him swerve from his atrocious purposes; but instead of deriving augmented resolution, as he had hoped, from the recollection, he experienced an emotion of alarm, of consternation; so that even, as a relief from the torment of retrospection, he thought of Lucy. "She lives still," said he, "she is here; there is yet time. I have it in my power to say to her, Go in peace! I can also ask her forgiveness. Forgiveness! I ask forgiveness of a woman! Ah, if in that word existed the power to drive this demon from my soul, I would say it; yes, I feel that I would say it. To what am I reduced? I am no longer myself! Well, well! many a time have such follies passed through my head; this will take its flight also."

And to procure the desired forgetfulness, he endeavoured to busy himself with some new project; but in vain: all appeared changed! that which at another time would have been a stimulus to action, had now lost its charm; his imagination was overwhelmed with the insupportable weight of remembered crimes. Even the idea of continuing to associate with those whom he had employed as the instruments of his daring and licentious will was revolting to his soul; and, disgusted and weary, he found relief only in the thought that by the dawn of morning he would set at liberty the unfortunate Lucy.

"I will save her; yes, I will save her. As soon as the day breaks, I will fly to her, and say, Go, go in peace. But my promise! Ay, who is Don Roderick that I should hold sacred a promise made to *him*?" With the perplexity of a man to whom a superior addresses unexpectedly an embarrassing question, the Unknown endeavoured to reply to this his own, or, rather, that was whispered by this new principle, that had of a sudden sprung up so awfully in his soul, to pass judgment upon him. He wondered how he could have resolved to engage himself to inflict suffering, without any motive of hatred or fear, on an unfortunate being whom he did not know, only to render a service to this man. He could not find any excuse for it; he could not even imagine how he had been led to do it. The hasty determination had been the impulse of a mind obedient to its habitual feelings, the consequence of a thousand previous deeds; and from an examination of the motives which had led him to commit a single deed, he was led to the retrospection of his whole life.

In looking back from year to year, from enterprise to enterprise, from crime to crime, from blood to blood, each one of his actions appeared abstracted from the feelings which had induced their perpetration, and therefore exposed in all their horrible deformity, but which those feelings had hitherto veiled from his view. They were all his own, he was responsible for all; they comprised his life; the horror of this thought filled him with despair; he grasped his pistol, and raised it to his head—but at the moment in which he would have terminated his miserable existence, his thoughts rushed onwards to the time that must continue to flow on after his end. He thought of his disfigured corpse, without sense or motion, in the power of the vilest men; the astonishment and confusion which would take place in the castle, the conversation it would excite in the neighbourhood and afar off, and, more than all, the rejoicing of his enemies. The darkness and silence of the night inspired him with other apprehensions still; it appeared to him that he would not have hesitated to perform the deed in open day, in the presence of others. "And, after all, what was it? but a moment, and all would be over." And now another thought rose to his mind: "If that other life, of which they tell, is an invention of priests, is a mere fabrication, why should I die? Of what consequence is all that I have done? It is a trifle—but if there should be another life!"

At such a doubt, he was filled with deeper despair, a despair from which death appeared no refuge. The pistol dropped from his grasp—both hands were applied to his aching head—and he trembled in every limb. Suddenly the words he had heard a few hours before came to his memory, "God pardons so many deeds for one act of mercy." They did not come to him clothed in the humble tone of supplication, with which he had heard them pronounced, but in one of authority which offered some gleam of hope. It was a moment of relief: he brought to mind the figure of Lucy, when she uttered them; and he regarded her, not as a suppliant, but as an angel of consolation. He waited with anxiety the approach of day, that he might hear from her mouth other words of hope and life. He imagined himself conducting her to her mother, "And then, what shall I do to-morrow? what shall I do for the rest of the day? what shall I do the day after, and the next day? and the night? the night which will so soon return? Oh, the night! let me not think of the night!" And, plunged in the frightful void of the future, he sought in vain for some employment of time, some method of living through the days and nights. Now he thought of abandoning his castle, and flying to some distant country, where he had never been heard of; but, could he fly from himself? Then he felt a confused hope of recovering his former courage and habits; and that he should regard these terrors of his soul but as a transient delirium: now, he dreaded the approach of day, which should exhibit him so miserably changed to his followers; then he longed for its light, as if it would bring light also to his troubled thoughts. As the day broke, a confused sound of merriment broke upon his ear. He listened; it was a distant chiming of bells, and he could hear the echo of the mountains repeat the harmony, and mingle itself with it. From another quarter, still nearer, and then from another, similar sounds were heard. "What means this?" said he. "For what are these rejoicings? What joyful event has taken place?" He rose from his bed of thorns, and opened the window.

The mountains were still half veiled in darkness, the heavens appeared enveloped in a heavy and vast cloud; but he distinguished, through the faint dawn of the morning, crowds passing towards the opening on the right of the castle, villagers in their holyday garments. "What are those people doing? what has happened to cause all this joy?" And calling a bravo, who slept in the adjoining room, he asked him the cause of the commotion. The man replied that he was ignorant of it, but would go immediately and enquire. His master remained at the window, contemplating the moving spectacle, which increasing day rendered more distinct every moment. He saw crowds passing in succession; men, women, and children, as guided by one impulse, directing their steps in one direction. They appeared animated by a common joy; and the bells, with their united sound of merriment, seemed to be an echo of the general hilarity. The Unknown looked on intently, and felt an eager curiosity to know what could have communicated such happiness to such a multitude of people.

Chapter XXII.

The bravo hastened back with the intelligence, that the Cardinal Frederick Borromeo, Archbishop of Milan, had arrived the evening before, and was expected to pass the day there. The report of his arrival being spread abroad, the people had been seized with a desire to see him; and the bells were rung in testimony of the happiness his presence conferred, and also to give wider notice of his arrival. The Unknown, left alone, continued to look down into the valley—"For a man! all crowding, all eager to see a man! And, nevertheless, each one of them has some demon that torments him; but none, none, a demon like mine; not one has passed such a night as I have. What is there in this man to excite such joy? Some silver which he will scatter among them.—But *all* are not actuated by such a motive. Well, a few words—Oh! if he had a few words of consolation for me! Yes—why should I not go to him? Why not? I *will* go. What better can I do? I will go and speak to him; speak to him alone. What shall I say to him? Why, why, that which—I will hear what he will say to me."

Having come to this vague determination, he threw over his shoulders a military cloak, put his pistol and dagger in his girdle, and took from the wall, where it hung, a carabine almost as famous as himself; thus accoutred, he proceeded to Lucy's chamber, and leaving his carabine at the door, he knocked and demanded admittance. The old woman hastened to open the door; he entered, and looking around the room saw Lucy tranquil and silent in the corner of it.

"Does she sleep?" asked he in a low voice. "Why did you suffer her to sleep there? Were these my orders?"

"I did all I could; but she would neither eat nor come—"

"Let her sleep then in peace; be careful not to trouble her, and when she wakes—Martha will be in the next chamber, and you must send her for whatever she may want—when she wakes—tell her I—that the signor has gone out for a little while, that he will return, and that—he will do all that she wishes."

The old woman was astonished; "She must be some princess," thought she.

The Unknown departed, took his carabine, gave orders to Martha to be in waiting, and to a bravo to guard the chamber, and not suffer any one to approach; then leaving the castle, with rapid steps he descended into the valley. The bravoes whom he met ascending the hill, stopped respectfully at his approach, expecting and awaiting orders for some expedition, and were astonished at his whole appearance, and the looks with which he returned their salute.

When he reached the public road, his presence made a very different impression; at his approach every one gave way, regarding him with looks of suspicion and wonder; each individual whom he met, cast at him a troubled look, bowed, and slackened his pace, in order to remain behind. He arrived at the village in the midst of the throng; his name quickly spread from mouth to mouth, and a passage was instantly made for him to pass. He enquired of one near him where the cardinal was. "In the house of the curate," replied the person, respectfully pointing to it. He went to it, entered a small court where there were several priests, who looked at him with astonishment and suspicion. He saw, opposite to him, a door open, which led to a small hall, in which were also a great collection of priests. He left his carabine in a corner of the court, and entered the hall. He was received here, likewise, with doubting looks, and whispers; and his name was repeated with infinite awe. He accosted one of them, asking to be directed to the cardinal, as he wished to speak with him.

"I am a stranger," replied the priest; and looking around upon the assembly, he called the cross-bearer, who at the time was saying to one near him, "He here!—the famous—What can have brought him here? Make room!" At this call, which resounded in the general silence, he felt himself compelled to advance. He bowed before the Unknown, raised his eyes in uneasy curiosity to his face, and understanding his request, he stammered out, "I do not know if his illustrious lordship—at this time—is—can—however, I will go and see." And he went, against his will, to carry the message to the cardinal.

At this period of our history we cannot do otherwise than rest a while, as the traveller worn out and weary with a long journey through a sterile and savage land, refreshes himself for a season under the shade of a tree, near a fountain of living water. We are about to introduce a person whose name and memory cause an emotion of respect and sympathy; and this emotion is the more grateful from our previous contemplation of wickedness and crime. We trust our readers will excuse our devoting a few moments to this great and good man.

Frederick Borromeo, born in the year 1564, was one of those rare characters who have employed a fine genius, the resources of great wealth, the advantages of privileged rank, and unceasing industry, for the discovery and practice of that which was for the good of mankind. His life was like a stream, which, issuing limpid from its native rock, moves on undefiled over various lands; and, clear and limpid still, unites itself with the ocean. In the midst of the pomps and pleasures of the world, he applied himself from his earliest youth to study and obey the precepts of religion; and this application produced in his heart its legitimate fruits. He took truth for the rule of his thoughts and actions. He was taught by it not to look upon this life as a burthen to the many, and a pleasure to the few; but as a scene of activity for all, and of which all must render their account; and the chief aim of his thoughts had ever been to render his life useful and holy.

In 1580, he declared his resolution to devote himself to the ministry of the church, and he took the habit from the hands of his cousin Carlos, whom the public voice, even to the present day, has uniformly acknowledged as a saint. He entered a short time after into the college at Pavia, founded by that holy man, and which still bears the name of the family. There, whilst applying himself with assiduity to the occupations prescribed by its rules, he voluntarily imposed on himself, in addition, the task of instructing the poor and ignorant in the principles of the Christian religion, and of visiting, consoling, and aiding the sick. He made use of the authority which was conceded to him by all, to induce his companions to second him in these deeds of benevolence; he steadily refused all worldly advantages, and led a life of self-denial and devotion to the cause of religion and virtue. The complaints of his kindred, who thought the dignity of the house degraded by his plain and simple habits of life, were unavailing. He had another conflict to sustain with the ecclesiastical authorities, who wished to impel him forward to distinction, and make him appear as the prince of the place. From all this, however, he carefully withdrew himself, although at the time but a youth.

It would not have been astonishing that, during the life of his cousin Carlos, Frederick should have imitated the example and followed the counsel of so good a man; but it was surprising, that after his death no one could perceive that Frederick, although only twenty years of age, had lost his guardian and guide. The increasing splendour of his talents, his piety, the support of many powerful cardinals, the authority of his family, the name itself, to which Carlos had caused to be associated an idea of sanctity and sacerdotal superiority, all concurred to point him out as a proper subject for ecclesiastical dignity. But he, persuaded in the depth of his soul of that which no true Christian can deny, that a man has no real superiority over others, but in devotion to their good, dreaded distinction, and sought to avoid it. He did not wish to escape from the obligation to serve his neighbour; his life was but one scene of such services; but he did not esteem himself worthy of so high and responsible an office. Governed by such feelings, in 1595, when Clement VIII. offered him the archbishopric of Milan, he refused it without hesitation, but was finally obliged to yield to the express command of the pope.

Such demonstrations are neither difficult nor rare; it is no greater effort for hypocrisy to assume them, than for raillery to deride them. But are they not also the natural expression of wise and virtuous feeling? The life is the test of sincerity; and though all the hypocrites in the world had assumed the expression of virtuous sentiments, yet the sentiments themselves will always command our respect and veneration, when their genuineness is evinced by a life of disinterestedness and self-sacrifice.

Frederick, as archbishop, was careful to reserve for himself only that which was barely necessary, of his time and his wealth: he said, as all the world says, that the ecclesiastical revenues are the patrimony of the poor; and we shall see how he put this maxim in practice. He caused an estimate to be made of the sum necessary for his expenses, and for those employed in his service: finding it to be 600 sequins, he ordered that amount to be taken from his patrimonial revenues for the supply of his table. He exercised such minute economy with regard to himself, that he did not relinquish any article of dress until it was entirely worn out; but he joined to these habits of extreme simplicity, an exquisite neatness, which was remarkable in this age of luxury and uncleanliness. He did more: in order that nothing should be lost from the fragments of his frugal table, he assigned them to a hospital for the poor, and a servant came every day to gather the remnants for that purpose. From the attention which he paid to such minutiæ, we might form a contracted idea of his mind, as being incapable of elevating itself to more extensive designs, were it not for the Ambrosian library, which remains a monument of his liberality and magnificence. To furnish it with books and manuscripts, besides those which he had already collected, he sent eight of the most skilful and learned men to make purchases of them in France, Spain, Germany, Italy, Flanders, Greece, Lebanon, and Jerusalem. He succeeded in collecting 30,000 printed volumes, and 14,000 manuscripts. He joined to the library a college of doctors: these doctors were nine in number, and supported by him as long as he lived; after his death, the ordinary revenues not being sufficient for the expense, they were reduced to two. Their duty consisted in the cultivation of the various branches of human knowledge, theology, history, belles lettres, ecclesiastical antiquities, and Oriental languages. Each one was obliged to publish some work on the subject to which he had particularly applied himself. He added to this a college, which he called *Trilingue*, for the study of the Greek, Latin, and Italian languages; and a college of pupils, who were instructed in these languages to become professors in their turn. He united to these also a printing establishment for the Oriental languages, for Hebrew, Chaldee, Arabic, Persian, and Armenian; a gallery of pictures, and another of statues; and a school for the three principal arts of design. For the latter, he was at no loss to find professors; but this was not the case with regard to the Eastern languages, which were at this time but little cultivated in Europe. In the orders which he left for the government and regulations of the library, we perceive a perpetual attention to utility, admirable in itself, and much in advance of the ordinary ideas of his time. He prescribed to the librarian the cultivation of a regular correspondence with the learned men of Europe, to keep himself acquainted with the state of science, and to procure every new and important work; he also charged him to point out to young students the books necessary for them, and, whether natives or foreigners, to afford them every possible facility in making use of those of the library. There is a history of the Ambrosian library by one Pierpaolo Bosca, who was librarian after the death of Frederick, in which all the excellent regulations are minutely detailed. Other libraries existed in Italy, but with little benefit to the studious: the books were carefully concealed from view in their cases, and inaccessible to all, except on rare occasions, and with the utmost difficulty. A book might then be seen, but not studied. It is useless to enquire what were the fruits of these establishments of Borromeo, but we must admire the generosity, judgment, and benevolence of the man who could undertake and execute such things, in the midst of the ignorance, inertness, and general indifference which surrounded him. And in attention to public, he was not unmindful of private benevolence; indeed, his whole life was a perpetual almsgiving; on the occasion of the famine of which our history has spoken, we may have to relate more than one instance of his wisdom and generosity.

The inexhaustible charity of the man shone as much in his private charities, as in his splendid and magnificent public establishments already recorded. On one occasion he saved a young lady from being immured in a convent against her wish. Her selfish father pretended he could not marry her suitably without a portion of 4000 crowns. The bishop advanced the money.

Easy of access, he made it a principle to receive the poor who applied to him, with kindness and affection. And on this point he was obliged to dispute with the nobility, who wished to keep him to their standard of action. One day, whilst visiting among the mountaineers, and instructing some poor children, Frederick bestowed caresses on them. A nobleman who was present, warned him to be careful, as the children were dirty and disgusting. The good bishop, not without indignation, replied, "These souls are committed to my care; these children may never see me again; and are you not willing that I should embrace them?"

He, however, seldom felt indignation or anger: he was admired for a placability, a sweetness of manner nearly imperturbable; which, however, was not natural to him, but the effect of continual combat against a quick and hasty disposition. If ever he appeared harsh, it was to those subordinate pastors, whom he found guilty of avarice, or negligence, or any other vice opposed to the spirit of their high calling. With regard to his own interests or temporal glory, he exhibited no emotion, either of joy or regret; admirable indeed, if his spirit was in reality not affected by these emotions; but more admirable still, if viewed as the result of continued and unremitted effort to subdue them. And amidst all the important cares with which he was occupied, he did not neglect the cultivation of his mind; he devoted himself to literature with so much ardour, that he became one of the most learned men of his time.

We must not, however, conceal that he adopted with firm persuasion, and maintained with constancy, certain opinions, which at this day would appear singular and ill-founded; these, however, were the errors of his time, and not his own.

Our readers may perhaps enquire, if so learned and studious a man has left no monument of his labours and studies? His works, great and small, Latin and Italian, printed as well as manuscript, amount to more than a hundred; they are preserved with care in the library which he founded. They are composed of moral treatises, sermons, historical dissertations, sacred and profane antiquities, literature, the fine arts, &c.

And what is the reason that they are so little known, so little sought for? We cannot enter into the causes of this phenomenon, as our explanation might not be satisfactory to our readers. So that we had better resume the course of our history, in relating facts concerning this extraordinary man.

Chapter XXIII.

The Cardinal Frederick was engaged in study, as was his custom, preparatory to the hour of divine service, when the cross-bearer entered, with a disturbed and unquiet air.

"A strange visit,—strange indeed, most illustrious signor."

"From whom?" asked the cardinal.

"From the signor —," replied the chaplain; pronouncing the name which we are unable to repeat to our readers. "He is without, in person, and asks admittance to the presence of your lordship."

"Indeed!" said the cardinal, closing his book and rising from his seat, his countenance brightening; "let him come in, let him come in immediately."

"But—," replied the chaplain, "does your lordship know who this man is? It is the famous outlaw —."

"And is it not a happy circumstance for a bishop, that such a man should have come to seek him?"

"But—," insisted the chaplain, "we never dare speak of certain things, because my lord says they are idle tales. However, in this case it appears to be a duty—. Zeal makes enemies, my lord, and we know that more than one ruffian has boasted that sooner or later—"

"And what have they done?"

"This man is an enterprising, desperate villain, who is in strict correspondence with other villains, as desperate as himself, and who, perhaps, have sent him—"

"Oh! what discipline is this!" said the cardinal, smiling; "the soldiers exhort the general to cowardice!" Then, with a grave and pensive air, he resumed, "Saint Carlo would not have deliberated a moment, whether he should receive such a man; he would have gone to seek him. Let him enter immediately; he has already waited too long."

The chaplain moved towards the door, saying in his heart, "There is no remedy; these saints are always obstinate."

He opened the door, and reaching the hall, where he had left the ecclesiastics, he beheld them collected together in one corner of the room, and the Unknown standing alone in another. As he approached him, he eyed him keenly to ascertain whether he had not arms concealed about his person. "Truly, before introducing him, we might at least propose—," but his resolution failed him. He spoke—"My lord expects your lordship. Be kind enough to come with me." And he led the way into the presence of Frederick, who came forward to meet the Unknown with a pleased and serene countenance, making a sign to the chaplain to quit the room.

The Unknown and the cardinal remained for some moments silent and undecided; the former experienced at the same time a vague hope of finding some relief to his internal torments, and also a degree of irritation and shame at appearing in this place as a penitent, to confess his sins, and implore pardon of a man. He could not speak; indeed, he hardly wished to do so. However, as he raised his eyes to the cardinal's face, he was seized with an irresistible sentiment of respect, which increasing his confidence, and subduing his pride without offending it, nevertheless kept him silent.

The person of Frederick was indeed fitted to inspire respect and love. His figure was naturally majestic and noble, and was neither bent nor wasted by years; his eye was grave and piercing, his brow serene and pensive; his countenance still shone with the animation of youth, notwithstanding the paleness of his face, and the visible traces it presented of abstinence, meditation, and laborious exertion. All his features indicated that he had once been more than ordinarily handsome; the habit of solemn and benevolent thought, the internal peace of a long life, love for mankind, and the influence of an ineffable hope, had substituted for the beauty of youth, the more dignified and superior beauty of an old age, to which the magnificent simplicity of the *purple* added an imposing and inexpressible charm. He kept his eyes for a few moments fixed on the Unknown, as if to read his thoughts; and imagining he perceived in his dark and troubled features something corresponding to the hope he had conceived, "Oh!" cried he in an animated voice, "what a welcome visit is this! and how I ought to thank you for it, although it fills me with self-reproach."

"Reproach!" cried the Unknown, in astonishment; but he felt re-assured by his manner, and the gentleness of his words, and he was glad that the cardinal had broken the ice, and commenced the conversation.

"Certainly, it is a subject of self-reproach that I should have waited till you came to me! How many times I might, and ought to have sought *you*!"

"You! seek *me*! Do you know who I am? Have they told you my name?"

"Do you believe I could have felt this joy, which you may read in my countenance—do you believe I could have felt it, at the sight of one unknown to me? It is you who are the cause of it—you, whom it was my duty to seek—you, for whom I have so wept and prayed—you, who are that one of my children (and I love them all with the whole strength of my affections)—that one, whom I would most have desired to see and embrace, if I could have ever dared to indulge the hope of so doing. But God alone can work miracles, and he supplies the weakness and tardiness of his poor servants."

The Unknown was amazed at the kindness and warmth of this reception; agitated and bewildered by such unlooked-for benevolence, he kept silence.

"And," resumed Frederick, more affectionately, "you have some good news for me; why do you hesitate to tell it me?"

"Good news! I! I have hell in my soul, and how can I bring you good news! Tell me, tell me, if you know, what good news could you expect from such a one as I?"

"That God has touched your heart, and is drawing you to himself," replied the cardinal calmly.

"God! God! If I could see! If I could hear him! Where is God?"

"Do you ask me? you! And who more than yourself has felt his presence? Do you not now feel him in your heart, disturbing, agitating you, not leaving you a moment of repose, and at the same time drawing you towards him, and imparting a hope of tranquillity and of consolation; of consolation which shall be full and unlimited, as soon as you acknowledge *Him*, confess your sins, and implore his mercy!"

"Oh! yes, yes; something indeed oppresses, something consumes me. But God—if it be God, if it be He, of whom you speak, what can he do with me?"

These words were uttered in a tone of despair; but Frederick calmly and solemnly replied, "What can God do with you? Through you he can exhibit his power and goodness. He would draw from you a glory, which none other could render him; you, against whom, the cries of the world have been for so long a time raised—you, whose deeds are detested—" (The Unknown started at this unaccustomed language, but was astonished to find that it excited no anger in his bosom, but rather communicated to it a degree of alleviation.) "What glory," pursued Frederick, "will accrue to God? A general cry of supplication has risen against you before his throne; among your accusers, some no doubt have been stimulated by jealousy of the power you have exercised; but more, by the deplorable security of your own heart, which has endured until this day. But, when *you* yourself shall rise to condemn your life, and become your own accuser, then, oh! then, God will be glorified! And you ask what he can do with you? What am I, feeble mortal! that I should presume to tell you what are his designs respecting you; what he will do with this impetuous will, and imperturbable constancy, when he shall have animated and warmed it with love, hope, and repentance? Who are you, feeble mortal, that you should think yourself able to execute and imagine greater things for the promotion of evil and vice, than God can make you accomplish for that of good and virtue? What can God do with you? Forgive you! save you! accomplish in you the work of redemption! Are not these things worthy of him? Oh! speak. If I, an humble creature—I, so miserable, and nevertheless so full of myself—I, such as I am,—if I so rejoice at your salvation, that to assure it, I would joyfully give (God is my witness) the few years that remain to me in life, Oh! think! what must be the love of Him who inspires me with the thought, and commands me to regard you with such devotion as this!"

The countenance and manner of Frederick breathed celestial purity and love, in accordance with the vows which came from his mouth. The Unknown felt the stormy emotions of his soul gradually calming under such heavenly influence, and giving place to sentiments of deep and profound interest. His eyes, which from infancy "had been unused to tears, became swoln;" and burying his face in his hands, he wept the reply he could not utter.

"Great and good God!" cried Frederick, raising his hands and eyes to heaven, "what have I ever done—I, thy unprofitable servant—that thou shouldst have invited me to this banquet of thy grace,—that thou shouldst have thought me worthy of being thy instrument to the accomplishment of such a miracle!" So saying, he extended his hand to take that of the Unknown.

"No!" cried he; "no! Approach me not! Pollute not that innocent and beneficent hand! You know not what deeds have been committed by the hand you would place within your own!"

"Suffer," said Frederick, taking it with gentle violence,—"suffer me to clasp this hand, which is about to repair so many wrongs, to scatter so many blessings; which will comfort so many who are in affliction, which will offer itself, peaceably and humbly, to so many enemies."

"It is too much," said the Unknown, sobbing aloud; "leave me, my lord! good Frederick! leave me! Crowds eagerly await your presence, among whom are pure and innocent souls, who have come from far to see and hear you, and you remain here to converse—with whom?"

"We will leave the ninety and nine sheep," replied the cardinal; "they are in safety on the mountain. I must now remain with the one which was lost. These people are perhaps now more satisfied than if they had the poor bishop with them; perhaps God, who has visited you with the riches and wonders of his grace, may even now be filling their hearts with a joy, of which they divine not the cause; perhaps they are united to us without knowing it; perhaps the Holy Spirit animates their hearts with the fervour of charity and benevolence; inspires them with a spirit of prayer; with, on your account, a spirit of thanksgiving of which you are the unknown object."

So saying, he passed his arm around the neck of the Unknown, who, after resisting a moment, yielded, quite vanquished by this impulse of kindness, and fell on the neck of the cardinal, in an agony of repentance. His burning tears dropped on the stainless purple of Frederick, and the pure hands of the bishop were clasped affectionately around him, who had hitherto been only habituated to deeds of violence and treachery.

The Unknown, after a long embrace, covering his face with his hands, raised his head, exclaiming, "Oh! God! Thou who art truly great and good! I know myself now; I comprehend what I am; my iniquities are all before me; I abhor myself; but still—still I experience a consolation, a joy—yes, a joy which I have never before known in all my horrible life!"

"God accords to you this grace," said Frederick, "to attract you to his service, to strengthen you to enter resolutely the new way he has opened to you, where you have so much to undo, to repair, to weep for!"

"Miserable that I am!" cried he, "there is so much—so much—that I can only weep over. But at least, there are some things but just undertaken, that I can arrest—yes, there is at least one evil that I can repair."

He then briefly related, in the most energetic terms of self-execration, the story of Lucy, with the sufferings and terrors of the unfortunate girl; her entreaties, and the species of frenzy that her supplications had excited in his soul; adding, that she was still in the castle.

"Ah! let us lose no time!" cried Frederick, moved with pity and solicitude. "What happiness for you! You may behold in this, the pledge of pardon! God makes you the instrument of safety to her, to whom you were to have been the instrument of ruin. God has indeed blessed you!—Do you know the native place of the unhappy girl?"

The Unknown named the village.

"It is not far from this," said the cardinal; "God be praised! And probably—" so saying, he approached a table, and rang a little bell. The chaplain entered, with an unquiet look; in amazement he beheld the altered countenance of the Unknown, on which the traces of tears were still visible; and glancing at that of the cardinal, he perceived, through its wonted calmness, an expression of great satisfaction, mingled with extraordinary solicitude. He was roused from the astonishment which the contemplation excited, by a question of the cardinal, if, among the curates in the hall, "there was one from ?"

"There is, most illustrious lord," replied the chaplain.

"Bring him hither immediately," said Frederick, "and with him, the curate of this parish."

The chaplain obeyed, and went to the hall where the priests were assembled. All eyes were turned towards him. He cried aloud, "His most illustrious and reverend lordship asks for the curate of this parish and the curate of ."

The former advanced immediately, and at the same time was heard, amidst the crowd, a *me?* uttered in a tone of surprise.

"Are you not the curate of ?" said the chaplain.

"Certainly; but—"

"His most illustrious and reverend lordship asks for you."

"Me?" replied he, and Don Abbondio advanced from the crowd with an air of amazement and anxiety. The chaplain led the way, and introduced them both to the presence of the cardinal.

The cardinal let go the hand of the Unknown as they entered, and taking the curate of the parish aside, related in few words the facts of the story, asking him if he knew some kind female, who would be willing to go to the castle in a litter, to remove Lucy thence; a devoted, charitable woman, capable of acting with judgment in so novel an expedition, and of exerting the best means to tranquillise the poor girl, to whom deliverance itself, after such anguish and alarm, might produce new and overwhelming apprehensions. After having reflected a moment, the curate took upon himself the affair, and departed. The cardinal then ordered the chaplain to have a litter prepared, and two mules ready saddled. The chaplain quitted the room to obey his orders, and the cardinal was left alone with Don Abbondio and the Unknown. The former, who had kept himself aloof, regarding with eager curiosity the faces of the Unknown and the cardinal, now came forward, saying, "I was told that your illustrious lordship wished to see me; but I suppose it was a mistake."

"There is no mistake;" replied Frederick, "I have both a novel and agreeable commission to give you. One of your parishioners, whom you have regarded as lost, Lucy Mondella, is found; she is near this, in the house of my good friend here. I wish you to go with him, and a good woman whom the curate of this parish will provide, and bring the poor girl, who must be so dear to you, to this place."

Don Abbondio did his best to conceal the extreme alarm which such a proposition caused him; and bowed profoundly, in sign of obedience, first to the cardinal, and then to the Unknown, but with a piteous look, which seemed to say, "I am in your hands; be merciful: *parcere subjectis.*"

The cardinal asked him of Lucy's relations.

"She has no near relation but her mother, with whom she lives," replied Don Abbondio.

"Is *she* at home?"

"Yes, my lord."

"Since," replied Frederick, "this poor child cannot yet go home, it would be a great consolation for her to see her mother; if the curate of this village does not return before I go to church, I beg you will desire him to send some prudent person to bring the good woman hither."

"Perhaps I had better go myself," said Don Abbondio.

"No, no; I have other employment for you."

"Her mother," resumed Don Abbondio, "is a very sensitive woman, and it will require a good deal of discretion to prepare her for the meeting."

"That is the reason that I have named some prudent person. You, however, will be more useful elsewhere," replied the cardinal. He could have added, had he not been deterred by a regard to the feelings of the Unknown—"This poor child needs much to behold some person whom she knows, after so many hours of alarm, and in such terrible uncertainty of the future."

It appeared strange, however, that Don Abbondio should not have inferred it from his manner, or that he should not have thought so himself; the reluctance he evinced to comply with the request of the cardinal appeared so out of place, that the latter imagined there must be some secret cause for it. He looked at the curate attentively, and quickly discovering the fears of the poor man at becoming the companion of this formidable lord, or entering his abode, even for a few moments, he felt an anxiety to dissipate these terrors; and in order to do this, and not injure the feelings of his new friend by talking privately to Don Abbondio in his presence, he addressed his conversation to the Unknown himself, so that Don Abbondio might perceive by his answers, that he was no longer a man to be feared.

"Do not believe," said he, "that I shall be satisfied with this visit to-day. You will return, will you not, in company with this worthy ecclesiastic?"

"*Will* I return!" replied the Unknown: "Oh! if ever you should refuse to see me, I would remain at your door as a beggar. I must talk to you, I must hear you, I must see you, I cannot do without you!"

Frederick took his hand, and pressing it affectionately, said, "Do us the favour, then, the curate of the village and myself, to dine with us; I shall expect you. In the mean time, whilst you are gathering the first fruits of repentance and compassion, I will go and offer supplications and thanksgivings to God with the people."

Don Abbondio, at this exhibition of confidence and affection, was like a timid child, who beholds a man caressing fearlessly a rough-looking mastiff, renowned for his ferocity and strength. It is in vain that the master assures him the dog is a good quiet beast: he looks at him, neither contradicting nor assenting; he looks at the dog, and dares not approach him, lest the good beast might show his teeth, if only from habit; he dares not retreat, from fear of the imputation of cowardice; but he heartily wishes himself safe "at home!"

The cardinal, as he was quitting the room, still holding the Unknown by the hand, perceived that the curate remained behind, embarrassed and motionless, and thinking that perhaps he was mortified at the little attention that was paid to him, compared with that which was bestowed on one so criminal, he turned towards him, stopped a moment, and with an amiable smile said, "Signor Curate, you have always been with me in the house of our Father; but this man *perierat, et inventus est*."

"Oh! how I rejoice at it!" said the curate, bowing to them both very reverently.

The archbishop passed on, and entering the hall, the admirable pair presented themselves to the eager gaze of the clergy who were there assembled. They regarded with intense curiosity those two countenances, on which were depicted different, but equally profound emotions. The venerable features of Frederick breathed a grateful and humble joy; in those of the Unknown might be traced an embarrassment blended with satisfaction, an unusual modesty, a keen remorse, through which, however, the lingerings of his severe and savage nature were apparent. More than one of the spectators thought of that passage of Isaiah, "The wolf also shall dwell with the lamb, and the leopard shall lie down with the kid." Behind them came Don Abbondio, whom no one noticed.

When they had reached the middle of the apartment, the servant of the cardinal entered, to inform him that he had executed the orders of the chaplain, that the litter was ready, and that they only waited for the female whom the curate was to bring. The cardinal told him to inform Don Abbondio when the curate should have arrived, and that afterwards all would be subject to his orders and those of the Unknown, to whom he bade an affectionate farewell, saying, "I shall expect you." Bowing to Don Abbondio, he directed his steps, followed by the clergy in procession, to the church.

Don Abbondio and the Unknown were left alone in the apartment; the latter was absorbed in his own thoughts, impatient for the moment to arrive when he should take *his* Lucy from sorrow and prison; for she was indeed *his* Lucy, but in a sense very different from the preceding night. His countenance expressed concentrated agitation, which to the suspicious eye of Don Abbondio appeared something worse: he looked at him with a desire to begin a friendly conversation. "But what can I say to him?" thought he. "Shall I repeat to him that I rejoice? I rejoice! at what? That having been a demon, he has formed the resolution to become an honest man? A pretty salutation, indeed! Eh! eh! *however* I should arrange my words, my *I rejoice* would signify nothing else! And can one believe that he has become an honest man all in a moment! Assertions prove nothing; it is so easy to make them! But, nevertheless, I must go with him to the castle! Oh! who would have told me this, this morning! Oh! if ever I am so happy as to get home again, Perpetua shall answer for having urged me to come here! Oh! miserable that I am! I must however say something to this man!" He had at least thought of something to say,—"I never expected the pleasure of being in such respectable company,"—and had opened his mouth to speak, when the servant entered with the curate of the village, who informed them that the good woman was in the litter awaiting them. Don Abbondio, approaching the servant, said to him, "Give me a gentle beast, for, to say truth, I am not a skilful horseman."

"Be quite easy," replied the valet, with a smile; "it is the mule of the secretary, a grave man of letters."

"Well," replied Don Abbondio, and continued to himself, "Heaven preserve me!"

The Unknown had advanced towards the door, but looking back, and seeing Don Abbondio behind, he suddenly recollected himself, and bowing with a polite and humble air, waited to let him pass before. This circumstance re-assured the poor man a little; but he had scarcely reached the little court, when he saw the Unknown resume his carbine, and fling it over his shoulder, as if performing the military exercise.

"Oh! oh! oh!" thought Don Abbondio, "what does he want with this tool? That is a strange ornament for a converted person! And if some whim should enter his head! what would become of me! what would become of me!"

If the Unknown had had the least suspicion of the thoughts that were passing in the mind of his companion, he would have done his utmost to inspire him with confidence; but he was far from such an imagination, as Don Abbondio was very careful not to let his distrust appear.

They found the mules ready at the door: the Unknown mounted one which was presented to him by a groom.

"Is she not vicious in the least?" asked Don Abbondio of the servant, with his foot in the stirrup.

"Be quite easy, she is a lamb," replied he. Don Abbondio climbed to the saddle, by the aid of the servant, and was at last safely mounted.

The litter, which was a few steps in advance, moved at a call from the driver, and the convoy departed.

They had to pass before the church, which was crowded with people, and through a small square, which was filled with villagers from abroad, who had not been able to find a place within the walls of the church. The report had already spread; and when they saw the carriage appear, and beheld the man who a few hours before had been the object of terror and execration, a confused murmur of applause rose from the crowd. They made way to let him pass; at the same time each one endeavoured to obtain a sight of him. When he arrived in front of the church, he took off his hat, and bowed his head in reverence, amidst the tumultuous din of many voices, which exclaiming "God bless you!" Don Abbondio took off his hat also, bent his head, and commended himself to the protection of heaven; and, hearing the voices of his brethren in the choir, he could not restrain his tears.

But when they reached the open country, in the windings of the almost deserted road, a darker veil came over his thoughts; there was nothing that he could regard with confidence but the driver, who, belonging to the establishment of the cardinal, must certainly be honest, and moreover did not look like a coward. From time to time they passed travellers crowding to see the cardinal. The sight of them was a transient balm to Don Abbondio; but still he approached this formidable valley, where they would meet none but the vassals of the Unknown! And what vassals! He desired more than ever to enter into conversation with his companion, to keep him in good humour; but, seeing him preoccupied, he dared not attempt to interrupt his thoughts. He was then obliged to hold colloquy with himself, of which we will transcribe a part for the benefit of the reader.

"Is it not an astonishing thing that the saints, as well as the wicked, have always quicksilver in their veins; and, not contented with making a bustle themselves, they would make all mankind, if they could, join the dance with them! Is there not a fatality in it, that the most troublesome come to me,—to me who never meddled with any body; they take me almost by the hair, and thrust me into their concerns! me! who desire nothing, but to live tranquilly, if they will let me do so. This mad knave Don Roderick. What was there wanting to make him the happiest man in the world, but a little prudence? He is rich, young, respected, courted; but happiness is a burthen to him, it seems; so that he must seek trouble for himself and his neighbour. He must set up, forsooth, for a molester of women,—the most silly, the most villanous, the most insane conduct in the world. He might ride to paradise in a coach; and he prefers to go halting to the devil's dwelling. And this man before me," continued he, regarding him as if he feared he could hear his thoughts, "and this man, after having, by his villanies, turned the world upside down, now turns it upside down by his conversion—if he is really converted! Meanwhile, it is I who am to put it to the test! Some people always want to make a noise! Is it so difficult to act an honest part, all one's life, as I have? Not at all! but they prefer to murder, kill, and play the devil.—Oh! unhappy man that I am! they must always be in a bustle, even in doing penance! just as if one could not repent at home, in private, without so much noise,—without giving others so much trouble.—And his illustrious lordship! to receive him all at once with open arms; to call him his dear friend, his worthy friend; to listen to his least words as if he had seen him work miracles, to give him his public approbation to assist him in all his undertakings; I should call this precipitation! And without any pledge or security, to place a poor curate in his hands! A holy bishop—and he is such assuredly—a holy bishop should regard his curates as the apple of his eye. A little prudence, a little coolness, a little charity, are things which, in my opinion, are not inconsistent with sanctity. And should this be all hypocrisy? Who can tell the designs of such a man? To think that I must accompany him into the castle! There must be some deviltry in it! Am I not unhappy enough? Let me not think of it. But how has Lucy fallen into the clutches of this man? It is a secret between him and my lord the cardinal, and they don't deign to inform me concerning it: I don't care to meddle with the affairs of others, but when one's life is in danger one has a right to know something.—But poor Lucy—I shall be satisfied if she escapes. Heaven knows what she has suffered. I pity her, but she was born to be my ruin. And if this man is really converted, what need has he of me? Oh! what a chaos! But Heaven owes me its protection, since I did not get myself into the difficulty. If I could only read in the countenance of this man what passes in his soul! Look at him; now he looks like Saint Anthony in the desert, and now like Holofernes himself."

In truth, the thoughts which agitated the Unknown passed over his countenance, as in a stormy day the clouds fly over the face of the sun, producing a succession of light and shade. His soul, calmed by the gentle language of Frederick, felt elated at the hope of mercy, pardon, and love; but then he sank again under the weight of the terrible past. Agitated and uneasy, he retraced in his memory those iniquities which were reparable, and considered what remedies would be the safest and quickest. And this unfortunate girl! how much she has suffered! how much he had caused her to suffer! At this thought his impatience to deliver her increased, and he made a sign to the coachman to hasten.

They entered at last into the valley. In what a situation was now our poor Don Abbondio! to find himself in this famous valley, of which he had heard such black and horrible tales. These famous men, the flower of the bravoes of Italy, these men without pity or fear, to see them in flesh and blood,—to meet them at every step! They bowed, it is true, respectfully, in the presence of their lord, but who knows what passed in their hearts, and what wicked design against the poor priest might, even then, be forming in their brains.

They reached *Malanotte*; bravoes were at the door, who bowed to the Unknown, glancing with eager curiosity at his companion, and the litter. If the departure of their master alone, at the break of day, had been regarded as extraordinary, his return was considered not less so. Is it a prize which he conducts? And how has he taken possession of it alone? And what is this strange litter? And whose is this livery? They did not stir, however; knowing, from the countenance of their master, that their silence was what he desired.

They reached the castle; the bravoes who were on the esplanade and at the door, retired on both sides to leave the passage free. The Unknown made a sign to them not to go farther off. Spurring his mule, he passed before the litter, and beckoning to Don Abbondio and the coachman to follow him, he entered a first court, and thence a second: approaching a small door, and with a gesture keeping back a bravo, who advanced to hold his stirrup, he said, "Remain there yourself, and let none approach nearer." He dismounted, and with the reins in his hand, drew near the woman, who had withdrawn the curtains of the litter, saying to her in a low voice, "Hasten to comfort her; and make her understand at once that she is free, and with friends. God will reward you!" He then advanced to the curate, and helping him to dismount, said, "Signor Curate, I will not ask your forgiveness for the trouble you have taken on my account; you suffer for one who will reward you well, and for this poor girl."

His countenance not less than his words restored the courage of Don Abbondio; drawing a full breath, which had been long pent up in his breast, he replied, "Your lordship jests, surely? But—but—" and accepting the hand offered to him so courteously, he slid from the saddle. The Unknown took the bridle, and gave both animals to the care of the driver, ordering him to wait there until their return. Taking a key from his pocket, he opened the little door, and followed by his two companions, the curate and the female, ascended the stairs.

Chapter XXIV.

Lucy had just risen. She was endeavouring to collect her senses, to separate the turbid visions of sleep from the remembrance of the sad reality, which appeared to her a dismal dream, when the old woman, in a voice which she meant to be humble and gentle, said to her, "Ah! you have slept! You would have done better to go to bed; I told you so a hundred times." Receiving no answer, she continued, "Eat a little; you have need of something; if you do not, he will complain of me when he returns."

"No, no, I wish to go to my mother. Your master promised me, he said, *to-morrow morning*. Where is he?"

"He has gone away; but he left word that he would return soon, and do all that you should desire."

"Did he say so? did he say so? Well; I wish to go to my mother, now, now."

Suddenly they heard steps in the adjoining chamber, and a knock at the door. The old woman demanded, "Who is there?"

"Open," replied the well-known voice.

The old woman drew the bolt, and holding the door open, the Unknown let Don Abbondio and the good woman pass in; then closing the door, and remaining outside himself, he sent away the old woman to a distant part of the castle. The first appearance of other persons increased the agitation of Lucy, to whom any change brought an accession of alarm. She looked, and beholding a priest and a female, felt somewhat reassured; she looked again! Can it be? Recognising Don Abbondio, her eyes remained fixed as by the wand of an enchanter. The kind woman bent over her, and with an affectionate and anxious countenance, said, "Alas! my poor child! come, come with us."

"Who are you?" said Lucy,—but, without waiting her reply, she turned again to Don Abbondio, exclaiming, "Is it you? Is it you indeed, Signor Curate? Where are we? Oh! unhappy girl! I am no longer in my right mind!"

"No, no, it is I, in truth; take courage. We have come to take you away. I am indeed your curate, come for this purpose—"

As if restored to strength in an instant, Lucy stood up, and fixing her eyes again on their faces, she said, "The Virgin has sent you, then!"

"I have no doubt of it," said the good lady.

"But is it true, that we may go away? Is it true indeed?" resumed Lucy, lowering her voice to a timid and fearful tone. "And all these people," continued she, with her lips compressed, and trembling from alarm and horror; "and this lord—this man—he promised me indeed."

"He is here also in person with us," said Don Abbondio. "He is without, expecting us; let us go at once; we must not make such a man wait."

At this moment the Unknown appeared at the door. Lucy, who, a few moments before, had desired earnestly to see him—nay, having no other hope in the world, had desired to see none but him—now that she was so unexpectedly in the presence of friends, was, for a moment, overcome with terror. Shuddering with horror, she hid her face on the shoulder of the good dame. Beholding the innocent girl, on whom the evening before he had not had resolution to fix his eyes; beholding her countenance, pale, and changed, from fasting and prolonged suffering, the Unknown hesitated; but perceiving her impulse of terror, he cast down his eyes, and, after a moment's silence, exclaimed, "It is true! forgive me!"

"He comes to save you; he is not the same man; he has become good. Do you hear him ask your forgiveness?" whispered the dame in the ear of Lucy.

"Could any one say more? Come, lift up your head; do not play the child. We can go away now, immediately," said Don Abbondio.

Lucy raised her head, looked at the Unknown, and beholding his humble and downcast expression, she was affected with a mingled feeling of gratitude and pity: "Oh! my lord! may God reward you for your compassion to an unfortunate girl!" cried she; "and may he recompense you a hundred-fold for the consolation you afford me by these words!" So saying, he advanced towards the door, and went out, followed by Lucy; who, quite encouraged, was supported by the arm of the good lady, Don Abbondio bringing up the rear. They descended the stairs, passed through the courts, and reached the litter; into which, the Unknown with almost timid politeness (a new thing for him!) assisted Lucy and her new companion to enter. He then aided Don Abbondio to reseat himself in the saddle. "Oh! what complaisance!" said the latter, moving much more lightly than he had done on first mounting.

The convoy resumed their way; as soon as the Unknown was mounted, his head was raised, and his countenance resumed its accustomed expression of command and authority. The robbers whom they met on their road discovered in it marks of strong thought and extraordinary solicitude; but they did not, they could not, comprehend the cause. They knew nothing as yet of the great change which had taken place in the soul of the man, and certainly such a conjecture would not have entered into their minds.

The good dame hastened to draw the curtains around the litter; pressing the hands of Lucy affectionately, she endeavoured to encourage her by words of piety, congratulation, and tenderness. Seeing, however, that besides the exhaustion from so much suffering, the confusion and obscurity of all that had happened prevented the poor girl from being alive to the satisfaction of her deliverance; she said what she thought would be most likely to restore her thoughts to their ordinary course. She mentioned the village to which she belonged, and towards which they were hastening.

"Yes, indeed!" said Lucy, remembering that this village was but a short distance from her own. "Oh! holy Virgin! I render thee thanks. My mother! my mother!"

"We will send for her immediately," said her friend, not knowing that it had already been done.

"Yes, yes; God will reward you. And you,—who are you? How is it that you have come here?"

"Our curate sent me, because this lord, whose heart God has touched, (blessed be his holy name!) came to our village to see the cardinal archbishop, who is visiting among us, the dear man of God! This lord has repented of his horrible sins, and wishes to change his life; and he told the cardinal that he had carried off an innocent girl, with the connivance of another, whose name the curate did not mention to me."

Lucy raised her eyes to heaven.

"You know it, perhaps," continued the lady. "Well, the lord cardinal thought, that a young girl being in the question, a female should be found to accompany her; he told the curate to look for one, and the curate kindly came to me—"

"Oh! may God reward you for your goodness!"

"And the curate desired me to encourage you, my poor child, to relieve you from uneasiness at once, and to make you understand, how the Lord has miraculously preserved you."

"Oh! miraculously indeed, through the intercession of the Virgin!"

"He told me to comfort you, to advise you to pardon him who has done you this evil, to rejoice that God has shown compassion towards him, and even to pray for him; for, besides its being a duty, you will derive comfort from it to your own heart."

Lucy replied with a look which expressed assent as clearly as if she had made use of words, and with a sweetness which words could not have expressed.

"Worthy young woman!" resumed the friend. "And as your curate was also in our village, the lord cardinal judged it best to send him with us, thinking that he might be of some assistance. I had already heard that he was a poor sort of a timid man; and on this occasion, he has been wholly taken up with himself, like a hen with one chick."

"And he—he who is thus changed—who is he?"

"How! do you not know?" said the good dame, repeating his name.

"Oh! merciful heaven!" cried Lucy. For many times had she heard this name repeated with horror, in more than one story, in which he had appeared like the *Ogre* of the fairy tale. At the idea of having been in his terrible power, and of now being under his protection,—at the thought of such peril, and such deliverance, in reflecting who this man was that had appeared to her so ferocious, and then so humble and so gentle, she was lost in astonishment, and could only exclaim, from time to time, "Oh! merciful Heaven!"

"Yes, it is indeed a great mercy! it is a great happiness for half the world in this neighbourhood, and afar off. When one thinks how many people he kept in continual alarm; and now, as our curate says—But you have only to look in his face to know that he is truly changed. And, besides, by 'their works' ye shall know them."

We should not tell the truth, did we say that the good dame had no curiosity to learn more of an affair in which she played so important a part; but, to her praise it must be added, that, feeling a respectful pity for Lucy, and estimating the weight and dignity of the charge confided to her, she did not for a moment think of asking her an indiscreet or idle question. All her discourse in their short journey was composed of expressions of tenderness and interest for the poor girl.

"It must be long since you have eaten any thing."

"I do not remember—It must indeed be some time."

"Poor child! you must need something to restore your strength."

"Yes," replied Lucy, in a faint voice.

"At my house, thanks be to God, we shall find something presently. Be of good cheer, it is but a short distance off."

Lucy, wearied and exhausted by her various emotions, fell languidly to the bottom of the litter, overcome by drowsiness; and her kind companion left her to a short repose.

As to Don Abbondio, the descent from the castle did not cause him so much fright as the ascent thither; but it was nevertheless not agreeable. When his alarm had first ceased, he felt relieved from an intolerable burthen; but he now began to torment himself in various ways, and found materials for such an operation in the present as well as in the future. His manner of travelling, to which he was not accustomed, he found to be exceedingly unpleasant, especially in the descent from the castle to the valley. The driver, obedient to a sign from the Unknown, made his beasts set off at a quick pace; the two mules kept up with the litter; and thus poor Don Abbondio, subjected to the unusual bounding and rebounding, which was more perilous from the steepness of the declivity they were descending, was obliged to hold fast by the saddle in order to keep his seat, not daring to ask his companions to abate somewhat of their speed. Moreover, if the road lay on a height, along a ridge, the mule, according to the custom of these animals, would obstinately keep on the outside, and place his feet literally on the very edge of the precipice. "Thou also," said he in his heart to the beast, "thou also hath this cursed desire to seek danger, when there are so many other paths!" He tightened the rein on the other side, but in vain; so that, although dying of vexation and fear, he suffered himself, as was his custom, to be led by the will of another. The bravoes no longer caused him much uneasiness now that he felt confidence in their master. "But," thought he, nevertheless, "if the news of this great conversion spreads, while we are yet here, who knows how these people may take it? Who knows what might be the result? Perhaps they might take it in their heads to think I had come as a missionary! and then (heaven preserve me!) they would make me suffer martyrdom!" But we have said enough of the terrors of Don Abbondio.

The company at last arrived at the extremity of the valley; the countenance of the Unknown became more serene, and Don Abbondio recovered in some degree his usual composure; but still his mind was occupied with more distant evils. "What will this fool Don Roderick say? To be exposed thus to scoffs and jests—how sorely will he feel it! he'll certainly play the devil outright! Perhaps he will seek another quarrel with me because I have been engaged in this cursed business! Having had the heart to send those two demons to attack me in the road, what he will do now, heaven knows. He cannot molest my lord the cardinal, because he is obviously beyond his reach; he will be obliged to champ the bit. However, the poison will be in his veins, and he will need to discharge it somewhere. It is well known how these affairs end; the blows always fall on the weakest. The cardinal will busy himself with placing Lucy in safety; this other poor devil is beyond his reach, but what is to become of me? And what will the cardinal do to defend me, after having engaged me in the business? Can he hinder this atrocious being from serving me a worse turn than before? And then he has so many things to think of! he cannot pay attention to every body! They who do good, do it in the gross, and enjoy their satisfaction without regarding minute consequences: but your evil-doer is more diligent; he lingers behind till he sees the last result, because of the fear that torments him. Shall I say I have acted by my lord archbishop's command, and against my own will? But it will seem that I favour villany! I—for the pleasure it gives me! Heaven forbid! but enough—I'll tell Perpetua the whole story, and leave her to circulate it—if indeed, his reverend lordship should not take up the fancy to make the whole matter public, and thrust me forward as a chief actor. However, I am determined on one thing: I will take leave of my lord the cardinal as soon as we arrive at the village, and go to my home. Lucy has no longer any need of me; she is under good protection; and, after so many fatigues, I may claim the right to take some repose.—But, should my lord be seized with the desire to know all her story, and I be compelled to relate the affair of the marriage! there would then be nothing wanting to complete my misery. And if he should visit my parish! Oh! let come what will, I will not torment myself beforehand! I have cares enough. For the present I shall shut myself up at home. But I foresee too well that my last days must be passed in trouble and vexation."

The little troop arrived before the services of the church were over; and passing, as they had previously done, through the crowd, they proceeded to the house of Lucy's companion.

Hardly had Don Abbondio alighted from his mule, when, making the most profuse compliments to the Unknown, he begged him to apologise for him to the cardinal, as he was obliged to return directly to his parish on some urgent business. He then went in search of a staff that he had left in the hall, and which he was accustomed to call his horse, and proceeded homewards. The Unknown remained at the cardinal's house, awaiting his return from the church.

The good dame hastened to procure Lucy some refreshment to recruit her exhausted powers; she put some dry branches under a kettle which she replaced over the fire, and in which swam a good fowl; after having suffered it to boil a moment, she filled a plate with the soup, and offered it to Lucy, congratulating herself that the affair had happened on a day, when, as she said, "the cat was not on the hearth." "It is a day of feasting for all the world," added she, "except for those unfortunate creatures who can hardly obtain bread of vetches, and a polenta of millet; they hope, however, to receive something from our charitable cardinal. As for us, thank heaven, we are not in that situation; between the trade of my husband and a small piece of land, we manage to live comfortably. Eat, then, poor child, with a good appetite; the fowl will be done presently, and you shall have something better." She then set about making preparations for dinner for the family.

As Lucy's spirits and strength returned, the necessity of arranging her dress occurred to her mind; she therefore tied up her long disordered tresses, and adjusted the handkerchief about her neck; in doing this, her fingers entwined themselves in the chaplet, which was there suspended: she gazed at it with much emotion, and the recollection of the vow she had made, this recollection which had been suspended by so many painful sensations, now rose clearly and distinctly to her mind. All the newly-awakened powers of her soul were again in a moment subdued. And if she had not been prepared for this by a life of innocence, resignation, and confidence, the consternation she experienced would have terminated in despair. After the first tumult of her thoughts had in some measure subsided, she exclaimed, "Oh! unhappy girl! what have I done!"

But hardly had she pronounced the words, when she was terrified at having done so; she recalled all the circumstances of her vow, her intolerable anguish, without hope of human aid, the fervour of her petition, the fulness of resolution with which the promise had been made; and to repent of this promise, after having obtained the favour she had implored, appeared to her sacrilegious ingratitude, perfidy towards God and the Virgin. It seemed to her that such infidelity would certainly draw upon her new and more terrible evils, and if these should indeed be its consequences she could no longer hope for an answer to her prayers; she therefore hastened to abjure her momentary regret, and drawing the chaplet reverently from her neck, and holding it in her trembling hand, she confirmed her vow; at the same time fervently praying to God that he would grant her strength to fulfil it, and to drive from her thoughts circumstances which might, if they did not move her resolution, still increase but too much the severity of the sacrifice. The absence of Renzo, without any probability of his return, which had at first been so bitter, appeared now to her a design of Providence, to make the two events conduce to the same end, and she endeavoured to find in one a consolation for the other. She also remembered that Providence would, to finish the work, find means to make Renzo resigned, and cause him to forget—But scarcely had this idea entered her mind, when a new terror overwhelmed her. Conscious that her heart had still need of repentance, the unfortunate girl again had recourse to prayer, and mental conflict; and at length arose, if the expression may be allowed, like a victor wearied and wounded, having disarmed his enemy.

Suddenly footsteps and joyous exclamations were heard; they proceeded from the children of the family, who were returning from church. Two little girls and a little boy ran into the room; stopping a moment to eye the stranger, they then came to their mother, one asking the name of their unknown guest, another wanting to relate the wonders they had seen. The good dame replied to them all with "Be quiet; silence!" The master of the house then entered with a calmer step; but with joy diffused over his countenance. He was the tailor of the village and its environs; a man who knew how to read, and who had even read, more than once, the Legend of the Saints and the *Reali di Francia*; he was regarded by the peasants as a man of knowledge, and when they lavished their praises on him, he repelled them with much modesty, only saying that he had indeed mistaken his vocation, and that, perhaps, if he had studied— Notwithstanding this little vanity he was the best natured man in the world. He had been present when the curate requested his wife to undertake her benevolent journey, and had not only given his approbation, but would have added his own persuasions, if that had been necessary; and now that the ceremonies of the church, and above all, the sermon of the cardinal, had given an impetus to his amiable feelings, he returned home with an ardent desire to know if the enterprise had succeeded, and to see the poor innocent girl in safety.

"See here!" said his wife to him as he entered, pointing to Lucy, who rose from her seat blushing, and stammering forth some apology. He advanced towards her, and, with a friendly tone, cried, "You are welcome! welcome! You bring the blessing of Heaven on this house! How glad I am to see you here! I knew that you would arrive safely to a haven, because I have never known the Lord commence a miracle without accomplishing it; but I am well content to see you here. Poor child! It is a great thing however to have been the subject of a miracle!"

We must not believe he was the only one who characterised the event by this term, and that because he had read the legendary. Throughout the village, and the surrounding country, it was spoken of in no other terms, as long as its remembrance lasted; and to say truth, if we regard its attendant circumstances, it would be difficult to find another name for it.

He then approached his wife, who was employed in taking the kettle from off the fire, and said in a low voice, "Has all gone well?"

"Very well. I will tell you another time."

"Well, well, at your leisure."

When the dinner was ready, the mistress of the house made Lucy sit down with them at the table, and helping her to a wing of the chicken, entreated her to eat. The husband began to dilate with much animation on the events of the day; not without many interruptions from the children, who stood round the table eating their dinner, and who had seen too many extraordinary things to be satisfied with playing the part of mere listeners. He described the solemn ceremonies, and then recurred to the miraculous conversion; but that which had made the most impression on his mind, and of which he spoke the oftenest, was the sermon of the cardinal.

"To see him before the altar," said he, "a lord like him, to see him before the altar, as a simple curate—"

"And that golden thing he had on his head," said one of the little girls.

"Hush, be quiet. When one thinks, I say, that a lord like him, a man so learned, who, as they say, has read all the books in the world, a thing which no one else has done, not even in Milan; when one thinks that he has adapted himself so to the comprehension of others, that every one understood him—"

"I understood, I did," said the other little chatterer.

"Hush, be quiet. What did you understand, you?"

"I understood that he explained the Gospel, instead of the curate."

"Be quiet. I do not say that he was understood by those only who know something, but even those who were the most stupid and ignorant, caught the sense perfectly. You might go now, and ask them to repeat his discourse; perhaps they might not remember a single word, but they would have its whole meaning in their head. And how easy it was to perceive that he alluded to this *signor*, although he never pronounced his name! But one might have guessed it from the tears which flowed from his eyes. And all the people wept—"

"That is true," cried the little boy. "But why did they all cry like little children?"

"Be quiet. And there are, nevertheless, hard hearts in this country. He has made us feel that although there is a scarcity, we must return thanks to God, and be satisfied; be industrious; do what we can, and then be content, because unhappiness does not consist at all in suffering and poverty; unhappiness is the result of wicked actions. These are not fine words merely; it is well known that he lives like a poor man, that he takes the bread from his mouth to give to those that are in need, when he might live an easier life than any one. Oh, then, there is great satisfaction in hearing him speak. He is not like many others, who say, 'Do as I say, and not as I do;' and besides, he has made it very apparent, that those even who are not what they call *gentlemen*, but who have more than is necessary, are bound to impart to those who are in want."

And here he stopped, as if pained by some recollection; after a moment's silence, he filled a plate with meat from the table, and adding a loaf of bread to it, tied up the whole in a napkin. "Take that," said he to the oldest of the children, and putting in her other hand a bottle of wine, "carry that to the widow Martha, and tell her to feast with her children. But be very careful what you say to her, don't seem to be doing a charity, and don't say a word of it, should you meet any one; and take care not to break any thing."

Lucy was touched, even to tears, and her soul was filled with a tenderness that withdrew her from the contemplation of her own sorrows. The conversation of this worthy man had already imparted a relief, that a direct appeal to her feelings would have failed to procure. Her spirit, yielding to the charm of the description of the august pomp of the church, of the emotions of piety there excited, and partaking of the enthusiasm of the narrator, forgot its woes, and, when obliged to recur to them, felt itself strengthened. The thought even of the great sacrifice she had imposed on herself, without having lost its bitterness, had assumed the character of austere and solemn tranquillity.

A few moments after, the curate of the village entered, saying that he was sent by the cardinal for intelligence concerning Lucy, and also to inform her that he desired to see her that day; then he thanked, in his lordship's name, her kind hosts for their benevolence and hospitality. All three, moved to tears, could not find words to reply to such a message from such a person.

"Has your mother not yet arrived?" said the curate to Lucy.

"My mother!" cried she.

Learning that the good archbishop had sent for her mother, that it was his own kind thought, her heart was overpowered, she raised her apron to her eyes, and her tears continued to flow long after the departure of the curate. As these tumultuous emotions, called forth by such unexpected benevolence, gradually subsided, the poor girl remembered that she had expressly solicited this very happiness of again beholding her mother, as a condition to her vow. "*Return me safely to my mother.*" These words recurred distinctly to her memory. She was confirmed more than ever in her purpose to keep her vow, and repented again bitterly of the regret which she had for a moment experienced.

Agnes, indeed, even whilst they were speaking of her, was very near; it is easy to imagine the feelings of the poor woman at so unexpected an invitation, at the intelligence, necessarily confused and incomplete, of a peril which was passed, but of a frightful peril, of an obscure adventure, of which the messenger knew not the circumstances, and could give no explanation, and for which she could find no clue from previous facts. "Ah, great God! ah, holy Virgin!" escaped from her lips, mingled with useless questions, during the journey. On the road she met Don Abbondio, who, by the aid of his staff, was travelling homewards. Uttering an exclamation of surprise, Agnes made the driver stop. She alighted, and with the curate withdrew into a grove of chestnuts, which was on the side of the road. Don Abbondio informed her of all he had seen and known: much obscurity still rested upon his statement, but at least Agnes ascertained that Lucy was now in safety.

Don Abbondio then introduced another subject of conversation, and would have given her ample instruction on the manner of conducting herself with the archbishop, if he, as was probable, should wish to see her and her daughter. He said it would not answer for her to speak of the marriage; but Agnes, perceiving that he spoke only from his own interest, was determined to promise nothing, because she said, "she had other things to think of," and bidding him farewell, she proceeded on her journey.

The carriage at last reached the house of the tailor, and the mother and daughter were folded in each other's arms. The good wife, who was the only witness of the scene, endeavoured to soothe and calm their feelings; and then prudently left them alone, saying that she would go and prepare a bed for them.

Their first tumultuous joy having in some measure subsided, Agnes requested to hear the adventures of Lucy, who attempted to relate them; but the reader knows that it was a history with which no one was entirely acquainted, and to Lucy herself there was much that was inexplicable, particularly the fatal coincidence of the carriage being at that place precisely at the moment that Lucy had gone there by an extraordinary chance. With regard to this, the mother and daughter lost themselves in conjecture, without even approaching the real cause. As to the principal author of this plot, however, they neither of them doubted that it was Don Roderick.

"Ah, that firebrand!" cried Agnes; "but his hour will come. God will reward him according to his works, and then he will know—"

"No, no, mother, no!" cried Lucy. "Do not wish harm to him! do not wish it to any one! If you knew what it is to suffer! if you had experienced it! No, no! rather let us pray to God and the Virgin for him, that God would touch his heart as he has done that of the other lord, who was worse than he, and who is now a saint."

The horror that Lucy felt in retracing events so painful and recent made her hesitate more than once. More than once she said she had not the heart to proceed, and, choked by her tears, she with difficulty went on with her narrative. But she was embarrassed by a different sentiment at a certain point of her recital, at the moment when she was about to speak of her vow. She feared her mother would accuse her of imprudence and precipitation; she feared that she would, as she had done in the affair of the marriage, bring forward her broad rules of conscience, and make them prevail; she feared that the poor woman would tell it to some one in confidence, if it were only to gain light and advice, and thus render it public. These reflections made Lucy experience insupportable shame, and an inexplicable repugnance to speak on the subject. She therefore passed over in silence this important circumstance, determining in her heart to communicate it first to Father Christopher; but how great was her sorrow at learning that he was no longer at the convent, that he had been sent to a distant country, a country called—

"And Renzo?" enquired Agnes.

"He is in safety, is he not?" said Lucy, hastily.

"It must be so, since every one says so. They say that he has certainly gone to Bergamo, but no one knows the place exactly, and there has been no intelligence from himself. He probably has not been able to find the means of informing us."

"Oh, if he is in safety, God be thanked!" said Lucy, commencing another subject of conversation, which was, however, interrupted by an unexpected event—the arrival of the cardinal archbishop.

After having returned from the church, and having learnt from the Unknown the arrival of Lucy, he had seated himself at table, placing the Unknown on his right hand; the company was composed of a number of priests, who gazed earnestly at the countenance of their once formidable companion, so softened without weakness, so humbled without meanness, and compared it with the horrible idea they had so long entertained of him.

Dinner being over, the Unknown and the cardinal retired together. After a long interview, the former departed for his castle, and the latter sent for the curate of the parish, and requested him to conduct him to the house where Lucy had received an asylum.

"Oh, my lord," replied the curate, "suffer me, suffer me. I will send for the young girl and her mother, if she has arrived,—the hosts themselves, if my lord desires it."

"I wish to go to them myself," replied Frederick.

"There is no necessity that you should inconvenience yourself; I will send for them immediately," insisted the curate, who did not understand that, by this visit, the cardinal wished to do honour to misfortune, innocence, hospitality, and to his own ministry. But the superior repeating his desire, the inferior bowed, and they proceeded on their way.

When they appeared in the street, a crowd immediately collected around them. The curate cried, "Come, come, back, keep off."—"But," said Frederick, "suffer them," and he advanced, now raising his hands to bless the people, now lowering them to embrace the children, who obstructed his progress. They reached the house, and entered it, whilst the crowd remained without. But amidst the throng was the tailor, who had followed with others; his eyes fixed, and his mouth open, wondering where the cardinal was going. When he beheld him entering his own house, he bustled his way through the crowd, crying out, "Make room for those who have a right to enter," and followed into the house.

Agnes and Lucy heard an increasing murmur in the street; and whilst they were surmising the cause, the door opened, and, behold, the cardinal and the curate!

"Is this she?" asked the former of the curate, and at a sign in the affirmative he approached Lucy, who with her mother was standing, motionless and mute with surprise and extreme diffidence: but the tones of the voice, the countenance, and above all, the words of Frederick, soon removed their embarrassment. "Poor young woman," said he, "God has permitted you to be subjected to a great trial; but he has also made you see that he watches over you, and has never forgotten you. He has saved you, and in addition to that blessing, has made use of you to accomplish a great work through you, to impart the wonders of his grace and mercy to one man, and at the same time to comfort the hearts of many."

Here the mistress of the house entered the room with her husband: perceiving their guests engaged in conversation, they respectfully retired to a distant part of the apartment. The cardinal bowed to them courteously, and continued the conversation with Lucy and her mother. He mixed with the consolation he offered many enquiries, hoping to find from their answers some way of rendering them still farther services after their sufferings.

"It is a pity all the clergy were not like your lordship, and then they would take the part of the poor, and not help to bring them into difficulty for the sake of drawing themselves out of it," said Agnes, encouraged by the familiar and affable manner of Frederick, and vexed that Don Abbondio, after having sacrificed others to his own selfishness, should dare to forbid her making the least complaint to one so much above him, when by so fortunate a chance the occasion presented itself.

"Say all that you think," said the cardinal; "speak freely."

"I would say, that if our curate had done his duty, things would not have been as they are."

The cardinal begging her to explain herself more clearly, she found some embarrassment in relating a history, in which she had at one time played a part, which she felt very unwilling to communicate to such a man. However, she got over the difficulty; she related the projected marriage, the refusal of Don Abbondio, and the pretext he had offered with respect to his *superiors* (oh, Agnes!); and passing to the attempt of Don Roderick, she told in what manner, being informed of it, they had been able to escape. "But, indeed," added she in conclusion, "it was escaping to fall into another snare. If the curate had told us sincerely the difficulty, and had married my poor children, we would have left the country immediately, and gone where no one would have known us, not even the wind. Thus time was lost, and that which has happened, has happened."

"The curate shall render me an account of this," said the cardinal.

"No, my lord, no," resumed Agnes. "I did not speak on that account, do not reprove him; because what is done, is done; and it would answer no purpose. He is a man of such a character, that if the thing were to do over again, he would act precisely in the same way."

But Lucy, dissatisfied with this manner of telling the story, added, "We have also been to blame; it is plain that it was the will of God the thing should not succeed."

"How can you have been to blame, my poor child?" said Frederick.

Lucy, notwithstanding the winks of her mother, related in her turn the history of the attempt made in the house of Don Abbondio, saying, as she concluded, "We did wrong, and God has punished us."

"Accept from his hand the chastisement you have endured, and take courage," said Frederick; "for who has a right to rejoice and hope, if not those who have suffered, and who accuse themselves?"

He then asked where was the betrothed; and learning from Agnes (Lucy stood silent with downcast eyes) the fact of his flight, he expressed astonishment and displeasure, and asked the reason of it. Agnes told what she knew of the story of Renzo.

"I have heard of him before," said the cardinal; "but how could a man, who was engaged in affairs of this nature, be in treaty of marriage with this young girl?"

"He was a worthy young man," said Lucy, blushing, but in a firm voice.

"He was a peaceable youth, too peaceable, perhaps," added Agnes; "your lordship may ask any one if he was not, even the curate. Who knows what intrigues and plots may have been going on at Milan? There needs little to make poor people pass for rogues."

"That is but too true," said the cardinal; "I will enquire about him, without doubt." He took a memorandum of the name of the young man, adding that he expected to be at their village in a few days; that during his sojourn there, Lucy could return home without fear, and in the mean while he would procure her an asylum till all was arranged for the best.

Turning to the master and mistress of the house, they came forward; he renewed the thanks he had addressed to them by the mouth of the curate, and asked them if they would be willing to keep the guests God had sent them for a few days.

"Oh yes, my lord," replied the dame, with a manner which said more than this timid reply; but her husband, quite animated by the presence of such a man, by the desire to do himself honour on an occasion of such importance, studied to make a fine answer. He wrinkled his forehead, strained his eyes, and compressed his mouth, but nevertheless felt a confusion of ideas, which prevented him from uttering a syllable. But time pressed; the cardinal appeared to have interpreted his silence. The poor man opened his mouth, and said, "Imagine—" Not a word more could he say. His failure not only filled him with shame on that day, but ever after, the unfortunate recollection intruded itself to mar the pleasure of the great honour he had received. How many times, in thinking of this circumstance, did a crowd of words come to his mind, every one of which would have been better than "*Imagine!*" But the cavities of our brains are full enough of thoughts when it is too late to employ them.

The cardinal departed, saying, "May the blessing of Heaven rest on this house!"

That evening he asked the curate in what way it would be best to indemnify the tailor, who could not be rich, for his hospitality. The curate replied, that truly neither the profits of his trade, nor his income from some little fields that the good tailor possessed, would at this time have enabled him to be liberal to others; but from having saved something the few years previous, he was one of the most easy in circumstances in the district; that he could allow himself to exercise some hospitality without inconvenience, and that he would do it with pleasure; and that he was confident he would be hurt if money was offered to him.

"He has probably," said the cardinal, "some demands on people who are unable to pay."

"You may judge, my lord; the poor people pay with the overplus of the harvest; this year there has been no overplus; on the contrary, every one is behind in point even of necessities."

"Well, I take upon myself all these debts. You will do me the favour to obtain from him the memoranda, and cancel them."

"It may be a very large sum."

"So much the better. And perhaps you have but too many who are more miserable, having no debts, because they have no credit?"

"Oh yes! indeed too many! they do what they can; but how can they supply their wants in these hard times?"

"Have them clothed at my expense; it is true that it seems to be robbery to spend any thing this year, except for bread; but this is a particular case."

We cannot finish our record of the history of this day without briefly relating the conduct of the Unknown. Before his second return to the castle, the report of his conversion had preceded him; it had spread through the valley, and excited surprise, anxiety, and numerous conjectures. As he approached the castle he made a sign to all the *bravoes* he met to follow him: filled with unusual apprehension, but with their accustomed submission, they obeyed; their number increased every moment. Reaching the castle, he entered the first court, and there, resting on his saddle bow, in a voice of thunder he gave a loud call, the wonted signal which all habitually obeyed. In a moment those who were scattered about the castle hastened to join the troop collected around their leader.

"Go and wait for me in the great hall," said he; as they departed, he dismounted from his beast, and leading it himself to the stable, thence approached the hall. The whispering which was heard among them ceased at his appearance; retiring to one corner they left a large space around him.

The Unknown raised his hand to enforce the silence that his presence alone had already effected; then raising his head, which yet was above that of any of his followers, he said, "Listen to me, all of you; and let no one speak, unless I ask him a question. My friends, the way which we have followed until to-day leads to hell. I do not wish to reproach you, I could not effect the important change, inasmuch as I have been your leader in our abominable career; I have been the most guilty of all; but listen to what I am about to say.

"God in his mercy has called me to a change of life, and I have obeyed his call. May this same God do as much for you! Know, then, and hold for certain, that I would rather now die than undertake any thing against his holy law. I recall all the iniquitous orders which I may have given any one of you; you understand me. And farther, I order you to do nothing which I have hitherto prescribed to you. Hold equally for certain, that no one can hereafter commit evil under my protection, and in my service. Those who will remain with me on these conditions, I shall regard as children. I should be happy, in the day of famine, to share with them the last mouthful that remained to me. To those who do not wish to continue here, shall be paid what is due of their salaries, and a further donative; they have liberty to depart, but they must never return, unless they repent and intend to lead a new life, and under such circumstances they shall be received with open arms. Think of it this night; to-morrow morning I will receive your answer, and then I will give you your orders. Now, every one to his post. May God, who has shown compassion towards me, incline your hearts to repentance and good dispositions."

He ceased, and all kept silence. Although strange and tumultuous thoughts fermented in their minds, no indication of them was visible. They had been habituated to listen to the voice of their lord, as to a manifestation of absolute authority, to which it was necessary to yield implicit obedience. His will proclaimed itself changed, but not enfeebled: it did not therefore enter their minds, that because he was converted they might become bold in his presence, or reply to him as they would to another man. They regarded him as a saint, indeed, but a saint sword in hand.

In addition to the fear with which he inspired them, they felt for him (especially those who were born in his service, and these were the greater number) the affection of vassals. Their admiration partook of the nature of love, mingled with that respect which the most rebellious and turbulent spirits feel for a superior, whom they have voluntarily recognised as such. The sentiments he expressed were certainly hateful to their ears, but they knew they were not false, neither were they entirely strange to them. If their custom had been to make them subjects of pleasantry, it was not from disbelief of their verity, but to drive away, by jesting, the apprehensions the contemplation of them might otherwise have excited. And now, there was none among them who did not feel some compunction at beholding their power exerted over the invincible courage of their master. Moreover, some of them had heard the extraordinary intelligence beyond the valley, and had witnessed and related the joy of the people, the new feeling with which the Unknown was regarded by them, the veneration which had succeeded their former hatred—their former terror. They beheld the man whom they had never regarded without trembling, even when they themselves constituted, to a great degree, his strength; they beheld him now, the wonder, the idol of the multitude,—still elevated above all others, in a different manner, no doubt, but in one not less imposing,—always above the world, always the first. They were confounded, and each was doubtful of the course he should pursue. One reflected hastily where he could find an asylum and employment; another questioned with himself his power to accommodate himself to the life of an honest man; another, moved by what he had said, felt some inclination for it; and another still was willing to promise any thing so as to be entitled to the share of a loaf, which had been so cordially proffered, and which was so scarce in those days. No one, however, broke the silence. The Unknown, at the conclusion of his speech, waved his hand imperiously for them to retire: obedient as a flock of sheep, they all quietly left the hall. He followed them, and stopping in the centre of the court, saw them all branch off to their different stations. He returned into the castle, visited the corridors, halls, and every avenue, and, finding all quiet, he retired to sleep,—yes, to sleep, for he was very sleepy. In spite of all the urgent and intricate affairs in which he was involved, more than at any former conjuncture, he was sleepy. Remorse had banished sleep the night before; its voice, so far from being subdued, was still more absolute—was louder—yet he was sleepy. The order of his household so long established, the absolute devotion of his faithful followers, his power and means of exercising it, its various ramifications, and the objects on which it was employed, all tended to create uncertainty and confusion in his mind,—still he was sleepy.

To his bed then he went, that bed which the night before had been a bed of thorns; but first he knelt to pray. He sought, in the remotest corner of his memory, the words of prayer taught him in his days of childhood. They came one by one: an age of vice had not effaced them. And who shall define the sentiments that pervaded his soul at this return to the habits of happy innocence? He slept soundly.

Chapter XXV.

The next morning, in the village of Lucy, and throughout all the territory of Lecco, nothing was talked of but herself, the Unknown, the archbishop, and another person, who, although generally desirous to be talked of, would willingly have been forgotten on this occasion,—we mean Don Roderick.

Not that, previous to this period, the villagers had not conversed much of his actions, in secret, to those in whom they had perfect confidence; but now they could no longer contain themselves, nor surpress many enquiries on the marvellous events in which two persons so famous had played a part. In comparison of these two personages, Signor Don Roderick appeared rather insignificant, and all agreed in rejoicing over the ill success of his iniquitous designs; but these rejoicings were still, in some measure, moderated by fears of the *bravoes* by whom he was surrounded.

A good portion of the public censure was bestowed on his friends and courtiers. It did not spare the Signor *Podestà*, always deaf and dumb and blind to the deeds of this tyrant, but these opinions were expressed in an under-tone, because the *Podestà* had his officers. Such regard was not paid to Doctor *Azzecca Garbugli*, who had only his *tricks* and his *verbiage* to employ for his defence; and as to the whole tribe of sycophants, resembling him, they were so pointed at, and eyed askance, that for some time they thought it most prudent to keep themselves within doors.

Don Roderick, struck, as by a thunderbolt, with the unexpected intelligence, so different from that which he had been anticipating from day to day, kept himself shut up in his castle, alone with his bravoes, devouring his rage for the space of two days, and on the third set off for Milan. If there had only existed the murmurs of the people, notwithstanding things had gone so far, he would perhaps have remained expressly to brave them; but he felt himself compelled to quit the field of contest, by the certain information that the cardinal was coming to the village. The count, his uncle, who knew nothing of the story but what Attilio had told him, would certainly require him to be one of the first to visit the cardinal, in order to obtain in public the most distinguished reception from him. The count would require it, because it was an important opportunity for making known in what esteem the house was held by his powerful eminence. To escape such a dilemma, Don Roderick, having risen before the sun, threw himself into a carriage with Griso, and, followed by the rest of the *bravoes*, retired like a fugitive, like (if we may be permitted to elevate him by such a comparison), like Catiline from Rome, foaming with rage, and threatening a speedy return to accomplish his revenge.

Meanwhile the cardinal approached, visiting every day one of the parishes situated in the territory of Lecco. On the day he was expected in the village, great preparations were made for his reception. At the entrance of the village, near the cottage of Agnes, a triumphal arch was erected, constructed of wood, covered with moss and straw, and ornamented with green boughs of birch and holly. The front of the church was adorned with tapestry; from every window of the houses were suspended quilts and sheets, intended for drapery; every thing, in short, whether in good taste or bad, was displayed in honour of this extraordinary occasion. At the hour of vespers (which was the hour Frederick usually selected to arrive at the churches which he visited), those who had not gone to church, the old men, women, and the youngest of the children, went forth, in procession, to meet their expected guest, headed by Don Abbondio. The poor curate was sad in the midst of the public joy; the tumult bewildered him; the movement of so many people, before and behind, disturbed him; and, moreover, he was tormented by the secret apprehension that the women had tattled, and that he should be obliged to render an account of his conduct to the cardinal.

Frederick appeared at last, or rather the crowd appeared, in the midst of which was his litter, and the retinue surrounding it. The persons who followed Don Abbondio scattered and mingled themselves with the crowd, notwithstanding all his remonstrances; and he, poor man, finding himself deserted by them, went to the church, there to await the cardinal's approach.

The cardinal advanced, bestowing benedictions with his hands, and receiving them in return from the mouths of the people, who were with difficulty kept back by his attendants. Being of the same village as Lucy, these peasants were desirous of rendering to the archbishop peculiar demonstrations of respect, but this was not practicable, inasmuch as, wherever he went, he was received with every possible honour. In the very commencement of his pontificate, at his first solemn entrance into the cathedral, the concourse had been so great that his life was in peril. Some gentlemen, who were near him, drew their swords to keep back and alarm the crowd. Such was the rude violence of the times, that even in the general disposition to do honour to their archbishop, they were on the point of crushing him: and this defence would not have been sufficient, if two priests, of great vigour and presence of mind, had not raised him in their arms, and carried him from the church door to the foot of the great altar. His very first entrance into the church, therefore, might be recorded amidst his pastoral labours and the dangers he had run.

Entering the church, the cardinal advanced to the altar, and after having prayed some time, he addressed, as was his custom, some words to the people, on his love for them, on his desire for their salvation, and how they should dispose their minds for the duties of the morrow. He then withdrew to the house of the curate, and among other questions which he put to him, he interrogated him with regard to the character and conduct of Renzo. Don Abbondio replied that he was rather choleric and obstinate: but as the cardinal made more special and precise enquiries, he was obliged to confess that he was an honest peaceable youth, and even he himself could not comprehend how he had committed at Milan the conduct which had been imputed to him.

"As to the young girl," continued the cardinal, "do you think she can return now with safety to her house?"

"At present," replied Don Abbondio, "she can come and remain for a while. I say, at present, but," added he with a sigh, "your illustrious lordship should be always near at hand."

"God is always present," said the cardinal. "But I will use my efforts to secure a place of safety for her."

Before dismissing Don Abbondio, he ordered him to send a litter, on the following day, for Lucy and her mother.

Don Abbondio went away quite pleased that the cardinal had talked to him of the young couple, without even alluding to his refusal to marry them. "He knows nothing of it," said he; "Agnes has kept silence! wonderful! She will see him again, 'tis true, but she shall have further instructions from me, so she shall." He little thought, poor man, that Frederick had only deferred the enquiry until he should have more leisure to learn the reasons of his conduct.

But the solicitude of the good prelate for the disposal of Lucy had been rendered useless, by a circumstance which we will relate.

The two females had as far as possible resumed, for the few days they had to pass under the hospitable roof of the tailor, their usual manner of life. As she had done at the monastery, Lucy, in a small chamber apart, employed herself in sewing; and Agnes, keeping much at home, remained for the most part with her daughter. Their conversations were affectionate and sorrowful; both were prepared for a separation, since the sheep could not dwell in the neighbourhood of the wolf. But how long was this separation to continue? The future was dark and inexplicable, but Agnes, notwithstanding, was full of agreeable anticipation. "After all," said she, "if no irreparable misfortune has befallen Renzo, we shall soon hear from him. If he has found employment, (and who can doubt it?) and if he keeps the faith he has sworn to you, why cannot we go and live with him?" Her daughter felt as much sorrow in listening to her hopes, as difficulty in replying to them. She still kept her secret in her heart; and although troubled at the idea of concealment with so good a mother, she was nevertheless restrained by a thousand fears from communicating it. Her plans were, indeed, very different from those of her mother, or rather, she had none, having committed the future into the hands of Providence; she therefore endeavoured to change the subject, saying in general terms that her only hope was to be permanently re-united to her mother.

"Do you know why you feel thus?" said Agnes; "you have suffered so much, that it seems impossible to you that things can turn out happily. But let God work; and if— Let a ray of hope come—a single ray, and then we shall see that you will think differently."

Lucy and her mother entertained a lively friendship for their kind hosts, which was warmly reciprocated; and between whom can friendship exist more in its purity, than between the benefactor and the recipients of the benefit, when both have kind hearts! Agnes, especially, had long gossips with the mistress of the house, and the tailor afforded them much amusement by his tales and moral discourses; at dinner particularly he had always something to relate of the sword of Roland, or of the Fathers of the Thebaid.

At some miles' distance from the village there dwelt a certain Don Ferrante, and Donna Prassede his wife; the latter was a woman of high birth, somewhat advanced in age, and exceedingly inclined to do good; which is surely the most praiseworthy employment one can be engaged on in this world; but which, indulged in without judgment, may be rendered hurtful, like all other good things. To do good, we must have correct ideas of good in itself considered, and this can be acquired only by control over our own hearts. Donna Prassede governed herself with her ideas, as some do with their friends; she had very few, but to these she was much attached. Among these few, were a number unfortunately a little narrow and unreasonable, and they were not those she loved the least. Thence it happened that she regarded things as good, which were not really so, and that she used means which were calculated to promote the very opposite of that which she intended; to this perversion of her intellect may also be attributed the fact, that she esteemed all measures to be lawful to her who was bent on the performance of duty. In short, with good intentions, her moral perceptions were in no small degree distorted. Hearing the wonderful story of Lucy, she was seized with a desire to know her, and immediately sent her carriage for the mother and daughter. Lucy, having no desire to go, requested the tailor to find some excuse for her; if they had been *common people*, who desired to make her acquaintance, the tailor would willingly have rendered her the service, but, under such circumstances, refusal appeared to him a species of insult. He uttered so many exclamations, such as, that it was not customary—that it was a high family—that it was out of the question to say *No* to such people—that it might make their fortune—and that, in addition to all this, Donna Prassede was a saint,—that Lucy was finally obliged to yield, especially as Agnes seconded the remonstrances and arguments of the tailor.

The high-born dame received them with many congratulations; she questioned and advised them with an air of conscious superiority, which was, however, tempered by so many soft and humble expressions, and mingled with so much zeal and devotion, that Agnes and Lucy soon felt themselves relieved from the painful restraint her mere presence had at first imposed on them. In brief, Donna Prassede, learning that the cardinal wished to procure an asylum for Lucy, and impelled by the desire to second, and at the same time to anticipate, his good intention, offered to take the young girl to her house, where there would be no other service required of her than to direct the labours of the needle or the spindle. She added, that she herself would inform the cardinal of the arrangement.

Besides the obvious and ordinary benefit conferred by her invitation, Donna Prassede proposed to herself another, which she deemed to be peculiarly important; this was to school impatience, and to place in the right path a young creature who had much need of guidance. The first time she heard Lucy spoken of, she was immediately persuaded that in one so young, who had betrothed herself to a robber, a criminal, a fugitive from justice such as Renzo, there must be some corruption, some concealed vice. *"Tell me what company you keep, and I will tell you who you are."* The visit of Lucy had confirmed her opinion; she appeared, indeed, to be an artless girl, but who could tell the cause of her downcast looks and timid replies? There was no great effort of mind necessary to perceive that the maiden had opinions of her own. Her blushes, sighs, and particularly her large and beautiful eyes, did not please Donna Prassede at all. She regarded it as certain as if she had been told it by having authority, that the misfortunes of Lucy were a punishment from Heaven for her connection with that villain, and a warning to withdraw herself from him entirely. That settled the determination to lend her co-operation to further so desirable a work; for as she frequently said to herself and others, "Was it not her constant study to second the will of Heaven?" But, alas! she often fell into the terrible mistake of taking for the will of Heaven, the vain imaginings of her own brain. However, she was on the present occasion very careful not to exhibit any of her proposed intentions. It was one of her maxims, that the first rule to be observed in accomplishing a good design, is to keep your motives to yourself.

Excepting the painful necessity of separation the offer appeared to both mother and daughter very inviting, were it only on account of the short distance from the castle to their village. Reading in each other's countenance their mutual assent, they accepted with many thanks the kindness of Donna Prassede, who renewing her kind promises, said she would soon send them a letter to present to the cardinal. The two females having departed, she requested Don Ferrante to write a letter, who, being a literary and learned man, was employed as her secretary on occasions of importance. In an affair of this sort, Don Ferrante did his best, and he gave the original to his wife in order that she could copy it; he warmly recommended to her an attention to the orthography, as orthography was among the great number of things he had studied, and among the small number over which he had control in his family. The letter was forthwith copied and sent to the tailor's house. These events occurred a few days before the cardinal had despatched a litter to bring the mother and daughter to their abode.

Upon their arrival they went to the parsonage; orders having been left for their immediate admittance to the presence of the cardinal. The chaplain, who conducted them thither, gave them many instructions with regard to the ceremony to be used with him, and the titles to be given him; it was a continual torment to the poor man to behold the little ceremony that reigned around the good archbishop in this respect. "This results," he was accustomed to say, "from the excessive goodness of this blessed man—from his great familiarity." And he added that he had "even heard people address him with *Yes, sir,* and *No, sir!*"

At this moment, the cardinal was conversing with Don Abbondio on the affairs of his parish; so that the latter had no opportunity to repeat his instructions to the females; however, in passing by them as they entered, he gave them a glance, to make them comprehend that he was well satisfied with them, and that they should continue, like honest and worthy women, to keep silence.

After the first reception, Agnes drew from her bosom the letter of Donna Prassede, and gave it to the cardinal, saying, "It is from the Signora Donna Prassede, who says that she knows your illustrious lordship well, my lord, as naturally is the case with great people. When you have read, you will see."

"It is well," said Frederick, after having read the letter, and extracted its meaning from the trash of Don Ferrante's flowers of rhetoric. He knew the family well enough to be certain that Lucy had been invited into it with good intentions, and that she would be sheltered from the snares and violence of her persecutor. As to his opinion of Donna Prassede, we do not know it precisely; probably she was not a person he would have chosen for Lucy's protectress; but it was not his habit to undo things, apparently ordered by Providence, in order to do them better.

"Submit, without regret, to this separation also, and to the suspense in which you are left," said he. "Hope for the best, and confide in God! and be persuaded, that all that He sends you, whether of joy or sorrow, will be for your permanent good." Having received the benediction which he bestowed on them, they took their leave.

Hardly had they reached the street, when they were surrounded by a swarm of friends, who were expecting them, and who conducted them in triumph to their house. Their female acquaintances congratulated them, sympathised with them, and overwhelmed them with enquiries. Learning that Lucy was to depart on the following morning, they broke forth in exclamations of regret and disappointment. The men disputed with each other the privilege of offering their services; each wished to remain for the night to guard their cottage, which reminds us of a proverb; " *If you would have people willing to confer favours on you, be sure not to need them.*" This warmth of reception served a little to withdraw Lucy from the painful recollections which crowded upon her mind, at the sight of her loved home.

At the sound of the bell which announced the commencement of the ceremonies, all moved towards the church. The ceremonies over, Don Abbondio, who had hastened home to see every thing arranged for breakfast, was told that the cardinal wished to speak with him. He proceeded to the chamber of his illustrious guest, who accosted him as he entered, with "Signor Curate, why did you not unite in marriage, Lucy to her betrothed?"

"They have emptied the sack this morning," thought Don Abbondio, and he stammered forth, "Your illustrious lordship has no doubt heard of all the difficulties of that business. It has been such an intricate affair, that it cannot even now be seen into clearly. Your illustrious lordship knows that the young girl is here, only by a miracle; and that no one can tell where the young man is."

"I ask if it is true, that, before these unhappy events, you refused to celebrate the marriage on the day agreed upon? and why you did so?"

"Truly—if your illustrious lordship knew—what terrible orders I received—" and he stopped, indicating by his manner, though respectfully, that it would be imprudent in the cardinal to enquire farther.

"But," said Frederick, in a tone of much more gravity than he was accustomed to employ, "it is your bishop, who, from a sense of duty, and for your own justification, would learn from you, why you have not done that which, in the ordinary course of events, it was your strict duty to do?"

"My lord," said Don Abbondio, "I do not mean to say,—but it appears to me, that as these things are now without remedy, it is useless to stir them up—However, however, I say, that I am sure your illustrious lordship would not betray a poor curate, because, you see, my lord, your illustrious lordship cannot be every where present, and I—I remain here, exposed—However, if you order me, I will tell all."

"Speak; I ask for nothing but to find you free from blame."

Don Abbondio then related his melancholy story, suppressing the name of the principal personage, and substituting in its place, "*a great lord*,"—thus giving to prudence the little that was left him in such an extremity.

"And you had no other motive?" asked the cardinal, after having heard him through.

"Perhaps I have not clearly explained myself. It was under pain of death that they ordered me not to perform the ceremony."

"And this reason appeared sufficient to prevent the fulfilment of a rigorous duty?"

"I know my obligation is to do my duty, even to my greatest detriment; but when life is at stake—"

"And when you presented yourself to the church," said Frederick, with increased severity of manner, "to be admitted to the holy ministry, were there any such reservations made? Were you told that the duties imposed by the ministry were free from every obstacle, exempt from every peril? Were you told that personal safety was to be the guide and limit of your duty? Were you not told expressly the reverse of all this? Were you not warned that you were sent as a lamb among wolves? Did you not even then know that there were violent men in the world, who would oppose you in the performance of your duty? He, whose example should be our guide, in imitation of whom we call ourselves shepherds, when he came on earth to accomplish the designs of his benevolence, did he pay regard to his own safety? And if your object be to preserve your miserable existence, at the expense of charity and duty, there was no necessity for your receiving holy unction, and entering into the priesthood. The world imparts this virtue, teaches this doctrine. What do I say? O shame! the world itself rejects it. It has likewise its laws, which prescribe good, and prohibit evil; it has also its gospel, a gospel of pride and hatred, which will not admit the love of life to be offered as a plea for the transgression of its laws. It commands, and is obeyed; but we, we children and messengers of the promise! what would become of the church, if your language was held by all your brethren? Where would she now be, if she had originally come forth with such doctrines?"

Don Abbondio hung down his head; he felt under the weight of these arguments as a chicken under the talons of a hawk, who holds him suspended in an unknown region, in an atmosphere he had never before breathed. Seeing that a reply was necessary, he said, more alarmed than convinced,—

"My lord, I have done wrong; since we should pay no regard to life, I have nothing more to say. But when one has to do with certain powerful people, who will not listen to reason, I do not see what is to be gained by carrying things with a high hand."

"And know you not that our gain is to suffer for the sake of justice? If you are ignorant of this, what is it you preach? What do you teach? What is the *good news* which you proclaim to the poor? Who has required this at your hand, to overcome force by force? Certainly you will not be asked at the day of judgment, if you have vanquished the powerful, for you have neither had the commission nor the means to do so. But, you *will* be asked, if you have employed the means which have been placed in your power, to do that which was prescribed to you, even when man had the temerity to forbid it."

"These saints are odd creatures," thought Don Abbondio; "extract the essence of this discourse, and it will be found that he has more at heart the love of two young people, than the life of a priest." He would have been delighted to have had the conversation terminate here, but he well perceived that such was not the intention of the cardinal, who appeared to be waiting a reply, or apology, or something of the kind.

"I say, my lord," replied he, "that I have done wrong—We cannot give ourselves courage."

"And why, then, I might say to you, have you undertaken a ministry which imposes on you the task of warring with the passions of the world? But, I will rather say, how is it that you have forgotten, that where courage is necessary to fulfil the obligations of this holy vocation, the Most High would assuredly impart it to you, were you earnestly to implore it? Do you think the millions of martyrs had courage naturally? that they had naturally a contempt for life, young Christians who had just begun to taste its charms, children, mothers! All had courage, simply because courage was necessary, and they trusted in God to impart it. Knowing your own weakness, have you ever thought of preparing yourself for the difficult situations in which you might be placed? Ah! if, during so many years of pastoral care, you had loved your flock, (and how could you refrain from loving them?) if you had reposed in them your affections, your dearest cares, your greatest delights, you would not have failed in courage: love is intrepid; if you had loved those who were committed to your spiritual guardianship, those whom you call children—if you had really loved them, when you beheld two of them threatened at the same time with yourself. Ah! certainly, charity would have made you tremble for them, as the weakness of the flesh made you tremble for yourself. You would have humbled yourself before God for the first risings of selfish terror; you would have considered it a temptation, and have implored strength to resist it. But, you would have eagerly listened to the holy and noble anxiety for the safety of others, for the safety of your children; you would have been unable to find a moment of repose; you would have been impelled, constrained to do all that you could to avert the evil that threatened them. With what then has this love, this anxiety, inspired you? What have you done for them? How have you been engaged in their service?"

And he paused for a reply.

Chapter XXVI.

Don Abbondio uttered not a word. It must be confessed that we ourselves, who have nothing to fear but the criticisms of our readers, feel a degree of repugnance in thus urging the unfashionable precepts of charity, courage, indefatigable solicitude for others, and unlimited sacrifice of self. But the reflection that these things were said by a man who practised what he preached, encourages us to proceed in our relation.

"You do not answer," resumed the cardinal. "Ah! if you had followed the dictates of charity and duty, whatever had been the result, you would now have been at no loss for a reply. Behold, then, what you have done; you having obeyed iniquity, regardless of the requirements of duty; you have obeyed her promptly; she had only to show herself to you, and signify her desire, and she found you ready at her call. But she would have had recourse to artifice with one who was on his guard against her, she would have avoided exciting his suspicion, she would have employed concealment, that she might mature at leisure her projects of treachery and violence; she has, on the contrary, boldly ordered you to infringe your duty, and keep silence; you have obeyed, you have infringed it, and you have kept silence. I ask you now, if you have done nothing more. Tell me if it is true, that you have advanced false pretences for your refusal, so as not to reveal the true motive—"

"They have told this also, the tattlers!" thought Don Abbondio, but as he gave no indication of addressing himself to speech, the cardinal pursued,—"Is it true, that you told these young people falsehoods to keep them in ignorance and darkness?—I am compelled, then, to believe it; it only remains for me to blush for you, and to hope that you will weep with me. Behold where it has led you, (merciful God! and you advanced it as a justification!) behold to what it has conducted you, this solicitude for your life! It has led you—(repel freely the assertion if it appear to you unjust: take it as a salutary humiliation if it is not) it has led you to deceive the feeble and unfortunate, to lie to your children!"

"This is the way of the world!" thought Don Abbondio again; "to this devil incarnate," (referring to the Unknown,) "his arms around his neck; and to me, for a half lie, reproaches without end! But you are our superiors; of course you are right. It is my star, that all the world is against me, not excepting the saints." He continued aloud,—"I have done wrong! I see that I have done wrong. But what could I do in so embarrassing a situation?"

"Do you still ask? Have I not told you? And must I repeat it? You should have loved, my son, you should have loved and prayed; you would then have felt that iniquity might threaten, but not enforce obedience; you would have united, according to the laws of God, those whom man desired to separate; you would have exercised the ministry these children had a right to expect from you. God would have been answerable for the consequences, as you were obeying His orders; now, since you have obeyed man, the responsibility falls on yourself. And what consequences, just Heaven! And why did you not remember that you had a superior? How would he now dare to reprimand you for having failed in your duty, if he did not at all times feel himself obliged to aid you in its performance? Why did you not inform your bishop of the obstacles which infamous power exerted to prevent the exercise of your ministry?"

"Just the advice of Perpetua," thought Don Abbondio vexed, to whose mind, even in the midst of these touching appeals, the images which most frequently presented themselves, were those of the bravoes and Don Roderick, alive and well, and returning at some future time, triumphant, and inflamed with rage. Although the presence, the aspect, and the language of the cardinal embarrassed him, and impressed him with a degree of apprehension, it was, however, an embarrassment and an apprehension which did not subjugate his thoughts, nor prevent him from reflecting that, after all, the cardinal employed neither arms nor bravoes.

"Why did you not think," pursued Frederick, "that if no other asylum was open to these innocent victims, I could myself receive them, and place them in safety, if you had sent them to me; sent them afflicted and desolate to their bishop; as therefore belonging to him, as the most precious part, I say not of his charge, but of his wealth! And as for you, I should have been anxious for you; I would not have slept until certain that not a hair of your head would be touched; and do you not suppose that this man, however audacious he may be, would have lost something of his audacity, when convinced that his designs were known by me, that I watched over them, and that I was decided to employ for your defence all the means within my power! Know you not, that if man promises too often more than he performs, he threatens also more than he dare execute? Know you not that iniquity does not depend solely on its own strength, but on the credulity and cowardice of others?"

"Just the reasoning of Perpetua," thought Don Abbondio, without considering that this singular coincidence in judgment of Frederick Borromeo and his servant, was an additional argument against him.

"But you," pursued the cardinal, "you have only contemplated your own danger. How is it possible that your personal safety can have appeared of importance enough to sacrifice every thing to it?"

"Because I saw them, I saw those frightful faces," escaped from Don Abbondio. "I heard those horrible words. Your illustrious worship talks well, but you should have been in the place of your poor priest, and have had the same thing happen to you."

No sooner had he uttered these words than he bit his tongue, perceiving that he had suffered himself to be overcome by vexation; he muttered in a low voice, "Now for the storm!" and raising his eyes timidly, he was astonished to see the cardinal, whom he never could comprehend, pass from the severe air of authority and rebuke, to that of a soft and pensive gravity.

"It is but too true," said Frederick. "Such is our terrible and miserable condition! We exact rigorously from others, that which it may be we would not be willing to render ourselves; we judge, correct, and reprimand, and God alone knows what we would do in the same situation, what we *have* done in similar situations. But, woe be to me, if I take my weakness for the measure of another's duty, for the rule of my instruction! Nevertheless it is certain, that while imparting precepts, I should also afford an example to my neighbour, and not resemble the pharisee, who imposes on others enormous burthens, which he himself would not so much as touch with his finger. Hear me then, my son, my brother; the errors of those in authority, are oftener better known to others than to themselves; if you know that I have, from cowardice, or respect to the opinions of men, neglected any part of my duty, tell me of it frankly, so that where I have failed in example, I may at least not be wanting in humble confession. Show me freely my weakness, and then words from my mouth will be more available, because you will be conscious that they do not proceed from me, but that they are the words of Him who can give to us both the necessary strength to do what He prescribes."

"Oh! what a holy man, but what a troublesome one!" thought Don Abbondio. "He censures himself, and wishes that I should examine, criticise, and control even *his* actions!" He continued aloud,—"Oh! my lord jests, surely! Who does not know the courage and indefatigable zeal of your illustrious lordship?" "Yes," added he to himself, "by far too indefatigable!"

"I do not desire praise that makes me tremble, because God knows my imperfections, and what I know of them myself is sufficient to humble me. But I would desire that we should humble ourselves together; I would desire that you should feel what your conduct has been, and that your language is opposed to the law you preach, and according to which you will be judged."

"All turns against me. But these persons who have told your lordship these things, have they not also told you that they introduced themselves treacherously into my house, for the purpose of compelling me to perform the marriage ceremony, in a manner unauthorised by the church?"

"They *have* told me, my son; but what afflicts and depresses me, is to see you still seeking excuses; still excusing yourself by accusing others; still accusing others of that which should have formed a part of your own confession. Who placed these unfortunates, I do not say under the necessity, but under the temptation, to do what they have? Would they have sought this irregular method, if the legitimate way had not been closed to them? Would they have thought of laying snares for their pastor, if they had been received, aided, and advised by him? of surprising him, if he had not concealed himself? And you wish to make them bear the blame; and you are indignant that, after so many misfortunes, what do I say? in the very midst of misfortune, they have suffered a word of complaint to escape before their pastor and yours? that the complaints of the oppressed and the afflicted should be hateful to the world, is not astonishing; but to us! and what advantage would their silence have been to you? Would you have been the gainer from their cause having been committed entirely to the judgment of God? Is it not an additional reason to love them, that they have afforded you the occasion to hear the sincere voice of your pastor; that they have provided for you the means to understand more clearly, and quite as far as may be in your power, the great debt you have contracted to them? Ah! if they had even been the aggressors, I would tell you to love them for that very reason. Love them, because they have suffered, and do suffer; love them, because they are a part of your flock, because you yourself have need of pardon and of their prayers."

Don Abbondio kept silence, but no longer from vexation, and an unwillingness to be persuaded; he kept silence from having more things to think of than to say. The words which he heard were unexpected conclusions, a new application of familiar doctrine. The evil done to his neighbour, which apprehension on his own account had hitherto prevented him from beholding in its true light, now made a novel and striking impression on his mind. If he did not feel all the remorse which the cardinal's remonstrances were calculated to produce, he experienced at least secret dissatisfaction with himself and pity for others; a blending of tenderness and shame; as, if we may be permitted to use the comparison, a humid and crushed taper at first hisses and smokes, but by degrees receives warmth, and imparts light, from the flame of a great torch to which it is presented. Don Abbondio would have loudly accused himself, and deplored his conduct, had not the idea of Don Roderick still obtruded itself into his thoughts; however, his feeling was sufficiently apparent to convince the cardinal that his words had at last produced some effect.

"Now," pursued Frederick, "one of these unfortunate beings is a fugitive afar off, the other on the point of departure; both have but too much reason to keep asunder, without any present probability of being re-united. Now, alas! they have no need of you; now, alas! you have no longer the opportunity to do them good, and our short foresight can assure us of but little of the future. But who knows, if God in his compassion is not preparing the occasion for you? Ah! do not let it escape; seek it, watch for it, implore it as a blessing."

"I shall not fail, my lord—I shall not fail to do so, I assure you," replied Don Abbondio, in a tone that came from the heart.

"Ah! yes, my son, yes!" cried Frederick with affectionate dignity; "Heaven knows that I would have desired to hold other converse with you. We have both had a long pilgrimage through life. Heaven knows how painful it has been to me, to grieve your old age by reproaches; how much more I should have loved to occupy the time of this interview in mutual consolation, and mutual anticipation of the heavenly hope which is so near our grasp! God grant that the language I have been obliged to hold may be useful to both of us! Act in such a manner, that He will not call me to account on the great and terrible day, for having retained you in a ministry of which you were unworthy. Let us redeem the time; the night is far spent; the spouse will not linger; let us keep our lamps trimmed and burning. Let us offer to God our poor and miserable hearts, that he may fill them with his love!" So saying he arose to depart; Don Abbondio followed him.

We must now return to Donna Prassede, who came, according to agreement, on the following morning, for Lucy, and also to pay her duty to the cardinal. Frederick bestowed many praises on Lucy, and recommended her warmly to the kindness of Donna Prassede; Lucy separated herself from her mother with many tears, and again bade farewell to her cottage and her village. But she was cheered by the hope of seeing her mother once more before their final departure, as Donna Prassede informed them that it was her intention to remain for a few days at her villa, and Agnes promised to visit it again to take a last farewell.

The cardinal was on the point of setting out for another parish, when the curate of the village near which the castle of the Unknown was situated, demanded permission to see him. He presented a small packet, and a letter from that lord, in which Frederick was requested to present to Lucy's mother a hundred crowns of gold, to serve as a dowry for the maiden, or for any other purpose she might desire. The Unknown also requested him to tell them, that if ever they should be in need of his services, the poor girl knew but too well the place of his abode, and as for him, he should consider it a high privilege to afford her protection and assistance. The cardinal sent immediately for Agnes, and informed her of the commission he had received. She heard it with equal surprise and joy.

"God reward this signor!" said she; "your illustrious lordship will thank him in our name, but do not say a word of the matter to any one, because we live in a world—you will excuse me, I know a man like your lordship does not tattle about such things, but—you understand me."

Returning to her house, she shut herself up in her chamber, and untied the packet; although she was prepared for the sight, she was filled with wonder at seeing in her own power and in one heap such a quantity of those coins which she had rarely ever seen before, and never more than one at a time. She counted them over and over again, and wrapping them carefully in a leather covering, concealed them under one corner of her bed. The rest of the day was employed in reverie and projects for the future, and desires for the arrival of the morrow; the night was passed in restless dreams, and vain imaginings of the blessings to be produced by this gold; at break of day, she arose, and departed for the villa of Donna Prassede.

The repugnance Lucy had felt to mention her vow, had not all diminished, but she resolved to overcome it, and to disclose the circumstance to her mother in this conversation, which would probably be the last they should have for a long time.

No sooner were they left alone, than Agnes, with an animated countenance, but in a low voice, said, "I have great news to tell you," and she related her unexpected good fortune.

"God bless this signor," said Lucy; "you have now enough to live comfortably yourself, and also to benefit others."

"Oh! yes, we can do a great deal with this money! Listen, I have only you, that is, I have only you two in the world, for from the moment that Renzo first addressed you, I have considered him as my son. We will hope that no misfortune has befallen him, and that we shall soon hear from him. As for myself, I would have wished to lay my bones in my own country, but now that you cannot stay here on account of this villain, (oh! even to think that he was near me, would make me dislike any place!) I am quite willing to go away. I would have gone with you to the end of the earth before this good fortune, but how could we do it without money? The poor youth had indeed saved a few pence, of which the law deprived him, but in recompence God has sent us a fortune. So then, when he has informed us that he is living, and where he is, and what are his intentions, I will go to Milan for you—yes, I will go for you. Formerly I would not have dreamt of such a thing, but misfortune gives courage and experience. I have been to Monza, and I know what it is to travel. I will take with me a man of resolution; for instance, Alessio di Maggianico; I will pay the expense, and—do you understand?"

But perceiving that Lucy, instead of exhibiting sympathy with her plans, could with difficulty conceal her agitation and distress, she stopped in the midst of her harangue, exclaiming, "What is the matter? are you not of my opinion?"

"My poor mother!" cried Lucy, throwing her arms around her neck, and concealing on her bosom her face, bathed in tears.

"What is the matter?" said Agnes, in alarm.

"I ought to have told you sooner, but I had not the heart to do it. Have pity on me."

"But speak, speak then."

"I cannot be the wife of that unfortunate youth."

"Why? how?"

Lucy, with downcast looks and flowing tears, confessed at last the vow which she had made. She clasped her hands, and asked pardon of her mother for having concealed it from her, conjuring her to speak of it to no one, and to lend her aid to enable her to fulfil it.

Agnes was overwhelmed with consternation; she would have been angry with her daughter for so long maintaining silence towards her, had not the grave thoughts that the circumstance itself excited, stifled all feeling of resentment. She would have blamed her for her vow, had it not appeared to her to be contending against Heaven; for Lucy described to her again, in more lively colours than before, that horrible night, her utter desolation, and unexpected preservation! Agnes listened attentively; and a hundred examples that she had often heard related, that she *herself* even had related to her daughter, of strange and horrible punishments for violated vows, came to her memory. "And what wilt thou do now?" said she.

"It is with the Lord that care rests; the Lord and the holy Virgin. I have placed myself in their hands; they have never yet abandoned me, they will not abandon me now that—The favour I ask of God, the only favour, after the safety of my soul, is to be restored to you, my beloved mother! He will grant it, yes, he will grant it. That fatal day—in the carriage—Oh! most holy Virgin! Those men—who would have thought I should be the next day with you?"

"But why not tell your mother at once?"

"Forgive me, I had not the heart—What use was there in afflicting you sooner?"

"And Renzo?" said Agnes, shaking her head.

"Ah!" cried Lucy, starting, "I must think no more of the poor youth. God has not intended—You see it appears to be his will that we should separate. And who knows?—But no, no; the Lord will preserve him from every danger, and render him, perhaps, happier without me."

"But, nevertheless, if you had not bound yourself for ever, provided no misfortune has happened to Renzo, with this money, I would have found a remedy for all our other evils."

"But, my mother, would this money have been ours if I had not passed that terrible night? It is God's will that all should be thus; his will be done!" And her voice became inarticulate through tears.

At this unexpected argument, Agnes maintained a mournful silence. After some moments, Lucy, suppressing her sobs, resumed,—"Now that the thing is done, we must submit cheerfully; and you, dear mother, you can aid me, first in praying to the Lord for your poor daughter, and then it is necessary that Renzo should know it. When you ascertain where he is, have him written to, find a man,—your cousin Alessio, for instance, who is prudent and kind, who has always wished us well, and who will not tattle. Make Alessio write to him, and inform him of the circumstance as it occurred, where I was, and how I suffered; tell him that God has ordered it thus, and that he must set his heart at rest; that, as for me, I can never be united to any one. Make him understand the matter clearly; when he knows that I have promised the Virgin—he always has been pious—And you, as soon as you hear from him, get some one to write to me, let me know that he is safe and well—and, nothing more."

Agnes, with much emotion, assured her daughter that all should be done as she desired.

"I would say something more; that which has befallen the poor youth, would never have occurred to him, if he had never thought of me. He is a wanderer, a fugitive; he has lost all his little savings; he has been deprived of every thing he possessed, poor fellow! and you know why—and we, we have so much money! Oh! mother, since the Lord has sent us wealth, and since the unfortunate—you regard him as your son, do you not? Ah! divide it, share it with him! Endeavour to find a safe man, and send him the half of it. God knows how much he may need it!"

"That is just what I was thinking of," replied Agnes. "Yes, I will do it certainly. Poor youth! And why did you think I was so pleased with the money, if it were not—but—I came here well pleased,'tis true; but, since matters are so, I will send it to him. Poor youth! he also—I know what I mean. Certainly money gives pleasure to those who have need of it; but this money—Ah! it is not this that will make him prosper."

Lucy returned thanks to her mother for her prompt and liberal accordance with her request, so fervently, that an observer would have imagined her heart to be still devoted to Renzo, more than she herself was aware of.

"And without thee, what shall I do—I, thy poor mother?" said Agnes, weeping in her turn.

"And I, without you, my dear mother? and in a house of strangers, at Milan? But the Lord will be with us both, and will re-unite us. In eight or nine months we shall see each other again; let us leave it to him. I will incessantly implore this favour from the Virgin; if I had any thing more to offer her, I would not hesitate; but she is so compassionate, she will surely grant my prayer."

The mother and daughter parted with many tears, promising to see each other again, the coming autumn, at the latest, as if it depended on themselves!

A long time elapsed before Agnes heard any thing of Renzo; neither message nor letter was received from him; the people of the village were as ignorant concerning him as herself.

She was not the only one whose enquiries had been fruitless; it was not a mere ceremony in the cardinal Frederick, when he promised Lucy and Agnes, to inform himself of the history and fate of Renzo; he fulfilled that promise, by writing immediately to Bergamo for the purpose. While at Milan, on his return from visiting his diocese, he received a reply, in which he was informed that little was known of the young man; that he had made, it was true, a short sojourn in such a place, but that one morning he had suddenly disappeared; that a relation of his, with whom he had lived while there, knew not what had become of him; he thought that he had probably enlisted for the Levant, or had passed into Germany, or, which was most likely, that he had perished in crossing the river. It was added, however, that should any more definite intelligence be received concerning him, his illustrious lordship should immediately be informed of it.

These reports eventually travelled to Lecco, and reached the ears of Agnes. The poor woman did her best to ascertain the truth of them; but she was kept in a state of suspense and anxiety by the contradictory accounts which were given, and which were, in fact, all without foundation.

The governor of Milan, lieutenant-general under Don Gonzalo Fernandez de Cordova, had complained bitterly to the lord resident of Venice at Milan, that a robber, a villain, an instigator of pillage and massacre, the famous Lorenzo Tramaglino, had been received in the Bergamascan territory. The resident replied, that he knew nothing of the matter, but that he would write to Venice for information concerning it, in order to give some explanation to his Excellency.

It was a maxim at Venice to encourage the tendency of the Milanese workmen in silk, to establish themselves in the Bergamascan territory, by making them find it to their advantage to do so. For this reason, Bortolo was warned confidentially, that Renzo was not safe in his present residence, and that he would do wisely to place him in some other manufactory, and even cause him to change his name for a while. Bortolo, who was quick of apprehension, made no objections, related the matter to his cousin, and taking him to another place fifteen miles off, he presented him, under the name of *Antonio Rivolta*, to the master of the manufactory, who was a native of Milan, and moreover his old acquaintance. He, although the times were hard, did not require much entreaty to induce him to receive a workman so warmly recommended by an old friend. He saw reason afterwards to congratulate himself on the acquisition, although, at first, the young man appeared rather heedless, because, when they called *Antonio*, he scarcely ever answered.

A short time after, an order arrived from Venice to the captain of Bergamo, to inform himself, and send word to government, whether there was not within his jurisdiction, and particularly in such a village, such an individual. The captain having obeyed in the best manner he could, transmitted a reply in the negative, which was transmitted to the resident at Milan, in order that he should transmit it to Don Gonzalo Fernandez de Cordova.

There were not wanting inquisitive people, who enquired of Bortolo why the young man had left him. The first time the question was put to him, he simply replied, "He has disappeared." To relieve himself, however, from the most persevering, he framed the stories we have already related, at the same time offering them as mere reports that he had heard; without, however, placing much reliance on them.

But when enquiry came to be made by order of the cardinal, or rather, by order of some great person, as his name was not mentioned, Bortolo became more uneasy, and judged it prudent to maintain his ordinary method of reply, with this addition, that he gave to the stories he had fabricated an air of greater verity and plausibility.

We must not conclude, however, that Don Gonzalo had any personal dislike to our poor mountaineer; we must not conclude that, informed perhaps of his disrespect and ill-timed jests upon his *Moorish king enchained by the throat*, he wished to wreak his vengeance on him, nor that he considered him a person dangerous enough to be pursued even in his flight, as was Hannibal by the Roman senate. Don Gonzalo had too many things to think of, to trouble himself with the actions of Renzo, and if he appeared to do so, it was the result of a singular concurrence of circumstances; by which the poor fellow, without wishing it, or even knowing why, found himself attached, as by an invisible thread, to numerous and important affairs.

Chapter XXVII.

We have had occasion to mention more than once a war which was then fermenting, for the succession to the states of the Duke Vincenzo Gonzaga, the second of the name; we have said that, at the death of this duke, his nearest heir, Carlos Gonzaga, chief of a younger branch transplanted to France, where he possessed the duchies of Nevers and Rhetel, had entered into possession of Mantua and Montferrat; the Spanish minister, who wished, at any price, to exclude from these two fiefs the new prince, and wanted some pretence to advance for his exclusion, had declared his intention to support the claims upon Mantua of another Gonzaga, Ferrante, Prince of Guastalla; and those upon Montferrat of Carlos Emanuel the First, Duke of Savoy, and Margherita Gonzaga, Duchess dowager of Lorraine. Don Gonzalo, who was descended from the great captain whose name he bore, had already made war in Flanders; and as he was desirous beyond measure to direct one in Italy, he made the greatest efforts to promote it. By interpreting the intentions, and by going beyond the orders of the minister, he had, in the mean time, concluded with the Duke of Savoy a treaty for the invasion and division of Montferrat; and easily obtained the ratification of it, by the count duke, by persuading him that the acquisition of Casale, which was the point the best defended, of the portion granted to the King of Spain, was extremely easy. However, he still continued to protest, in the name of his sovereign, that he desired to occupy the country only as a trust, until the decision of the emperor should be declared. But in the meantime the emperor, influenced by others as well as by motives of his own, had refused the investiture to the new duke, and ordered him to leave in sequestration, the states which had been the subject of contention; promising, after he should have heard both parties, to give it to the one whom he should deem justly entitled to it. The Duke of Nevers would not submit to these conditions.

The duke had high and powerful friends, being supported by the Cardinal Richelieu, the senate of Venice, and the pope. But the first of these, absorbed at the time by the siege of Rochelle, embarrassed in a war with England, thwarted by the party of the queen mother, Mary de' Medici, who, for particular reasons, was hostile to the house of Nevers, could only hold out hopes and promises. The Venetians would not stir in the contest, until a French army arrived in Italy; and while secretly aiding the duke, they confined themselves, in their negotiations with the court of Madrid, and the government of Milan, to protests, offers, or even threats, according to circumstances. Urban VIII. recommended the Duke of Nevers to his friends, interceded for him with his adversaries, and made propositions of peace; but he never afforded him any military aid.

The two powers, allied for offensive operations, could then securely begin their enterprise; Carlos Emanuel entered Montferrat, and Don Gonzalo gladly undertook the siege of Casale; but he did not meet with the success he had anticipated. The court did not afford him all the supplies he demanded; his ally, on the contrary, was too liberal in his aid to the cause; for, after having taken his own portion, he also took that which had been assigned to the King of Spain. Don Gonzalo, inexpressibly enraged, but fearing, if he made the least complaint, that Carlos, as active in intrigue, and as brave in arms, as he was fickle in disposition, and false to his promises, would throw himself on the side of France; was constrained to shut his eyes, to champ the bit, and to maintain a satisfied appearance. Whether from the firm resistance of the besieged, or from the small number of troops employed against them, or, according to some statements, from the numerous mistakes of Don Gonzalo, the siege, although protracted, was finally unsuccessful. It was at this very period that the sedition of Milan obliged Don Gonzalo to go thither in person.

In the relation that was there made to him, the flight of Renzo was mentioned, and the facts, real or supposed, which had caused his arrest; he was also informed that this man had taken refuge in the territory of Bergamo. This latter circumstance attracted the attention of Don Gonzalo; he knew that the Venetians had taken an interest in the insurrection of Milan, and that, in the beginning of it, they had imagined that, on that account alone, he would be obliged to raise the siege of Casale, and thus incur a heavy disappointment to his hopes. In addition to this, immediately after this event, the news was received, so much desired by the senate, and so much dreaded by Gonzalo, of the surrender of Rochelle. Stung to the quick, as a man and a politician, and vexed at his loss of reputation, he sought out every occasion to convince the Venetians, that he had lost none of his former boldness and determination; he therefore ventured to make loud complaints of the conduct of the senate. The resident of Venice, having come to pay his respects to him, and endeavouring to read in his features and deportment what was passing in his mind, Don Gonzalo spoke lightly of the tumult, as a thing already quieted, making use, however, of the reception of Renzo, in the Bergamascan territory, as a pretext for complaint against the Venetians. The result is known to our readers. When he had answered his own purposes, with the affair, it was entirely forgotten by him.

But Renzo, who was far from suspecting the little importance that was in reality attached to him, had, for a long time, no other thought but to keep himself concealed. It may well be supposed that he desired ardently to send intelligence to Lucy and her mother, and to hear from them in return. But to this, there were two very great obstacles. It was necessary to confide in an amanuensis, as he himself was unable to write,—an accomplishment in those days not very usual in his class; and how could he venture to do this where all were strangers to him? The other difficulty was to find a trusty messenger, to take charge of the letter. He finally succeeded in overcoming these difficulties, and found one of his companions who could write for him. But not knowing whether Lucy and Agnes were still at Monza, he thought it best to enclose the letter under cover to Father Christopher, with a few lines in addition to him. The writer engaged to send it, and gave it to a man who was to pass near Pescarenico, and who left it in an inn on the route, in a neighbouring place to the convent, and with many injunctions for its safe delivery. As the cover was directed to a capuchin, it was carried to Pescarenico, but it was never known what farther became of it. Renzo, not receiving an answer, caused another letter to be written, and enclosed it to one of his relations at Lecco. This time the letter reached its destination. Agnes requested her cousin Alessio to read it for her; and to write an answer, which was sent to Antonio Rivolta, at the place of his abode; all this, however, was not done so quickly as we tell it. Renzo received the answer, and wrote a reply; in short, there was a correspondence, however irregular, established between them. But the manner of carrying on such a correspondence, which is the same, perhaps, at this day, we will explain. The absent party who can't write, selects one who possesses the art, from amongst his own class, in which he can more securely trust. To him he explains with more or less clearness his subject and his thoughts. The man of letters comprehends part, guesses the rest, gives an opinion, proposes an alteration, and finishes with "leave it to me." Then begins the translation of the spoken into the written thoughts.—The writer corrects, improves, overcharges, diminishes, or even omits, according to his opinion of the graces of style. The finished letter is, accordingly, often wide of the mark aimed at. But when, at length, it reaches the hands of a correspondent, equally deficient in the art of reading running hand, he is under the like necessity of finding a learned clerk of the same calibre to interpret the hieroglyphics. Hereupon arise questions upon the various meanings. Towards their elucidation, the one supplies philological notices upon the text; the other, commentaries upon the hidden matter; so that, after mature discussion, they may come to the same understanding between themselves, however remote that may be from the intention of the originator of the perplexity.

This was precisely the condition of our two correspondents.

The first letter from Renzo contained many details; he informed Agnes of the circumstance of his flight, his subsequent adventures, and his actual situation. These events, however, were rather hinted at, than clearly explained, so that Agnes and her interpreter were far from drawing any definite conclusions from the relation of them. He spoke of secret information, of a change of name; that he was in safety, but that he was obliged to keep himself concealed; further, the letter contained pressing and passionate enquiries with regard to Lucy, with some obscure references to the reports which had reached him, mingled with vague expressions of hope, and plans for the future, and affectionate exhortations to constancy and patience.

Some time after the receipt of this letter, Agnes sent Renzo an answer, with the fifty crowns that had been assigned him by Lucy. At the sight of so much gold, he did not know what to think; and, with his mind agitated by reflections by no means agreeable, he went in search of his amanuensis, requesting him to interpret the letter, and afford him a clue to the developement of the mystery.

The amanuensis of Agnes, after some complaints on the want of clearness in Renzo's epistle, described the wonderful history of *this person* (so he called the Unknown), and thus accounted for the fifty crowns; then he mentioned the vow, but only periphrastically; adding more explicitly the advice, to set his heart at rest, and not to think of Lucy any more.

Renzo was very near quarrelling with his interpreter; he trembled; he was enraged with what he had understood, and with what he had not understood.

He made him read three or four times this melancholy epistle, sometimes understanding it better, sometimes finding obscure and inexplicable that which at first had appeared clear. In the delirium of his passion, he desired his amanuensis to write an answer immediately. After the strongest expressions of pity and horror at the misfortunes of Lucy; "Write," pursued he, "that I do not wish to set my heart at rest, and that I never will; that this is not advice to give me; and that, moreover, I will never touch the money, but will keep it in trust, as the dowry of the young girl; that Lucy belongs to me, and that I will not abide by her vow; that I have always heard that the Virgin interests herself in our affairs, for the purpose of aiding the afflicted, and obtaining favour for them; but that I have never heard that she will protect those who do evil, and fail to perform their promises; say that, as such cannot be the case, her vow is good for nothing; that with this money we can establish ourselves here, and that, if our affairs are now a little perplexed, it is a storm which will soon pass away."

Agnes received this letter, sent an answer, and the correspondence continued for some time, as we have related. When her mother informed Lucy that Renzo was well and in safety, she derived great relief from the intelligence, desiring but one thing more, which was, that he should forget, or rather, that he should endeavour to forget her. On her part she made a similar resolution, with respect to him, a hundred times a day; and employing every means of which she was mistress to accomplish so desirable an end, she applied herself incessantly to labour, endeavouring to give to it all the powers of her soul. When the image of Renzo occurred to her mind, she tried to banish it by prayer; but, while thinking of her mother, (and how could she avoid thinking of her mother?) the image of Renzo intruded himself as a third into the place so often occupied by the real Renzo. However, if she did not succeed in forgetting, she contrived at least to think less frequently of him; and in this she would have been more successful, had she been left to prosecute the work alone; but, alas! Donna Prassede, who, on her part, was determined to drive the poor youth from her mind, thought there was no better expedient for the purpose than to talk of him incessantly; "Well," said she, "do you still think of him?"

"I think of no one," said Lucy.

Donna Prassede, who was not a woman to be satisfied with such an answer, replied, "that she wanted actions, not words." Discussing at length, the tendencies of young girls, she said, "When they have once given their heart to a libertine, it is impossible to withdraw their affections. If their love for an honest man is, by whatever means, unfortunate, they are soon comforted, but love for a libertine is an incurable wound." And then beginning the panegyric of poor Renzo, of this rascal, who wished to deluge Milan in blood, and reduce it to ashes, she concluded, by insisting that Lucy should confess the crimes of which he had been guilty in his own country.

Lucy, with a voice trembling from shame, grief, and from as much indignation as her gentle disposition and humble station permitted her, declared and protested, that in her village this poor youth had always acted peaceably and honourably, and had obtained a good reputation. "She wished," she said, "that one of his countrymen were present to bear testimony to the truth." Even respecting the events at Milan, of which, 'twas true, she knew not the details, she defended him, and solely on account of the acquaintance she had had with his habits from infancy. She defended him (or rather, she *meant* to defend him) from the pure duty of charity, from love of truth, and as being her neighbour. But Donna Prassede deduced, from this defence, new arguments to convince Lucy, that this man still held a place in her heart, of which he was not worthy. At the degrading portrait which the old lady drew of him, the habitual feelings of her heart, with regard to him, and her knowledge and estimate of his character, revived with double force and distinctness. Her recollections, which she had had so much difficulty in subduing, returned vividly to her imagination; in proportion to the aversion and contempt manifested by Donna Prassede towards the unfortunate youth, just in such proportion did she recall her former motives for esteem and sympathy; this blind and violent hatred excited in her heart stronger pity and tenderness. Such conversations could not be much prolonged without resolving Lucy's words into tears.

If Donna Prassede had been led to this course of conduct by hatred towards Lucy, the tears of the latter, which flowed freely during these examinations, might have subdued her to silence, but as she was moved to speak by the desire of doing good, she never suffered herself to be softened by them; for groans and supplications may arrest the arm of an enemy, but not the friendly lance of the surgeon. After having reproached her for her wickedness, she passed to exhortations and advice, mingling also a few praises, to temper the bitter with the sweet, and obtain more certainly the effect she desired. These disputes, which had nearly the same beginning, middle, and end, did not, however, leave any trace of resentment against her severe lecturer in the gentle bosom of Lucy; she was, in other respects, treated with much kindness by the lady, and she believed her, even in this matter, to be guided by good, though mistaken intentions. There did follow them, however, such agitation, such uneasy awakening of slumbering thoughts, that much time and effort were requisite to restore her to any degree of tranquillity.

It was a happiness for Lucy that Donna Prassede's sphere of usefulness was somewhat extensive; consequently these tiresome conversations could not be so frequently repeated. Besides her immediate household, composed, according to her opinion, of persons that had more or less need of correction and regulation; and besides all the other occasions which presented themselves for her rendering the same office from pure benevolence to persons who required not the duty at her hands; she had five daughters, neither of whom lived at home, but they gave her the more trouble from that very cause. Three were nuns; and two were married. Donna Prassede consequently had three monasteries and two families to govern; a vast and complicated machinery, and the more troublesome, as two husbands, supported by a numerous kindred, three abbesses, defended by other dignitaries, and a great number of nuns, would not accept her superintendence. There was a continual warfare, polite indeed, but active and vigilant; a perpetual attention to avoid her solicitude, to close up the avenues to her advice, to elude her enquiries, and to keep her in as much ignorance as possible of their affairs. In her own family, however, her zeal could display itself freely; all were governed by her authority, and submissive to her, in every respect, with the exception of Don Ferrante; with him things were conducted in a peculiar manner.

A man of study, he neither loved to obey nor command; he was perfectly willing that his wife should be mistress in all things pertaining to household affairs, but not that he should be her slave; and if, at her request, he lent upon occasion the services of his pen, it was because he had a particular taste for such employments. And, moreover, he could refuse to do it, when not convinced of the propriety of her demand. "Well," he would say, "do it yourself, since the matter appears so plain to you." Donna Prassede, after vainly trying to induce him to submission, took refuge in grumbling against him as an original, a man who would have his own way, a mere scholar;

which latter title, however, she never gave him without a degree of complacency, mingling itself with her displeasure.

Don Ferrante passed much time in his study, where he had a considerable collection of choice books; he had selected the most famous works on many different subjects, in each of which he was more or less versed. In astrology he was justly considered more than an amateur, because he not only possessed the general notions, and the common vocabulary of influences, aspects, and conjunctions, but he could speak to the point, and, like a professor, of the twelve houses of heaven, of the great and lesser circles, of degrees, lucid and obscure, of exaltations, passages, and revolutions; in short, of the principles the most certain and most recondite of the science. For more than twenty years, in long and frequent disputes, he had sustained the pre-eminence of *Cardan* against another learned man attached to the system of *Alcabizio*, "from pure obstinacy," said Don Ferrante, who, in acknowledging voluntarily the superiority of the ancients, could not, however, endure the prejudice which would never accord to the moderns, even that which they evidently deserved. He had also a more than ordinary acquaintance with the history of the science; he could cite the most celebrated predictions which had been verified, and reason very skilfully and learnedly on other celebrated predictions which had *not* been verified, demonstrating that the failure was not owing to any deficiency in the science, but to the ignorance which could not apply its principles.

He had acquired as much ancient philosophy as would have contented a man of ordinary ambition, but he was continually adding to his stock from the study of Diogenes Laertius; however, as we cannot adhere to every system, and as, from among them all, a choice is necessary to him who desires the reputation of a philosopher, Don Ferrante made choice of Aristotle, who, as he was accustomed to say, was neither ancient nor modern. He possessed many works of the wisest and most subtle disciples of the school of Aristotle among the moderns; as to those of his opponents, he would not read them, "because it would be a waste of time," he said, "nor buy them, because it would be a waste of money." In the judgment of the learned, therefore, Don Ferrante passed for an accomplished peripatetic, although this was not the judgment he passed on himself, for, more than once, he was heard to declare, with singular modesty, that the essence, the universals, the soul of the world, and the nature of things, were not matters so clear as people thought.

As to natural philosophy, he had made it more a pastime than a study: he had rather read than digested the works of Aristotle himself on the subject. Nevertheless, with a slight acquaintance with that author, and the knowledge he had incidentally gathered from other treatises of general philosophy, he could, when necessary, entertain an assembly of learned persons in reasoning most acutely on the wonderful virtues and singular characteristics of many plants. He could describe exactly the forms and habits of the syrens, and the phoenix, the only one of its kind; he could explain how it was that the salamander lived in fire, how drops of dew became pearls in the shell, how the chameleon lived on air, and a thousand other secrets of the same nature.

He was, however, much more addicted to the study of magic and sorcery, as this was a science more in vogue, and withal more serviceable, and the facts of which were of pre-eminent importance. It is not necessary to add that, in devotion to such a science, he had no other purpose than to obtain an accurate knowledge of the worst artifices of the sorcerers, in order to guard himself against them. Guided by the great *Martino Delrio*, he was able to discourse, *ex professo*, on the enchantment of love, the enchantment of sleep, the enchantment of hatred, and on the innumerable species of these three chief enchantments, which, alas! are witnessed every day in their destructive and baneful effects.

His knowledge of history, especially universal history, was not less vast and solid. "But," said he often, "what is history without politics? a guide who conducts without teaching any one the way; as politics without history, is a man without a guide to conduct him." Here was then a small place on his shelf assigned to statistics; there, among others of the second rank, were seen Bodin, Cavalcanti, Sansovino, Paruta, and Boccalini. There were, however, two books that Don Ferrante preferred to all others on the subject; two, which he called, for a long time, the first of the kind, without deciding to which of the two this rank exclusively belonged. One was *Il Principe* and the *Discorsi* of the celebrated secretary of Florence. "A rascal, 'tis true," said he, "but profound;" the other, *La Ragion di Stato*, of the not less celebrated Giovanni Botero. "An honest man, 'tis true," said he, "but cunning." But, a short time before the period to which our history belongs, a work appeared which had terminated the question of pre-eminence; a work in which was comprised and condensed a relation of every vice, in order to enable men to avoid it, and every virtue, in order to enable men to practise it,—a book of few leaves, indeed, but all of gold; in a word, the *Statista Regnante* of *Don Valeriano Castiglione*; of the celebrated man upon whom the most learned men emulated each other in bestowing praises, and for whose notice the greatest personages contended; whom Pope Urban VIII. honoured with a magnificent eulogium; whom Cardinal Borghese and the Viceroy of Naples, Don Pietro de Toledo, solicited to write, the first, the life of Pope Paul V., the second, the wars of the Catholic king in Italy, and both in vain; whom Louis XIII., King of France, with the advice of Cardinal Richelieu, named his historiographer; upon whom the Duke Carlos Emanuel, of Savoy, conferred the same office; and in praise of whom the Duchess Christina, daughter to his most Christian majesty, Henry IV., added in a diploma, after many other titles, "the renown he had obtained in Italy as the first writer of the age."

But if Don Ferrante might be said to be well versed in all the above sciences, there was one in which he deserved, and really obtained, the title of professor, the science of chivalry. He not only spoke of it as a master, but was often requested to interfere in nice points of honour, and give his decision. He had in his library, and, we may add, in his head also, the works of the most esteemed writers on this subject, particularly Torquato Tasso, whom he had always ready; and he could, if required, cite from memory all the passages of the Jerusalem Delivered, which might be brought forward as authority in these matters. We might speak more at large of this learned man, but we feel it to be time to resume the thread of our history.

Nothing of importance occurred to any of the personages of our story before the following autumn, when Agnes and Lucy expected to meet again; but a great public event disappointed this hope. Other events followed, which produced no material change in their destiny. Then occurred new misfortunes, powerful and overwhelming, coming upon them like a hurricane, which impetuously tears up and scatters every object in its way, sweeping the land, and bearing off, with its irresistible and mighty power, every vestige of peace and prosperity. That the particular facts which remain to be related may not appear obscure, we must recur for awhile to the farther recital of general facts.

Chapter XXVIII.

After the famous sedition on St. Martin's day, it may be said that abundance flowed into Milan, as if by enchantment. The shops were well stored with bread, the price of which was no higher than in the most fruitful years; those who, on that terrible day, had howled through the streets, and committed every excess in their power, had now reason to congratulate themselves. But, with the cessation of their alarm, they had not resumed their accustomed quiet; on the squares, and in the inns, there were congratulations and boastings (although in an under tone) at having hit on a mode of reducing the price of bread. However, in the midst of these popular rejoicings, there reigned a vague apprehension and presentiment that this happiness would be of short duration. They besieged the bakers and vendors of flour with the same pertinacity as during the period of the former factitious and transient abundance, produced by the first tariff of Antony Ferrer. He who had some pence by him converted them immediately into bread and flour, which was piled in chests, in small casks, and even in vessels of earthen ware. In thus attempting to extend the advantages of the moment, their long duration was rendered, I do not say impossible, for it was so already; but even their momentary continuance thus became still more difficult.

On the fifteenth of November, Antony Ferrer, "*by the order of his excellency,*" published a decree in which it was forbidden to any one, having any quantity of grain or flour in his house, to purchase more; and to the rest of the people to buy bread beyond that which was necessary for two days, "*under pecuniary and corporal penalties at the discretion of his excellency.*" The decree ordered the *anziani* (officers of justice), and invited every body, as a duty, to denounce the offenders; it commanded the judges to cause search to be made in every house which might be mentioned to them, issuing at the same time a new command to the bakers to keep their shops well furnished with bread, "*under penalty of five years in the galleys, and still greater punishment at the discretion of his excellency.*" A great effort of imagination would be required to believe that such orders were easy of execution.

In commanding the bakers to make such a quantity of bread, means ought to have been afforded for the supply of the material of which it was to be made. In seasons of scarcity, there is always an endeavour to make into bread various kinds of aliment, which, under ordinary circumstances, are consumed under other forms. In this way rice was introduced into the composition of a bread which was called mistura. On the 23d of November, there was a decree issued, which placed at the order of the vicar and twelve members of provision the half of the rice that each possessed; under penalty for selling it without the permission of those lords of the loss of the entire commodity, and a fine of three crowns the bushel.

But this rice had to be paid for at a price very disproportioned to that of bread. The burden of supplying this enormous difference was imposed on the city: but the council of ten resolved to send a remonstrance to the governor, on the impossibility of sustaining such a tax; and the governor fixed, by a decree of the 13th of December, the price of rice at twelve livres the bushel. It is also probable, though nowhere expressly stated, that the maximum price for other sorts of grain was fixed by other proclamations. Whilst, by these various measures, bread and flour were kept at a low price in Milan, it consequently happened that crowds of people rushed into the city to supply their wants. Don Gonzalo, to remedy this inconvenience, forbade, by another decree of the 15th of December, the carrying out of the city bread to the value of more than twenty pence; the penalty was a fine of *"twenty-five crowns, and in case of inability, a public flogging, and greater punishments still, at the discretion of his excellency."*

The populace wished to procure abundance by pillage and conflagration, the legal power wished to maintain it by the galleys and the rope. Every method was resorted to to accomplish their purpose, but the reader will soon learn the total failure of them all. It is, besides, easy to see, and not useless to observe, that these strange means had an intimate and necessary connection with each other; each was the inevitable consequence of the preceding, and all, in fact, flowed from the first error, that of fixing upon bread a price so disproportioned to that which ought to have resulted from the real state of things. Such an expedient, however, has always appeared to the populace not only conformable to equity, but very simple and easy of execution; it is then very natural that in the agonies and misery which are the necessary effects of scarcity, they should, if it be in their power, adopt it. But as the consequences begin to be felt, the government is obliged to repair the evil by new laws, forbidding men to do that which previous laws had recently prescribed to them.

The principal fruits of the insurrection were these; the destruction or loss of much provision in the insurrection itself, and the rapid consumption of the small quantity of grain then on hand, which should otherwise have lasted until the next harvest. To these general effects may be added, the punishment of four of the populace, who were hung as leaders of the sedition, two before the baker's shop of the crutches, and two at the corner of the street in which was situated the house of the superintendent of provision.

The historical relations of this epoch are handed down to us with so little clearness, that it is difficult to ascertain when this arbitrary tariff ceased. But we have numerous accounts of the situation of the country, and especially the city, in the winter of that year and the following spring. In every quarter shops were closed; and the manufactories were, for the most part, deserted; the streets afforded a terrible spectacle of sorrow and desolation; mendicants by profession, now the smallest number, were confounded with the new multitude, disputing for alms with those from whom they had formerly been accustomed to receive them; clerks and servants, dismissed by the merchants and shopkeepers, hardly existing upon some scanty savings; merchants and shopkeepers themselves failing and ruined by the stoppage of trade; artificers wandering from door to door, lying along the pavement, by the houses and churches, soliciting charity, and hesitating between want and shame, emaciated and feeble, reduced by long fasting, and the rigours of the cold which penetrated their tattered clothing; servants, dismissed by their masters, who were incapable of maintaining their accustomed numerous and sumptuous establishments; and the numerous dependents upon the labour of these various classes, old men, women, and children, grouped around their former supporters, or wandered in search of support elsewhere.

Among the wretched crowds also might be distinguished, by their *long lock*, by the remnants of their magnificent apparel, by their carriage and gestures, and by the traces which habit impresses on the countenance, many *bravoes*, who, having lost in the common misery their criminal means of support, were reduced to an equality of suffering, and with difficulty dragged themselves along the city that they had so often traversed with a proud and ferocious bearing, magnificently armed and attired; they now extended with humility the hand which they had so frequently raised to menace with insolence, or to strike with treachery.

But the most dense, livid, and hideous swarm was that of the villagers. These were seen in entire families; husbands with their wives, dragging along their little ones, and supporting in their arms their wretched babies, whilst their own aged and helpless parents followed behind,—all flocked into the city in hopes of obtaining bread. Some, whose houses had been invaded and despoiled by the soldiery, had fled in despair; some, to excite compassion, and render their misery more striking, showed the wounds and bruises they had received in defending their homes; and others, whom this scourge had not reached, had been driven, by the two scourges from which no corner of the country was exempt, sterility and the consequent increase on the price of provisions, to the city, as to the abode of abundance and pious munificence. The new comers might be recognised by their air of angry astonishment and disappointment at finding such an excess of misery where they had hoped to be themselves the peculiar objects of compassion and benevolence. Here, too, might be recognised, in all their varieties of ragged habiliments, in the midst of the general wretchedness, the pale dweller of the marsh, the bronzed countenance of the plain or hill countryman, and the sanguine complexion of the mountaineer, all, however, alike in the hollow eye, ferocious or insane countenance, knotted hair, long and matted beard, attenuated body, shrivelled skin and bony breast,—all alike reduced to the lowest condition of languor, of infantine debility.

Heaps of straw and stubble were seen along the walls, and by the gutters, which appeared to be a particular provision of charity for these unfortunate creatures; there their limbs reposed during the night; and in the day they were occupied by those who, exhausted by fatigue and suffering, could no longer bear the weight of their emaciated bodies; sometimes, upon the damp straw a dead body lay extended; sometimes, the miserable spark of life was rekindled in its feeble tenement by timely succour from a hand rich in the means and in the disposition to do good, the hand of the pious Frederick.

He had made choice of six priests of ardent charity and robust constitution; and, dividing them into three companies, assigned to each the third of the city as their charge; they were accompanied by porters, laden with food, cordials, and clothing. Each morning these worthy messengers of benevolence passed through the streets, approached those whom they beheld stretched on the pavement, and gave to each their kindly assistance. Those who were too ill to be benefited by temporal succour received from them the last offices of religion.

Their assistance was not limited to present relief: the good bishop requested them, wherever it was possible, to furnish more efficacious and permanent comfort, by giving to those who should be in some measure restored to strength money for their future necessities, lest returning want should again plunge them into wretchedness and misery; and to obtain shelter for others who lay exposed in the street in the neighbouring houses, by requesting their inhabitants to receive the poor afflicted ones as boarders, whose expenses would be paid by the cardinal himself.

Frederick had not waited for the evil to attain its height, in order to exercise his benevolence, and to devote all the powers of his mind towards its amelioration. By uniting all his means, by practising strict economy, by drawing upon the sums destined to other liberalities, and which had now become of secondary importance, he endeavoured to amass money, in order to employ it entirely for those who were suffering from hunger and its consequences. He bought a quantity of grain, and sent it to the most destitute parts of his diocese; but as the succour was far from adequate to the necessity, he sent with it a great quantity of salt, "with which," says Ripamonti, relating the fact, "the herbs of the field and the leaves of trees were made food for men." He distributed grain and money to the curates of the city; and he himself travelled over it, administering alms, and secretly aiding many indigent families. In the episcopal palace, rice was boiled every day, and dealt out to the necessities of the people, to the extent of 2000 measures. Besides these splendid efforts of a single individual, many other excellent persons, though with less powerful means, strove to mitigate the horrible sufferings of the people: of these sufferers, thousands struggled to grasp the broth or other food provided at different quarters, and thus prolong for a day, at least, their miserable lives; but thousands were still left behind in the struggle, and these generally the weakest,—the aged women and children; and these might be seen, dead and dying from inanition, in every part. But in the midst of these calamities not the least disposition to insurrection appeared.

The void that mortality created each day in the miserable multitude was each day more than replenished; there was a perpetual concourse, at first from the neighbouring villages, then from the more distant territories, and, finally, from the Milanese cities.

The ordinary spectacle of ordinary times, the contrast of magnificent apparel with rags, and of luxury with poverty, had entirely disappeared. The nobility even wore coarse clothing; some, because the general misery had affected their fortune; others, because they would not insult the wretchedness of the people, or because they feared to provoke the general despair by the display of luxury at such a time.

Thus passed the winter and the spring; already had the Tribunal of Health remonstrated with the Tribunal of Provision on the danger to which such mass of misery exposed the city. To prevent contagious diseases, a proposal was made to confine the vagabond beggars in the various hospitals. Whilst this project was under discussion, some approving and others condemning, dead bodies incumbered the streets. The Tribunal of Provision, however, proposed another expedient as more easy and expeditious, which was, to shut up all the mendicants, healthy or diseased, in the lazaretto, and to maintain them there at the expense of the city. This measure was resolved upon, notwithstanding the remonstrances of the Tribunal of Health, who objected that, in so numerous an assemblage, the evil to which they wished to apply a remedy would be greatly augmented.

The little order that reigned in the lazaretto, the bad quality of the food, and the standing water which was drank plentifully, soon created numerous maladies. To these causes of mortality, so much the more active from operating on bodies already exhausted or enfeebled, was added the unfavourableness of the season; obstinate rains, followed by more obstinate drought, and violent heat. To these physical evils were added others of a moral nature, despair and wearisomeness in captivity, desire for accustomed habits, regret for cherished beings of whom these unfortunate beings had been deprived; painful apprehension for those who were living, and the continual dread of death, which had itself become a new and powerful cause of the extension of disease. It is not to be wondered at that mortality increased in this species of prison to such a degree as to assume the appearance and deserve the name of *pestilence*. The number of deaths in the lazaretto soon amounted to a hundred daily.

Whilst within these wretched walls, grief, fear, anguish, and rage prevailed, in the Tribunal of Provision, shame, astonishment, and irresolution were equally apparent. They consulted, and now listened to the advice of the Tribunal of Health: finding they could do no better than to undo what they had done, at so much expense and trouble, they opened the doors of the lazaretto, and released all who were well enough to leave it. The city was thus again filled with its former cries, but feebler, and more interrupted; the sick were transported to Santa Maria della Stella, which was then the hospital for the poor, and the greater part perished there.

However, the fields began to yield the harvest so long desired, and the troops of peasants left the city for their long prayed for and accustomed labours. The ingenious and inexhaustible charity of the good Frederick still exerted itself; he made a present of a giulio and a sickle to each peasant, who solicited it at the palace.

With a plentiful harvest, scarcity ceased to be felt; the mortality, however, continued, in a greater or less degree, until the middle of autumn. It was on the point of ceasing, when a new scourge overwhelmed the city and country.

Many events of high historical importance had occurred in this interval of time. The Cardinal Richelieu, after having taken Rochelle, and made a treaty of peace with England, had proposed, effected by his powerful influence in the councils of the French king, that efficacious aid should be sent to the Duke of Nevers; he had also persuaded the king to lead the expedition in person. Whilst the preparations were in progress, the Count of Nassau, imperial commissary, suggested to the new duke in Mantua the expediency of replacing his states in the hands of Ferdinand; intimating that, in case of refusal, an army would be immediately sent by the emperor to occupy them. The duke, who in the most desperate circumstances had rejected so hard a condition, encouraged now by the promised succours from France, was determined still longer to defend himself. The commissary departed, declaring that force would soon decide the matter.

In the month of March, the Cardinal Richelieu with the king, at the head of an army, demanded a free passage from the Duke of Savoy; he entered into treaties for the purpose, but nothing was concluded. After a rencounter, in which the French obtained the advantage, a new treaty was entered into, in which the duke stipulated that Don Gonzalo de Cordova should raise the siege of Casale, engaging, in case of his refusal, to unite with the French, and invade the duchy of Milan. Don Gonzalo raised the siege of Casale, and a body of French troops entered it, to reinforce the garrison. The Cardinal

Richelieu decided to return to France, on business which he regarded as more urgent; but Girolamo Soranzo, envoy from Venice, offered the most powerful reasons to divert him from this resolution. To these the king and the cardinal paid no attention; they returned with the greatest part of the army, leaving only 6000 men at Suza to occupy the passes and maintain the treaty.

Whilst this army departed on one side, that of Ferdinand, commanded by the Count of Collato, advanced on the other. It had invaded the country of the Grisons, and the Valtelline, and was preparing to come down on the Milanese. Besides the usual terrors which such an expectation was calculated to excite, the report was spread, that the plague lurked in the imperial army. Alessandro Tadino, one of the conservators of the public health, was charged by the tribunal to state to the governor the frightful danger which threatened the country, if this army should obtain the pass which opened on Mantua. It appears from all the actions of Gonzalo, that he was possessed by a desire to occupy a great place in history; but, as often happens, history has failed to register one of his most remarkable acts, the answer he returned to this Doctor Tadino; which was, "that he knew not what could be done; that reasons of interest and honour, which had induced the march of the army, were of greater weight than the danger represented; that he would, however, endeavour to act for the best, and that they must trust to Providence."

In order, then, to act for the best, their two physicians proposed to the tribunal to forbid, under the most severe penalty, the purchase of any articles of clothing from the soldiers who were about to pass. As to Don Gonzalo, his reply to Doctor Tadino was one of his last acts at Milan, as the ill success of the war, which had been instigated and directed by him, caused him to be displaced in the course of the summer. He was succeeded by Marquis Ambrosio Spinola, who had already acquired the military celebrity in the wars of Flanders which still endures.

Meanwhile the German troops had received definite orders to march upon Mantua, and in the month of September they entered the duchy of Milan.

At this epoch armies were composed, for the greater part, of adventurers, enlisted by *condottieri*, who held their commission from some prince, and who sometimes pursued the occupation on their own account, so as to be able to sell themselves and followers together. Men were drawn to this vocation much less by the pay which was assigned to them, than by the hope of pillage, and the charms of licence. There was no fixed or general discipline; and as their pay was very uncertain, the spoils of the countries which they over-ran were tacitly accorded to them by their commanders.

It was a saying of the celebrated Wallenstein's, that it was easier to maintain an army of 100,000 men than one of 12,000. And this army of which we are now speaking was part of that which in the thirty years' war had desolated all Germany; it was commanded by one of Wallenstein's lieutenants, and consisted of 28,000 infantry, and 7000 horse. In descending from the Valtelline towards Milan, they had to coast along the Adda, to the place where it empties into the Po; eight days' march in the duchy of Milan.

A great proportion of the inhabitants retired to the mountains, carrying with them their most precious possessions; some remained to watch the sick, or to preserve their dwellings from the flames, or to watch the valuable property which they had buried or concealed; and others remained because they had nothing to lose. When the first detachment arrived at the place where they were to halt, the soldiers scattered themselves through the country; and subjected it at once to pillage; all that could be eaten or carried off disappeared; fields were destroyed, and cottages burnt to the ground; every hiding-place, every method to which people had resorted, in their despair, for the defence of their property, became useless, nay, often resulted in the peculiar injury of the proprietor. Strict search was made throughout every house by the soldiers; they easily detected in the gardens the earth which had been newly dug; they penetrated the caverns in search of the opulent inhabitants, who had taken refuge there, and dragging them to their houses, forced them to declare where they had concealed their treasures.

At last they departed; their drums and trumpets were heard receding in the distance, and a temporary calm succeeded to these hours of tumult and affright; but, alas! the sound of drums was again heard, announcing the arrival of another detachment, the soldiers of which, furious at not finding booty, destroyed what the first work of desolation had spared; burned the furniture and the houses, and manifested the most cruel and savage disposition towards the inhabitants. This continued for a period of twenty days, the army containing that number of divisions.

Colico was the first territory of the duchy that these demons invaded; they then threw themselves on Bellano, from which they entered and spread themselves in the Valsassina, whence they marched into the territory of Lecco.

Chapter XXIX.

Here, among those who were expecting the arrival of the army in alarm and consternation, we find persons of our acquaintance. He who did not behold Don Abbondio on the day when the report was spread of the descent of the army, of its near approach, and its excesses, can have no idea of the power of fright upon a feeble mind. All sorts of reports were afloat. They are coming—thirty, forty, fifty thousand men. They have sacked Cortenova; burnt Primaluna; plundered Introbbio, Pasturo, Barsio. They have been seen at Balobbio; to-morrow they will be here. Such were the statements in circulation. The villagers assembled in tumultuous crowds, hesitating whether to fly or remain, while the women lamented aloud over their miserable fate.

Don Abbondio, to whom flight had immediately suggested itself, saw in it, nevertheless, invincible obstacles, and frightful dangers. "What shall I do?" cried he; "where shall I go?" The mountains, without speaking of the difficulty of ascending them, were not safe; the foot soldiers climbed them like cats, if they had the slightest indication or hope of booty; the waters of the lake were swollen; it was blowing violently; in addition to which, the greater part of the watermen, fearing to be forced to pass soldiers or baggage, had taken refuge with their boats on the opposite shore; the few barks that remained were already filled with people, and endangered by the weather. It was impossible to find a carriage or horse, or any mode of conveyance. Don Abbondio did not dare venture on foot, incurring, as he would, the probability of being stopped on the road. The confines of the Bergamascan territory were not so distant, but that he could have walked there in a little while; but a report had reached the village, that a squadron of *cappelletri* had been sent in haste from Bergamo, to guard the frontiers against the German foot-soldiers. These were not less devils incarnate than those they were commissioned to oppose. The poor man was beside himself with terror; he endeavoured to concert with Perpetua some plan of escape, but Perpetua was quite occupied in collecting and concealing his valuables; with her hands full, she replied, "Let me place this in safety; we will then do as other people do." Don Abbondio desired eagerly to discuss with her the best means to be pursued, but Perpetua, between hurry and fright, was less tractable than usual: "Others will do the best they can," said she, "and so will we. Excuse me, but you only hinder one. Do you not think they have skins to save as well as we?"

Relieving herself thus from his importunities, she went on with her occupation; the poor man, as a last resource, went to a window, and cried, in a piteous tone, to the people who were passing, "Do your poor curate the favour to bring him a horse or a mule; is it possible no one will come to help me? Wait for me at least; wait till I can go with you; abandon me not. Would you leave me in the power of these dogs? Know you not that they are Lutherans, and that the murder of a priest will seem to them a meritorious deed? Would you leave me here to be martyred?"

But to whom did he address this appeal? to men who were themselves incumbered with the weight of their humble movables, or, disturbed by the thoughts of what they had been obliged to leave behind, exposed to the ravages of the destroyer. One drove his cow before him; another conducted his children, who were also laden with burdens, his wife perhaps with an infant in her arms. Some went on their way without replying or looking at him; others merely said, "Eh, sir, do as you can; you are fortunate in having no family to think of; help yourself; do the best you can."

"Oh, poor me!" cried Don Abbondio, "oh, what savages! they have no feeling; they give not a thought to their poor curate!" And he went again in search of Perpetua.

"Oh, you are come just in time," said she, "where is your money?"

"What shall we do with it?"

"Give it to me; I will bury it in the garden with the plate."

"But—"

"But, but, give it to me; keep a few pence for necessity, and let me manage the rest."

Don Abbondio obeyed, and drawing his treasure from his strong box, gave it to Perpetua. "I will bury it in the garden, at the foot of the fig-tree," said she, as she disappeared. She returned in a few moments, with a large basket, full of provisions, and a small one, which was empty; into the latter she put a few articles of clothing for herself and master.

"You must take your breviary with you," said she.

"But where are we going?"

"Where every one else goes. We will go into the street, and then we shall hear and see what we must do."

At this moment Agnes entered with a small basket in her hand, and with the air of one about to make an important proposal.

She had decided not to wait the approach of the dangerous guests, alone as she was, and with the gold of the Unknown in her possession; but had remained some time in doubt where to seek an asylum. The residue of the crowns, which in time of famine would have been so great a treasure, was now the principal cause of her anxiety and irresolution; as, under the present circumstances, those who had money were worse off than others; being exposed at the same time to the violence of strangers, and the treachery of their companions. It is true, none knew of the wealth which had thus, as it were, fallen to her from heaven, except Don Abbondio, to whom she had often applied to change a crown, leaving him always some part of it for those more unfortunate than herself. But hidden property, above all, to those not accustomed to such a possession, keeps the possessor in continual suspicion of others. Now, whilst she reflected on the peculiar dangers to which she was exposed, by the very generosity itself of the Unknown, the offer of unlimited service, which had accompanied the gift, suddenly occurred to her recollection. She remembered the descriptions she had heard of his castle, as situated in a high place, where, without the concurrence of the master, none dared venture but the birds of heaven. Resolving to go thither, and reflecting on the means of making herself known to this signor, her thoughts recurred to Don Abbondio, who, since the conversation with the archbishop, had been very particular in his expression of good feeling towards her, as he could at present be, without compromising himself, there being but little probability, from the situation of affairs, that his benevolence would be put to the test. She naturally supposed, that in a time of such consternation, the poor man would be more alarmed than herself, and might acquiesce in her plan; this was, therefore, the purpose of her visit. Finding him alone with Perpetua, she made known her intentions.

"What do you say to it, Perpetua?" asked Don Abbondio.

"I say that it is an inspiration from Heaven, and that we must lose no time, and set off immediately."

"But then—"

"But then, but then; when we have arrived safely there, we shall be very glad, that's all. It is well known that this signor thinks of nothing now but doing good to others, and he will afford us an asylum with the greatest pleasure. There, on the frontiers, and almost in the sky, the soldiers will not trouble us. But then—but then, we shall have enough to eat, no doubt. On the top of the mountains, the provisions we have here with us would not serve us long."

"Is it true that he is really converted?"

"Can you doubt it, after all you have seen?"

"And if, after all, we should be voluntarily placing ourselves in prison?"

"What prison? With this trifling, excuse me, we shall never come to any conclusion. Worthy Agnes! your plan is an excellent one." So saying, she placed the basket on the table, and having passed her arms through the straps, swung it over her shoulders.

"Could we not procure," said Don Abbondio, "some man to accompany us? Should we encounter some ruffian on the way, what assistance would you be to me?"

"Not done yet! always losing time!" cried Perpetua. "Go then, and look for a man, and you will find every one engaged in his own business, I warrant you. Come, take your breviary, and your hat, and let us be off."

Don Abbondio was obliged to obey, and they departed. They passed through a small door into the churchyard. Perpetua closed it from custom; not for the security it could now give. Don Abbondio cast a look towards the church,—"It is for the people to guard it," thought he; "it is their church: let them see to it, if they have the heart." They took the by-paths through the fields, but were in continual apprehension of encountering some one, who might arrest their progress. They met no one, however; all were employed, either in guarding their houses, or packing their furniture, or travelling, with their moveables, towards the mountains.

Don Abbondio, after many sighs and interjections, began to grumble aloud: he complained of the Duke of Nevers, who could have remained to enjoy himself in France, had he not been determined to be Duke of Mantua, in despite of all the world; of the emperor, and above all, of the governor, whose duty it was to keep this scourge from the country, and not invoke it by his taste for war.

"Let these people be, they cannot help us now," said Perpetua. "These are your usual chatterings, excuse me, which mean nothing. That which gives me the most uneasiness—"

"What is it?"

Perpetua, who had been leisurely recalling to mind the things which she had so hastily concealed, remembered that she had forgotten such an article, and had not safely deposited such another; that she had left traces which might impart information to the depredators.

"Well done!" cried Don Abbondio, in whom the security he was beginning to feel with regard to his life allowed his anxiety to appear for his property; "well done! Is this what you have been doing? Where were your brains?"

"How!" replied Perpetua, stopping for a moment, and attempting, as far as her load would permit, to place her arms a-kimbo; "do you find fault, when it was yourself who teased me out of my wits, instead of helping me as you ought to have done? I have thought more of my master's goods than my own; and if there is any thing lost, I can't help it, I have done more than my duty."

Agnes interrupted these disputes by introducing her own troubles: she was obliged to relinquish the hope of seeing her dear Lucy, for some time at least; for she could not expect that Donna Prassede would come into this vicinity under such circumstances. The sight of the well-remembered places through which they were passing increased the anguish of her feelings. Leaving the fields, they had taken the high road, the same which the poor woman had travelled, in re-conducting, for so short a time, her daughter to her home, after having been with her at the tailor's. As they approached the village, "Let us go and visit these worthy people," said Agnes.

"And rest a little, and eat a mouthful," said Perpetua, "for I begin to have enough of this basket."

"On condition that we lose no time, for this is not by any means a journey for amusement," said Don Abbondio.

They were received with open arms, and cordially welcomed; Agnes, embracing the good hostess, wept bitterly; replying with sobs to the questions her husband and she asked concerning Lucy.

"She is better off than we are," said Don Abbondio; "she is at Milan, sheltered from danger, far from these horrible scenes."

"The signor curate and his companions are fugitives, are they not?" said the tailor.

"Yes," replied, at the same time, Perpetua and her master.

"I sympathise with your misfortunes."

"We are going to the castle of—"

"That is well thought of; you will be as safe as in Paradise."

"And are you not afraid here?"

"We are too much off the road. If they should turn out of their way, we shall be warned in time."

The three travellers decided to take a few hours' rest: as it was the hour of dinner, "Do me the honour," said the tailor, "to partake of my humble fare."

Perpetua said she had provisions enough in her basket wherewith to break her fast; after a little ceremony, however, on both sides, they agreed to seat themselves at the dinner table.

The children had joyfully surrounded their old friend Agnes; the tailor ordered one of them to roast some early chestnuts; "and you," said he to another, "go to the garden, and bring some peaches; all that are ripe. And you," to a third, "climb the fig-tree, and gather the best figs; it is a business to which you are well accustomed." As for himself, he left the room to tap a small cask of wine, while his wife went in search of a table-cloth. All being prepared, they seated themselves at the friendly board, if not with unmingled joy, at least with much more satisfaction than they could have anticipated from the events of the morning.

"What does the signor curate say to the disasters of the times? I can fancy I'm reading the history of the Moors in France," said the tailor.

"What do I say? That even that misfortune might have befallen me," replied Don Abbondio.

"You have chosen an excellent asylum, however; for none can ascend those heights without the consent of the master. You will find a numerous company there. Many people have already fled thither, and there are fresh arrivals every day."

"I dare to hope we shall be well received. I know this worthy signor: when I had the honour to be in his company he was all politeness."

"And," said Agnes, "he sent me word by his illustrious lordship, that if ever I should need assistance, I had only to apply to him."

"What a wonderful conversion!" resumed Don Abbondio. "And he perseveres? does he *not* persevere?"

The tailor spoke at length of the holy life of the Unknown, and said, that after having been the scourge of the country, he had become its best example and benefactor.

"And the people of his household—that band?" asked Don Abbondio, who had heard some contradictory stories concerning them, and did not feel, therefore, quite secure.

"The greater part have left him," replied the tailor, "and those who have remained have changed their manner of life; in short, this castle has become like the Thebaid. The signor curate understands me."

Then retracing with Agnes the visit of the cardinal, "What a great man!" said he, "a great man, indeed! what a pity he remained so short a time with us! I wished to do him honour. Oh, if I had only been able to address him again, more at my leisure!"

When they rose from table, he showed them an engraving of the cardinal, which he had hung on the door, from veneration to his virtues, and also to enable him to assure every body that it was no likeness; he knew it was not, as he had regarded him closely at his leisure in this very room.

"Did they mean that for him?" said Agnes. "The habit is the same, but—"

"It is no likeness, is it?" said the tailor; "that is what I always say, but other things being wanting, there is at least his name under it, which tells who it is."

Don Abbondio being impatient to be gone, the tailor went in search of a vehicle to carry the little company to the foot of the ascent, and returned in a few moments to inform them it was ready. "Signor curate," said he, "if you wish a few books to carry with you, I can lend you some; for I amuse myself sometimes with reading. They are not like yours, to be sure, being in the vulgar tongue, but—"

"A thousand thanks, but under present circumstances I have scarcely brains enough to read my breviary."

After an exchange of thanks, invitations, and promises, they bade farewell, and pursued, with a little more tranquillity of mind, the remainder of their journey.

The tailor had told Don Abbondio the truth, with regard to the new life of the Unknown. From the day that we took our leave of him, he had continued to put in practice his good intentions, by repairing injuries, reconciling himself with his enemies, and succouring the distressed and unfortunate. The courage he had formerly evinced in attack and defence he now employed in avoiding all occasion both for the one and the other. He went unarmed and alone; disposed to suffer the possible consequences of the violences he had committed; persuaded that it would be adding to his crimes to employ any methods of defence for himself, as he was a debtor to all the world; and persuaded also, that though the evil done to him would be sin against God, it would be but a just retribution against himself; and that he had left himself no right to revenge an injury, however unprovoked it might be at the time. But he was not less inviolable than when he bore arms to insure his safety; the recollection of his former ferocity, and the contrast of his present gentleness, the former exciting a desire of revenge, and the latter rendering this revenge so easy, conspired to subdue hatred, and, in its place, to substitute an admiration which served him as a safeguard. The man whom no one could humble, but who had humbled himself, was regarded with the deepest veneration. Those whom he had wronged had obtained, beyond their hopes, and without incurring any danger, a satisfaction which they could never have promised themselves from the most complete revenge, the satisfaction of seeing him repent of his wrongs, and participate, so to speak, in their indignation. In his voluntary abasement, his countenance and manner had acquired, without his own knowledge, something elevated and noble; his outward demeanour was as dauntless as ever.

This change, also, in addition to other reasons, secured him from public retribution at the instigation of those in authority. His rank and family, which had always been a species of defence to him, still prevailed in his favour; and to his name, already famous, was joined the personal esteem which was now due to him. The magistrates and nobility had rejoiced at his conversion, as well as the people; as this conversion produced compensations that they were neither accustomed to ask nor obtain. Probably, also, the name of the Cardinal Frederick, whose interest in his conversion, and subsequent friendship for him, were well known, served him as an impenetrable shield.

Upon the arrival of the German troops, when fugitives from the invaded countries fled to the castle, delighted that his walls, so long the object of dread and execration to the feeble, should now be regarded as a place of security and protection, the Unknown received them rather with gratitude than politeness. He caused it to be made public, that his doors would be open to all, and employed himself immediately in placing not only the castle but the valley beneath in a state of defence: assembling the servants who had remained with him, he addressed them on the opportunity God had afforded them, as well as himself, to serve those whom they had so frequently oppressed and terrified. With his old accent of command, expressing the certainty of being obeyed, he gave them general orders, as to their deportment, so that those who should take refuge with him might behold in them only defenders and friends. He gave their arms to them again, of which they had been deprived; as also to the peasants of the valley, who were willing to engage in its defence: he named officers, and appointed to them their duty and their different stations, as he had been accustomed to do in his former criminal life. He himself, however, whether from principle, or that he had made a vow to that effect, remained unarmed at the head of his garrison.

He also employed the females of the household in preparing beds, straw, mattresses, sacks, in various rooms intended as temporary dormitories. He ordered abundant provisions to be brought to the castle for the use of the guests God should send him; and in the mean while he was himself never idle, visiting every post, examining every defence, and maintaining the most perfect order by his authority and his presence.

Chapter XXX.

As our fugitives approached the valley, they were joined by many companions in misfortune, who were on the same errand to the castle with themselves: under similar circumstances of distress and anguish, intimacies are soon matured, and they listened to the relation of each other's peril with mutual interest and sympathy; some had fled, like the curate and our females, without waiting the arrival of the troops; others had actually seen them, and could describe, in lively colours, their savage and horrible appearance.

"We are fortunate, indeed," said Agnes; "let us thank Heaven. We may lose our property, but at least our lives are safe."

But Don Abbondio could not see so much reason for congratulation; the great concourse of people suggested new causes of alarm. "Oh," murmured he to the females when no one was near enough to hear him; "oh, do you not perceive that by assembling here in such crowds we shall attract the notice of the soldiery? As every one flies and no one remains at home, they will believe that our treasures are up here, and this belief will lead them hither. Oh, poor me! why was I so thoughtless as to venture here!"

"What should they come here for?" said Perpetua, "they are obliged to pursue their route; and, at all events, where there is danger, it is best to have plenty of company."

"Company, company, silly woman! don't you know that every lansquenet could devour a hundred of them? and then, if any of them should commit some foolish violence, it would be a fine thing to find ourselves in the midst of a battle! It would have been better to have gone to the mountains. I don't see why they have all been seized with a mania to go to one place. Curse the people! all here; one after the other, like a frightened flock of sheep!"

"As to that," said Agnes, "they may say the same of us."

"Hush, hush! it is of no use to talk," said Don Abbondio; "that which is done, *is* done: we are here, and here we must remain. May Heaven protect us!"

But his anxiety was much increased by the appearance of a number of armed men at the entrance of the valley. It is impossible to describe his vexation and alarm. "Oh, poor me!" thought he; "I might have expected this from a man of his character. What does he mean to do? Will he declare war? Will he act the part of a sovereign? Oh, poor me! poor me! In this terrible conjuncture he ought to have concealed himself as much as possible; and, behold, he seeks every method to make himself known. It is easy to be seen he wants to provoke them."

"Do you not see, sir," said Perpetua, "that these are brave men who are able to defend us? Let the soldiers come; these men are not at all like our poor devils of peasants, who are good for nothing but to use their legs."

"Be quiet," replied Don Abbondio, in a low but angry tone, "be quiet; you know not what you say. Pray Heaven that the army may be in haste to proceed on its march, so that they may not gain information of this place being disposed like a garrison. They would ask for nothing better; an assault is mere play to them, and putting every one to the sword like going to a wedding. Oh, poor me! perhaps I can secure a place of safety on one of these precipices. I will never be taken in battle! I will never be taken in battle! I never will!"

"If you are even afraid of being defended—" returned Perpetua; but Don Abbondio sharply interrupted her.

"Be quiet, and take care not to relate this conversation. Remember you must always keep a pleasant countenance here, and appear to approve all that you see."

At Malanotte they found another company of armed men. Don Abbondio took off his hat and bowed profoundly, saying to himself, "Alas, alas! I am really in a camp." They here quitted the carriage to ascend the pass on foot, the curate having in haste paid and dismissed the driver. The recollection of his former terrors in this very place increased his present forebodings of evil, by mingling themselves with his reflections, and enfeebling more and more his understanding. Agnes, who had never before trod this path, but who had often pictured it to her imagination, was filled with different but keenly painful remembrances. "Oh, signor curate," cried she, "when I think how my poor Lucy passed this very road."

"Will you be quiet, foolish woman?" cried Don Abbondio in her ear. "Are these things to speak of in this place? Are you ignorant that we are on his lands? It is fortunate no one heard you. If you speak in this manner—"

"Oh," said Agnes, "now that he is a saint—"

"Be quiet," repeated Don Abbondio: "think you we can tell the saints all that passes through our brains? Think rather of thanking him for the kindness he has done you."

"Oh, as to that I have already thought of it; do you think I have no manners, no politeness?"

"Politeness, my good woman, does not consist in telling people things they don't like to hear. Have a little discretion, I pray you. Weigh well your words, speak but little, and that only when it is indispensable. There is no danger in silence."

"You do much worse with all your—" began Perpetua. But "Hush," said Don Abbondio, and, taking off his hat, he bowed profoundly. The Unknown was coming to meet them, having recognised the curate approaching. "I could have wished," said he, "to offer you my house on a more agreeable occasion; but, under any circumstances, I esteem myself happy in serving you."

"Confiding in the great kindness of your illustrious lordship, I have taken the liberty to trouble you at this unhappy time; and, as your illustrious lordship sees, I have also taken the liberty to bring company with me. This is my housekeeper—"

"She is very welcome."

"And this is a female to whom your lordship has already rendered great benefits. The mother of—of—"

"Of Lucy," said Agnes.

"Of Lucy!" cried the Unknown, turning to Agnes; "rendered benefits! I! Just God! It is you who render benefits to me by coming hither; to me—to this dwelling. You are very welcome. You bring with you the blessing of Heaven!"

"Oh, I come rather to give you trouble." Approaching him nearer, she said, in a low voice, "I have to thank you—"

The Unknown interrupted her, asking with much interest concerning Lucy. He then conducted his new guests to the castle. Agnes looked at the curate, as if to say, "See if there is any need of your interfering between us with your advice."

"Has the army arrived in your parish?" said the Unknown to Don Abbondio.

"No, my lord, I would not wait for the demons. Heaven knows if I should have escaped alive from their hands, and been able to trouble your illustrious lordship!"

"You may be quite at ease; you are now in safety; they will not come here. If the whim should seize them, we are ready to receive them."

"Let us hope they will not come," said Don Abbondio. "And on that side," added he, pointing to the opposite mountains, "on that side, also, wanders another body of troops; but—but—"

"It is true. But, doubt not, we are ready for them also."

"Between two fires!" thought Don Abbondio, "precisely between two fires! Where have I suffered myself to be led? And by two women! And this lord appears to delight in such business! Oh, what people there are in the world!"

When they entered the castle, the Unknown ordered Agnes and Perpetua to be conducted to a room, in the quarter assigned to the women, which was three of the four wings of the second court, in the most retired part of the edifice. The men were accommodated in the wings of the other court to the right and left; the body of the building was filled, partly with provisions, and partly with the effects that the refugees brought with them. In the quarter devoted to the men was a small apartment destined to the ecclesiastics who might arrive. The Unknown accompanied Don Abbondio thither, who was the first to take possession of it.

Our fugitives remained three or four and twenty days in the castle, in the midst of continual bustle and alarm. Not a day passed without some reports; at each account, the Unknown, unarmed as he was, led his band beyond the precincts of the valley to ascertain the extent of the peril; it was a singular thing, indeed, to behold him, without any personal defence, conducting a body of armed men.

Not to encroach too far on the benevolence of the Unknown, Agnes and Perpetua employed themselves in performing services in the household. These occupations, with occasional conversations with the acquaintances they had formed at the castle, enabled them to pass away the time with less weariness. Poor Don Abbondio, who had nothing to do, was notwithstanding prevented from becoming listless and inactive by his fears: as to the dread of an attack, it was in some measure dissipated, but still the idea of the surrounding country, occupied on every side by soldiers, and of the numerous consequences which might at any moment result from such a state, kept him in perpetual alarm.

All the time he remained in this asylum he never thought of going beyond the defences; his only walk was on the esplanade; he surveyed every side of the castle, observing attentively the hollows and precipices, to ascertain if there were any practicable passage by which he might seek escape in case of imminent danger. Every day there were various reports of the march of the soldiers; some newsmongers by profession gathered greedily all these reports, and spread them among their companions. On such a day, such a regiment arrived in such a territory; the next day they would ravage such another, where, in the mean time, another detachment had been plundering before them. An account was kept of the regiments that passed the bridge of Lecco, as they were then considered fairly out of the country. The cavalry of Wallenstein passed, then the infantry of Marrados, then the cavalry of Anzalt, then the infantry of Brandenburgh, and, finally, that of Galasso. The flying squadron of Venetians also removed, and the country was again free from invaders. Already the inhabitants of the different villages had begun to quit the castle; some departed every day, as after an autumn storm the birds of heaven leave the leafy branches of a great tree, under whose shelter they had sought and obtained protection. Our three friends were the last to depart, as Don Abbondio feared, if he returned so soon to his house, to find there some loitering soldiers. Perpetua in vain repeated, that the longer they delayed, the greater opportunity they afforded to the thieves of the country to take possession of all that might have been left by the spoilers.

On the day fixed for their departure, the Unknown had a carriage ready at Malanotte, and, taking Agnes aside, he made her accept a bag of crowns, to repair the damage she would find at home; although she protested she was in no need of them, having still some of those he had formerly sent her.

"When you see your good Lucy," said he, "(I am certain that she prays for me, as I have done her much evil,) tell her that I thank her, and that I trust in God that her prayer will return in blessings on herself."

They finally departed; they stopped for a few moments at the house of the tailor, where they heard sad relations of this terrible march,—the usual story of violence and plunder. The tailor's family, however, had remained unmolested, as the army did not pass that way.

"Ah, signor curate!" said the tailor, as he was bidding him farewell, "here is a fine subject to appear in print!"

After having proceeded a short distance, our travellers beheld melancholy traces of the destruction they had heard related. Vineyards despoiled, not by the vintager, but as if by a tempest; vines trampled under foot; trees wounded and lopped of their branches; hedges destroyed; in the villages, doors broken open, window-frames dashed in, and streets filled with different articles of furniture and clothing, broken and torn to pieces. In the midst of lamentations and tears, the peasants were occupied in repairing, as well as they could, the damage done; while others, overcome by their miseries, remained in a state of silent despair. Having passed through these scenes of complicated woe, they at last succeeded in reaching their own dwellings, where they witnessed the same destruction. Agnes immediately occupied herself in reducing to order the little furniture that was left her, and in repairing the damage done to her doors and windows; but she did not forget to count over in secret her crowns, thanking God in her heart, and her generous benefactor, that in the general overthrow of order and safety she at least had fallen on her feet.

Don Abbondio and Perpetua entered their house without being obliged to have recourse to keys. In addition to the miserable destruction of all their furniture, whose various fragments impeded their entrance, the most horrible odours for a time drove them back; and when these obstacles were at last surmounted, and the rooms were entered, they found indignity added to mischief. Frightful and grotesque figures of priests, with their square caps and bands, were drawn with pieces of coal upon the walls in all sorts of ridiculous attitudes.

"Ah, the hogs!" cried Perpetua.—"Ah, the thieves!" exclaimed Don Abbondio. Hastening into the garden, they approached the fig-tree, and beheld the earth newly turned up, and, to their utter dismay, the tomb was opened, and the dead was gone. Don Abbondio scolded Perpetua for her bad management, who was not slack in repelling his complaints. Both pointing backwards to the unlucky hiding place, at length returned to the house, and set about endeavouring to purify it of some of its accumulated filth, as at such a time it was impossible to procure assistance for the purpose. With money lent them by Agnes, they were in some measure enabled to replace their articles of furniture.

For some time this disaster was the source of continual disputes between Perpetua and her master; the former having discovered that some of the property, which they supposed to have been taken by the soldiers, was actually in possession of certain people of the village, she tormented him incessantly to claim it. There could not have been touched a chord more hateful to Don Abbondio, since the property was in the hands of that class of persons with whom he had it most at heart to live in peace.

"But I don't wish to know these things," said he. "How many times must I tell you that what has happened has? Must I get myself into trouble again, because my house has been robbed?"

"You would suffer your eyes to be pulled from your head, I verily believe," said Perpetua; "others hate to be robbed, but you, you seem to like it."

"This is pretty language to hold, indeed! Will you be quiet?"

Perpetua kept silence, but continually found new pretexts for resuming the conversation; so that the poor man was obliged to suppress every complaint at the loss of such or such a thing, as she would say, "Go and find it at such a person's house, who has it, and who would not have kept it until now if he had not known what kind of a man he had to deal with."

But here we will leave poor Don Abbondio, having more important things to speak of than his fears, or the misery of a few villagers from a transient disaster like this.

Chapter XXXI.

The pestilence, as the Tribunal of Health had feared, did enter the Milanese with the German troops. It is also known that it was not limited to that territory, but that it spread over and desolated a great part of Italy. Our story requires us, at present, to relate the principal circumstances of this great calamity, as far as it affected the Milanese, and principally the city of Milan itself, for the chroniclers of the period confine their relations chiefly to this place. At the same time we cannot avoid giving a general though brief sketch of an event in the history of our country more talked of than understood.

Many partial narratives written at the time are still extant; but these convey but an imperfect view of the subject, historically speaking. It is true they serve to illustrate and confirm one another, and furnish materials for a history; but the history is still wanting. Strange to say, no writer has hitherto attempted to reduce them to order, and exhibit all the various events, public and private acts, causes and conjectures, relative to this calamity, in a concatenated series. Ripamonti's narrative, though far more ample than any other, is still very defective. We shall, therefore, attempt, in the following pages, to present the reader with a succinct, but accurate and continuous, statement of this fatal scourge.

In all the line of country which had been over-run by the army, dead bodies had been found in the houses, as well as on the roads. Soon after, throughout the whole country, entire families were attacked with violent disorders, accompanied with unusual symptoms, which the aged only remembered to have seen at the time of the plague, which, fifty-three years before, had desolated a great part of Italy, and principally the Milanese, where it was and still is known by the name of the Plague of San Carlo. It derives this appellation from the noble, beneficent, and disinterested conduct of that great man, who at length became its victim.

Ludovico Settala, a physician distinguished so long ago as during the former plague, announced to the Tribunal of Health, by the 20th of October, that the contagion had indisputably appeared at Lecco; but no measures were taken upon this report. Further notices of a like import induced them to despatch a commissioner, with a physician of Como, who, most unaccountably, upon the report of an old barber of Bellano, announced that the prevailing disease arose merely from the autumnal exhalation from the marshes, aggravated by the sufferings caused by the passage of the German troops.

Meanwhile, further intelligence of the new disease, and of the number of deaths, arriving from all parts, two commissioners were sent to examine the places where it had appeared, and, if necessary, to use precautions to prevent its increase. The scourge had already spread to such an extent, as to leave no doubt of its character. The commissioners passed through the territories of Lecco, the borders of the lake of Como, the districts of Monte-Brianza, and Gera-d'Adda, and found the villages every where in a state of barricade, or deserted, and the inhabitants flying, or encamped in the middle of the fields, or dispersed abroad throughout the country; "like so many wild creatures," says Doctor Tadino, one of the envoys, "they were carrying about them some imaginary safeguard against the dreaded disease, such as sprigs of mint, rue, or rosemary, and even vinegar." Informing themselves of the number of deaths, the commissioners became alarmed, and visiting the sick and the dead, recognised the terrible and infallible evidences of the *plague*!

Upon this information, orders were given to close the gates of Milan.

The Tribunal of Health, on the 14th of November, directed the commissioners to wait on the governor, in order to represent to him the situation of affairs. He replied, that he was very sorry for it; but that the cares of war were much more pressing: this was the second time he had made the same answer under similar circumstances. Two or three days after, he published a decree, prescribing public rejoicings on the birth of Prince Charles, the first son of Philip IV., without troubling himself with the danger which would result from so great a concourse of people at such a time; just as if things were going on in their ordinary course, and no dreadful evil was hanging over them.

This man was the celebrated Ambrose Spinola, who died a few months after, and during this very war which he had so much at heart,—not in the field, but in his bed, and through grief and vexation at the treatment he experienced from those whose interests he had served. History has loudly extolled his merits; she has been silent upon his base inhumanity in risking the dissemination of that worst of mortal calamities, plague, over a country committed to his trust.

But that which diminishes our astonishment at his indifference is the indifference of the people themselves, of that part of the population which the contagion had not yet reached, but who had so many motives to dread it. The scarcity of the preceding year, the exactions of the army, and the anxiety of mind which had been endured, appeared to them more than sufficient to explain the mortality of the surrounding country. They heard with a smile of incredulity and contempt any who hazarded a word on the danger, or who even mentioned the plague. The same incredulity, the same blindness, the same obstinacy, prevailed in the senate, the council of ten, and in all the judicial bodies. Cardinal Frederick alone enjoined his curates to impress upon the people the importance of declaring every case, and of sequestrating all infected or suspected goods. The Tribunal of Health, prompted by the two physicians, who fully apprehended the danger, did take some tardy measures; but in vain. A proclamation to prevent the entrance of strangers into the city was not published until the 29th of November. This was too late; the plague was already in Milan.

It must be difficult, however interesting, to discover the first cause of a calamity which swept off so many thousands of the inhabitants of the city; but both Tadino and Ripamonti agree that it was brought thither by an Italian soldier in the service of Spain, who had either bought or stolen a quantity of clothes from the German soldiers. He was on a visit to his parents in Milan, when he fell sick, and, being carried to the hospital, died on the fourth day.

The Tribunal of Health condemned the house he had lived in; his clothes and the bed he had occupied in the hospital were consigned to the flames. Two servants and a good friar, who had attended him, fell sick a few days after; but the suspicions from the first entertained of the nature of the malady, and the precautions used, prevented its extension for the present.

But in the house from which the soldier had been taken there were several attacked by the disease; upon which all the inhabitants of it were conducted to the lazaretto, by order of the Tribunal of Health.

The contagion made but little progress during the rest of this year and the beginning of the following. From time to time there were a few persons attacked, but the rarity of the occurrence diminished the suspicion of the plague, and confirmed the multitude in their disbelief of its existence. Added to this, most of the physicians joined with the people in laughing at the unhappy presages and threatening opinions of the smaller number of their brethren: the cases that did occur they pretended to explain upon other grounds; and the account of these cases was seldom presented to the Tribunal of Health. Fear of the lazaretto kept all on the alert; the sick were concealed, and false certificates were obtained from some subaltern officers of health, who were deputed to inspect the dead bodies. Those physicians, who, convinced of the reality of the contagion, proposed precautions against it, were the objects of general animadversion. But the principal objects of execration were Tadino and the senator Settala, who were stigmatised as enemies of their country, men whose best exertions had been directed towards mitigating the severity of the coming mischief. Even the illustrious Settala, the aged father of the senator, whose talents were equalled by his benevolence, was obliged to take refuge in a friend's house from the popular fury, because he had constantly urged the necessity of precautionary measures.

Towards the end of the month of March, at first in the suburb of the eastern gate, then in the rest of the city, deaths, attended by singular symptoms, such as spasms, delirium, livid spots and buboes, began to be more frequent. Sudden deaths, too, were frequent, without any previous illness. The physicians still perversely held out; but the magistracy were aroused. The Tribunal of Health called on them to enforce their directions; to raise the requisite funds for the growing expenses of the lazaretto, as well as the helpless poor. The malady advanced rapidly. In the lazaretto all was confusion, bad arrangement, and anarchy. In their difficulty on this point the Tribunal had recourse to the capuchins, and conjured the father provincial to give them a man capable of governing this region of desolation. He offered them Father Felice Casati, who enjoyed a high reputation for charity, activity, and kindness of disposition, added to great strength of mind, and as a companion to him, Father Michele Pozzobonelli, who, although young, was of a grave and thoughtful character. They were joyfully accepted, and on the 30th of March they entered on their duties. As the crowd in the lazaretto increased, other capuchins joined them, willingly performing every office both of spiritual and of temporal kindness, even the most menial; the Father Felice, indefatigable in his labours, watched with unceasing and parental care over the multitude. He caught the plague, was cured, and resumed his duties even with greater alacrity. Most of his brethren joyfully sacrificed their lives in this cause of afflicted humanity.

Not being able longer to deny the terrible effects of the malady, which had now reached the family of the physician Settala, and was spreading its ravages in many noble families, those medical men who had been incredulous were still unwilling to acknowledge its true cause, which would have been a tacit condemnation of themselves; they therefore imagined one entirely conformable to the prejudices of the time. It was at that period a prevailing opinion in all Europe, that enchanters existed, diabolical operators, who at this time conspired to spread the plague, by the aid of venomous poisons and witchcraft. Similar things had been affirmed and believed in other epidemics; particularly at Milan, in that of the preceding century. Moreover, towards the end of the preceding year, a despatch had arrived from King Philip IV. giving information that four Frenchmen, suspected of spreading poisons and pestilential substances, had escaped from Madrid, and ordering that watch should be kept to ascertain if by chance they had arrived at Milan.

The governor communicated the despatch to the senate, and the Tribunal of Health. It then excited no attention; but when the plague broke out, and was acknowledged by all, this intelligence was remembered, and it served to confirm the vague suspicion of criminal agency: two incidents converted this vague suspicion into conviction of a positive and real conspiracy. Some persons who imagined they saw, on the evening of the 17th of May, individuals rubbing a partition of the cathedral, carried the partition out of the church in the night, together with a great quantity of benches. The president of the senate, with four persons of his tribunal, visited the partition, the benches, and the basins of holy water, and found nothing which confirmed the ridiculous suspicion of poison. However, to satisfy the disturbed imaginations of the populace, it was decided that the partition should be washed and purified. But the incident became a text for conjecture to the people; it was affirmed, that the poisoners had rubbed all the benches and walls of the cathedral, and even the bell-ropes.

The next morning a new and more strange and significant spectacle struck the wondering eyes of the citizens. In all parts of the city the doors of the houses and the walls were plastered with long streaks of whitish yellow dirt, which appeared to have been rubbed on with a sponge. Whether it was a wicked pleasantry to excite more general and thrilling alarm, or that it had been done from the guilty design of increasing the public disorder; whatever was the motive, the fact is so well attested, that it cannot be attributed to imagination. The city, already alarmed, was thrown into the utmost confusion; the owners of houses purified all infected places; strangers were stopped in the streets on suspicion, and conducted to prison, where they underwent long interrogatories which naturally ended in proving none of these absurd and imaginary practices against them. The Tribunal of Health published a decree, offering a reward to whomsoever should discover the author or authors of this attempt; but they did this, as they wrote to the governor, only to satisfy the people and calm their fears,—a weak and dangerous expedient, and calculated to confirm the popular belief.

In the mean time many attributed this story of the poisoned ointment to the revenge of Gonsalvo Fernandez de Cordova; others to Cardinal Richelieu, in order the more easily to get possession of Milan; others again affixed the crime to various Milanese gentlemen.

There were still many who were not persuaded that it was the plague, because if it were, every one infected would die of it; whereas a few recovered. To dissipate every doubt, the Tribunal of Health made use of an expedient conformable to the necessity of the occasion; they made an address to the eyes, such as the spirit of the times suggested. On one of the days of the feast of Pentecost, the inhabitants of the city were accustomed to go to the burying ground of San Gregorio, beyond the eastern gate, in order to pray for the dead in the last plague. Turning the season of devotion into one of amusement, every one was attired in his best; on that day a whole family, among others, had died of the plague. At the hour in which the concourse was most numerous, the dead bodies of this family were, by order of the Tribunal of Health, drawn naked on a carriage towards this same burying ground; so that the crowd might behold for themselves the manifest traces, the hideous impress of the disease. A cry of alarm and horror arose wherever the car passed; their incredulity was at least shaken, but it is probable that the great concourse tended to spread the infection.

Still it was not absolutely the *plague*; the use of the word was prohibited, it was a pestilential fever, the adjective was preferred to the substantive,—then, not the true plague,—that is to say, the plague, but only in a certain sense,—and further, combined with poison and witchcraft. Such is the absurd trifling with which men seek to blind themselves, wilfully abstaining from a sound exercise of judgment to arrive at the truth.

Meanwhile, as it became from day to day more difficult to raise funds to meet the painful exigencies of circumstances, the council of ten resolved to have recourse to government. They represented, by two deputies, the state of misery and distress of the city, the enormity of the expense, the revenues anticipated, and the taxes withheld in consequence of the general poverty which had been produced by so many causes, and especially by the pillaging of the soldiery. That according to various laws, and a special decree of Charles V., the expense of the plague ought by right to devolve upon government. Finally, they proceeded to make four demands: that the taxes should be suspended; that the chamber should advance funds; that the governor should make known to the king the calamitous state of the city and province; and that the duchy, already exhausted, should be excused from providing quarters for the soldiery. Spinola replied with new regrets and exhortations; declaring himself grieved not to be able to visit Milan in person, in order to employ himself for the preservation of the city, but hoping that the zeal of the magistrates would supply his place: in short, he made evasive answers to all their requests. Afterwards, when the plague was at its height, he transferred, by letters patent, his authority to the high chancellor Ferrer, being, as he said, obliged to devote himself entirely to the cares of the war.

The council of ten then requested the cardinal to order a solemn procession, for the purpose of carrying through the streets the body of San Carlos. The good prelate refused; this confidence in a doubtful means disturbed him, and he feared that, if the effect should not be obtained, confidence would be converted into infidelity, and rebellion against God. He also feared that if there really were poisoners, this procession would be a favourable occasion for their machinations; and if there were not, so great a collection would have a tendency to spread the contagion.

The doors of public edifices and private houses had been again anointed as at first. The news flew from mouth to mouth; the people, influenced by present suffering, and by the imminence of the supposed danger, readily embraced the belief. The idea of subtle instantaneous poison seemed sufficient to explain the violence, and the almost incomprehensible circumstances, of the disease. Add to this the idea of enchantment, and any effect was possible, every objection was rendered feeble, every difficulty was explained. If the effects did not immediately succeed the first attempt, the cause was easy to assign: it had been done by those to whom the art was new;

and now that it was brought to perfection, the perpetrators were more confirmed in their infernal resolution. If any one had dared to suggest its having been done in jest, or denied the existence of a dark plot, he would have passed for an obstinate fool, if he did not incur the suspicion of being himself engaged in it. With such persuasions on their minds, all were on the alert to discover the guilty; the most indifferent action excited suspicion, suspicion was changed to certainty, and certainty to rage.

As illustrations of this, Ripamonti cites two examples which fell under his own observation, and such were of daily occurrence.

In the church of St. Antonio, on a day of some great solemnity, an old man, after having prayed for some time on his knees, rose to seat himself, and before doing so, wiped the dust from the bench with his handkerchief. "The old man is poisoning the bench," cried some women, who beheld the action. The crowd in the church threw themselves upon him, tore his white hair, and after beating him, drew him out half dead, to carry him to prison and to torture. "I saw the unfortunate man," says Ripamonti; "I never knew the end of his painful story, but at the time I thought he had but a few moments to live."

The other event occurred the next day; it was as remarkable, but not as fatal. Three young Frenchmen having come to visit Italy, and study its antiquities, had approached the cathedral, and were contemplating it very attentively. Some persons, who were passing by, stopped; a circle was formed around them; they were not lost sight of for a moment, having been recognised as strangers, and especially Frenchmen. As if to assure themselves that the wall was marble, the young artists extended their hands to touch it. This was enough. In a moment they were surrounded, and, with imprecations and blows, dragged to prison. Happily, however, they were proved to be innocent, and released.

These things were not confined to the city; the frenzy was propagated equally with the contagion. The traveller encountered off the high road, the stranger whose habits or appearance were in any respect singular, were judged to be poisoners. At the first intelligence of a new comer, at the cry even of a child, the alarm bell was rung; and the unfortunate persons were assailed with showers of stones, or seized and conducted to prison. And thus the prison itself was, during a certain period, a place of safety.

Meanwhile, the council of ten, not silenced by the refusal of the wise prelate, again urged their request for the procession, which the people seconded by their clamours. The cardinal again resisted, but finding resistance useless, he finally yielded; he did more, he consented that the case which enclosed the relics of San Carlos should be exposed for eight days on the high altar of the cathedral.

The Tribunal of Health and the other authorities did not oppose this proceeding; they only ordained some precautions, which, without obviating the danger, indicated too plainly their apprehensions. They issued severe orders to prevent people from abroad entering the city; and, to insure their execution, commanded the gates to be closed. They also nailed up the condemned houses; "the number of which," says a contemporary writer, "amounted to about five hundred."

Three days were employed in preparation; on the 11th of June the procession left the cathedral at daybreak: a long file of people, composed for the most part of women, their faces covered with silk masks, and many of them with bare feet, and clothed in sackcloth, appeared first. The tradesmen came next, preceded by their banners; the societies, in habits of various forms and colours; then the brotherhoods, then the secular clergy, each with the insignia of his rank, and holding a lighted taper in his hand. In the midst, among the brilliant light of the torches, and the resounding echo of the canticles, the case advanced, covered with a rich canopy, and carried alternately by four canons, sumptuously attired. Through the crystal were seen the mortal remains of the saint, clothed in his pontifical robes, and his head covered with a mitre. In his mutilated features might still be distinguished some traces of his former countenance, such as his portraits represent him, and such as some of the spectators remembered to have beheld and honoured. Behind the remains of the holy prelate, and resembling him in merit, birth, and dignity, as well as in person, came the Archbishop Frederick. The rest of the clergy followed him, and with them the magistrates in their robes, then the nobility, some magnificently clothed, as if to do honour to the pomp of the celebration, and others as penitents, in sackcloth and bare-footed, each bearing a torch in his hand. A vast collection of people terminated the procession.

The streets were ornamented as on festival days: the rich sent out their most precious furniture; and thus the fronts of the poorest houses were decorated by their more wealthy neighbours, or at the expense of the public. Here, in the place of hangings, and there, over the hangings themselves, were suspended branches of trees; on all sides hung pictures, inscriptions, devices; on the balconies were displayed vases, rich antiquities, and valuable curiosities; with burning flambeaux at various stations. From many of the windows the sequestrated sick looked out upon the procession, and mingled their prayers with those of the people as they passed. The procession returned to the cathedral about the middle of the day.

But the next day, whilst presumptuous and fanatical assurance had taken possession of every mind, the number of deaths augmented in all parts of the city in a progression so frightful, and in a manner so sudden, that none could avoid confessing the cause to have been the procession itself. However, (astonishing and deplorable power of prejudice!) this effect was not attributed to the assemblage of so many people, and to the increase of fortuitous contact, but to the facility afforded to the poisoners to execute their infernal purposes. But as this opinion could not account for so vast a mortality, and as no traces of strange substances had been discovered on the road of the procession, recourse was had to another invention, admitted by general opinion in Europe—magical and poisoned powders! It was asserted that these powders, scattered profusely in the road, attached themselves to the skirts of the gowns, and to the feet of those who had been on that day barefooted: thus the human mind delights itself with contending against phantoms of its own creating.

The violence of the contagion increased daily; in short, there was hardly a house that was not infected; the number of souls in the lazaretto amounted to 12,000, and sometimes to 16,000. The daily mortality, which had hitherto exceeded 500, soon increased to 1200 and 1500.

We may imagine the agony of the council of ten, on whom rested the weighty burden of providing for the public necessities, and of repairing what was reparable in such a disaster: they had to replace every day, and every day to add to the number of individuals charged with public services of all kinds. Of these individuals there were three remarkable classes; the first was that of the *monatti*: this appellation, of doubtful origin, was applied to those men who were devoted to the most painful and dangerous employment in times of contagion; the taking of the dead bodies from the houses, from the streets, and from the lazaretto, carrying them to their graves, and burying them; also, bringing the sick to the lazaretto, and burning and purifying suspected or infected objects; the second class was that of the *apparitori*, whose special function was to precede the funeral cars, ringing a bell to warn passengers to retire; and the third was that of the commissaries, who presided over both the other classes, under the immediate orders of the Tribunal of Health.

It was necessary to keep the lazaretto furnished with medicine, surgeons, food, and all the requisites of an infirmary; and it was also necessary to find and prepare new habitations for new cases. Cabins of wood and straw were hastily constructed in the interior enclosure of the lazaretto; then a second lazaretto, a little beyond, was erected, capable of containing 4000 persons. Two others were ordered, but means, men, and courage failed, and they were never completed: despair and weakness had attained such a point, that the most urgent and painful wants were unprovided for; each day, for example, children, whose mothers had perished of the plague, died from neglect. The Tribunal of Health proposed to found an hospital for these innocent creatures, but could obtain no assistance for the purpose; all supplies were for the army, "because," said the governor, "it is a time of war, and we must treat the soldiers well."

Meanwhile the immense ditch which had been dug near the lazaretto was filled with dead bodies; a number still remained without sepulture, as hands were wanting for the work. Without extraordinary aid this calamity must have remained unremedied. The president of the senate addressed himself in tears to the two intrepid friars who governed the lazaretto, and the Father Michele pledged himself to relieve in four days the city of the unburied dead, and to dig, in the course of a week, another ditch sufficient not only for present wants, but even for those which might be anticipated in future. Followed by another friar, and public officers chosen by the president, he went into the country to procure peasants, and partly by the authority of the tribunal, partly by that of his habit, he gathered 200, whom he employed to dig the earth. He then despatched *monatti* from the lazaretto to collect the dead. At the appointed time his promise was fulfilled.

At one time the lazaretto was left without physicians, and it was only after much trouble and time, and great offers of money and honours, that others could be prevailed on to supply their place. Provisions were often so scarce, as to create apprehensions of starvation, but more than once these necessities were unexpectedly supplied by the charity of individuals. In the midst of the general stupor, or the indifference to the miseries of others, occasioned by personal apprehension, some were found whose hands and hearts had ever been open to the wretched, and others with whom the virtue of benevolence had commenced with the loss of all their terrestrial happiness. So also, amidst the destruction of the flight of so many men charged with watching over and providing for the public safety, others were seen, who, well in body and firm in mind, ever remained faithful at their post, and some even, who, by an admirable self-devotion, sustained with heroic constancy cares to which their duty did not call them.

The most entire self-devotion was especially conspicuous among the clergy; at the lazarettos, in the city, their assistance was always at hand; they were found, wherever there was suffering, always in attendance on the sick and the dying; very often languishing and dying themselves: with spiritual, they bestowed, as far as they could, temporal succour. More than sixty clergymen in the city alone died from the contagion, which was nearly eight out of nine.

Frederick, as might be expected, was an example to all; after having seen all his household perish around him, he was solicited by his family, by the first magistrates, and by the neighbouring princes, to fly the peril, but he rejected their advice and their solicitations with the same firmness which induced him to write to the clergy of his diocese:—"Be disposed to abandon life rather than these sufferers, who are your children, and your family; go with the same joy into the midst of the pestilence, as to a certain reward, since you may, by these means, win many souls to Christ." He neglected no precaution compatible with his duty: he even gave instructions to his clergy on this point; but he betrayed no anxiety, nor did he even appear to perceive danger, where it was necessary to incur it, in order to do good. He was always with the ecclesiastics, to praise and direct the zealous, and to excite the lukewarm; he visited the lazarettos to console the sick, and encourage those who assisted them; he travelled over the city, carrying aid to the miserable who were sequestered in their houses, stopping at their doors and under their windows, to listen to their complaints, and to give them words of consolation and encouragement. Having thus thrown himself into the midst of the contagion, it was truly wonderful that he never was attacked by it.

In seasons of public calamity, when confusion takes the place of order, we often behold a display of the sublimest virtue, but more frequently, alas! an increase of vice and crime. Instances of the latter were not wanting during the present unhappy period. The profligate, spared by the plague, found in the common confusion, and in the slackening of the restraints of law, new occasions for mischief, and new assurances of impunity. And further, power itself had passed into the hands of the boldest among them. There were scarcely found for the functions of *monatti* and *apparitori* any, but those over whom the attraction of rapine and licence had more sway than dread of the contagion. Strict rules had been prescribed to them, and severe penalties threatened for infringing them, which had some power for awhile; but the number of deaths, and the increasing desolation, and the universal alarm, soon relieved them from all superintendence, and they constituted themselves (the *monatti* in particular) the arbiters of every thing. They entered houses as masters and enemies; and, not to mention their robberies, and the cruel treatment which those unhappy persons experienced whom the plague condemned to their authority, they applied their infected and criminal hands to those in health, threatening to carry them to the lazaretto, unless they purchased their exemption with money. At other times they refused to carry off the dead bodies already in a state of putrefaction, without a high price being paid them; it is even said, that they designedly let fall from their carts infected clothing, in order to propagate the infection from which their wealth was derived. Many ruffians, too, assuming the garb of these wretches, carried on extensive robberies in the houses of the sick, dying, and helpless.

In the same proportion as vice increased, folly increased; the foolish idea was again revived of *poisonings*; the dread of this fantastic danger beset and tormented the minds of men more than the real and present danger. "While," says Ripamonti, "the heaps of dead bodies lying before the eyes of the living made the city a vast tomb, there was something more afflicting and hideous still—reciprocal distrust and extravagant suspicion; and this not only between friends, neighbours, and guests; but husbands, wives, and children, became objects of terror to one another, and, horrible to tell! even the domestic board and the nuptial bed were dreaded as snares, as places were poison might be concealed."

Besides ambition and cupidity, the motives commonly attributed to the poisoners, it was imagined that this action included an indefinable, diabolical voluptuousness of enjoyment, an attractiveness stronger than the will. The ravings of the sick, who accused themselves of that which they had dreaded in others, were considered as so many involuntary revelations, which rendered belief irresistible.

Among the stories recorded of this delirium, there is one which deserves to be related, on account of the extensive credence it obtained.

It was said that on a certain day, a citizen had seen an equipage with six horses stop in the square of the cathedral. Within it was a person of a noble and majestic figure, dark complexion, eyes inflamed, and lips compressed and threatening. The spectator being invited to enter the carriage, complied. After a short circuit, it made a halt before the gate of a magnificent palace. Entering it he beheld mingled scenes of delight and horror, frightful deserts and smiling gardens, dark caverns and magnificent saloons. Phantoms were seated in council. They showed him large boxes of money, telling him he might take as many of them as he chose, provided he would accept at the same time a little vase of poison, and consent to employ it against the citizens. He refused, and in a moment found himself at the place from which he had been taken. This story, generally believed by the people, spread all over Italy. An engraving of it was made in Germany. The Archbishop of Mayence wrote to Cardinal Frederick, asking him what credence might be attached to the prodigies related of Milan. He received for answer, that they were all idle dreams.

The dreams of the learned, if they were not of the same nature as those of the vulgar, did not exceed them in value; the greater part beheld the forerunner and the cause of these calamities, in a comet which appeared in 1628, and in the conjunction of Jupiter and Saturn. Another comet that appeared in June in the same year announced the poisonous anointings. All writings were ransacked that contained any passages respecting poisons; amongst the ancients, Livy was cited, Tacitus, Dionysius, even Homer and Ovid were searched. Among the moderns, Cesalpino, Cardan, Grevino, Salio, Pareo Schenchio, Zachia, and lastly the fatal Delrio, whose *Disquisitions on Magic* became the text book on such subjects, the future rule, and, in fact, the powerful impulse to horrible and frequent legal murders.

The physicians yielded to the popular belief, and attributed to poison and diabolical conjurations the ordinary symptoms of the malady. Even Tadino himself, one of the most celebrated physicians of his day, who had witnessed the entrance of the disorder, anticipated its ravages, studied its symptoms, and admitted it to be *the plague*, even he, such is the strange perversity of human reason, drew from all these facts an argument in proof of the dissemination of some subtle poison, by means of ointments. Nor was the enlightened Cardinal Frederick himself altogether uninfected by the general mania. In a small tract of his on the subject in the Ambrosian Library, he says, "Of the mode of compounding and dispensing these ointments, various statements have been made, some of which we hold for true, while others appear imaginary."

On the other hand, Muratori tells us, that he had met with well-informed persons in Milan, whose ancestors were decidedly convinced of the absurdity of this widely spread and extraordinary error, but whose safety rendered it imperative on them to keep their sentiments on the subject to themselves.

The magistrates employed the little vigilance and resolution which remained to them in searching out the poisoners, and unhappily thought they had detected them. A recital of these and similar cases would form a remarkable feature in the history of jurisprudence. But it is high time we should resume the thread of our story.

Chapter XXXII.

One night, towards the end of the month of August, in the very height of the pestilence, Don Roderick returned to his house at Milan, accompanied by his faithful Griso, one of the small number of his servants who still survived. He had just left a company of friends, who were accustomed to assemble together, to banish by debauchery the melancholy of the times; at each meeting there were new guests added, and old ones missing. On that day Don Roderick had been one of the gayest, and, among other subjects of merriment which he introduced, he had made the company laugh at a mock funeral sermon on Count Attilio, who had been carried off by the pestilence a few days before.

After leaving the house where he had held his carousal, he was conscious of an uneasiness, a faintness, a weariness of his limbs, a difficulty of breathing, and an internal heat, which he was ready to attribute to the wine, the late hour, and the influence of the season. He spoke not a word during the whole route. Arriving at his house, he ordered Griso to light him to his chamber. Griso, perceiving the change in his master's countenance, kept at a distance, as, in these dangerous times, every one was obliged to keep for himself, as was said, a medical eye.

"I feel very well, do you see," said Don Roderick, reading in the features of Griso the thoughts which were passing through his mind,—"I feel very well; but I have drank a little too much. The wine was so fine! With a good sleep all will be well again. I am overcome by sleep. Take away the light; I cannot bear it; it troubles me."

"It is the effect of the wine, signor," said Griso, still keeping at a distance; "but go to bed, sleep will do you good."

"You are right; if I could sleep— I am well, were it not for the want of sleep. Place the little bell near me, in case I should want something; and be attentive if I ring. But I shall need nothing. Carry away that cursed light," added he; "it troubles me more than I can tell."

Griso carried off the light; and, wishing his master a good night, he quitted the apartment as Don Roderick crouched beneath the bed-clothes.

But the bed-clothes weighed upon him like a mountain; throwing them off, he endeavoured to compose himself to sleep; hardly had he closed his eyes when he awoke with a start, as if he had been roused by a blow, and he felt that the pain and fever had increased. He endeavoured to find the cause of his sufferings in the heat of the weather, the wine, and the debauch in which he had just been engaged; but one idea involuntarily mingled itself with all his reflections, an idea at which he had been laughing all the evening with his companions, as it was easier to make it a subject of raillery than to drive it away,—the idea of the plague.

After having struggled a long time, he at last fell asleep, but was tormented by frightful dreams. It appeared to him that he was in a vast church, in the midst of a crowd of people. How he came there he could not tell, nor how the thought to do so could have entered his head, especially at such a time. Looking on those by whom he was surrounded, he perceived them to be lean, livid figures, with wild and glaring eyes; the garments of these hideous creatures fell in shreds from their bodies, and through them might be seen frightful blotches and swellings. He thought he cried, "Give way, you rascals!" as he looked towards the door, which was far, far off, accompanying the cry with a menacing expression of countenance, and wrapping his arms around his body to prevent coming in contact with them, for they seemed to be touching him on every side. But they moved not, nor even seemed to hear him: it appeared to him, however, that some one amongst them, with his elbow, pressed his left side near his heart, where he felt a painful pricking. Trying to withdraw himself from so irksome a situation, he experienced a recurrence of the sensation. Irritated beyond measure, he stretched out his hand for his sword, and, behold, it had glided the whole length of his body, and the hilt of it was pressing him in this very place. Vainly did he endeavour to remove it, every effort only increased his agonies. Agitated and out of breath, he again cried aloud; at the sound, all those wild and hideous phantoms rushed to one side of the church, leaving the pulpit exposed to view, in which stood, with his venerable countenance, his bald head and white beard, Father Christopher. It appeared to Don Roderick that the capuchin, after having looked over the assembly, fixed his eyes upon him, with the same expression as on the well-remembered interview in his castle, and, at the same time, raised his arm, and held it suspended above his head; making an effort to arrest the blow, a cry which struggled in his throat escaped him, and he awoke. He opened his eyes; the light of day, which was already advanced, pressed upon his brain, and imparted as keen an anguish as the torch of the preceding night. Looking around on his bed and his room, he comprehended that it was a dream; the church, the crowd, the friar, all had vanished; but not so the pain in his left side. He was sensible of an agonising and rapid beating of his heart, a buzzing in his ears, an internal heat which consumed him, and a weight and weariness in his limbs greater than when he went to bed. He could not resolve to look at the spot where he felt the pain; but, finally gathering courage to do so, he beheld with horror a hideous tumour of a livid purple.

Don Roderick saw that he was lost. The fear of death took possession of him, and with it came the apprehension, stronger perhaps than the dread of death itself, of becoming the prey of the *monatti*, and of being thrown into the lazaretto. Endeavouring to think of some means of avoiding this terrible fate, he experienced a confusion and obscurity in his ideas which told him that the moment was fast approaching when he should have no feeling left but of despair. Seizing the bell, he shook it violently. Griso, who was on the watch, appeared immediately; stopping at a distance from the bed, he looked attentively at his master, and became certain of that which he had only conjectured the night before.

"Griso," said Don Roderick, with difficulty raising himself in his bed, "you have always been my favourite."

"Yes, my lord."

"I have always done well by you."

"The consequence of your goodness."

"I can trust you, I think. I am ill, Griso."

"I perceived that you were."

"If I am cured, I will do still more for you than I have ever yet done."

Griso made no answer, waiting to see to what this preamble would lead.

"I would not trust any one but you," resumed Don Roderick; "do me a favour."

"Command me."

"Do you know where the surgeon Chiodo lives?"

"I do."

"He is an honest man, who, if he be well paid, keeps secret the sick. Go to him; tell him I will give him four or six crowns a visit,—more, if he wishes it.

Tell him to come here immediately; act with prudence; let no one get knowledge of it."

"Well thought of," said Griso; "I will return immediately."

"First, Griso, give me a little water; I burn with thirst."

"No, my lord, nothing without the advice of a physician. This is a rapid disease, and there is no time to lose. Be tranquil. In the twinkling of an eye, I will be here with the signor Chiodo." So saying, he left the room.

Don Roderick followed him in imagination to the house of Chiodo, counted his steps, measured the time. He often looked at his side, but, horror-struck, could only regard it a moment. Continuing to listen intently for the arrival of the surgeon, this effort of attention suspended the sense of suffering, and left him the free exercise of his thoughts. Suddenly he heard a noise of small bells, which appeared to come from some of the apartments, and not from the street. Listening again, he heard it louder, and at the same time a sound of steps. A horrible suspicion darted across his mind. He sat up, listened still more attentively, and heard a sound in the next chamber, as of a chest carefully placed on the floor; he threw his limbs out of bed, so as to be ready to rise; and kept his eyes fastened on the door; it opened, and, behold, two *monatti* with their diabolical countenances, and cursed liveries, advancing towards the bed, whilst from the half-open door was seen the figure of Griso, awaiting the success of his sordid treachery.

"Ah, infamous traitor! Begone, rascals! Biondino, Carlotto, help! murder!" cried Don Roderick, extending his hand under his pillow for his pistol.

At his very first cry the *monatti* had rushed towards the bed, and the most active of the two was upon him before he could make another movement; jerking the pistol from his hand, and throwing it on the floor, he forced him to lie down, crying in an accent of rage and mockery, "Ah, scoundrel! against the *monatti*! against the ministers of the tribunal!"

"Keep him down until we are ready to carry him out," said the other, as he advanced to a strong box. Griso entered the room, and with him commenced forcing its lock. "Villain!" shouted Don Roderick, struggling to get free: "let me kill this infamous rascal," said he to the *monatti*, "and then you may do with me what you will." He then called again loudly on his other servants, but in vain; the abominable Griso had sent them far away with orders as if from his master, before he himself went to propose this expedition, and a share of its spoils, to the *monatti*.

"Be quiet, be quiet," said the man, who held him extended on the bed, to the unhappy Don Roderick; then, turning to those who were taking the booty, he said, "Behave like honest men."

"You! you!" murmured Don Roderick to Griso, "you! after— Ah, demon of hell! I may still be cured! I may still be cured!"

Griso spoke not a word, and was careful to avoid looking at his master.

"Hold him tight," said the other *monatto*, "he is frantic."

The unfortunate man, after many violent efforts, became suddenly exhausted; but from time to time was seen to struggle feebly and vainly, for a moment, against his persecutors.

The *monatti* deposited him on a hand-barrow which had been left in the outer room; one of them returned for the booty, then raising their miserable burden, they carried him off. Griso remained awhile to make a selection of such articles as were valuable and portable; he had been very careful not to touch the *monatti*, nor be touched by them; but, in his thirst for gain, his prudence forsook him; taking the different articles of his master's dress from off the bed, he shook them, for the purpose of ascertaining if there was money in them.

He had, however, occasion to remember his want of caution the next day; whilst carousing in a tavern, he was seized with a shivering, his eyes grew dim, his strength failed, and he fell lifeless. Abandoned by his companions, he fell into the hands of the *monatti*, who, after having plundered him, threw him on a car, where he expired, before arriving at the lazaretto to which his master had been carried.

We must leave Don Roderick in this abode of horror, and return to Renzo, whom our readers may remember we left in a manufactory under the name of Antony Rivolta. He remained there five or six months; after which, war being declared between the republic and the King of Spain, and all fear on his account having ceased, Bortolo hastened to bring him back, both because he was attached to him, and because Renzo was a great assistance to the *factotum* of a manufactory, without the possibility of his ever aspiring to be one himself, on account of his inability to write. Bortolo was a good man, and in the main generous, but, like other men, he had his failings; and as this motive really had a place in his calculations, we have thought it our duty to state it. From this time Renzo continued to work with his cousin. More than once, and especially after having received a letter from Agnes, he felt a desire to turn soldier; and opportunities were not wanting, for at this epoch the republic was in want of recruits. The temptation was the stronger, as there was a talk of invading the Milanese, and it appeared to him that it would be a fine thing to return there as a conqueror, see Lucy again, and have an explanation with her; but Bortolo always diverted him from this resolution. "If they go there," said he, "they can go without you, and you can go afterwards at your leisure. If they return with broken heads, you will be glad to have been out of the scrape. The Milanese is not a mouthful to be easily swallowed; and then the question, my friend, turns on the power of Spain. Have a little patience. Are you not well here? I know what you will say; but if it is written above that the affair shall succeed, succeed it will, without your committing more follies. Some saint will come to your assistance. Believe me, war is not a trade for you. It needs men expressly trained to the business."

At other times Renzo thought of returning home in disguise, under a false name, but Bortolo dissuaded him from this project also.

The plague afterwards spreading over all the Milanese, and advancing to the Bergamascan territory—don't be alarmed, reader, our design is not to relate its history; all that we would say is, that Renzo was attacked with it, and recovered. He was at death's door; but his strong constitution repelling the disease, in a few days he was out of danger. With life, the hopes and recollections and projects of life returned with greater vigour than ever; more than ever were his thoughts occupied with his Lucy: what had become of her in these disastrous times? "To be at so short distance from her, and to know nothing concerning her, and to remain, God knows how long, in this uncertainty! and then her vow! I will go myself, I will go and relieve these terrible doubts," said he. "If she lives, I will find her; I will hear herself explain this promise; I will show her that it is not binding; and I will bring her here, and poor Agnes also, who has always wished me well, and I am sure does so still,—yes, I will go in search of them."

As soon as he was able to walk, he went in search of Bortolo, who had kept himself shut up in his house, on account of the pestilence. He called to him to come to the window.

"Ah, ah," said Bortolo, "you have recovered. It is well for you."

"I have still some weakness in my limbs, as you see, but I am out of danger."

"Oh, I wish I was on your legs. Formerly, when one said, *I am well*, it expressed all that could be desired; but now-a-days that is of little consequence. When one can say *I am better*, that's the word for you!"

Renzo informed his cousin of his determination.

"Go now, and may Heaven bless you," replied he; "avoid the law as I shall avoid the pestilence; and if it is the will of God, we shall see each other again."

"Oh, I shall certainly return. If I were only sure of not returning alone! I hope for the best."

"Well, I join in your hopes; if God wills, we will work, and live together here. Heaven grant you may find me here, and that this devilish disease may have ceased."

"We shall meet again, we shall meet again, I am sure."

"I say again, God bless you."

In a few days Renzo, finding his strength sufficiently restored, prepared for his departure; he put on a girdle in which he placed the fifty crowns sent him by Agnes, together with his own small savings; he took under his arm a small bundle of clothes, and secured in his pocket his certificate of good conduct from his second master; and having armed himself with a good knife, a necessary appendage to an honest man in those days, he commenced his journey towards the end of August, three days after Don Roderick had been carried to the lazaretto. He took the road to Lecco, before venturing into Milan, as he hoped to find Agnes there, and learn from her some little of what he desired so much to know.

The small number of those who had been cured of the plague formed a privileged class amidst the rest of the population; those who had not been attacked by the disease lived in perpetual apprehension of it; they walked about with precaution, with an unquiet air, with a hurried and hesitating step; the former, on the contrary, nearly certain of security (for to have the plague twice was rather a prodigy than a rarity), advanced into the very midst of the pestilence with boldness and unconcern. With such security, tempered, however, by his own peculiar anxieties, and by the spectacle of the misery of a whole people, Renzo travelled towards his village, under a fine sky, and through a beautiful country; meeting on the way, after long intervals of dismal solitude, men more like shadows and wandering phantoms than living beings; or dead bodies about to be consigned to the trench without funeral rites. Towards the middle of the day he stopped in a grove to eat his meat and bread; he was bountifully supplied with fruits from the gardens by the road, for the year was remarkably fertile, the trees along the road were laden with figs, peaches, plums, apples, and other various kinds, with hardly a living creature to gather them.

Towards evening he discovered his village; although prepared for the sight, he felt his heart beat, and he was assailed in a moment by a crowd of painful recollections and harrowing presentiments: a deathlike silence reigned around. His agitation increased as he entered the churchyard, and became hardly supportable at the end of the lane—it was there, where stood the house of Lucy—one only of its inmates could now be there, and the only favour he asked from Heaven was to find Agnes still living; he hoped to find an asylum at her cottage, as he judged truly that his own roust be in ruins.

As he went on he looked attentively before him, fearing, and at the same time hoping, to meet some one from whom he might obtain information. He saw at last a man seated on the ground, leaning against a hedge of jessamines, in the listless attitude of an idiot. He thought it must be the poor simpleton Jervase, who had been employed as a witness in his unsuccessful expedition to the curate's house. But approaching nearer, he recognised it to be Anthony. The disease had affected his mind, as well as his body, so that in every act a slight resemblance to his weak brother might be traced.

"Oh, Tony," said Renzo, stopping before him, "is it you?" Tony raised his eyes, but not his head.

"Tony, do you not know me?"

"Is it my turn? Is it my turn?" replied he.

"Poor Tony! do you indeed not know me?"

"Is it my turn? Is it my turn?" replied he, with an idiotic smile, and then stood with his mouth open.

Renzo, seeing he could draw nothing from him, passed on still more afflicted than before. Suddenly, at a turn of the path, he beheld advancing towards him a person whom he recognised to be Don Abbondio. His pale countenance and general appearance showed that he also had not escaped the tempest. The curate, seeing a stranger, anxiously examined his person, whose costume was that of Bergamo. At length he recognised Renzo with much surprise.

"Is it he, indeed?" thought he, and raised his hands with a movement of wonder and dismay. His wasted arms seemed trembling in his sleeves, which before could hardly contain them.

Renzo, hastening towards him, bowed profoundly; for, although he had quitted him in anger, he still felt respect for him as his curate.

"You here! you!" cried Don Abbondio.

"Yes, I am here, as you see. Do you know any thing of Lucy?"

"How should I know? nothing is known of her. She is at Milan, if she is still in this world. But you—"

"And Agnes, is she living?"

"Perhaps she is; but who do you think can tell? she is not here. But—"

"Where is she?"

"She has gone to Valsassina, among her relatives at Pasturo; for they say that down there the pestilence has not made such ravages as it has here. But you, I say—"

"I am glad of that. And Father Christopher?"

"He has been gone this long time. But you—"

"I heard that,—but has he not returned?"

"Oh no, we have heard nothing of him. But you—"

"I am sorry for it."

"But you, I say, what do you do here? For the love of Heaven, have you forgotten that little circumstance of the order for your apprehension?"

"What matters it? people have other things to think of now. I came here to see about my own affairs."

"There is nothing to see about; there is no one here now. It is the height of rashness in you to venture here, with this little difficulty impending. Listen to an old man who has more prudence than yourself, and who speaks to you from the love he bears you. Depart at once, before any one sees you, return whence you came. Do you think the air of this place good for you? Know you not that they have been here on the search for you?"

"I know it too well, the rascals."

"But then—"

"But, I tell you, they think no more about it. And *he*, does *he* yet live? is *he* here?"

"I tell you there is no one here; I tell you to think no more of the affairs of this place; I tell you that—"

"I ask you if *he* is here;"

"Oh, just Heaven! Speak in another manner. Is it possible you still retain so much warmth, after all that has happened?"

"Is *he* here, or is *he* not?"

"He is not. But the plague, my son, the plague keeps every one from travelling at present."

"If the pestilence was all that we need fear—I speak for myself, I have had it, and I fear it not."

"You had better render thanks to Heaven. And—"

"I do, from the bottom of my heart."

"And not go in search of other evils, I say. Listen to my advice."

"You have had it also, sir, if I am not mistaken."

"That I have, truly! most terrible it was! it is by a miracle I am here; you see how it has left me. I have need of repose to restore my strength; I was beginning to feel a little better. In the name of Heaven, what do you do here? Go away, I beseech you."

"You always return to your *go away*. If I ought to go away, I would not have come. You keep saying, *What do you come for? what do you come for?* Sir, I am come home."

"Home!"

"Tell me, have there been many deaths here?"

"Many!" cried Don Abbondio; and beginning with Perpetua, he gave a long list of individuals, and even whole families. Renzo expected, it is true, a similar recital; but hearing the names of so many acquaintances, friends, and relations, he was absorbed by his affliction, and could only exclaim, from time to time, "Misery! misery! misery!"

"And it is not yet over," pursued Don Abbondio. "If those who remain do not listen to reason, and calm the heat of their brains, it will be the end of the world."

"Do not concern yourself; I do not intend to remain here."

"Heaven be praised! you talk reason at last. Go at once—"

"Do not trouble yourself about it; the affair belongs to me. I think I have arrived at years of discretion. I hope you will tell no one that you have seen me. You are a priest, and I am one of your flock; you will not betray me?"

"I understand," said Don Abbondio, angrily, "I understand. You would ruin yourself, and me with you. What you have suffered, what I have suffered, is not sufficient. I understand, I understand." And continuing to mutter between his teeth, he proceeded on his way.

Renzo, afflicted and disappointed, reflected where he should seek another asylum. In the catalogue of deaths given to him by Don Abbondio, there was a family which had all been carried off by the pestilence, with the exception of a young man nearly of his own age, who had been his companion from infancy. The house was a short distance off, a little beyond the village; he bent his steps thither, to seek the hospitality which it might afford him. On his way he passed his own vineyard. The vines were cut, the wood carried off. Weeds of various kinds and most luxuriant growth, principally of the parasitical order, covered the place, displaying the most brilliant flowers above the loftiest branches of the vines, and obstructing the progress of the miserable owner. The garden beyond presented a similar scene of varied and luxuriant wildness. The house, that had not escaped the visitation of the lansquenets, was deformed with filth, dust, and cobwebs. Poor Renzo turned away with imbittered feelings, and moved slowly onwards to his friend's. It was evening. He found him seated before the door, on a small bench, his arms crossed on his breast, with the air of a man stupified by distress, and suffering from solitude. At the sound of steps he turned, and the twilight and the foliage not permitting him to distinguish objects distinctly, he said, "Are there not others besides me? Did I not do enough yesterday? Leave me in quiet; it will be an act of charity."

Renzo, not knowing what this meant, called him by name.

"Renzo?" replied he.

"It is indeed," said Renzo, and they ran towards each other.

"Is it you indeed?" said his friend: "oh, how happy I am to see you! who would have thought it? I took you for one of those persons who torment me daily to help to bury the dead. Know you that I am left alone? alone! alone as a hermit!"

"I know it but too well," said Renzo. They entered the cottage together, each making numerous enquiries of the other. His friend began to prepare the table for supper; he went out, and returned in a few moments with a pitcher of milk, a little salt meat, and some fruit. They seated themselves at table, at which the polenta was not forgotten, mutually congratulating each other on their interview. An absence of two years, and the circumstances under which they met, revived and added new vigour to their former friendship.

No one, however, could supply the place of Agnes to Renzo, not only on account of the particular affection she bore him, but she alone possessed the key to the solution of all his difficulties. He hesitated awhile whether he had not best go in search of her, as she was not very far off; but recollecting that he knew nothing of the fate of Lucy, he adhered to his first intention of gaining all the information he could concerning her, and carrying the result to her mother. He learnt from his friend, however, many things of which he was ignorant, others were explained which he only knew by halves, with regard to the adventures of Lucy, and the persecutions she had undergone. He was also informed that Don Roderick had left the village, and had not returned. Renzo learnt, moreover, to pronounce the name of Don Ferrante properly; Agnes, it is true, had caused it to be written to him, but Heaven knows how it was written; and the Bergamascan interpreter had given it so strange a sound, that if he had not received some instruction from his friend, probably no one in Milan would have guessed whom he meant, although this was the only clue he had to guide him to Lucy. As far as the law was in question his mind was set at rest. The signor Podestà was dead, and most of the officers; the others were removed, or had other matters too pressing to occupy their attention. He related, in his turn, his own adventures to his friend, receiving in exchange an account of the passage of the army, the pestilence, the poisoners, and the prodigies. "Dreadful as are our afflictions," said he, as he led him for the night to a little chamber which the epidemic had deprived of its inhabitants, "there is a mournful consolation in speaking of them to our friends."

At the break of day they both arose, and Renzo prepared to depart. "If all goes well," said he, "if I find her living—if—I will return. I will go to Pasturo and carry the joyful news to poor Agnes, and then—but if, by a misfortune, which may God avert—then, I know not what I shall do, nor where I shall go; but you will never see me here again."

As he stood on the threshold of the door, about to resume his journey, he contemplated for a moment, with a mixture of tenderness and anguish, his village, which he had not beheld for so long a time. His friend accompanied him a short distance on his road, and bade him farewell, prognosticating a happy return, and many days of prosperity and enjoyment.

Renzo travelled leisurely, because there was ample time for him to arrive within a short distance of Milan, so as to enter it on the morrow. His journey was without accident, except a repetition of the same wretched scenes that the roads at that time presented. As he had done the day before, he stopped in a grove to make a slight repast, which the generosity of his friend had bestowed on him. Passing through Monza, he saw loaves of bread displayed in the window of a shop; he bought two of them, but the shopkeeper called to him not to enter; stretching out a shovel, on which was a small bowl of vinegar and water, he told him to throw the money into it; then with a pair of tongs he reached the bread to him, which Renzo put in his pocket.

Towards evening he passed through Greco, and quitting the high road, went into the fields in search of some small house where he might pass the night, as he did not wish to stop at an inn. He found a better shelter than he anticipated; perceiving an opening in a hedge which surrounded the yard of a dairy, he entered it boldly. There was no one within: in one corner of it was a barn full of hay, and against the door of it a ladder placed. After looking around, Renzo ascended the ladder, settled himself for the night, and slept profoundly until the break of day. When he awoke, he descended the ladder very cautiously, and proceeded on his way, taking the dome of the cathedral for his polar star. He soon arrived before the walls of Milan near the eastern gate.

Chapter XXXIII.

Renzo had heard vague mention made of severe orders, forbidding the entrance of strangers into Milan, without a certificate of health; but these were easily evaded, for Milan had reached a point when such prohibition was useless, even if it could have been put into execution. Whoever ventured there, might rather appear careless of his own life, than dangerous to that of others.

With this conviction, Renzo's design was to attempt a passage at the first gate, and in case of difficulty to wander on the outside of the walls until he should find one easy of access. It would be difficult to say how many gates he thought Milan had.

When he arrived before the ramparts, he looked around him; there was no indication of living being, except on a point of the platform, a thick cloud of dense smoke arising; this was occasioned by clothing, beds, and infected furniture, which were committed to the flames; every where along the ramparts appeared the traces of these melancholy conflagrations.

The weather was close, the air heavy, the sky covered by a thick cloud, or fog, which excluded the sun, without promising rain. The surrounding country was neglected and sterile; all verdure extinct, and not a drop of dew on the dry and withering leaves. The depth, solitude, and silence, so near a large city, increased the gloom of Renzo's thoughts; he proceeded, without being aware of it, to the gate *Nuova*, which had been hid from his view by a bastion, behind which it was then concealed. A noise of bells, sounding at intervals, mingled with the voices of men, saluted his ear; turning an angle of the bastion, he saw before the gate a sentry-box, and a sentinel leaning on his musket, with a wearied and careless air. Exactly before the opening was a sad obstacle, a hand-barrow, upon which two *monatti* were extending an unfortunate man, to carry him off; it was the chief of the toll-gatherers, who had just been attacked by the pestilence. Renzo awaited the departure of the convoy, and no one appearing to close the gate, he passed forwards quickly; the sentinel cried out "Holla!" Renzo stopping, showed him a half ducat, which he drew from his pocket; whether he had had the pestilence, or that he feared it less than he loved ducats, he signed to Renzo to throw it to him;

seeing it at his feet, he cried, "Go in, quickly," a permission of which Renzo readily availed himself. He had hardly advanced forty paces when a toll-collector called to him to stop. He pretended not to hear, and passed on. The call was repeated, but in a tone more of anger than of resolution to be obeyed—and this being equally unheeded, the collector shrugged his shoulders and turned back to his room.

Renzo proceeded through the long street opposite the gate which leads to the canal *Naviglio*, and had advanced some distance into the city without encountering a single individual; at last he saw a man coming towards him, from whom he hoped he might gain some information; he moved towards him, but the man showed signs of alarm at his approach. Renzo, when he was at a little distance, took off his hat, like a polite mountaineer as he was, but the man drew back, and raising a knotty club, armed with a spike, he cried, "Off! off! off!" "Oh! oh!" cried Renzo; he put on his hat, and having no desire for a greeting of this fashion, he turned his back on the discourteous passenger and went on his way.

The citizen retired in an opposite direction, shuddering and looking back in alarm: when he reached home he related how a poisoner had met him with humble and polite manners, but with the air of an infamous impostor, and with a phial of poison or the box of powder (he did not know exactly which) in the lining of his hat, to poison him, if he had not kept him at a distance. "It was unlucky," said he, "that we were in so private a street; if it had been in the midst of Milan, I would have called the people, and he would have been seized: but alone, it was enough to have saved myself—but who knows what destruction he may not already have effected in the city:"—and years after, when the poisoners were talked of, the poor man maintained the truth of the fact, as "he had had ocular proof."

Renzo was far from suspecting the danger he had escaped; and, reflecting on this reception, he was more angry than fearful. "This is a bad beginning," thought he; "my star always seems unpropitious when I enter Milan. To enter is easy enough, but, once here, misfortunes thicken. However—by the help of God—if I find—if I succeed in finding—all will be well."

The streets were silent and deserted; no human being could he see; a single disfigured corpse met his eye in the channel between the street and the houses. Suddenly he heard a cry, which appeared addressed to him; and he perceived, not far off, on the balcony of a house, a woman, surrounded by a group of children, making a sign to him to approach. As he did so, "O good young man!" said she, "do me the kindness to go to the commissary, and tell him that we are forgotten here. They have nailed up the house as suspected, because my poor husband is dead; and since yesterday morning no one has brought us any thing to eat, and these poor innocents are dying of hunger."

"Of hunger!" cried Renzo. "Here, here," said he, drawing the two loaves from his pocket. "Lower something in which I may put them."

"God reward you! wait a moment," said the woman, as she went in search of a basket and cord to suspend it.

"As to the commissary, my good woman," said he, putting the loaves in the basket, "I cannot serve you, because, to tell truth, I am a stranger in Milan, and know nothing of the place. However, if I meet any one a little humane and tractable, to whom I can speak, I will tell him."

The woman begged him to do so, and gave him the name of the street in which she lived.

"You can also render me a service, without its costing you any thing," said Renzo. "Can you tell me where there is a nobleman's house in Milan, named ?"

"I know there is a house of that name, but I do not know where it is. Further on in the city you will probably find some one to direct you. And remember to speak of us."

"Do not doubt me," said Renzo, as he passed on.

As he advanced, he heard increasing a sound that had already attracted his attention, whilst stopping to converse with the poor woman; a sound of wheels and horses' feet, with the noise of little bells, and occasionally the cracking of whips and loud cries.

As he reached the square of San Marco, the first objects he saw were two beams erected, with a cord and pulleys. He recognised the horrible instrument of torture! These were placed on all the squares and widest streets, so that the deputies of each quarter of the city, furnished with the most arbitrary power, could subject to them whoever quitted a condemned house, or neglected the ordinances, or by any other act appeared to merit the punishment; it was one of those extreme and inefficacious remedies, which, at this epoch, were so absurdly authorised. Now, whilst Renzo was gazing at this machine, he heard the sounds increasing, and beheld a man appear, ringing a little bell; it was an *apparitore*, and behind him came two horses, who advanced with difficulty, dragging a car loaded with dead; after this car came another, and another, and another; *monatti* walked by the side of the horses, urging them on with their whips and with oaths. The bodies were for the most part naked; some were half covered with rags, and heaped one upon another; at each jolt of the wretched vehicles, heads were seen hanging over, the long tresses of women were displayed, arms were loosened and striking against the wheels, thrilling the soul of the spectator with indescribable horror!

The youth stopped at a corner of the square to pray for the unknown dead. A frightful thought passed over his mind. "There, perhaps, there, with them—O God! avert this misfortune! let me not think of it!"

The funeral convoy having passed on, he crossed the square, and reached the Borgo Nuovo by the bridge Marcellino. He perceived a priest standing before a half-open door, in an attitude of attention, as if he were confessing some one. "Here," said he, "is my man. If a priest, and in the discharge of his duty, has no benevolence, there is none left in the world who has." When he was at a few paces distance from him, he took off his hat, and made a sign that he wished to speak with him, keeping, however, at a discreet distance, so as not to alarm the good man unnecessarily. Renzo having made his request, was directed to the hotel. "May God watch over you now and for ever!" said Renzo, "and," added he, "I would ask another favour." And he mentioned the poor forgotten woman. The worthy man thanked him for affording him the opportunity to bestow help where it was so greatly needed, and bade him farewell.

Renzo found it difficult enough to recollect the various turnings pointed out by the priest, disturbed as his mind was by apprehensions for the issue of his enquiries. An end was about to be put to his doubts and fears; he was to be told, "she is living," or, "she is dead!" This idea took such powerful possession of his mind, that at this moment, he would rather have remained in his former ignorance, and have been at the commencement of the journey, to the end of which he so nearly approached. He gathered courage, however. "Ah!" cried he, "if I play the child now, how will it end!" Plunging therefore into the heart of the city, he soon reached one of its most desolated quarters, that which is called the *Carrobio di Porta Nuova*. The fury of the contagion here, and the infection from the scattered bodies, had been so great, that those who had survived had been obliged to fly: so that, whilst the passenger was struck with the aspect of solitude and death, his senses were painfully affected by the traces of recent life. Renzo hastened on, hoping to find an improvement in the scene, before he should arrive at the end of his journey. In fact, he soon reached what might still be called the city of the living, but, alas! what living! Every door was closed from distrust and terror, except such as had been left open by the flight of the inhabitants, or by the *monatti*; some were nailed on the outside, because there were within people dead, or dying of the pestilence; others were marked with a cross, for the purpose of informing the *monatti* that their services were required, and much of this was done more by chance than otherwise; as a commissary of health happened to be in one spot rather than in another, and chose to enforce the regulations. On every side were seen infected rags and bandages, clothes and sheets, which had been thrown from the windows; dead bodies which had been left in the streets until a car should pass to take them up, or which had fallen from the cars themselves, or been thrown from the houses; so much bad the long duration and the violence of the pest brutalised men's minds, and subdued every spark of human feeling or sympathy. The customary sounds of human occupation or pleasure had ceased; and this silence of death was interrupted only by the funeral cars, the lamentations of the sick, the shrieks of the frantic, or the vociferations of the *monatti*.

At the break of day, at noon, and at night, a bell of the cathedral gave the signal for reciting certain prayers, which had been ordered by the archbishop, and this was followed by the bells of the other churches. Then persons were seen at the windows, and a confused blending of voices and groans was heard, which inspired a sorrow, not however unmixed with consolation. It is probable that at this time not less than two thirds of the inhabitants had died, and of the remainder many were sick or had left the city. Every one you met exhibited signs of the dreadful calamity. The usual dress was changed of every order of persons. The cloak of the gentleman, the robe of the priest, the cowl of the monk, in short, every loose appendage of dress that might occasion contact, was carefully dismissed; every thing was as close on the person as possible. Men's beards and hair were alike neglected, from fear of treachery on the part of the barbers. Every man walked with a stick, or even a pistol, to prevent the approach of others. Equal care was shown in keeping the middle of the street to avoid what might be thrown from windows, and in avoiding the noxious matters in the road. But if the aspect of the uninfected was appalling, how shall we describe the condition of the wretched sick in the street, tottering or falling to rise no more—beggars, children, women.

Renzo had travelled far on his way, through the midst of this desolation, when he heard a confused noise, in which was distinguishable the horrible and accustomed tinkling of bells.

At the entrance of one of the most spacious streets, he perceived four cars standing; *monatti* were seen entering houses, coming forth with burthens on their shoulders, and laying them on the cars; some were clothed in their red dress, others without any distinctive mark, but the greater number with a mark, more revolting still than their customary dress,—plumes of various colours, which they wore with an air of triumph in the midst of the public mourning, and whilst people from the different windows around were calling to them to remove the dead. Renzo avoided, as much as possible, the view of the horrid spectacle; but his attention was soon attracted by an object of singular interest; a female, whose aspect won the regards of every beholder, came out of one of the houses, and approached the cars. In her features was seen beauty, veiled and clouded, but not destroyed, by the mortal debility which seemed to oppress her; the soft and majestic beauty which shines in the Lombard blood. Her step was feeble, but decided; she wept not, although there were traces of tears on her countenance. There was a tranquillity and profundity in her grief, which absorbed all her powers. But it was not *her* appearance alone which excited compassion in hearts nearly closed to every human feeling; she held in her arms a young girl about nine years of age, dead, but dressed with careful precision; her hair divided smoothly on her pale forehead, and clothed in a robe of the purest white. She was not lying, but was seated, on the arm of the lady, her head leaning on her shoulder; you would have thought she breathed, if a little white hand had not hung down with inanimate weight, and her head reposed on the shoulder of her mother, with an abandonment more decided than that of sleep. Of her mother! it was indeed her mother! If the resemblance of their features had not told it, you would have known it by the expression of that fair and lovely countenance!

A hideous *monatto* approached the lady, and with unusual respect offered to relieve her of her burthen. "No," said she, with an appearance neither of anger nor disgust, "do not touch her yet; it is I who must place her on the car. Take this," and she dropped a purse into the hands of the *monatto*; "promise me not to touch a hair of her head, nor to let others do it, and bury her thus."

The *monatto* placed his hand on his heart, and respectfully prepared a place on the car for the infant dead. The lady, after having kissed her forehead, placed her on it, as carefully as if it were a couch, spread over her a white cloth, and took a last look; "Farewell! Cecilia! rest in peace! To-night we will come to you, and then we shall be separated no more!" Turning again to the *monatto*, "As you pass to-night," said she, "you will come for me; and not for me only!"

She returned into the house, and a moment after appeared at a window, holding in her arms another cherished child, who was still living, but with the stamp of death on her countenance. She contemplated the unworthy obsequies of Cecilia, until the car disappeared from her eyes, and then left the window with her mournful burthen. And what remained for them, but to die together, as the flower which proudly lifts its head, falls with the bud, under the desolating scythe which levels every herb of the field.

"O God!" cried Renzo, "save her! protect her! her and this innocent creature! they have suffered enough! they have suffered enough!"

He then proceeded on his way, filled with emotions of distress and pity. Another convoy of wretched victims encountered him at a cross street on their way to the lazaretto. Some were imploring to be allowed to die on their own beds in peace; some moving on with imbecile apathy, women as usual with their little ones, and even some of these supported and encouraged with manly devotion by their brothers a little older than themselves, and whom alone the plague had for a time spared for this affecting office. When the miserable crowd had nearly passed, he addressed a commissary whose aspect was a little less savage than the rest; and enquired of him the street and the house of Don Ferrante. He replied, "The first street to the right, the last hotel to the left."

The young man hastened thither, with new and deeper trouble at his heart. Easily distinguishing the house, he approached the door, raised his hand to the knocker, and held it suspended awhile, before he could summon resolution to knock.

At the sound, a window was half opened, and a female appeared at it, looking towards the door with a countenance which appeared to ask, "Is it *monatti*? thieves? or poisoners?"

"Signora," said Renzo, but in a tremulous voice, "is there not here in service a young villager of the name of Lucy?"

"She is no longer here; begone," replied the woman, about to close the window.

"A moment, I beseech you. She is no longer here! Where is she?"

"At the lazaretto."

"A moment, for the love of Heaven! With the pestilence?"

"Yes. It is something very uncommon, is it not? Begone then."

"Wait an instant. Was she very ill? Is it long since?"

But this time the window was closed entirely.

"Oh! signora, signora! one word, for charity! Alas! alas! one word!" But he might as well have talked to the wind.

Afflicted by this intelligence, and vexed with the rude treatment of the woman, Renzo seized the knocker again, and raised it for the purpose of striking. In his distress, he turned to look at the neighbouring houses, with the hope of seeing some one, who would give him more satisfactory information. But the only person he discovered, was a woman, about twenty paces off, who, with an appearance of terror, anger, and impatience, was making signs to some one to approach; and this she did, as if not wishing to attract Renzo's notice. Perceiving him looking at her, she shuddered with horror.

"What the devil!" said Renzo, threatening her with his fist, but she, having lost the hope of his being seized unexpectedly, cried aloud, "A poisoner! catch him! catch him! stop the poisoner!"

"Who? I! old sorceress! be silent," cried Renzo, as he approached her in order to compel her to be so. But he soon perceived that it was best to think of himself, as the cry of the woman had gathered people from every quarter; not in so great numbers as would have been seen three months before under similar circumstances, but still many more than one man could resist. At this moment, the window was again opened, and the same discourteous woman appeared at it, crying, "Seize him, seize him; he must be one of the rascals who wander about to poison the doors of people."

Renzo determined in an instant that it was better to fly than to stop to justify himself. Rapidly casting his eyes around to see on which side there were the fewest people, and fighting his way through those that opposed him, he soon freed himself from their clutches.

The street was deserted before him; but behind him the terrible cry still resounded, "Seize him! stop him! a poisoner!" It gained on him, steps were close at his heels. His anger became rage; his agony, despair; drawing his knife from his pocket, and brandishing it in the air, he turned, crying aloud, "Let him who dares come here, the rascal, and I will poison him indeed with this."

But he saw, with astonishment and pleasure, that his persecutors had already stopped, as if some obstacle opposed their path; and were making frantic gestures to persons beyond him. Turning again, he beheld a car approaching, and even a file of cars with, their usual accompaniments. Beyond them was another little band of people prepared to seize the poisoner, but prevented by the same obstacle. Seeing himself thus between two fires, it occurred to Renzo, that *that* which was an object of terror to these people, might be to him a source of safety. Reflecting that this was not a moment for fastidious scruples, he advanced towards the cars, passed the first, and perceiving in the second a space large enough to receive him, threw himself into it.

"Bravo! bravo!" cried the *monatti* with one shout. Some of them were following the convoy on foot, others were seated on the cars, others on the dead bodies, drinking from an enormous flagon, which they passed around. "Bravo! that was well done!"

"You have placed yourself under the protection of the *monatti*; you are as safe as if you were in a church," said one, who was seated on the car into which Renzo had thrown himself.

The enemy was obliged to retreat, crying, however, "Seize him! seize him! he is a poisoner!"

"Let me silence them!" said the *monatto*; and drawing from one of the dead bodies a dirty rag, he tied it up in a bundle, and made a gesture as if intending to throw it among them, crying, "Here, rascals!" At the sight, all fled away in horror!

A howl of triumph arose from the *monatti*.

"Ah! ah! you see we can protect honest people," said the *monatto* to Renzo, "one of us is worth a hundred of those cowards."

"I owe my life to you," said Renzo, "and I thank you sincerely."

"'Tis a trifle, a trifle; you deserve it; 'tis plain to be seen you're a brave fellow; you do well to poison this rabble; extirpate the fools, who, as a reward for the life we lead, say, that the plague once over, they will hang us all. They must all be finished, before the plague ceases; the *monatti* alone must remain to sing for victory, and to feast in Milan."

"Life to the pestilence, and death to the rabble!" cried another, putting the flagon to his mouth, from which he drank freely, and then offered it to Renzo, saying, "Drink to our health."

"I wish it to you all," said Renzo, "but I am not thirsty, and do not want to drink now."

"You have been terribly frightened, it seems," said the *monatto*; "you appear to be a harmless sort of a person; you should have another face than that for a poisoner."

"Give me a drop," said a *monatto*, who walked by the side of the cars; "I would drink to the health of the nobleman, who is here in such good company—in yonder carriage!" And with a malignant laugh he pointed to the car in which poor Renzo was seated. Then brutally composing his features to an expression of gravity, he bowed profoundly, saying, "Will you permit, my dear master, a poor devil of a *monatto* to taste a little wine from your cellar? Do now, because we lead rough lives, and moreover, we are doing you the favour to take you a ride into the country. And besides, you are not accustomed to wine, and it might harm your lordship; but the poor *monatti* have good stomachs."

His companions laughed loudly; he took the flagon, and before he drank, turned again to Renzo, and with an air of insulting compassion said, "The devil with whom you have made a compact, must be very young; if we had not saved you, you would have been none the better for his assistance."

His companions laughed louder than before, and he applied the flagon to his lips.

"Leave some for us! some for us!" cried those from the forward car. After having taken as much as he wanted, he returned the flagon to his companions, who passed it on; the last of the company having emptied it, threw it on the pavement, crying, "Long live the pestilence!" Then they commenced singing a lewd song, in which they were accompanied by all the voices of the horrible choir. This infernal music, blended with the tingling of the bells, the noise of the wheels, and of the horses' feet, resounded in the empty silence of the streets, echoed through the houses, wringing the hearts of the very few who still inhabited them!

But the danger of the preceding moment had rendered more than tolerable to Renzo, the company of these wretches and the dead they were about to inter; and even this music was almost agreeable to his ears, as it relieved him from the embarrassment of such conversation. He returned thanks to Providence for having enabled him to escape from his peril, without receiving or doing an injury; and he prayed God to help him now to deliver himself from his liberators. He kept on the watch to seize the first opportunity of quietly quitting the car, without exciting the opposition of his protectors.

At last they reached the lazaretto. At the appearance of a commissary, one of the two *monatti* who were on the car with Renzo jumped to the ground, in order to speak with him: Renzo hastily quitting the ear, said to the other, "I thank you for your kindness; God reward you."

"Go, go, poor poisoner," replied he, "it will not be you who will destroy Milan!"

Fortunately no one heard him. Renzo hastened onwards by the wall, crossed the bridge, passed the convent of the capuchins, and then perceived the angle of the lazaretto. In front of the inclosure a horrible scene presented itself to his view. Arrived in front of the lazaretto, throngs of sick were pressing into the avenues which led to the building; some were seated or lying in the ditch, which bordered the road on either side, their strength not having sufficed to enable them to reach their asylum, or who, having quitted it in desperation, were too weak to go further; others wandered by themselves, stupified, and insensible to their condition; one was quite animated, relating his imaginations to a miserable companion, who was stretched on the ground, oppressed by suffering; another was furious from despair; a third, more horrible still! was singing, in a voice above all the rest, and with heart-rending hilarity, one of the popular songs of love, gay and playful, which the Milanese call *villanelle*.

Already weary, and confounded at the view of so much misery concentrated within so small a space, our poor Renzo reached the gate of the lazaretto. He crossed the threshold, and stood for a moment motionless under the portico.

Chapter XXXIV.

The reader may imagine the lazaretto, peopled with sixteen thousand persons infected with the plague: the vast enclosure was encumbered with cabins, tents, cars, and human beings. Two long ranges of porticoes, to the right and left, were crowded with the dying or the dead, extended upon straw; and from the immense receptacle of woe, was heard a deep murmur, similar to the distant voice of the waves, agitated by a tempest.

Renzo went forward from hut to hut, carefully examining every countenance he could discern within—whether broken down by suffering, distorted by spasm, or fixed in death. Hitherto he met none but men, and judged, therefore, that the women were distributed in some other part of, the inclosure. The state of the atmosphere seemed to add to the horror of the scene: a dense and dark fog involved all things. The disc of the sun, as if seen through a veil, shed a feeble light in its own part of the sky, but darted down a heavy deathlike blast of heat: a confused murmuring of distant thunder might be heard. Not a leaf moved, not a bird was seen—save the swallow only, which descended to the plain, and, alarmed at the dismal sounds around, remounted the air, and disappeared. Nature seemed at war with human existence—hundreds seemed to grow worse—the last struggle more afflictive—and no hour of bitterness was comparable to that.

Renzo had, in his search, witnessed, as he thought, every variety of human suffering. But a new sound caught his ear—a compound of children's crying and goats' bleating: looking through an opening of the boards of a hut, he saw children, infants, lying upon sheets or quilts upon the floor, and nurses attending them; but the most singular part of the spectacle, was a number of she-goats supplying the maternal functions, and with all the appearance of conscious sympathy hastening, at the cries of the helpless little ones, to afford them the requisite nutrition. The women were aiding these efficient coadjutors, in rendering their supplies available to the poor bereft babies. Whilst observing this wretched scene, an old capuchin entered with two infants, just taken from their lifeless mother, to seek among the flock for one to supply her place. Quitting this spot, and looking about on every side, a sudden apparition struck his sight, and set his thoughts in commotion. He saw at some distance, among the tents, a capuchin, whom he instantly recognised to be Father Christopher!

The history of the good friar, from the moment in which we lost sight of him until this meeting, may be related in few words. He had not stirred from Rimini, and he would not now have thought of doing so if the plague breaking out at Milan had not afforded him the opportunity, so long desired, of sacrificing his life for the benefit of others. He demanded, as a favour, permission to go and assist those who were infected with the disease. The count, he of the secret council, was dead; and moreover, at this time, there was a greater want of guardians to the sick, than of politicians: his request was readily granted. He had now been in the lazaretto nearly three months.

But the joy of Renzo at seeing the good father was not unalloyed. It was he indeed; but, alas! how changed! how wan! Exhausted nature appeared to be sustained for a while by the mind, that had acquired new vigour from the perpetual demand on its sympathies and activity.

"Oh, Father Christopher!" said Renzo, when he was near enough to speak to him.

"You here!" said the friar, rising.

"How are you, my father, how are you?"

"Better than these unfortunate beings that you see," replied the friar. His voice was feeble—hollow and changed as his person. His eye alone "had not lost its original brightness"—benevolence and charity appeared to have imparted to it a lustre superior to that which bodily weakness was gradually extinguishing.

"But you," pursued he, "why are you here? Why do you thus come to brave the pestilence?"

"I have had it, thank Heaven! I come—in search of—Lucy."

"Lucy! Is Lucy here?"

"Yes. At least I hope so."

"Is she thy wife?"

"My dear father! alas! no, she is not my wife. Do you know nothing, then, of what has happened?"

"No, my son. Since God removed me from you, I have heard nothing. But now that he sends you to me, I wish much to know. And your banishment?"

"You know, then, what they did to me?"

"But you, what did *you* do?"

"My father, if I were to say I was prudent on that day at Milan, I should tell a falsehood; but I committed no bad action wilfully."

"I believe you; I have always thought so."

"Now then I will tell you all."

"Wait a moment."

He approached a cabin, and called " *Father Victor*."

In a few moments a young capuchin appeared. "Do me the favour, Father Victor," said he, "to take my place in watching over our poor patients for a little while. If, however, any should particularly ask for me, be so good as to call me."

The young friar complied, and Father Christopher, turning to Renzo, "Let us enter here," said he. "But," added he, "you appear much exhausted, you have need of food."

"It is true. Now that you make me think of it, I have not tasted any thing to-day."

"Wait, then, a moment." He soon brought Renzo a bowl of broth, from a large kettle, the common property of the establishment, and making him sit down on his bed, the only seat his cabin afforded, and placing some wine on a little table by his side, he seated himself next him. "Now tell me about my poor child," said he, "and be in haste, for time is precious, and I have much to do, as you perceive."

Renzo related the history of Lucy; that she had been sheltered in the convent of Monza, and carried off from her asylum. At the idea of such treatment and peril, and at the thought, too, that it was he who had unwittingly exposed her to it, the good friar was breathless with attention; but he recovered his tranquillity when he heard of her miraculous deliverance, her restoration to her mother, and her having been placed under the protection of Donna Prassede.

Renzo then briefly related his journey to Milan, his flight, and his return home; that he had not found Agnes there; and at Milan had learned that Lucy was in the lazaretto. "And I am here," concluded he, "I am here in search of her; to see if she yet lives, and if—she still thinks of me—because—sometimes—"

"But what direction did they give you? Did they tell you where she was placed when she came here?"

"I know nothing, dear father, nothing; only that she is here, if she still lives, which may God grant!"

"Oh, poor child! But what have you done here until now?"

"I have searched, and searched, but have seen hardly any but men. I think the females must be in another part by themselves; you can tell me if this is the case?"

"Know you not that it is forbidden to men to enter there unless their duty calls them?"

"Oh, well! what can happen to me if I should attempt?"

"The law is a good one, my dear son; and if our weight of affliction does not permit us to enforce it, is that a reason why an honest man should infringe it?"

"But, Father Christopher, Lucy should have been my wife; you know how we have been separated; it is twenty months since I have suffered, and taken my misfortunes patiently; I have come here, risking every thing to behold her, and now—"

"I know not what to say," resumed the friar; "you are, no doubt, guided by a praiseworthy motive; would to God that all those who have free access to these places conducted themselves as well as I am sure you will. God, who certainly blesses thy perseverance of affection, thy fidelity in desiring and seeking her whom he has given thee, God, who is more rigorous than man, but also more indulgent, will not regard what may be irregular in this enquiry for one so dear."

So saying, he arose, and Renzo followed him. While listening to him, he had been confirmed in his resolution not to acquaint the father with Lucy's vow. "If he learns that," thought he, "he will certainly raise new difficulties. Either I shall find her, and we can then disclose, or—and then—what use would it be?"

After having conducted him to the opening of the cabin, towards the north, "From yonder little temple," said he, "rising above the miserable tents, Father Felix is about to lead in procession the small remnant who are convalescent, to another station, to finish their quarantine. Avoid notice, but watch them as they pass. If she is not of the number, this side," added he, pointing to the edifice before them, "this side of the building and a part of the field before it are assigned to the women. You will perceive a railing which divides that quarter from this, but so broken, in many places, that you can easily pass through. Once there, if you do nothing to offend, probably no one will speak to you. If, however, there is any difficulty, say that Father Christopher knows you, and will answer for you. Seek her, then, seek her with confidence—and with resignation; for remember, it is an unusual expectation, a person alive within the walls of the lazaretto! Go, then, and be prepared for whatever result—"

"Yes, I understand!" said Renzo, a dark cloud overshadowing his countenance; "I understand, I will seek in every place, from one end of the lazaretto to the other—And if I do not find her!"

"If you do not find her?" repeated the father, in a serious and admonitory tone.

But Renzo, giving vent to the wrath which had been for some time pent up in his bosom, pursued, "If I do not find her, I will find *another* person. Either at Milan, or in his abominable palace, or at the end of the world, or in the house of the devil, I will find the villain who separated us; but for whom Lucy would have been mine twenty months ago; and if we had been destined to die, at least we should have died together. If he still lives, I will find him—"

"Renzo!" said the friar, seizing him by the arm, and looking at him severely.

"And if I find him," continued Renzo, entirely blinded by rage, "if the pestilence has not already done justice—the time is past when a poltroon, surrounded by bravoes, can reduce men to despair, and laugh at them! the time is come when men meet face to face, and I will do myself justice."

"Unhappy youth!" cried Father Christopher, with a voice which had suddenly become strong and sonorous, his head raised, and eyes darting forth more than their wonted fire; "unhappy youth! look around you! Behold who punishes and who judges; who punishes and pardons! But you, feeble worm, you would do yourself justice! Do you know what justice is? Unhappy youth! begone! I hoped—yes, I hoped that before I died, God would afford me the consolation to learn that my poor Lucy still lived; to see her, perhaps, and to hear her promise that she would send a prayer to yonder grave where I shall rest. Begone, you have taken away my hope. God has not left her on the earth for thee, and you certainly have not the audacity to believe yourself worthy that God should think of consoling you. Go, I have no time to listen to you farther." And he dropped the arm of Renzo, which he had grasped, and moved towards a cabin.

"Oh, my father!" said Renzo, following him with a supplicating look, "will you send me away thus?"

"How!" resumed the capuchin, but in a gentler tone, "would you dare ask me to steal the time from these poor afflicted ones, who are expecting me to speak to them of the pardon of God, in order to listen to thy accents of rage—thy projects of vengeance? I listened to you, when you asked consolation and advice, but now that you have revenge in your heart, what do you want with me? Begone, I have listened to the forgiveness of the injured, and the repentance of the aggressor; I have wept with both; but what have I to do with thee?"

"Oh, I pardon him! I pardon him! I pardon him for ever!" said the young man.

"Renzo," said the friar, in a calmer tone, "think of it, and tell me how often you have pardoned him?"

He kept silence some time, and not receiving an answer, he bowed his head, and, with a voice trembling from emotion, continued, "You know why I wear this habit?"

Renzo hesitated.

"You know it?" repeated the old man.

"I know it."

"I likewise hated, I, who have reprimanded you for a thought, a word. The man I hated, I killed."

"Yes, but it was a noble, one of those—"

"Silence!" interrupted the friar. "If that were justification, believe you I should not have found it in thirty years? Ah! if I could now make you experience the sentiment I have since had, and that I now have for the man I hated! If *I* could *I*!—but God can. May he do it! Hear me, Renzo. He is a better friend to you, than you are to yourself; you have thought of revenge, but He has power enough, pity enough, to prevent it; you know you have often said that he can arrest the arm of the powerful; but learn, also, that he can arrest that of the vindictive. And because you are poor, because you are injured, can he not defend against you a man created in his image? Will he suffer you to do all you wish? No! but he can cast you off for ever; he can, for this sentiment which animates you, embitter your whole life, since, whatever happens to you, hold for certain, that all will be punishment until you have pardoned, pardoned freely and for ever!"

"Yes, yes," said Renzo, with much emotion, "I feel that I have never truly pardoned him; I have spoken as a brute and not as a Christian; and now, by the help of God, I pardon him from the bottom of my soul."

"And should you see him?"

"I would pray God to grant me patience, and to touch his heart."

"Do you remember that the Lord has not only told us to pardon our enemies, but to love them? Do you remember that he loved them so as to die for them?"

"Yes, I do."

"Well, come and behold him. You have said you would find him; you shall do so; come, and you will see against whom you preserve hatred, to whom you desire evil, against what life you would arm yourself!"

He took the hand of Renzo, who followed him, without daring to ask a question. The friar led the way into one of the cabins. The first object Renzo beheld was a sick person seated on a bed of straw, who appeared to be convalescent. On seeing the father, he shook his head, as if to say *No*. The father bowed his with an air of sorrow and resignation. Renzo, meanwhile, gazing with uneasy curiosity around the cabin, beheld in the corner of it a sick person lying on a feather bed, wrapped up in a sheet, and covered with a cloak. Looking attentively, he recognised Don Roderick! The unfortunate man lay motionless; his eyes wide open, but without any cognisance of the objects around him; the stamp of death was on his face, which was covered with black spots; his lips were swollen and black: you would have thought it the face of the dead, if a violent contraction about the mouth had not revealed a tenacity of life; his respiration was painful, and his livid hand, extending on the outside of the covering, was firmly grasping his cloak, and pressing it upon his heart, as if conscious that *there* was his deepest agony.

"Behold!" said the friar, in a low solemn voice; "the sentiment you hold towards this man, who has offended you, such will God hold towards you on the great day. Bless him, and be blessed! For four days he has been here in this condition, without giving any sign of perception. Perhaps the Lord is disposed to grant him an hour of repentance, but he would have you pray for it; perhaps he desires that you should pray for him with this innocent girl; perhaps he reserves this favour for thy prayer alone, for the prayer of an afflicted and resigned heart. Perhaps the salvation of this man and thine own depend at this moment upon thyself, upon thy pity, upon thy love." He kept silence, and clasping his hands, bowed his head as in prayer, and Renzo, completely subdued, followed his example. Their supplications were interrupted in a short time by the striking of a bell: they immediately arose and left the cabin.

"The procession is about to move," said the father; "go then, prepared to make a sacrifice, to praise God, whatever may be the issue of your search; and whatever that may be, return to me, and we will praise him together."

Here they separated; the one to resume his painful duties, the other to the little temple, which was close at hand.

Chapter XXXV.

Who would have told Renzo some moments before, that at the very time of his greatest suspense and anxiety, his heart should be divided between Lucy and Don Roderick? And nevertheless it was so. The thought of him mingled itself with all the bright or painful images which hope or fear called up as he proceeded. The words the friar had uttered by that bed of pain, blended themselves with the cruel uncertainty of his soul. He could not utter a prayer, for the happy issue of his present undertaking, without adding to it one for the miserable object of his former resentment and revenge.

He saw the Father Felix on the portico of the church, and by his attitude comprehended that the holy man was addressing the assembled convalescents. He placed himself where he could overlook the audience. In the midst were the women, covered with veils; Renzo gazed at them intently, but finding that, from the place where he stood, it would be a vain scrutiny, he directed his attention to the father. He was touched by his venerable figure; and listened with all the attention his own solicitude would allow, to the reverend speaker, who thus proceeded in his affecting address:—

"Let us think for a moment," said he, "of the thousands who have gone forth thither," pointing to a gate behind him, leading to the burying ground of San Gregory, which was then but one mighty grave. "Let us look at the thousands who remain here, uncertain of their destiny; let us also look at ourselves! May the Lord be praised! praised in his justice! praised in his mercy! praised in death! praised in life! praised in the choice he has made of us! Oh! why has he done it, my children, if not to preserve a people corrected by affliction, and animated by gratitude? That we may be deeply sensible that life is his gift, that we may value it accordingly, and employ it in works which he will approve? That the remembrance of our sufferings may render us compassionate, and actively benevolent to others. May those with whom we have suffered, hoped, and feared, and among whom we leave friends and kindred, may they as we pass amidst them derive edification from our deportment! May God preserve us from any exhibition of self-congratulation, or carnal joy, at escaping that death against which they are still struggling! May they see us depart, rendering thanks to Heaven for ourselves, and praying for them; that they may say, *Even beyond these walls they will remember us, they will continue to pray for us!* Let us begin from this moment, from the first step we shall take into the world, a life of charity! Let those who have regained their former strength, lend a fraternal arm to the feeble; let the young sustain the old; let those who are left without children become parents to the orphan, and thus your sorrows will be softened, and your lives will be acceptable to God!"

Here a deep murmur of sighs and sobs, which had been increasing in the assembly, was suddenly suspended, on seeing the friar place a cord around his neck and fall on his knees. All was intense attention and profound silence.

"For myself," said he, "and for all my companions, who have been chosen to the high privilege of serving Christ in you, I humbly ask your forgiveness if we have not worthily fulfilled so great a ministry. If indolence, or the waywardness of the flesh, has rendered us less attentive to your wants, less prompt to your call than duty demanded; if unjust impatience, or culpable disgust, have caused us sometimes to appear severe and wearied in your presence; if, indeed, the miserable thought that you had need of us, has led us to be deficient in humility towards you; if our frailty has made us commit any action which may have given you pain, pardon us! May God remit also your offences, and bless you!"

We have here related, if not the very words, at least the sense of that which he uttered; but we cannot describe the accent which accompanied them. It was that of a man who called it a privilege to serve the afflicted, because he really considered it such; who confessed not to have worthily exercised this privilege, because he truly felt his deficiency; who asked pardon, because he was persuaded he had need of it. But his hearers, who had beheld these capuchins only occupied in serving them, who had beheld so many of them die in the service, and he who now spoke in the name of all, always the first in toil as he was the first in authority, his hearers could only answer him with tears. The good friar then took a cross which rested against a pillar, and holding it up before him, took off his sandals, passing through the crowd, which opened respectfully to give him a passage, and placed himself at their head.

Renzo, overcome with emotion, drew on one side, and placed himself near a cabin, where, half concealed, he awaited, with his eyes open, his heart palpitating, but with renewed confidence, the result of the emotion excited by the touching scene of which he had been a witness.

Father Felix proceeded barefooted at the head of the procession, with the cord about his neck, bearing that long and heavy cross; he advanced slowly but resolutely, as one who would spare the weakness of others, but whose ideas of duty enabled him to rise above his own. The largest children followed immediately behind him, for the most part barefooted, and very few entirely clothed; then came the women, nearly all of them leading a child, and singing alternately the *miserere*. The feeble sound of the voices, the paleness and languor of the countenances, would have excited commiseration in the heart of a mere spectator. But Renzo was occupied with his own peculiar anxieties; the slow progress of the procession enabled him to scan with ease every face as it passed. He looked and looked again, and always in vain! His eye wandered from rank to rank, from face to face—they came, they passed—in vain, in vain—none but unknown features! A new ray of hope dawned upon his mind as he beheld some cars approaching, in which were the convalescents who were still too feeble to support the fatigue of walking. They approached so slowly that Renzo had full leisure to examine each in turn. But he was again disappointed; the cars had all passed, and Father Michael, with his staff in his hand, brought up the rear as regulator of the procession.

Thus nearly vanished his hopes, and with them his resolution. His only ground of hope now was to find Lucy still under the power of the disease; to this sad and feeble hope, he clung with all the ardour of his nature. He fell on his knees at the last step of the temple, and breathed forth an unconnected, but fervent prayer; he arose, strengthened in hope; and passing the railing pointed out by the father, entered into the quarter allotted to the women. As he entered it, he saw on the ground one of the little bells that the *monatti* carried on their feet, with its leather straps attached to it. Thinking it might serve him as a passport, he tied it to his foot, and then began his painful search. Here new scenes of sorrow met his eye, similar in part to those he had already witnessed, partly dissimilar. Under the weight of the same calamity, he discerned a more patient endurance of pain, and a greater sensibility to the afflictions of others; they to whom bodily suffering is a lot and an inheritance, acquire from it fortitude to bear their own woes, and sympathy to bestow on the woes of others.

Renzo had proceeded some distance on his search, when he heard behind him a "Ho!" which appeared to be addressed to him. Turning, he saw at a distance a commissary, who cried, "Go there into those rooms; they want you there; they have not finished carrying all off."

Renzo perceived that he took him for a *monatto*, and that the little bell had caused the mistake. He determined to extricate himself from it as soon as he could. Making a sign of obedience, he hid himself from the commissary, by passing between two cabins which were very near each other.

As he stooped to unloose the strap of the little bell, he rested his head against the straw wall of one of the cabins; a voice reached his ear. O Heaven! is it possible? His whole soul was in his ear, he scarcely breathed. Yes! yes! it was that voice! "Fear of what?" said that gentle voice; "we have passed through worse dangers than a tempest. He who has watched over us until now, will still continue to do so."

Renzo scarcely breathed, his knees trembled, his sight became dim; with a great effort recovering his faculties, he went to the door of the cabin, and beheld her who had spoken! She was standing, leaning over a bed; she turned at the sound of his steps, and gazed for a moment bewildered; at last she exclaimed, "Oh! blessed Lord!"

"Lucy! I have found you again! I have found you again! It is, indeed, you! You live!" cried Renzo, advancing with trembling steps.

"Oh! blessed Lord!" cried Lucy, greatly agitated; "is it indeed you? How? Why? the pestilence—"

"I have had it. And you?"

"Yes. I have had it also. And my mother?"

"I have not seen her yet; she is at Pasturo. I believe, however, that she is well. But you are still suffering! how feeble you appear! you are cured, however; you are, is it not so?"

"The Lord has seen fit to leave me a little longer here below," said Lucy. "But, Renzo! why are you here?"

"Why?" said Renzo, approaching her, "do you ask me why I am here? Must I tell you? Whom do I think of then? Am I not Renzo? Are you no longer Lucy?"

"Oh! why speak thus! Did not my mother write to you?"

"Yes! she wrote to me! kind things, truly, to write to a poor unfortunate man, an exile from his native land, one, at least, who never injured you!"

"But Renzo! Renzo! since you knew—why come, why?"

"Why come! O Lucy! why come, do you say! After so many promises! Are we no longer the same! Is all forgotten?"

"O God!" cried Lucy, sorrowfully clasping her hands, and raising her eyes to heaven; "why didst thou not take me to thyself! O Renzo! what have you done! Alas! I hoped—that with time—I should have driven from my memory—"

"A kind hope indeed! and to say so to me!"

"Oh! what have you done! in this place! in the midst of these sorrows! Here, where there is nothing but death, you have dared—"

"We must pray to God for those who die, and trust that they will be happy; but their calamity is no reason why those who live must live in despair—"

"But Renzo! Renzo! you know not what you say; a promise to the Virgin! a vow!"

"I tell you, such promises are good for nothing."

"Oh! where have you been all this time? with whom have you associated, that you speak thus?"

"I speak as a good Christian. I think better of the Virgin than you do, because I do not believe vows to the injury of others are acceptable to her. If the Virgin had spoken herself, oh! then indeed—but it is simply an idea of your own!"

"No, no, you know not what you say; you know not what it is to make a vow! Leave me, leave me, for the love of Heaven!"

"Lucy!" said Renzo, "tell me at least, tell me, if this reason did not exist—would you feel the same towards me?"

"Unfeeling man!" said Lucy, with difficulty restraining her tears; "would it satisfy you to hear me confess that which might be sinful, and would certainly be useless! Leave me, oh! leave me! forget me! we were not destined for each other. We shall meet again above; we have not long to remain in the world. Go! tell my mother that I am cured, that even here God has assisted me, that I have found a good soul, this worthy woman who has been a mother to me; tell her we shall meet *when* it is the will of God, and *as* it is his will. Go! for the love of Heaven! and remember me no more—except when you pray to God!"

And as if wishing to withdraw from the temptation to prolong the conversation, she drew near the bed where the female was lying of whom she had spoken.

"Hear me, Lucy, hear me!" said Renzo, without however approaching her.

"No, no; go away! for charity!"

"Hear me, Father Christopher—"

"How!"

"He is here."

"Here! where? how do you know?"

"I have just spoken with him; a man like him it appears to me—"

"He is here! to assist the afflicted, no doubt. Has he had the plague?"

"Ah! Lucy! I fear, I greatly fear—" As Renzo hesitated to utter his fears, she had unconsciously again approached him, with a look of anxious enquiry—"I fear he has it now!"

"Oh! poor man! But what do I say? poor man! he is rich, rich in the favour of God! How is he? Is he confined to his bed? Has he assistance?"

"He is, on the contrary, still assisting others—but if you were to see him! Alas! there can be no mistake!"

"Oh! is he indeed within these walls?" said Lucy.

"Here, and not far off; hardly farther than from your cottage to mine—if you remember—"

"Oh! most holy Virgin!"

"Shall I tell you what he said to me? He said I did well to come in search of you, that God would approve it, and that he would assist me to find you—Thus, then, you see—"

"If he spoke thus, it was because he did not know—"

"What use would there be in his knowing a mere imagination of your own? A man of sense, such as he is, never thinks of things of that sort. But oh! Lucy! Shall I tell you what I have seen?"—And he related his visit to the cabin.

Lucy, although familiarised in this abode of horrors to spectacles of wretchedness and despair, was shocked at the recital.

"And at the side of that bed," said Renzo, "if you could have heard the holy man! He said, that God has perhaps resolved to look in mercy on this unfortunate—(I can now give him no other name)—that he designs to subdue him to himself, but that he desires that we should pray together for him—together! do you understand?"

"Yes, yes, we will pray each, there where the Lord shall place us. He can unite our prayers."

"But if I tell you his very words—"

"But, Renzo, he does not know—"

"But can you not comprehend, when such a man speaks, it is God who speaks in him, and that he would not have spoken thus, if it ought not to be exactly so? And the soul of this unfortunate! I have prayed, and will pray for him; I have prayed with all my heart, as if he were my brother. But what, think you, will be his condition in the other world, if we do not repair some of the evil he has done? If you return to reason, all will be set in order. That which has been, has been—he has had his punishment here below—"

"No, Renzo, no! God would not have us do evil that good may come. Leave to him the care of this unfortunate man; our duty is to pray for him. If I had died that fatal night, would not God have been able to pardon him? And if I am not dead, if I have been delivered—"

"And your mother, poor Agnes, who desired so much to see us man and wife, has she not told you it was a foolish imagination?".

"My mother! think you my mother would advise me to break a vow? Would you desire that she should? But, Renzo, you are not in your right mind!"

"Oh! you women cannot be made to comprehend reason! Father Christopher told me to return, and inform him whether I had found you—I will go, and get his advice—"

"Yes, yes, go to the holy man! Tell him I pray for him, and that I desire his prayers! But, for the love of Heaven! for your soul's sake, and for mine, do not return here, to trouble, to—tempt me! Father Christopher will explain matters to you, and make you return to yourself; he will set your heart at rest."

"My heart at rest! Oh! don't encourage an idea of that sort! You have, before now, caused such language to be written to me! and the suffering it caused me! and now you have the heart to tell it to me! As for me, I declare to you plainly, that I will never set my heart at rest. Lucy! you have told me to forget you; forget you! how can I do it? After so many trials! so many promises! Who have I thought of ever since we parted? Is it because I have suffered, that you treat me thus? because I have been unfortunate? because the world has persecuted me? because I have been so long away from you? because the first moment I was able, I came to seek you?"

"Oh! holy Virgin!" exclaimed Lucy, as the tears flowed from her eyes, "come to my help. You have aided me hitherto; aid me now. Since that night such a moment as this have I never passed."

"Yes, Lucy, you do well to invoke the Virgin. She is the mother of compassion, and will take no pleasure in our sufferings. But, if this is an excuse—if I have become odious to you—tell me, speak frankly—"

"For pity, Renzo, for pity, stop—stop. Do not make me die. Go to Father Christopher; commend me to him. Do not return here—do not return here."

"I go, but think not I will not return. I would return from the end of the world; yes, I would return!" and he disappeared.

Lucy threw herself on the floor near the bed, upon which she rested her head, and wept bitterly. The good woman, who had been a silent spectator of the painful scene, demanded the cause of her anguish and her tears? But, perhaps, the reader will wish to know something of this benevolent person: we will satisfy the desire in a few words.

She was a rich tradeswoman, about thirty years of age: she had beheld her husband and children die of the plague. Attacked by it herself, she had been brought to the lazaretto, and placed in the cabin with Lucy, who was just beginning to recover her senses, which had forsaken her from the commencement of her attack in the house of Don Ferrante. The humble roof could only accommodate two guests, and there grew up, in their affliction, a strict and intimate friendship between them. They derived great consolation from each other's society, and had pledged themselves not to separate, after quitting the lazaretto. The good woman, whose wealth was now far more ample than were her desires, wished to retain Lucy with her as a daughter: the proposition was received with gratitude, and accepted, on condition of the permission and approval of Agnes. Lucy had, however, never made known to her the circumstances of her intended marriage, and her other extraordinary adventures; but now she related, as distinctly as tears permitted her to do so, her sad story.

Meanwhile Renzo went in search of Father Christopher: he found him with no small difficulty, and engaged in administering consolation to a dying man. The scene was soon closed. The father remained a short time in silent prayer. He then arose, and seeing Renzo approach, exclaimed, "Well, my son!"

"She is there; I have found her!"

"In what state?"

"Convalescent, and out of danger."

"God be praised!" said the friar.

"But—" said Renzo, "there is another difficulty!"

"What do you mean?"

"I mean that—you know how good this poor girl is; but she is sometimes a little fanciful. After so many promises, she tells me now she cannot marry me, because on that night of fear she made a vow to the Virgin! These things signify nothing, do they? Is it not true that they are not binding, at least on people such as we are?"

"Is she far from this?"

"Oh no; a few steps beyond the church."

"Wait a moment," said the friar, "and we will go together."

"Will you give her to understand that—?"

"I know not, my son: I must hear what she will say." And they proceeded to Lucy's cabin.

The clouds were gathering in the heavens, and a tempest coming on. Rapid lightning, cleaving the increasing darkness, illumined at moments the long roofs and arcades of the building, and the cupola of the little church: loud claps of thunder resounded with prolonged echoes through the heavens. Renzo suppressed his impatience, and accommodated his steps to the strength of the father, who, exhausted by fatigue, oppressed by disease, and breathing in pain, could, with difficulty, drag his failing limbs to the performance of this last act of benevolence.

As they reached the door of the cabin, Renzo stopped, saying, in a trembling voice, "She is there!" They entered. Lucy arose, and ran towards the old man, crying—"Oh, what I do see! Oh, Father Christopher!"

"Well, Lucy! through how much peril has God preserved you! you must be rejoiced that you have always trusted in Him."

"Ah! yes.—But you, my father! how you are changed! how do you feel? say, how are you?"

"As God wills, and as, through his grace, I will also," replied the friar, with a serene countenance. Drawing her aside, he said, "Hear me, I have but a few moments to spare. Are you disposed to confide in me, as in times past?"

"Oh, are you not still my father?"

"Well, my child, what is this vow of which Renzo speaks?"

"It is a vow I made to the Virgin never to marry."

"But did you forget that you were bound by a previous promise? God, my daughter, accepts of offerings from that which is our own. It is the heart he desires, the will; but you cannot offer the will of another to whom you had pledged yourself."

"I have done wrong."

"No, poor child, think not so; I believe the holy Virgin has accepted the intention of your afflicted heart, and has offered it to God for you. But tell me, did you ask the advice of any one about this matter?"

"I did not deem it a sin, or I would have confessed it, and the little good one does, one ought not to mention."

"Have you no other motive for preventing the fulfilment of your promise to Renzo?"

"As to that—for myself—what motive?—no other," replied Lucy, with a hesitation which implied any thing rather than uncertainty; and a blush passed over her pale and lovely countenance.

"Do you believe," resumed the old man, "that God has given the church authority to remit the obligations that man may have contracted to him?"

"Yes, I believe it."

"Learn, then, that the care of souls in this place, being committed to us, we have the most ample powers from the church; and I can, if you ask it, free you from the obligation you have contracted by this vow."

"But is it not a sin to repent of a promise made to the Virgin?" said Lucy, violently agitated by unexpected hope.

"Sin, my child," said the father, "sin, to recur to the church, and to ask her minister to use the authority which he has received from her, and which she receives from God! I bless him that he has given me, unworthy that I am, the power to speak in his name, and to restore to you your vow. If you ask me to absolve you from it, I shall not hesitate to do so; and I even hope you will."

"Then—then—I ask it," said Lucy, with a modest confidence.

The friar beckoned to Renzo, who was watching the progress of the dialogue with the deepest solicitude, to approach, and said aloud to Lucy, "With the authority I hold from the church, I declare you absolved from your vow, and liberate you from all the obligations you may have contracted by it."

The reader may imagine the feelings of Renzo at these words. His eyes expressed the warmth of his gratitude to him who had uttered them; but they sought in vain for Lucy's.

"Return in peace and safety to your former attachment," said the father. "And do you remember, my son, that in giving you this companion, the church does it not to insure simply your temporal happiness, but to prepare you both for happiness without end. Thank Heaven that you have been brought to this state through misery and affliction: your joy will be the more temperate and durable. If God should grant you children, bring them up in his fear, and in love to all men—for the rest you cannot greatly err. And now, Lucy, has Renzo told you whom he has beheld in this place?"

"Yes, father, he has told me."

"You will pray for him, and for me also, my children. You will remember your poor friar?" And drawing from his basket a small wooden box, "Within this box are the remains of the loaf—the first I asked for charity—the loaf of which you have heard; I leave it to you; show it to your children; they will come into a wicked world; they will meet the proud and insolent. Tell them always to forgive, always! every thing, every thing! And let them pray for the poor friar!"

Lucy took the box from his hands with reverence, and he continued, "Now tell me what you mean to do here at Milan? and who will conduct you to your mother?"

"This good lady has been a mother to me," said Lucy; "we shall leave this place together, and she will provide for all."

"May God bless her!" said the friar, approaching the bed.

"May he bestow his blessing upon you!" said the widow, "for the joy you have given to the afflicted, although it disappoints my hope of having Lucy as a companion. But I will accompany her to her village, and restore her to her mother, and," added she, in a low voice, "I will give the outfit. I have much wealth, and of those who should have enjoyed it with me none are left."

"The service will be acceptable to God," said the father, "who has watched over you both in affliction. Now," added he, turning to Renzo, "we must begone; I have remained too long already."

"Oh, my father," said Lucy, "shall I see you again? I have recovered from this dreadful disease, I who am of no use in the world; and you—"

"It is long since," replied the old man with a serious and gentle tone, "I asked a great favour from Heaven; that of ending my days in the service of my fellow-men. If God grants it to me now, all those who love me should help me to return him thanks. And now give Renzo your commissions for your mother."

"Tell her all," said Lucy to her betrothed; "tell her I have found here another mother, and that we will come to her as soon as we possibly can."

"If you have need of money," said Renzo, "I have here all that you sent—"

"No, no," said the widow, "I have more than sufficient."

"Farewell, Lucy, and you, too, good signora, till we meet again," said Renzo, not having words to express his feelings at this moment.

"Who knows whether we shall all meet again?" cried Lucy.

"May God ever watch over you and bless you!" said the friar, as he quitted the cabin with Renzo.

As night was not far distant, the capuchin offered the young man a shelter in his humble abode: "I cannot bear you company," said he, "but you can at least repose yourself, in order to be able to prosecute your journey."

Renzo, however, felt impatient to be gone; as to the hour or the weather it might be said that, night or day, rain or shine, heat or cold, were equally indifferent to him; the friar pressed his hand as he departed, saying, "If you find, which may God grant! the good Agnes, remember me to her; tell her, as well as all those who remember Friar Christopher, to pray for me."

"Oh, dear father, shall we never meet again?"

"Above, I hope. Farewell, farewell!"

Chapter XXXVI.

As Renzo passed without the walls of the lazaretto, the rain began to fall in torrents. Instead of lamenting, he rejoiced at it: he was delighted with the refreshing air, and with the sound of the falling drops from the plants and foliage which seemed to have new life imparted to them; and breathing more freely in this change of nature, he felt more vividly the change that had occurred in his own destiny.

But much would his enjoyment have been increased, could he have surmised what would be seen a few days after. This water carried off, washed away, so to speak, the contagion. If the lazaretto did not restore to the living all the living it still contained, at least from that day it received no more into its vast abyss. At the end of a week, shops were opened, people returned to their houses, quarantine was hardly spoken of, and there remained of the pestilence but a few scattered traces.

Our traveller proceeded on full of joy, without having thought *where* or *when* he should stop for the night; anxious only to go forward to reach the village, and to proceed immediately to Pasturo in search of Agnes. In the midst of the reminiscences of the horrors and the dangers of the day, there was always present the thought, "I have found her! she is well! she is mine!"

And then again he recalled his doubts, his difficulties, his fears, his hopes, that had agitated him that eventful morning! He fancied himself with his hand on the knocker of Don Ferrante's house! And the unfavourable answer! And then those fools who were about to attack him in their madness! And the lazaretto, that vast sepulchre! To have hurried thither to find her, and to have found her! And the procession! What a moment! And now it appeared nothing to him! And the quarter set apart for the women! And there, behind that cabin when he least expected it, that voice! that voice itself! And to see her there! But then her vow! It exists no longer. And his violent hatred against Don Roderick, which had augmented his grief, and shed its venom over his hopes! That also was gone. Indeed, had it not been for his uncertainty concerning Agnes, his anxiety about Father Christopher, and the consciousness that the pestilence still existed, his happiness would have been without alloy.

He arrived at Sesto in the evening; the rain had as yet no appearance of ceasing. But Renzo did not stop, his only inconvenience was an extraordinary appetite, which the vicinity of a baker's shop enabled him to mitigate the violence of. When he passed through Monza it was dark night; he succeeded, however, in leaving it by the right road; but what a road! buried between two banks, almost like the bed of a river, it might then, indeed, have been called a river, or rather, an aqueduct; in numerous places were deep holes, from which Renzo could with difficulty extricate himself. But he did as well as he could, without impatience or regret. He reflected that every step brought him nearer to the end of his journey; that the rain would cease when God should please; that day would come in its own time; and that in the mean time the road he had passed over he should not have to travel again. At the break of day he found himself near the Adda. It had not ceased raining; there was still a drizzling shower; the light of the dawn enabled Renzo to see around him. He was in his own country! Who can express his sensations? Those mountains, the *Resegone*, the territory of Lecco, appeared to belong to him, to be his own! But, looking at himself, he felt that his outward aspect was rather at variance with the exuberant joyousness of his heart; his clothes were wet and clinging to his body, his hat bent out of shape and full of water; his hair hanging straight about his face; while his lower man was encased in a dense covering of mud.

He reached Pescate; travelled along the Adda, giving a melancholy glance at Pescarenico; passed the bridge, and crossed the fields, to the house of his friend, who, just risen, was at the door, looking out upon the weather. He beheld the strange figure, covered with mud, and wet to the skin, and yet, so joyous and animated! in his life he had never seen a man, so accoutred, appear so satisfied with himself.

"How!" said he, "already here! and in such weather! How have things gone with you?"

"She is there! she is there! she is there!"

"Well and safe?"

"Convalescent, which is better! I have wonderful things to tell you."

"But what a state you are in!"

"A pretty pickle indeed!"

"In truth you might squeeze water enough from your upper half to wash away the mud from the lower. But wait a moment; I will make a fire."

"I shall be glad to feel its warmth, I assure you. Do you know where the rain overtook me? Precisely at the door of the lazaretto; but no matter, the weather does its business, and I mine."

His friend soon kindled a bright blaze. "Now do me another favour," said Renzo, "bring me the bundle I left above; for before my clothes dry—"

Returning with the bundle, his friend said, "You must be hungry; you have had drink enough, no doubt, on the way, but as to eating—"

"I bought two loaves yesterday at dusk, but truly, I have not eaten them."

"Well, I will provide for you." He poured some water in a kettle which hung over the fire, adding, "I will go and milk the cow, and when I return with the milk, the water will be ready, and we will have a good *polenta*. You, in the mean while, change your clothes." After having allowed him time to perform the troublesome operation, his friend returned, and commenced making the *polenta*. "I have much to tell you," said Renzo. "If you were to see Milan! and the lazaretto! She is there! you will soon see her here; she will be my wife; you shall be at the wedding, and, pestilence or not, we will be happy for a few hours."

On the following morning Renzo set out for Pasturo. On his arrival, he asked concerning Agnes, and learnt that she was in health and safety. He approached her residence, which had been pointed out to him, and called her by name from the street. At the sound of his voice, she rushed to the window, and Renzo, without allowing her time to speak, cried, "Lucy is well; I saw her the day before yesterday; she will be at home shortly; oh, I have so many things to tell you."

Overcome by various emotions, Agnes could only articulate, "I will open the door for you."

"Stop, stop," said Renzo. "You have not had the plague, I believe?"

"No. Have you?"

"Yes; but you ought to be prudent. I come from Milan; and have been for two days in the midst of it. It is true I have changed my clothes, but the contagion attaches itself to the flesh, like witchcraft; and since God has preserved you until now, you must take care of yourself until all danger is over; for you are our mother, and I trust we shall live long together as a compensation for the sufferings we have endured, *I* at least."

"But—"

"There is no longer any *but*; I know what you would say. You will soon see there is no longer any *but*; come into the open air, where I may speak to you in safety, and I will tell you all about it."

Agnes pointed to a garden adjoining the house. Renzo entered it, and was immediately joined by the anxious and impatient Agnes. They seated themselves opposite each other on two benches. The events he described are already known to our reader, and we will leave to his imagination the numerous exclamations of grief, horror, surprise, and joy, that interrupted the progress of the narrative every moment. The result, however, was an agreement to settle all together at Bergamo, where Renzo had already an advantageous engagement; *when* would depend on the pestilence and other circumstances; Agnes was to remain where she was, until it should be safe for her to return home; and in the interval she should have regular information of all their movements.

He departed, with the additional consolation of having found one so dear to him safe and well. He remained the rest of that day and the following night with his friend, and on the morrow set out for the country of his adoption.

He found Bortolo in good health, and in less apprehension of losing it, as within a few days things had rapidly changed for the better. The malignity of the distemper had subsided, and given place to fever indeed, accompanied with tumours, but much more easily cured. The country presented a new aspect; those who had survived the pestilence began to resume their business; masters were preparing for the employment of workmen in every trade; and, above all, in that of weaving silk. Renzo made some preparations for the accommodation of his family, by purchasing and furnishing a neat little cottage, from his hitherto untouched treasure, which the ravages of the plague enabled him to do at small cost.

After a few days' stay, he returned by the way of Pasturo, and conducted Agnes to her village home: we will not attempt to describe her feelings at beholding again those well remembered places. She found all things in her cottage as she had left them: it seemed as if angels had watched over the poor widow and her child. Her first care was to get ready with all speed an apartment in her humble abode for that kind friend who had been to her child a second mother. Renzo, on his side, was not idle. He laboured alternately at the widow's garden, and in the service of his hospitable friend. As to his own cottage, it pained him to witness the scene of desolation it presented; and he resolved to dispose of it, and transfer its value to his new country. His re-appearance in the village was a cause of much congratulation to those who had survived the plague. All were anxious to learn his adventures, which had given rise to so many reports among the neighbours. As to Don Abbondio, he exhibited the same apprehension of the marriage as before; the mention of which conjured up to his affrighted fancy the dreaded Don Roderick and his train on the one side, and the almost equally feared cardinal and his arguments on the other.

We will now transport the reader for a few moments to Milan. Some days after the visit of Renzo to the lazaretto, Lucy left it with the good widow. A general quarantine having been ordered, they passed the period of it together in the house of the latter. The time was employed in preparing Lucy's wedding clothes; and, the quarantine terminated, they set off on their journey. We could add, *they arrived*, but, notwithstanding our desire to yield to the impatience of the reader, there are three circumstances which we must not pass over in silence.

The first is, that while Lucy was relating her adventures more minutely to the good widow, she recurred to the signora, who had afforded her an asylum, in the convent of Monza, and in return learnt many things which afforded her the solution to numerous mysteries, and filled her with sorrow and astonishment. She learnt, too, that the unfortunate signora, falling afterwards under the most horrible suspicions, had been, by order of the cardinal, transferred to a convent at Milan; that there, after having given herself up for a time to rage and despair, she had at last made her confession and repented of her crimes; and that her present life was one of severe and voluntary penance. If any one desires to know the details of her sad history, it will be found in the author we have so often quoted.

The second is, that Lucy, making enquiries concerning Father Christopher, of every capuchin from the lazaretto, learnt with more grief than surprise that he had died of the pestilence.

And the third is, that before quitting Milan, Lucy had a desire to know something concerning her former patrons. The widow accompanied her to their house, where they were informed that both had died of the plague. When we say of Donna Prassede she *died*, we have said all that is necessary; not so with Don Ferrante, he deserves a little more of our attention, considering his learning.

From the commencement of the pestilence, Don Ferrante was one of the most resolute in denying its existence, not indeed like the multitude, with cries of rage, but with arguments which none could accuse of want of concatenation. "In *rerum natura*," said he, "there are but two kinds of things, substances and accidents; and if I prove that the contagion can neither be one nor the other of these I shall have proved that it does not exist; that it is a chimera. Thus, then: substances are either material or spiritual; that the contagion is a spiritual substance, is so absurd an opinion, that no one would presume to advance it; it is, then, useless to speak of it. Material substances are either simple or compound. Now, the contagion is not a simple substance, and I will prove it in three words. It is not an aerial substance, because, if it were, instead of passing from one body to another, it would fly off to its sphere; it is not a watery substance, because it would be dried up by the wind; it is not igneous, because it would burn; it is not earthy, because it would be visible. Moreover, it is not a compound substance, because it would be sensible to the eye, or to the touch; and who has seen it? or touched it? It remains to see if it be an accident. This is still less probable. The doctors say it is communicated from body to body; this is their Achilles; the pretext for so many useless regulations. Now, supposing it an accident, it would be a transferable accident, which is an incongruity. There is not in all philosophy a more evident thing than this, that an accident cannot pass from one subject to another; so if, to avoid this Scylla, they are reduced to call it an accident produced, they avoid Scylla by falling into Charybdis, because if it be produced, it does not communicate itself, it does not propagate, as they declare. These principles allowed, what is the use of talking of botches and carbuncles?"

"It is folly," said one of his hearers.

"No, no," resumed Don Ferrante, "I do not say so. Science is science; we must only know how to employ it. Swellings, purple botches, and black carbuncles, are respectable terms, which have a good and proper signification; but I say they have nothing to do with the question. Who denies that there may be and are such things? We must only prove whence they come."

Here began the vexations of Don Ferrante. So long as he laughed at the contagion, he found respectful and attentive listeners; but when he came to distinguish and demonstrate that the error of the doctors was, not in affirming that there existed a general and terrible disease, but rather in assigning its cause, then he found them intractable and rebellious, then he no longer dared expose his doctrine, but by shreds and patches.

"Here is the true reason," said he, "and those even who maintain other fancies are obliged to acknowledge it. Let them deny, if they can, that there is a fatal conjunction of Jupiter and Saturn. And when has it been said that influences propagate? And would these gentlemen deny the existence of influences? Will they say there are no planets? or will they say that they keep up above, doing nothing, as so many pins in a pincushion? But that which I cannot understand from these doctors is, that they confess we are under so malign a conjunction, and then they tell us, don't touch this, don't touch that, and you will be safe! as if, in avoiding the material contact of terrestrial bodies, we could prevent the virtual effect of celestial bodies. And such a work in burning rags! Poor people! will you burn Jupiter? will you burn Saturn?"

His fretus, that is to say, on these grounds, he took no precautions against the pestilence; he caught it, and died, like Metastasio's hero, complaining of the stars.

Chapter XXXVII.

One fine evening Agnes heard a carriage drive up to the door of her cottage. It was Lucy and the good widow. We can easily imagine the joy of the meeting.

The following morning Renzo made his appearance, at an early hour, little expecting to find Lucy with her mother. "How are you, Renzo?" said Lucy, with downcast eyes, and in a tone—oh how different from that with which she addressed all besides! Renzo was conscious that it was meant for him alone.

"I am always well when I see you," replied the young man.

"Our poor Father Christopher," said Lucy, "pray for his soul, although we may be almost sure he is now in heaven, praying for us."

"I expected no less," said Renzo mournfully, "I expected to hear that he was taken away from this world of sorrow and trouble."

Notwithstanding the sadness of their recollections, joy was the predominant feeling of their hearts. The good widow was an agreeable addition to the little company. When Renzo saw her in the miserable cabin at the lazaretto, he could not have believed her to be of so facile and gay a disposition; but the lazaretto and the country, death and a wedding, are not at all the same things. During the evening Renzo left them, for the purpose of visiting the curate. "Signor Curate," said he, with a respectful but jocular air, "the headache, which, you said, prevented you from marrying us, has it passed off? The bride is here, and I am come to have you appoint an hour, but, I pray you, not to let it be far distant."

Don Abbondio did not say he would not; but he began to offer excuses and insinuations. "Why come forward into public view with this order for his apprehension hanging over him? and the thing could be easily done elsewhere, and then this, and then that."

"I understand," said Renzo, "you have still a little pain in your head, but listen to me." And he described the state in which he had seen Don Roderick.

"That has nothing to do with us," said Don Abbondio. "Did I say no to you? However, while there is life there is hope, you know. Look at me; I have also been nearer the other world than this, and here I am nevertheless; and if new troubles do not fall upon me, I hope to remain here a little longer."

The conversation was prolonged some time, without coming to any satisfactory conclusion, and Renzo returned home to relate it. "I came off," said he, "because I feared I should lose all patience. At times he behaved exactly as he did before, and I verily believe if I had remained a little longer, he would have spoken Latin again. I see that all this portends a tedious business. It would be better to do as he says, and go and be married where we intend to live."

"Let us go and see what we can do," said the widow, "perhaps he will be more tractable to the ladies."

They followed this advice, and in the afternoon proceeded to the parsonage. The curate evinced much pleasure on seeing Lucy and Agnes, and much politeness towards the stranger. He endeavoured to divert the discourse from that which he knew to be the purport of their visit. He begged from Lucy a recital of all her woes, and availed himself of the account of the lazaretto to draw the stranger into the conversation. He then expatiated on his own miseries, which he detailed at full length. The pause so long watched for came at last. One of the widows broke the ice; but Don Abbondio was no longer the same man; he did not say *no*; but he returned to his doubts and his difficulties, jumping like a bird from branch to branch. "It would be necessary," said he, "to get free from this unlucky order. You, signora, who live at Milan, you ought to know the course of these things; if we had the protection of some powerful man, all wounds would be healed. After all, the shortest way would be to have the ceremony performed where these young people are going, and where this proscription cannot affect them. Here, with this order, which is known to every one, to utter from the altar the name of Lorenzo Tramaglino is a thing I should be very unwilling to do. I wish him too well; it would be rendering him an ill service."

While Agnes and the widow were endeavouring to reply to these reasons, which the subtle curate as often reproduced under another form, Renzo entered the room, with the air of one bringing important intelligence, "The Lord Marquis has arrived!" said he.

"What do you mean? arrived! where?" said Don Abbondio, rising.

"He has arrived at his castle, which was Don Roderick's: he is the heir by feoffment of trust, as they say. So that there is no longer a doubt on the subject. And as to the marquis, he is a most worthy man."

"That he is," said Don Abbondio; "I have often heard him spoken of as an excellent lord. But is it really true that—"

"Will you believe your sexton?"

"Why—"

"Because he saw him with his own eyes. Will you hear Ambrose? I made him wait without expressly."

Renzo called the sexton, who confirmed the intelligence.

"Ah, he is dead then! he is really gone!" said Don Abbondio. "You see, my children, the hand of Providence. It is a happy thing for this poor country: we could not live with this man. The plague has been a great scourge, but it has also been, as it were, a serviceable broom; it has swept off certain people, of whom, my children, we could never have delivered ourselves. In the twinkling of an eye they have disappeared by the hundred. We shall no longer see him wandering about with that haughty air, followed by his cut throats, and looking at every body as if they were all placed on earth for his pleasure. He is gone, and we are still here! He will send no more messages to honest people. He has made us all pass a sad life; and now we are at liberty to say so."

"I pardon him," said Renzo, "with all my heart."

"And you do well; it is your duty; but we may also thank Heaven for delivering us from him. Now, if you wish to be married, I am ready. As to the *order for your seizure*, that is of little importance; the plague has carried off that too. If you choose—to-day is Thursday—on Sunday, I will publish the banns, and then I shall have the happiness of uniting you."

"You know we came for that purpose," said Renzo.

"Very well; and I will send word of it to his Eminence."

"Who is his Eminence?" asked Agnes.

"His Eminence? our lord cardinal archbishop, whom may God preserve!"

"Oh, as to that, you are mistaken; I can tell you they do not call him so, because the second time we went to speak with him, one of the priests drew me aside, and told me I must call him your illustrious lordship, and my lord."

"And now, if that same priest were to tell you, he would say you must call him *Your Eminence*; the pope has ordered, that this title be given to the cardinals. And do you know why? Because *Most Illustrious* was assumed by so many people who had no right to it. By and by, they will call the bishops *Your Eminence*, then the abbots will claim it, then the canons—"

"And the curates," said the widow.

"No, no, let the curates alone for that; they will be only *Your Reverence* to the end of the world. But to return to our affairs. On Sunday, I will publish the banns at the church, and obtain, in the mean time, a dispensation for omitting the two other publications. There will be plenty of similar applications, if things go on elsewhere as they do here; the fire has taken; no one will wish to live alone, I imagine; I have already three marriages on hand besides yours; what a pity Perpetua is dead, she might find a husband! And at Milan, signora, I imagine it is the same thing."

"Yes, indeed. In my parish alone there were fifty marriages last Sunday."

"Well, the world wo'n't end yet. And you, signora, has no butterfly begun to fly around you?"

"No, no, I think not of it; I do not mean to think of it."

"Oh, yes, yes; would you be alone indeed? Agnes also, Agnes also—"

"You have a mind to jest," said Agnes.

"To be sure I have; it is high time. We may hope that the few days that remain to us will be less sad. As for me, poor old man! there is no remedy for years, as they say, *Senectus ipsa est morbus*."

"Oh, now," said Renzo, "you may speak Latin as much as you like; I don't care about it now."

"You still quarrel with Latin, do you? Well, I will not forget you. When you come before me with Lucy, to pronounce some little words in Latin, I will say to you, You do not like Latin, go in peace. Eh?"

"Ah, it is not that Latin I dislike, pure and holy like that of the mass; I speak of the Latin which falls on one as a traitor, in the very midst of conversation. For example, now that we are here, and all is past, the Latin you spoke there, in that corner, to make me understand that you could not, and—I know not what. Tell me now in language I can understand, will you?"

"Hush! you mischievous fellow, hush!" said Don Abbondio. "Do not stir up old grievances: if we were to settle our accounts, I do not know which of us would be in debt to the other. I have forgiven you, but you also played me an ill turn. As for you, it did not astonish me, because you are a good-for-nothing fellow; but I speak of this silent—this little saint; one would have thought it a sin to distrust her. But I know who advised her; I know I do," added he, pointing to Agnes.

It is impossible to describe the change which had come over him. His mind, so long the slave of continual apprehension, was now emancipated from its fetters, and his tongue, liberated from its bonds, recurred to its former habits. He playfully prolonged the conversation, even following them to the door, with some parting jest.

The following morning, Don Abbondio received a visit, as agreeable as it was unexpected, from the lord marquis, whose appearance confirmed all that report had said of him. "I come," said he, "to bring you the salutations of the cardinal archbishop."

"Oh, what condescension in both of you!"

"When I took leave of that incomparable man, who honours me with his friendship, he spoke to me of two young people of this parish who have suffered much from the unfortunate Don Roderick. My lord wishes to hear of them. Are they living? Are their affairs settled?"

"Their affairs are settled; and I had thought of writing to his Eminence about it, but now that I have the honour—"

"Are they here?"

"Yes; and as soon as possible, they will be man and wife."

"I request you to tell me what I can do for them, and the best manner of doing it. You will render me a service by enabling me to dispose of some of my superfluous wealth for their benefit."

"May Heaven reward you! I thank you in the name of my children," said Don Abbondio; "and since your lordship allows me, I have an expedient to suggest which perhaps will not displease you. These good people have resolved to establish themselves elsewhere, and to sell the little that belongs to them here. The best charity you can render them, is to buy their property, as otherwise it will be sold for little or nothing. But your lordship will decide, I have spoken in obedience to your commands."

The marquis thanked Don Abbondio, telling him he should leave it to him to fix the price, and to do so entirely to their advantage, as it was an object with him to make the amount as large as possible. He then proposed that they should go together to the cottage of Lucy.

On their way, Don Abbondio, quite overjoyed continued the conversation,—"Since your lordship is so disposed to benefit this people, there is another service you can render them. The young man has an order for his apprehension out against him, for some folly he committed two years ago at Milan, on the day of the great Tumult. A recommendation, a word, from a man like yourself, might hereafter be of service to him."

"Are there not heavy charges against him?"

"They made a great deal of noise about it; but really there was nothing in it."

"Well, well; I will take it upon myself to free him from all embarrassment."

We may imagine the surprise of our little company, at a visit from such a guest. He entered agreeably into conversation with them and after a while, made his proposal. Don Abbondio, being requested by him to fix the price, did so; the purchaser said he was well satisfied, and, if he had not understood him, in repeating it, doubled the sum. He would not hear of rectifying the mistake, and ended the conversation by inviting the company to dinner the day after the wedding, when the affair could be settled with every necessary formality.

"Ah!" thought Don Abbondio when he returned home, "if the pestilence acted everywhere with so much discrimination, it would be a pity to speak ill of it. We should want one every generation."

The happy day at length arrived. The betrothed went to the church where they were united by Don Abbondio. The day after, the wedding party made their visit at the castle. We will leave the reader to imagine their reflections on entering those walls! In the midst of their joy, however, they felt that the presence of the good Father Christopher was wanting to complete it. "But," said Lucy, "he is even happier than we are, assuredly."

The contract was drawn up by a doctor, but not *Azzecca Garbugli!* He was gone to *Canterelli.* For those who are not of this country, an explanation of this expression may be necessary.

About half a mile above Lecco, and nearly on the borders of the other territory, called Castello, is *Canterelli.* This was a spot where two roads cross. Near the point of junction there is a small eminence, an artificial hill, surmounted by a cross. This was a heap of bodies, dead of this epidemic. It is true, tradition simply says, *the dead of the epidemic;* but it must have been this one, as it was the last, and most severe within the memory of man: and we know that tradition says very little of itself, unless we render it some assistance.

On their return, no other inconvenience was felt, than the weight of the money which Renzo had to sustain. However, he did not look upon this as one of the greatest hardships he had had to encounter. There was, however, one matter which perplexed him not a little. How should he employ it? Should it be in agriculture? Should it be in business? Or why choose at all? Were not both in turn, like one's legs, better than either singly?

It will be asked, Did they feel no regrets on quitting their native village—their native mountains? Don Roderick and his wretched agents could no longer disturb them. Regrets they did feel; but the old recollections of happiness enjoyed amidst its scenes, had been greatly weakened by recent distresses and apprehensions, and new hopes had arisen connected with their new country; so that they could look to their change of abode without any feelings of grief.

The little company now thought only of preparing for their journey,—the *Tramaglino* family to their new country, and the widow to Milan. Many tears were shed, many thanks given, and many promises to meet again. The separation of Renzo and the friend who had treated him so hospitably, was not less tender. Neither did they part coldly from Don Abbondio: they had always preserved a certain respect for their curate, and he, in his heart, had always wished them well. It is these unfortunate affairs of the world which perplex our affections. But who would believe that, in this new abode, where Renzo had expected such happiness, he should find only vexation! This was the result of trifles, doubtless; but it requires so little to disturb a state of happiness in this life!

The reports the Bergamascans had heard of Lucy, together with Renzo's extraordinary attachment to her—perhaps, too, the representations of some partial friend—had contributed to excite an extravagant idea of her beauty. When Lucy appeared, they began to shrug their shoulders, and say, "Is this the woman? We expected something very different! What is she, after all? A peasant, like a thousand others! Women like her, and fairer than she, are to be found every where!"

Unfortunately, some kind friends told Renzo these things, perhaps added to what they had heard, and roused his indignation. "And what consequence is it to you?" said he. "Who told you what to expect? Did I ever do so? Did I tell you she was beautiful? She is a peasant, forsooth! Did I ever say I would bring a princess here? She does not please you. Do not look at her, then: you have beautiful women; look at them." Thus did he make himself unhappy; and believing that all were disposed to criticise his Lucy, he showed ill nature in return. It would have gone ill with him, if he had been condemned to remain in the place; but fortune smiled on him in this respect.

The master of another manufactory, situated near the gates of Bergamo, being dead, the inheritor of it, a young libertine, was willing to sell it half price, for ready money. Bortolo proposed to his cousin that they should make the purchase together. They did so; and when they entered into possession, Lucy was much pleased, and Renzo also, and not the less so for having heard that more than one person amongst his neighbours had said, "Have you seen this beautiful simpleton who is just come?"

Their affairs now went on prosperously. Before the year was completed, a beautiful little creature made her appearance, as if to give them the earliest opportunity of fulfilling Lucy's vow. Be assured it was named Maria. In the course of time, they were surrounded by others of both sexes, whom Agnes was delighted to carry about one after the other, calling them little rogues, and loading them with kisses. They were all taught to read and write; "for," said Renzo, "as this notion is in the country, we may as well take advantage of it."

It was highly pleasing to hear him relate his adventures: he always concluded by naming the great things he had learnt, by which to govern his conduct for the future. "I have learnt," said he, "not to mix in quarrels; not to preach in public; not to drink more than I want; not to keep my hand on the knocker of a door, when the inhabitants of the place are all crazy; not to tie a little bell to my feet, before I think of the consequences."

"And I!" said Lucy, who thought that the doctrine of her moralist, though sound, was rather confused, and certainly incomplete—"what have I learnt?" said she. "I have not sought misfortunes, they have sought me. Unless you say," smiling affectionately, "that my error was in loving you, and promising myself to you."

They settled the question, by deciding that misfortunes most commonly happen to us from our own misconduct or imprudence; but sometimes from causes independent of ourselves; that the most innocent and prudent conduct cannot always preserve us from them; and that, whether they arise from our own fault or not, trust in God softens them, and renders them useful in preparing us for a better life. Although this was said by poor peasants, it appears to us so just, that we offer it here as the moral of our story.